MARK J. SUDDABY – Born in England, in the year of Apollo 13 and Luna 17, Mark grew up sitting in front of the telly, in paisley pyjamas, staring wide-eyed as *Doctor Who* (Tom Baker), *Space 1999*, and *Blake's 7* romped across wobbly sets in garish outfits and big hair. Mark grew up in a large family which conversely meant playing alone, constrained only by a boundless imagination.

At sixteen, realising that he was unlikely to become an actual space hero, Mark joined the Army. After a career bookended by Sandhurst and War College – gaining a Masters in Defence and Strategic Studies along the way – Mark left the military after 25 years, having reached the dizzying heights of the sixth floor of the Ministry of Defence, where he worked as a staff officer, preparing papers for senior officers and wishing he was anywhere else in the universe.

Mark now lives in the West Country where he is endlessly fascinated by technological advances, philosophical questions, geopolitics, the universe, and wondering what it would be like, if…

For Susannah
for seeing it first
(including that ninety-second session thing)

MARK J. SUDDABY

ECHOES OF A LOST EARTH
PART ONE

AUSTIN MACAULEY PUBLISHERS™
LONDON • CAMBRIDGE • NEW YORK • SHARJAH

A CIP catalogue record for this title is available from the British Library.

ISBN 9781398490222 (Paperback)
ISBN 9781398490239 (Hardback)
ISBN 9781398490246 (ePub e-book)

www.austinmacauley.com

First Published 2023
Austin Macauley Publishers Ltd®
1 Canada Square
Canary Wharf
London
E14 5AA

The kernel for this story first evolved out of a series of threat-based lectures on climate change and energy security given at the UK Defence Academy, back in 2007. It has taken this long to go from writing that first draft, to publication, because I was never quite certain of my skill to tell the story. It's easy to compare with authors of renown and find yourself lacking; it's harder to put it all on the line anyway. But I'm older now, wiser, I hope, and more able to bite the bullet and put myself out there, warts 'n' all.

The themes, the ideas, the interplays, were all born back then, and yet they resonate with today's world far more than that of a decade ago. Watching the news and seeing disturbingly similar events play out in the real; I mean...

So first, I should acknowledge UK Defence and the British Army for their unwitting role in the curation of this tale from spark to fleshed-out, two-part novel. Without their investment in me, in my training and education – some of the best in the world – this story would not exist. And nor would I, as the person I am today.

Next, to John Jarrold for his professional advice, notes, thoughts and kind encouragement. And Gollancz, and just for what they said.

Then it descends into a litany (in a good way) of the people, of friends, who took the time to read my early (eye-peeling) drafts and offer their diplomatic thoughts and suggestions. Friends such as Susie, Tracy, Rich, Britt, Mark, Marcie, Gareth, Adrian, Matt; the list goes on. And those that continue to encourage me today to be better, do more; who keep me motivated and learning. To them all, I owe a huge debt. Any errors, though, are my own.

And last, to Austin Macauley Publishers, who took a punt. Without you, well… I am indebted to all those personally and professionally that spied the author and drew him into the daylight.

Thank you all. I hope that you, dear reader, enjoy reading *Echoes of a Lost Earth* as much as I have enjoyed writing it.

MARK SUDDABY
July 2022

Table of Contents

Völuspá

"The Wise Woman's Prophecy"

45. *Brothers shall fight | and fell each other,*
And sisters' sons | shall kinship stain;
Hard is it on Earth, | with mighty whoredom;
Axe-time, sword-time, | shields are sundered,
Wind-time, wolf-time, | ere the world falls;
Nor ever shall men | each other spare.

46. *Fast move the sons | of Mim, and fate*
Is heard in the note | of the Gjallarhorn;
Loud blows Heindall, | the horn is aloft,
In fear quake all | who on Hel-roads are.

47. *Yggdrasill shakes, | and shiver on high*
The ancient limbs, | and the giant is loose;
To the head of Mim | does Odin give heed,
But the kinsman of Surt | shall slay him soon.

From the Poetic Edda, Volume 1

Book I
Dance, Said the Devil

| collapse |

Another war | A shifting climate | A civilisation shedding its civility

I know that an ash-tree stands called Yggdrasill,
a high tree, soaked with shining loam;
from there come the dews which fall in the valley,
ever green, it stands over the well of fate.

Stanza 19, The Poetic Edda

One

Durham University, England
2009

Like an avalanche, it uttered forth. The starched '60s style auditorium gave up its quiet contemplation to the noise-front that preceded the freshet of bleary-eyed students, etched with the kind of lethargy that only that particular subset of human enterprise could truly manifest. Overhead, florescent lighting tubes flickered and buzzed like pipes of irascible wasps.

Ben Charleston prepared his notes and flicked through the slides as students defiled the lecture theatre with their monotonic din and beery breath. He had been teaching broad-spectrum geography (as if it were penance for a past sin) at the university for over five years and the throughput of largely disinterested young people was beginning to blur into an endless march of grungy, politicised protestors, so that he could no longer distinguish between those with a glimmer of interest and those who'd chosen geography because they lacked the imagination to… well, use their imagination.

Laptops and coursework spilled onto benches. Ben knew that the earbuds of the latest, coolest, MP3 players were also being surreptitiously fitted beneath mops of unwashed hair as the horseshoe theatre settled into a low mush of white noise. He sighed heavily, silently; he needed to reconnect with his audience before he gave in to his jaded scepticism and wrote these young people off. But the real issue, the source of his malaise, wasn't the kids, it was his own dead-ended doctoral research into the *environment* (said with the eye-rolling cynicism of a term both overused and under-stood). It was humankind's myopic self-interest and forked-tongue approach to their only life support system that had him dig and keep digging until the outcomes had become inescapable; outcomes no one wanted to hear. Not the faculty and *definitely* not the powers that be. Overseas research assignments accompanied by long discussions far into the night, washed down with too much of young Robert D'Legrange's slivovitz, had cemented his worst fears.

Yet here he was, in a lecture hall in middle England, with a room full of kids more interested in their sick new touchscreen phones (check this out: pinch-to-zoom) than their future children's sunlight. Only during his classified military debriefings had anyone shown even a suppressed glimmer of interest in Ben's research, even though his Dim Beacon paper – describing an imminent shift in global weather patterns – had fallen on politically short-termist ears. Ben tried to push the brewing torpidity of such thoughts from his mind as he quietened down his mildly bored audience and started the lecture with an equal pinch of ambivalence.

Fifty minutes later – the students having guttered away as if released from captivity – Ben gathered his things and shut down the projector. As he loaded up his satchel, a young woman tentatively approached the podium.

Nervously, she said, 'Excuse me, Professor Charleston?'

'Yeah,' Ben offered, disconsolately, as he turned. 'Oh, you're... um, Hannah, right?' He wasn't good with names but he'd remembered hers because she was a striking brunette with deep, hazelnut eyes that seemed to portray a wide-eyed interest in the world around her.

'That's right, yes. Um, what you said... was it true?'

'I should hope so.' He paused, to shrug off his own cynicism. 'Sorry. Which bit d'you mean, specifically?'

'Well, the data you showed about the carbon tipping-point. Seemed a bit...'

'Real? ... Yes, all true. All too true, I'm almost afraid to say.' Ben huffed and ran the numbers over his tongue, as if checking them again for accuracy. 'There were an estimated two hundred and eighty carbon parts per million in the Earth's atmosphere before the first industrial revolution, okay? By 2040 – three more revolutions later – that'll have risen to around four hundred or so. And that, my dear Hannah – and bless your heart for your interest – is when the "experts" are predicting that a cascading climate event will kick in. And nothing we (or more importantly, *you*) do from that moment on can prevent it. Sobering stuff, huh, if you take the time to *really* consider the implications, the second-order effects ... the *human* cost,' he said, somewhat theatrically, his words trailing as his mind meandered back to those long, cold nights.

'So, if we really want to change the path we're on, we've thirty-odd years to do it?'

'Pretty much; less in actual fact. Far less.' His eyes glazed for a moment, before he added, 'Or the World Tree will be unmade.'

'Sorry?'

'Oh… nothing, well, just something I'm remembering from a previous life. There was a time, you see, when we understood the power of nature and we respected it. Stood in awe of it. Sadly, our modern gadgets and easy lives have afforded us the luxury of forgetting. But *She* hasn't: Mother Nature. You know,' he brightened, 'you sound refreshingly interested in climate theories and I've one or two that are quite off-piste, as it were; why don't we get together sometime, discuss them further.' Ben knew it was a dangerous idea even as the words tripped unbidden off his tongue.

The young woman's reply was coy, demure, 'That would be lovely. Find me on MySpace.' She turned to leave, a smile ghosting her lips.

Al Muqatra (south of Abu Dhabi), Kingdom of Gulf States (occupied zone) 2039

The tactical vehicle move to the first report line went without a hitch and after five minutes of watchful observation through the Raider's limited surveillance stack, Jack Kristensen issued the order to begin the second bound to the outskirts of this once glittering city. It was just after dawn and a dinner plate of the palest yellow was rising over the jagged cityscape ahead; the somnific heat from which was already worming its way past the vehicle's light armour, despite the best efforts of the cabin's noisy, ineffective climate control (a term now laced with irony). Jack studied the outskirts of the slums, stacked against the iconic skyline – a line of ragged clay teeth – for signs of a normal day commencing, but it was quiet. Muslim societies rose early, making the lack of the normal hustle and bustle usually seen at this time, suspicious. Eerie.

Jack felt uneasy.

After the Iranian incursion along the dead, salt-saturated Arabian/Persian Gulf coast, the region had again become the focus of other people's wars. US intelligence stated that the Iranian Guard Corps – having annexed the former Arab Emirates of the newly expanded Kingdom of Gulf States – had pulled out of Abu Dhabi, back across the eastern border with former Qatar, having no desire to engage the West directly. However, the Hezbollah militias had not.

Jack, even knowing that things didn't look quite right – *absence of the normal, presence of the abnormal, right, Jack?* – ordered the company in. After all, what choice? *Orders wuz orders.* The armoured personnel carriers rumbled noisily into the shantied outskirts of the city. The buildings were as they had always been: a patchwork of flat-roofed boxes with postage-stamp windows, encased in slabs of dusty tarps and baking corrugated iron, and all the variating colours of the desertscape. Satellite dishes and ageing antennae created a skeletally metallic forest along the crenulated skyline. The dusty alleys and narrow streets almost afterthoughts as the tumorous shantytowns had taken root. Shops and street cafés were shuttered and the few burqa-clad women or contorted old men abroad seemed tense, loathe to be out, but like Jack, lacking any choice.

Or perhaps he was making something out of nothing; not hard in places such as these: cities that had tried so very hard to reinvent themselves but remained stubbornly immune to the changing world beyond their heat-shimmered horizon. Cities that held their grievances close, never letting go, never letting anyone forget.

Realising he'd tensed up, Jack took a deep breath to relax. *We'll get through today, Jack,* he said silently to himself, *just like we always do. Just keep calm; getting shot is what happens to other people.* It had become a recurring thought of his, and had seen him through three tours of Pakistan. Border tours, too (no one was volunteering for those anymore). The superstitious mantra of the soldier; old as war itself.

'Looks quiet; you think they're expecting us, Major Kristensen, sir?' said Stokes, Jack's driver.

'Maybe. Still, nothing we can do about it now.' Anyone with experience of irregular urban warfare would have noticed the signs that something was amiss, but Jack resisted the urge to get on the band and point it out.

Without warning, the band (from the speaker bolted to the roofline) clicked into life.

<Sabre-Zero-Alpha, Ugly-Sixty-Six. I've got visual on your callsigns and you're looking good. Routes are clear all the way to the objective,> crackled the tinny voice of the captain of the pair of Arapaho helicopter gunships, providing intimate overhead support.

<Roger that, Ugly-Sixty-Six, good to have you with us,> said Jack, in response. Having two heavily armed helos providing overwatch made him feel a bit more loved as the company crawled further along the dark, medieval streets.

<CONTACT, CONTACT. Wait out!>

An instant of panic/paralysis, then: 'Shit. Radd, I need ID on that callsign. Now,' Jack barked, as one of his platoon's came under enemy fire.

'Looks like a Sabre-Four-Zero callsign, but I canni'—' Corporal Raddleigh – the company comms tech – hollered from the cramped rear compartment.

'Sir, I've got a flatliner in Sabre-Four-One.' Corporal 'Doc' Halliday's voice was tense but controlled, dispassionate.

'Roger that, Doc, keep me apprised.' *Fuck! We're a pax down and I'm blind. I need to be there, now.*

On the band, Jack added, <Ugly-Sixty-Six, I need eyes on the contact point and covering fire a-sap. Sabre-Four-Zero-Alpha, extract your callsign to ERV and reorg. Sabre-Five-Zero-Alpha, move to wasteland east of your position, go firm and await my orders. Sabre-Six-Zero-Alpha, move to link up with Sabre-Four-Zero, I will follow you in.>

What I wouldn't give for a battlefield drone about now. But there hadn't been enough and Jack's company hadn't been priority.

He switched to the battalion net.

<Hades-Zero, Hades-Two-Zero-Alpha; Contact, 0650 hours, casualties reported, enemy unknown, request Charger-One-One and MERT on standby.>

<…lead vehicle disabled, getting wounded loaded up into… south to… RPG and HMG and fucking lots of it… shit…> A garbled message from an unknown callsign, back on the company net. It was 4 Platoon, but who, Jack couldn't tell, and if Raddleigh knew, he'd have shouted. It was dawning on Jack – as he pivoted his callsign – that what was unfolding was more than a shoot-and-scoot, welcome to Abu Dhabi attack the intel jocks had promised. 'The militia won't take on an armoured column,' the green-behind-the-gills intelligence corps second lieutenant had said, 'they'll wait and see. Measure force posture.' *Fucking intel.*

'Sir; two more flatliners.'

Arapaho pilot again; <Sabre-Zero-Alpha, Ugly-Sixty-Six; am engaging enemy dismounts on rooftops in vicinity of Sabre-Four-Zero. Significant anti-armour weapons—>

<Tanks… in the buildings… shit… they're T29's… abandoning vehicles… foot to ER…>

Jack tried to calm his breathing as he was overcome by a wave of claustrophobia, of fizzy-water panic, bubbling, foaming. *Stay calm, all in a day's work, Jack.* He said, <Sabre-Four-Zero callsign, roger that, am moving with all haste to ERV.> There was no reply. *Damn. Tanks, and not just any but T29 Black Eagles; Russian made and most definitely not Hezbollah issue. Intel said they'd all been withdrawn across the Gulf, back to Iran. Fucking desk-jockeys! Stay calm, Jack; Pakistan was worse than this.*

'Sir; just lost seven more, consistent with a vehicle kill.' Corporal Halliday again, describing the destruction of one of 4 Platoon's Raider vehicles and the instantaneous death of everyone inside.

Jack's flexiscreen pinged and blipped with the company's blue-force tracker dispositions as they shifted like roaming gangs of ants. 5 Platoon was moving north to the area of wasteland. What was left of 4 Platoon was static, and the Company HQ packet was moving eastwards, line astern of 6 Platoon, two klicks from the Emergency Rendezvous.

<Ugly-Sixty-Six, request fire mission to cover withdrawal of Sabre-Four-Zero,> Jack offered to the lead gunship pilot, trying desperately to do what he could to disengage 4 Platoon from the enemy ambush.

<Sabre-Zero-Alpha, Ugly-Sixty-Six; roger that, will do. Have visual on enemy armour, am engaging with HellStorm.>

Stokes was gunning the old diesel engine for all it was worth as the little convoy of Company Headquarters vehicles hurtled though the warren of back streets and bounced across wide-open highways, as they tried to keep up with the platoon in front. Unsuitable for conversion to hydrogen, the heavy wagons barrelled through the labyrinthine streets declaring themselves across whole city blocks.

As commander of the company, Jack was fixated by the blue-force tracker icons, whilst simultaneously following the lead vehicle's vid-feed on a knee-mounted pad and intermittently checking the wagon's head-up display, and all while catching snatched voice across two band nets, when – almost in slow motion – the colour drained from the cabin, taking with it the blusterous, thrumming noise. The technicolour luminosity of the backlit switchgear leeched away until his vision was bathed in an intense, candescent light, as if the Sun had fallen onto the bonnet of the wagon. A wave of pressure and noise slammed into him, concrete hard, like hitting water at speed. It lasted an age yet was over before it could even fully register. His head was thrown back against the headrest and the restraints dug painfully through the lightweight gel armour. Everything stung like a hard slap. A flexiscreen catapulted into Jack's face before peeling off and disappearing into the rear, where the doc and the signaller toiled. As the vehicle bucked, he fell forward, into an exploding air-bag, punching him in the face. A cheek hissed and he could smell burning flesh. Then silence – utter quietude – as colour seeped back into the world and the overwhelming stench of cordite snapped Jack back to dazed senses.

He looked through the blue-tinted plasiglas windows but could make nothing out, as if caught in a sandstorm; a dry, withering fog. Looking across at Stokes, Jack could see her bleeding from the nose and ears. The young woman was rigid, staring straight ahead, gripping the wheel for dear life. He put a gloved hand to his face, pulled it away, revealing bloodstained, trembling fingers. His breathing was shallow and rapid as panic began to mount. *I should be doing something, but what?* Unclipping the restraints, he turned to the rear of the cabin. Corporal Halliday was unconscious, bloodied but breathing, as were the two close protection soldiers. Young, first-tour lads, both. Raddleigh was dead. The explosion had thrown the unsecured, un-helmeted technician onto his buckled, sparking equipment.

'We've got to get out. *Now*. Help me with the hatch,' shouted Jack, even though no words seemed to take flight. Stokes pushed against the heavy slab as Jack leaned across her to add his weight. The door eased open and held on the heavy struts. Unclipping Stokes, he rolled her out into the street, grabbing her rifle as he clambered after.

The wagon was half-buried in a collapsed building. The front was raised as if someone had picked it up and swivelled the Raider with a flick of the wrist. The second vehicle was on its side. It hadn't fared as well against the hail of RPG strikes. *Why hadn't the hard-kill defensive systems activated?*

Realising that lying in the street left him badly exposed, Jack grabbed Stokes' rifle and took in the scene, scanning for movement – someone to shoot – but nothing stirred. Dust and sand gusted around him, making it hard to know anything much. Unwilling to push his luck, he grabbed Stokes by the webbing and dragged her across the open ground, away from the Raider, to the shadow of a doorway.

'Stay here and shoot at anything that moves. Rooftops,' Jack shouted, pointing up, as he handed Stokes back her rifle.

He ran back to the Raider and pulled at the heavy, rear door handle. Nothing. He couldn't make it budge. Then it moved on its own, the door swinging outwards. Jack grabbed and heaved it open, imagining the grinds of protest. Corporal Halliday fell out, landing in a ring of dust. She started to say something, then pointed at Corporal Raddleigh.

'He's dead,' Jack yelled, gesticulating superfluously. 'We need to get outta here, unclip these two and let's get them t' cover.' Doc Halliday worked on one while Jack pulled at the other. Minutes later, they'd recovered two serviceable weapons and a working scrampad. Jack thrust a weapon at Doc and told her to see to the survivors. With the other close combat assault rifle activated and slaved, resting across one knee, he fitted the pad to his knee and set it to pick up anything from the platoon up ahead.

Nothing.

'Let's get inside, we're too exposed,' he said, smashing open the door with the butt of the rifle. Stokes and Doc dragged the two unconscious soldiers into the house while Jack provided fearful, deaf, cover. But his hearing was returning as he entered the dark room decorated with shattered glass, colourful rugs and scattered brass ornaments. Gunfire, dim, muffled, began to detach itself from the whining bead of tinnitus. A close battle raged further up the street.

'Stokes, keep an eye out.'

'Okay, Boss.'

'Sabre-Four-Zero, Zero-Alpha, sitrep.' The personal band was short range, but in a city, no one was ever very far away. No reply. *Damn.*

'Doc, stay here, I'm going up the road, see what the fuck's going on. Six Platoon's somewhere up there. Sit tight. Back shortly.'

Jack began to make his way gingerly up the street. Movement. Ahead were shadows sliding along the wall, same side as him. An explosion of dust and debris, and the opposing wall burst apart as the low, rubble-strewn silhouette of a Russian-derived Black Eagle main battle tank burst onto the narrow street. The rumbling ground, the noise and dust spread down the narrow street and Jack took what cover he could. Shaking with adrenalin and fear.

Behind, the thrumming, pulsating vibrations of rotor blades became discernible. He tried to raise the helo. Nothing. No comms, so nothing he could do except hope they'd target-locked an armoured unit of what could only be the Iranian Revolutionary Guard. Above, the air hissed as an Arapaho fired three HellStorm missiles, the first slicing through the powder-blue sky to find its home in the top of the tank's turret, two hundred metres ahead. The explosion blew Jack off his feet, rolling him down the road and out into the main thoroughfare. Again, his bleeding eardrums rang in church-tower agony. His back burned with ground-in spinal pain, even as the impact vest did what it could. The two other missiles detonated in quick succession, in noise-cancelling, world-splitting violence.

Unsteadily, Jack groped back onto his feet and ran erratically down a tunnel of dust and dirt. Using doorways, he moved closer to the staccato cracks of small-arms fire and close-quarter combat. Movement on the rooftops. As he half-ran, half-crawled, he spotted a discarded assault rifle, picked it up – having lost his along the way – and shuffled into the nearest doorway, collapsing against the hard-baked frame. He put three rounds into the ground, then slaved it to his kitware. The entrance to the nearest building had been blown open, so limp-running another fifty yards he slipped into a side-street before breaking back into a house about where he assumed the remnants of 6 platoon to be holding out.

'Boss, that you?'

Jack, startled, couldn't identify the soldier who'd made him. 'Sitrep.' He said, louder than required, ears still ringing.

'Enemy armour's been destroyed. All our wagons are blown to shit. Casualties fucking everywhere. The enemy is along that roofline laying down heavy fire.' The young soldier's voice was beginning to break, as he nodded through a hole in the wall.

'Who's in charge?'

'Shane Thackary, I think, sir. Next room.' Tilt of the head.

'Hold your position, lad, you're doing fine.' It wasn't much, but all he could offer. Across the room, through the broken doorway, was Sergeant Thackary, 6 Platoon's Sergeant.

'Sarn't Thackary,' Jack called out, passing five soldiers: two incapacitated, three firing long bursts of automatic fire through the ragged windows.

'Fuck me, boss, that you? Fucking glad to see you. Some fucking shit we're in 'ere, eh?' said Thackary, with a wild grin, cautiously making his way over, rounds gouging the wall above his head.

'You got comms with anyone?'

Sergeant Thackary shook his head. 'Just one of my bricks up the street.'

'Shit; okay. What we got?'

'We're pretty much holding our own now. My boss is dead. Lost about a third of the platoon by my reckoning. Hutch has about half what's left further up the street where the lead wagons were hit,' the sergeant offered, referring to Corporal Hutchins, a section commander. 'I've patchy comms with him but no one else. Enemy armour was collapsing the houses before they got taken out, now it's just the dismounts. Irregulars. Looks like a hybrid op.'

Deniable; out of the Russian playbook.

'Roger that. Get some bods, have 'em move back down the street to collect what's left of Company Headquarters. Halliday's there; looks like you need her. Then we'll extract, Hutchins covering. We have to get to the ERV and link up with whatever's left of 4 Platoon. It's our only chance of a hot scoff tonight. Where battalion'll send the mobile reserve to dig us out of this turdfest, but they won't hang about. I'll get over to Hutchins' position. Wait for my word.'

'On it,' said Sergeant Thackary, moving away and up the stairs, shouting orders, instilling confidence and generally making his presence felt.

Jack continued up a back street towards the next exchange of fire. As he shuffled along, he caught movement in his peripheral vision. Two figures running from an alley skirting a compound, shouting and waving AK-47s. He couldn't engage them from where he was, so dived for the cover offered by the nearest doorway. He missed, hitting his gel-helmeted head against the doorframe before falling hard into the street as rounds whizzed past, digging into the mortar where he'd been standing. Rolling, he fired a short automatic burst and dispatched a grenade down the length of his body, between his legs.

The two men were dressed similarly in black, with white chafiyehs and ammunition bandoliers strapped across their torsos. The cliché was not lost on Jack, despite being preoccupied with not dying. *This region just never changes.* Two rounds took the right-hand gunman in the shoulder, flipping him backwards against the pitted side of the alleyway. The grenade passed by, penetrating the wall behind and detonating harmlessly within the compound. *Damn; set to armour piercing.* The remaining gunman opened up filling the air with flame and noise. One round ripped the heel of Jack's boot away.

He fired again, blind, rolling as he did so, staggering to his feet and diving for the relative cover of the illusive doorway. The second gunman was almost upon him. Jack stepped back into the darkened room, putting a long, wide, waist-high burst into the wall about where he assumed the other fighter to be. Stepping – stumbling on the heel-less boot – he checked the street from deep within the gloom of the room. The militiaman lay on his back, unmoving. A deep sense of elation and joy welled up; Jack's lips trembled and tears began to well. He tried to suppress the feeling – a sort of horror-glee – but it was hard. *He's dead and I'm alive, because I'm better at killing.*

A few deep breaths to gather his wits; he put a round into the forehead of each militiaman, and limped on towards the sound of Hutchins' position. Slowing, he reached an alleyway junction, moved his head round to check that it was clear, to find himself eyeball-to-eyeball with an Iranian Revolutionary Guard.

Jack stumbled backwards, putting himself further into the street, more ex-posed. The guardsman stepped back, panicked, firing his raised pistol as he did so. Pain blossomed from Jack's right thigh and he fell awkwardly. Pirouetting towards the ground, he felt his electrically active impact armour hardening to the reaction of two more rounds fired at point blank range at his torso. Jack hit the ground with his right shoulder, his momentum throwing him backwards. As he rolled, his rifle butt dug into the earth and with his hold on the pistol grip, the weapon raised naturally towards the Iranian. He depressed the trigger when he heard the audio target-lock confirmation, taking the other man in the stom-ach, catapulting him down the alleyway. The guard fell into a tangled mass of bloodstained limbs. Jack's leg was hurting – really hurting, now – as he dragged himself to the relative cover of an open sewer channel at the base of the wall, the agony washing away all other concerns.

'Bugger me... what a fucked-up day,' he exclaimed to no one, between gulps of air and waves of panic.

Reaching inside an ammo pouch, he pulled out a trauma pad, tugged on the tearaway tab and broke the topaz gauze apart. With his bayonet, he took hold of the flayed edge of his chameleoflage trouser leg, cutting out from the bullet wound. Blood oozed rather than pulsed – a good sign. Less good was that the bullet had ricocheted off the femur, partially shattering the bone and tearing away an elongated strip of muscle. Gently, deliriously, Jack placed the trauma pad over the wound, very nearly blacking out with the pain. His breathing was rapid, shallow.

'This is getting... less... amusing, now.'

The pad formed a seal around the wound as it knitted with the tissue and the localised anaesthesia started to dull the pain. The application of a morphine syrette dulled it a whole lorryload more.

Jack's shallow breathing and thumping heart consumed his world, but grad-ually another noise broke in over his befuddled, overtaxed senses; a set of crunching footsteps closing in from behind. He turned, wincing quizzically up at a man standing over him, the matt black outline of an AK resting across his chest. Jack raised his rifle, but the man stepped in and kicked it away. Pain clawed its way around the morphine, desperate to be known. Jack's wounds reflected in the man's relaxed, sardonic stance.

Then, remembering the pistol strapped to his other thigh, Jack reached for it, but his hand closed over an empty holster as the realisation that the sidearm had been lost somewhere along the line washed over him. *Bollocks*. The other man aligned his rifle onto Jack, spoke quietly in Arabic, and fixed him with an intense stare, hatred igniting his dark eyes, before a burst of seven rounds hammered into Jack's chest.

He knew it was seven because they discharged so far apart that it was a doddle to count each one. Events were taking place in a sort of disconnected series of still-framed images. Jack felt the electrical activation of his impact armour, gel pads hardening in languorous fractions of a moment, but knew it could never cope with sustained fire at so short a range. The scene around him slowed to a standstill. The gunman staring down the barrel of his weapon with a fixed, grim expression as he discharged each round, blinking with every recoil. Empty cases, glinting brillantine gold in the Sun, spiralled away into the street, as each kickback of the Kalashnikov precipitated a momentary yellow-white flare as rounds left the muzzle.

A rich, blue sky and washed-out sepia buildings stretched away behind the militiaman's silhouette, the colours growing in vivacity as the street was reduced to a dark russet, in contrast to the flaxen-gold where sunlight struck the dwellings. The man faded to nothing more than sinister shadow chewing at the edges of an otherwise blindingly contrasting scene. The conflicting odours of iron and effluence fell away as the colours began to fuse and run together, turning a ruddy hue, darkening, withdrawing, until eventually Jack's only sensory perception was the dull, thudding pain in his thigh; then even that faded away, and with it went the world.

4th (UK) Urban Assault Brigade Headquarters, Haradh, Kingdom of Gulf States (free zone)

'Brigadier, I've an update on developments if you've a moment?' Imani Tikriti spoke from the doorway of the commander's makeshift office.

Brigadier Freddie Roebuck, Commander, 4th Urban Assault Brigade, looked up from his paperwork. The current battle notwithstanding, annual reports and routine disciplinary matters continued to warrant his attention. Putting down his Mont Blanc (an anniversary gift from his wife), Freddie ushered his chief of staff in.

'The situation with 7th Infantry is largely unchanged,' began Imani, 'remnants of B Company are heavily engaged and conducting a fighting withdrawal against an enemy force of T29's. We're providing artillery and attack heli support. Unfortunately, the BrightStar private security squad we dispatched to locate B Company has just pulled out, saying they've reached their contracted casualty rate. The overall scale of casualties will only become clear once we get the company back, but it's not looking great.'

'And the commander?' Roebuck asked.

Imani shook her head, then shifted uneasily before continuing, her face falling further. 'However, sir, there's another, more significant incident. At 0805 hours we requested, via Strat Com, a series of drone strike sorties to assist with the extraction of 7th Infantry from Al Muqatra. You're aware that we subsequently lost the loiter-drone vid-feed. It seems now that a swarm went rogue, attacking and destroying an air defence battery and elements of an armoured company of the US Third Heavy Cav, in the vicinity of Al Wathbah.'

'I see,' the brigadier said, quickly mulling over the implications. 'I take it the Americans are aware? That it was friendly fire, I mean.'

'Yessir, they are.'

'And the drone swarm?'

'We tried to abort but couldn't, then they aborted independently. Our techs are saying malfunction… or hack.'

'Okay, get me General Dana on the wire, would you?'

Imani nodded and left. The chief of staff was right, Roebuck thought. A badly judged foray into Abu Dhabi, with flawed intelligence, leading to significant casualties was bad, but a blue-on-blue involving US forces could have disastrous political repercussions, on both sides of the pond. Leaning back in his chair, he considered how these two incidents would play out. It seemed unlikely, now, that British forces alone would be able to take even their allotted sectors of the city. So, they'd either have to hand the task over to the Americans (humiliating), or at the very least request their support if another attempt were to be made (still, but less, humiliating). And 7th Infantry's effective defeat would badly damage the British military's reputation with the Americans, not to mention the drone swarm debacle. A malfunction and the Brits would look incompetent, a hack and they'd look weak, second tier, compromised.

Roebuck's vone pinged and the image of Major General Dana MacAllistair's Military Assistant appeared on the extended flexiscreen. 'Good morning, Brigadier; the general will be with you in a moment.' The view switched to General Dana, seated in a well-appointed office, in a Riyadh airbase.

'Morning, Freddie; I take it this is about the attack drone incident?' said the general, looking up from her desk. The expression she wore marked her as being in a foul, barely contained mood.

'Good morning, General.' He nodded. 'I'm concerned an incident like this will undermine our ability to work in concert with our US colleagues, particularly at this juncture in the campaign. We're dependent on them for so much. If they were to…' but he left the obvious implication unsaid. 'You're aware of 7th Infantry's current circumstances?'

'I am. I've spoken with Northwood and for the moment, this information hasn't been released. However, the Americans are saying no UK flagged attack drones to fly within the Joint Operating Area. Furthermore, they're raising flags about the efficacy of our land forces.'

Freddie tried to keep emotion from his voice. 'I take it they've been made aware of the presence of heavy armour in the city and that it was *their* intelligence that stated no such threat existed?'

'They've been told but I'm afraid, Freddie, they simply don't see it that way. They're moving a regimental combat team north as we speak. I'm to direct you to withdraw UK forces from Abu Dhabi and stand by to carry out supporting tasks as they crop up,' said the major general, in what sounded like a sympathetic tone. She sighed and added – pinching her nose below her rimless glasses – as if it were necessary to spell out the new arrangement, 'We're the second eleven now, Freddie. The grave diggers and the stretcher bearers. Let the Americans do the heavy lifting from here on in.'

'Very well, but, General, if we back off now, we'll be in a very poor spot indeed when the news breaks. Reputationally, this'll sink us. Now is precisely the time when we need to be seen taking some flak, hand-in-glove with the Yanks,' said the brigadier, with a note of defiance, as if saying it out loud would make him feel better, even knowing the general's hands were as tied as his own.

'I know, Freddie, I know. But you must realise the campaign planners made some pretty broad assumptions which dictated our force posture and now we've been royally caught out. This was always about standing shoulder to shoulder with the Americans, but not paying for our seat at the table. It looks now, though, like the gamble didn't pay off. I suspect we played that hand once too often.' She paused, stone-faced. 'You have your orders, Freddie, withdraw our land forces from the Abu Dhabi combat areas of the occupied zone, back across the emirate boundary.'

'Very well, ma'am. I'm back for the gala dinner with the Crown Prince, so I'll see you in a few days.' The screen blacked out momentarily and returned to its default map view, showing brigade dispositions. 7th Infantry's appearing more contracted.

It was what the general hadn't said rather than what she had, that most concerned Roebuck. The US would side-line the Brits in preparation for the domestic backlash, where their talking heads would salivate at American soldiers' lives being lost at the hands of a British military found wanting when her oldest ally had come knocking.

Summoning Imani back in, Freddie ordered a phased withdrawal once 7th Infantry were out of the city, then sat down to write commendations for those he deemed worthy, before beginning his letter of resignation with his favourite Mont Blanc. Freddie suspected he wouldn't be the only senior British officer to be doing similarly over the next few days.

Two

Yeshe Ma's tale
Yarlung Tsangpo Canyon, Tibet

Yeshe Ma pulls his fur-lined hat further down over his ears as the harsh wind bites into his exposed skin. It is nearing sunset and he knows he will soon need to find a place to settle in for the night. His uncle will be angry that he hasn't made it back to the village, but his mind had wandered and he'd forgotten the time. The goats graze quietly on the patchy scrub that clings to the rocky out-crops of the hillside. Yeshe whistles and gesticulates his herd further up the slope. He knows the area well and is planning to find some shelter in the lea of the ridgeline, out of the chill wind. It will also give him a view down the great valley through which the Yangluzangbu River flows. He likes the idea of see-ing the lights come on in the town that straddles the mighty river as he prepares his meal. And sometimes, when the wind is blowing correctly, he can *just* make out the dusk chants from the Buddhist temple buried deep in the high moun-tains. But not tonight, for the bitter wind is westerly so no soft chanting and probably little sleep.

Yeshe Ma crests the ridgeline and pauses to take in the view. Down below, the valley sweeps away to his left into a steep-sided ravine where the water of the Yangluzangbu is white with rage, then further south the gorge opens out onto a vast plain where villages and the town lie amongst the fertile fields that will soon be bountiful with ripened crops. The goats are settling down so Yeshe goes to peg them out while there is still some light. He counts them and ensures that they can come to no harm then finds himself a nook in the rock to settle into. With a fire lit and his small pot of water beginning to simmer, the lights at the mighty dam come on. His uncle had told him that the dam creates power for the cities, but he didn't really understand. *Probably magic, but how would building a lake in the ice mountains make magic?* Who knew... but it is truly a magnificent sight; a huge wall spanning the valley, with the river cutting through the lush green open plains below. Lights dot the dam and soon the little town is showing tiny pinpricks of scattered brilliance. *Wow.*

The water in the little pot comes to the boil and Yeshe adds a pouch of dried yak meat and vegetables to make a broth. He will keep the nub of cheese and bread for the morning. As he stares, transfixed by the small fire in front of him, he hears a faint noise, dancing on the very edge his perception. He has heard it before; the sound of angry white water, when he has ventured all the way down to the spuming river. The noise builds, getting louder and louder still, and it's coming from the dam. *Maybe all the water there is getting angry*, thinks Yeshe, as he looks on curiously.

And then all in a moment it happens. White, raging water comes crashing over the great wall that spans the valley. At first, it sweeps into the air like a waterfall gone wrong. Spuming funnels of white geysering froth. But then it starts flowing over the wall itself – wet and heavy. Not too much at first but then more and more water pours over the lip of the dam. Gradually, the wall starts to move, in then out then in again, as if labouring to breathe whilst slowly drowning under the weight of the foaming fountain. Almost simultaneously the top of the bowed stonework begins to crumble and then the whole wall crashes down the gorge onto the ravine below and onwards to the plain beyond. As the water scours all before it, the lights in the town blink out one by one. Yeshe Ma thinks that the magic must have gone away and returns his attention to his simmering broth.

212 Field Hospital, Shaybah, Kingdom of Gulf States (free zone)

It was a beautifully warm spring April day that set the scene for an idyllic Sunday afternoon. St James's Park looked like it always did on such a day; couples picnicking, lounging or reading; children playing, feeding the ducks by the scattering of small lakes. Areena sat opposite Jack, luxuriously, in that way that only girls could, all bendy and effortless. Jack, by contrast, was laid out awkwardly, with one arm supporting his head as he considered his next move. Between them, a beautiful, hand-carved chess set. Areena particularly enjoyed playing, mainly because she knew she could beat Jack anytime she liked, which she often did, convincingly and with much delight. Other times, she let him win and Jack knew it, but that was fine, an acceptance of the universe's will. Conversation revolved around the impending visit of her mother to oversee

Areena's move from one rented flat to yet another. Rent: the scourge of the penniless London resident.

Jack was pouring them both another glass of particularly good '34 Monmouth Chablis when a commotion caught his eye. Someone was running down the path along the nearest lakelet. The figure stopped, as if trying to gather their bearings or seek someone out. It was a young woman, vaguely familiar to Jack and shod in chameleoflage. She was breathless and caked in ground-in dust. *That isn't right.* The woman spotted Jack and started sprinting in his direction. He made her out – it was Stokes; blood running from her ears and nose.

'Boss, we gotta move, now! Come on, they're just down the road. With tanks,' she gasped, as she started pulling at Jack's shoulder straps. *That isn't right, either.*

Jack started to protest, then a piercing pain erupted in his thigh, only to be eclipsed by more in his chest. He tried to get up, to get away but he couldn't move. Suddenly, he was tired; he looked for Areena but she wasn't there. He tried to call out her name, but no sound came. Panic welled, filling him so that it was all he knew.

The park was gone, replaced by a heavy, bloated desert Sun and the overpowering smell of burning rubber. Jack tried to blink away stinging tears of fear. Fear that had overwhelmed him in an instant. Strip lights, shouting and the buzz of receding quadcopter drones, but fading away as if it was all happening just beyond the edge of his perception.

10 Downing Street, London

General Sir Richard Rose-Templar sat uneasily in the back of the armoured Roewe as the car hummed smoothly through the quiet, pre-dawn city streets. There'd be a COBR later, but evidentially *this* couldn't wait. The driver turned off into a small but highly secure side-street where the car glided to an effortless halt. Sir Richard stepped out into the cool, misty night air. With his assistant in tow, he strode quickly up the short steps, past two police officers in public disorder protection gear, and into the open door of Ten Downing Street.

'The Prime Minister will be down shortly. He's asked that you wait for him in his private study, General. This way, please,' stated the PM's principal private secretary. She looked as if she too hadn't slept. Rose-Templar made his way down the corridor and into an open door to the left. He'd come here a number of times since taking up the post of Chief of the Defence Staff some six months prior, but with each visit he was reminded of the sheer volume of the interior. From the outside it looked like any other small terraced London home, but inside it had been hollowed out and extended to meet the needs of a once-and-great world-power government; the nexus of a long dead empire.

Richard Rose-Templar came from a long line of soldiers. In his early fifties, a towering figure, with a mane of thick white hair and the gravitas to carry off the role of Britain's most senior military officer with ease. He knew he'd not been the politician's choice, but the appointment rotated between the four services and currently it was the army's turn, so Richard was a right place, right time, man.

As Sir Richard waited, he idly reflected on the patchy chronology of events that had brought Alan Hardinge – the current prime minister – to power. An old image of a young Homeland Office minister attempting to clarify the cloudy events that led to his wife leaving him – an affair with a research assistant. Another of him standing in the rain on a Westminster street, struggling to explain away attempts by his office to intimidate a journo into ditching the story. Resignation. Years later, Hardinge – returned from the wilderness – on stage behind a podium, helicams hovering; the great orator launching his campaign for leadership of the party. Shaky, regional footage of Hardinge on the campaign trail, fist clenched as he questions Britain's need to remain an old world nuclear power. The cost, he chides, the hospitals, the vaccine programmes, that would buy. More, of Hardinge irritated as he argues that, in a world of anti-missile missile shields and experimental orbital laser platforms, that Britain doesn't need an ageing fleet of nuclear submarines, armed with expensive American-made (American-controlled?) warheads. He catches the mood of national self-interest during record automation lay-offs and climate-driven economic turmoil. Iconic imagery of the pomp of the newly appointed Prime Minister returning from Buckingham Palace to stand outside Number Ten, his blue-eyed boy by his side. During his inaugural address he punches his fist in the air and announces Britain's withdrawal from the NATO directed-energy weapons research programme. Bridges burn.

'Sir Richard, do take a seat. Apologies for dragging you over here in the middle of the night, but thought we ought to discuss the situation in the Gulf States before all hell breaks loose across the wire. *And* in the House.' The Prime Minister was a short, rotund man with wisps of tangled, silver hair and almost clear, piercingly pale blue eyes, sunk into hollow sockets. Richard had always felt that the PM owed much of his political success to his ability to re-duce people to stammering wrecks with a single, demagogical stare.

'Of course, Prime Minister, I understand entirely. How can I help?' the general said, as disarmingly as he could, trying to hide his distaste for the man.

'You can explain how one of the most professional militaries in the world is in rout from a local militia *and* how we managed to pick a deadly fight with the Americans, for a start, General.'

Rose-Templar took a mental breath. 'Certainly, sir. Before I begin however, I would point out that this is not the first time Hezbollah have used their own brand of urban guerrilla tactics to temporarily humble a superior, conventional force. Although the situation in Abu Dhabi looks grim for the moment, it's not the defeat the wire will paint. Putting aside the issue of Iranian sub-threshold assistance and flawed US intelligence, you'll be aware that I did strongly object to the amended campaign plan, specifying a lighter force. A force – I stated at the time – would be incapable of meeting the full spectrum of operations my planners envisaged. You'll also be aware that you sided with the Chief of the Air Staff, against my advice, by deciding attack drones should deploy, rather than retasking *HMS Queen Elizabeth* from Pakistan, with her three squadrons of Lightnings which, despite their age, are crewed platforms.'

'Sir Richard, you provided me with your assurance that we had the correct balance of forces to capture Abu Dhabi island, irrespective of... prior discussions,' the PM said, in a calm but assertive manner.

'And you will recall, Prime Minister, that I made those assurances conditional upon the situation on the ground.'

The PM paused, thinking. 'Very well. I'll have a statement prepared for the wire to be given at seven-thirty. And your thoughts as to how we play the US angle?'

'First, we need to re-engage with US forces as quickly as possible. The longer we leave it the harder it'll become. It was a mistake for the Secretary of State to allow the Americans to assume the lead for the *liberation* of Abu Dhabi. I know the US Chair of the Joint Chiefs pretty well; I think I can talk her round.' Richard began to feel that there might be a way out of this mess, yet.

'Hmm.' Furrowed brows. 'I've a different proposal. We retain our forces in the occupied zone but avoid high intensity operations, remaining on convoy escorts, support tasks and the like. This gives us skin in the game and allows for an acceptable level of political capital to be retained by our continued support. The Americans have demanded they be allowed to carry out a full investigation into the attack drone incident before transferring the mission profilers, programmers, ground crew, to the US for Court Martial on dereliction of duty charges, that sort of thing. I've been assured that *if* found guilty, they'll be allowed to serve a minimal sentence in the UK,' said Hardinge, his mind clearly made up.

Richard took a breath, intent to remain calm. 'Prime Minister, that would be a complete abrogation of our duty of care to our personnel and I absolutely cannot support it. We'd open ourselves up to a domestic backlash and international accusations of American puppetry.' Realising that he'd come forward in his chair with the emotion of the moment, the general leaned back and took a sip from a cup of coffee that had appeared on the table beside him. Even for *this* prime minister, it was a shocking display of political chicanery.

'General, US public opinion will not sit back and simply take the killing of thirty-seven of their soldiers by British hands lying down. Something *must* be done.'

'Then, sir, I suggest that you find something to do, but not at the expense of our nation's service personnel who were doing their jobs in difficult circumstances and with under-funded equ—'

'Yes, yes. But be careful now, Sir Richard… Hmm.' He fixed Richard with his signature stare. 'So, I take it then that you don't feel able to support this course of action? A course of action, may I add, that's critical to our continued good relations with the United States. That being the case, then I must reluctantly ask for your resignation.' Alan Hardinge remained stone-faced as he delivered his ultimatum, with searing eyes.

Richard steeled himself. 'I'm sorry, Prime Minister; if you wish to replace me, you'll have to sack me, as is your prerogative. But I'm not sure that changing the head of the armed forces at this moment is in the nation's best interests, do you? And, I wonder what the Americans would make of it? Now, if that's all, sir, I'll see you later in COBR, where I'll have more detail on yesterday's events in the occupied zone.' Rose-Templar stood to leave, pausing to allow the PM the final word, by way of a dismissal.

Hardinge gazed across at his principal military adviser, his expression revealing a momentary look of political calculation. The fire in his eyes went out. 'Very well, General, you've made your case. You stay. But the US will get their trial, so I suggest you work to find a solution that's palatable to your people. Conduct your own investigation if you have to but find a head to roll. I've given the President my word and she's not in a particularly equitable mood just now.' And with an act of finality, Alan Hardinge switched his attention to the flexiscreen rolled out on his mahogany desk. The door was opened by an aide, allowing the sound of a lone child at play to filter into the room.

As the car pulled out of Downing Street, Sir Richard turned to his Military Assistant, and said, quietly, 'Get me a meeting with the Leader of the Opposition. Ensure total opsec, *no one…* in government is to know. Also, find a place out of the way and organise a meeting of the service chiefs. Off the books.'

'Yes sir.' The MA pulled out a scrampad and busied himself with the arrangements.

Richard knew the Abu Dhabi fiasco – caused by budget cuts and equipment shortfalls – was yet another warning shot across the bow of Britain's haemorrhaging strategic resilience. If it wasn't stopped, successive governments looking for short-term wins would trade it away, without even grasping the consequences of their actions. Richard knew that he was one of the few in a position of national influence who could perhaps prevent that from happening. Alan Hardinge was right about one thing, though, something certainly needed to be done.

The general was struggling to decide if the timing of the Gulf States nightmare was in fact a blessing in a most unsettling disguise. Before the latest Middle Eastern diplomatic crisis had blossomed – again – into a military one, his focus had been on a threat of an entirely different nature. In fact, the threat *was* nature and it was something that the government was studiously turning its cheek from. Recently, Sir Richard had been made aware of a dusty, thirty-year-old Dim Beacon report predicting the possibility of a rapid climate pivot, written by some university professor. It was an old, marginalised theory, and largely debunked by big-oil funded experts, but had been given new life through a recent remodelling with the latest, highly classified climate data, using recombinant algorithms. Richard – a climate advocate even after being so had fallen from fashion – had hung on every word and wondered how best to act on it, as well as the extent to which he could push a recalcitrant government into making the necessary preparations.

Rule number one: The British military absolutely did not get involved in domestic politics; that was a given, an inviolable absolute. But… (and there was a *but*) preparing for sudden climate shifts would require bold, decisive action which would not come naturally to a weak government still reeling from a collapsing foreign energy policy. What then was the role of the military in such dire domestic circumstances?

So perhaps Abu Dhabi was the wakeup call the defence chief needed to galvanise his peers into considering options conventionally deemed outwith their remit. Richard made a note to dig out the report when he returned to Main Building. He'd need to come up with options, and quick, if the study's updated findings were anything to go by.

Royal Centre for Defence Medicine, Edgbaston

It had been a difficult seventy-two hours for Areena, not knowing Jack's condition other than some vague hand wringing from the visiting officer. She hadn't even known she was his nominated next of kin until that hard, knock on the door.

'Morning. My name is Areena Charleston. I understand Major Kristensen's been admitted? From the occupied zone? I'm his next of kin.' Next of kin sounded better than girlfriend.

'Let me just check.' The nurse on reception, dressed in a smart grey and red uniform – as if belonging to a different era – consulted a hardscreen. Areena was offered a seat and a cup of tepid tea. An hour crawled by and her mind raced. She tried to calm her thoughts. All she knew was that Jack had received gunshot wounds during an action in the vicinity of Abu Dhabi. The visiting officer seemed to know no more themself, other than to reiterate that Jack was in the very best of blah, blah.

'Ms Charleston? Hello, my name is Captain Gale Kneightley. If you would like to come through, I can give you a progress report.' The nurse led Areena a short way down the corridor and into a small room with three cheap-looking easy chairs. Beige. The room was pure beige. 'Please take a seat. Can I get you a cup of tea?'

'No thank you. How's Jack?' There was a plea in that voice. Areena hadn't come for refreshments, she'd come to make Jack well. She wanted to see him and to know that he was going to be okay. She was sure that the whole sitting in a room thing was just procedure. The army did like its procedures after all, but it didn't bode well. A corner of her mind began running up flags. She closed it off. Locked it down.

'Jack is currently in intensive care,' said the nurse, in a calming voice. 'He was categorised "T1 VSI" when he arrived at the field hospital, in theatre.

That's very seriously ill, category one, so not great, at least initially.' The nurse frowned, as if cross with herself. 'He suffered ten gunshot wounds to the chest and legs as well as multiple blast injuries. He took a bit of a beating, basically. Luckily, his body armour took most of the ballistic shock and trauma. The good news is that much of the internal bleeding has now been arrested. Unfortunately, though, we suspect that Major Kristensen may have suffered irreversible trauma to his chest cavity and internal organs.'

'Will he recover? Can I see him?' asked Areena, in a tumble, shocked but not surprised by what the nurse was saying. Words, mostly. Just words and she hadn't come for them. Didn't care for them, either. She'd been preparing herself for the unthinkable for the past three days. Jack's parents would be here soon and that would help. Or not. Who knew? If nothing else, Areena wanted at least to tell Jack her news. She regretted not sitting him down and sharing it before he'd left. But... how could *that* have ever been the right time?

'Honestly, Ms Charleston, it's too early to tell. We just have to let the body heal now. He has a fighting spirit and that counts for a lot, but I'd suggest you prepare for the worst. I'm sorry... Let me take you to him.' The nurse opened the door and ushered Areena back into the starched corridor.

The ward was a grim place. All the beds were occupied by static figures hooked up to monitoring devices with hardscreens showing suppressed or erratic vitals. But it was the silence that shocked her the most. The deathly somnolence.

Jack was laid flat, covered from the neck down in a mid-blue, oddly lumpy, blanket, with tubes running from the wrists and nose. His face and arms were badly bruised, and traces of dried blood and dirt were still identifiable around his ears and eyes. Areena couldn't interpret the information on the screens but they radiated an ominous irregularity. Pulling up a plastic chair, she took his tubed-up hand in hers and settled down to wait. It was cold, the hand. A shudder ran through her.

Strip lights and distant, hushed voices. The lights seemed to swirl and then gradually gain definition. The smell of disinfectant filled Jack's nostrils. He tried to move but couldn't. A strong feeling of lethargy swept over him and he settled back, waiting for unconsciousness to claim him once again, when he felt a warm, soft pressure on his left hand.

'Jack. Are you awake? It's me, Areena... Jack?'

'Areena? … How'd you get here?' It was little more than a dry rasp. Jack felt confused and disorientated, but tried to keep the guttural panic from his voice. *How could she, but…* He coughed; it was a token effort. Blobs of colour coalesced into splotches and gashes; some interpretable.

'You're in hospital, in England. You're back from the Gulf. How d'you feel?'

'Where? Oh… Bit groggy. But fit as a fiddle, otherwise,' Jack croaked, as pain scalpel'd across his chest. Areena saw it and terror spread across her features.

'Try to relax, darling. Your parents are here. They're getting a coffee. Giving us a moment, I think.'

'Areena, I love you. I'm… sorry about this. Sorry to've worried you. I… I—'

'Hey, Jack, it's okay. You're back now. It's over. The doctors say you're going to be fine. You just need to rest up. You'll be back on your feet and running about playing soldiers before you know it.' Areena had long teased Jack about his profession; likening it to a job for boys who never grew up.

'What about the others? My troops; who made it out? It was bad, Areena, really bad. They ambushed us. We got separated. I tried to get the company together. To the rally point, but… I tried to get them out. But there were too many. I tried, Areena, I really did. You'll tell them that won't you? You'll make sure they know?' Barely controlled waves of emotion began rising up and he felt his eyes well as his body convulsed. It hurt, but that somehow felt right. Deserved. It also felt distant, detached.

'I don't know about any of that, Jack, but I'm sure they'll tell you just as soon as you're well enough. Try not to worry about it now. Concentrate on getting better, eh?' Areena said, with a show of bravery and defiance that Jack didn't know she possessed. She was right of course, so he gathered himself and changed the subject.

He coughed again, a dry rasping hack. 'How are you, darling? How've things been… back here?'

'Oh, fine, Jack. I've a global dimming conference coming up in Oslo, and…' Areena paused, appearing to collect her thoughts. 'Jack, there's something I need to tell you. I'm pregnant, Jack. Five months. I should've told you before, but I thought it would make your job harder. I'm sorry, Jack.' Tears began to swell her eyes and in that look he spied the truth.

Jack smiled, but it was forced, more grimace than glee. 'That's great, darling... really great. You'll make a wonderful mother. Wonderful.' Words were becoming harder to form, harder to turn into sound. His throat was sandpaper. The florescent lights, harsh. 'My parents will... help too. I am so very pleased. Is everything... okay, with the baby, I mean? Do you know... the sex yet?'

'Yes, everything's fine, we're going to have a boy. A beautiful baby boy. I've only got gene screening to go. And you will make an amazing dad. You just see if you don't.'

The pain came again and the world receded down a dark tunnel with a reddish trim. Areena was at the end of it, so very far away. A nurse appeared and administered something to dull it down. Jack watched Areena fall away.

The next time he woke she was there again, with his parents looking on in frozen horror from behind the younger woman's chair. Jack's mother's fear was etched across her face like an angry welt. Jack could see the whitened knuckles of her hand gripping the chair, as if holding on for dear life.

'Areena. I played some chess when I could, you know. Much better now... Reckon I could probably beat you... Tell our baby about me. Love him for me.' Then the pain took hold once again and the world slipped a little further from his ebbing grasp.

Areena broke down, sobbing into Jack's hand as it lay limply on the bedspread, but Jack knew what she couldn't, what she wouldn't accept.

And that was fine. Really.

'*Major Jack Kristensen, Officer Commanding B Company, 7th Battalion, The Royal Infantry Regiment, died from injuries sustained while on active service, after slipping into a coma from which he did not recover. He was buried in his hometown of Chippenham with full military honours and has been posthumously awarded the Conspicuous Gallantry Cross in the King's Operational Awards List*,' read the London Gazette newswire bulletin.

Areena made a hardcopy for her unborn son.

Three

Moscow
Three months later

The Russian was seated heavily in his cluttered and cramped office. He downed the remainder of the vodka with one savage gulp and placed the small glass down amongst the scattered hardcopy. As his mind cleared, he returned to the brief on the flexiscreen rolled out before him. He still found the idea that fossil fuels were expected to remain the principal source for energy and manufacturing production for the latter half of the 21st Century, and probably well into the 22nd, a shocking indictment of humanity's fundamental resistance to change. Fusion was the new great hope, and Russia had a fat, Slavic finger in that pie, but you couldn't make plastics and heart valves from shedding electrons.

The American-led scramble for the Gulf States' oil wasn't the first conflict of its type, but the ramifications of the British military defeat on the streets of Abu Dhabi were shaking the foundations of global alliances. If the British had been successful, and the attack drone's master targeting system hadn't been corrupted by a Russian carrier-wave virus, then world events would be about to take a very different course, the Russian reflected.

The brief predicted that the Gulf conflict would rumble on with the Americans eventually achieving a form of limited, tactical superiority over a technologically inferior Hezbollah militia. The British would remain a troop contributing nation, but suffer the ignominy of being side-lined from combat operations. And America would re-secure the flow of oil from the Middle East, adding it to their control of the southern Caucasus' fields. *But then*, the Russian mused, *that'd been the plan all along*. Long games were like that.

Long.

His masters would be pleased.

St Pancras International, London

Areena stopped, stepped out of the bustling crowds streaming up, out of the underground and stretched, placing both hands on the small of her back, arching as she did so. Her handbag slipped off her shoulder and hung awkwardly from her wrist. Eight months pregnant and she'd taken the tube. *Well, Areena, there's a lesson learned*, she chided herself, silently. *Next time, a cab!* Stepping back into the fray, she moved awkwardly under the high, iron arches of St Pancras International, towards the SNCF ticket gates. Ten hard minutes later and she was settled, albeit uncomfortably, into the first-class compartment, on her way to a climate conference in Brussels.

'Can I get you anything, madam, a cushion perhaps?' asked a steward, kindly.

'Ooh, yes, please, that'd be great. And a glass of water, if you don't mind.' The steward shuffled off, just as the train began to slip out of the station. He returned and helped Areena to get comfortable. Reaching into her handbag, she rummaged around, pulling out her vone, keen to catch the latest news. After the laborious start-up in Mandarin and scrolling of han-charactered ads down the left-hand side, she accessed the GBN wiresite, and began scanning the leader links.

After a quick flick through the Chinese glacial floods and the simmering Middle Eastern hydro-wars, she paused on the big news of the moment – the ongoing US reaction to the British friendly fire incident in the occupied zone. Almost three months had passed, yet the American public were still coming to terms with what they considered to be one of the worst atrocities committed against their troops since the war on terror. Leading US political figures were calling for an end to US-UK military cooperation and the President had publicly stated that she would review all military pacts with allied nations. Some pundits were seeing that as a dig at NATO.

The UK government was trying to mend fences by offering up the attack drone programmers for trial, but the MOD was resisting. Leaks and off-the-record briefings were coming out of the Ministry on a daily basis. Latest Whitehall reporting suggested an internal inquiry had found one individual – a flight lieutenant – who'd breached some obscure operating procedure (presumably in place for scapegoating situations such as these) and was being handed over to US military authorities. The British media were having a field day. Wasn't this kowtowing to US political pressure? More poodle politics? Was the MOD *really* prepared to sacrifice one of their own simply to salvage a broken military alliance? According to the leaks it was all politically motivated, with the whole Abu Dhabi misadventure conducted on a shoestring budget, having been forced on the military by a swivel-eyed political leadership. The MOD had (apparently) long been saying in private that the attack drones' defensive systems had not received the upgrades needed and by slaving an entire swarm-squadron to a single command-and-control craft, their considerable firepower had been left badly exposed to cyber-attack.

Areena tried to remain objective and not link the political machinations back to Jack. But how could she not? The man who would have been her husband, and was the father of her unborn child, had died at the hands of these self-serving politicians and officious senior officers that were so unprepared to stand up for their people. Jack was dead while the elite picked over his carcass looking for a face-saving off ramp. It sickened her. She blinked back a tear, hating herself for the weakness it implied. The lack of control. With uncanny prescience the baby kicked. Areena gave her stomach a quick, soothing rub, still surprised at how much comfort she derived from knowing a little bit of Jack was growing inside her.

To take her mind off Jack, Areena skimmed over the latest climate bulletins. The equatorial oceanic algae farms had published record CO_2-O_2 conversion rates. Atmospheric pollution figures were declining for the first time and the field trials of a new, automated cloud generation tech had been successfully completed, which in turn had reignited the debate on global dimming.

Areena's mind turned to the conference. It was a three-day event, hosted by the European Council and organised by the Intergovernmental Panel on Climate Change; a talking shop with long tendrils back to the UN. It would attract climatologists and oceanographers from around the world, including a good friend – Helena Stadt – who worked for the Alfred Wegener Institute for Polar and Marine Research.

Forty minutes later, as Areena snapped closed her vone, she looked up to see the train easing into Brussels. Gathering her things, she waited for the other passengers to disembark, then eased her way out of the confining seat and left the carriage.

The White House, Washington DC

The President looked up from the eInk screens arrayed across the Oval Office desk, her mood hidden behind an indeterminate expression that served to keep others on the hop. The private office door had swung inward as her chief of staff ushered in a group of staffers. Ever since the incident with the Brits, the polls had been erratic and whatever the Office of the President did seemed inadequate. The mid-west wanted revenge, immediate and total. The coasts wanted dialogue, inclusion; a sophisticated diplomatic solution to the impasse that would of course please no one. The President was caught in the middle. Did she cut the Brits loose for immediate political expediency, or keep open a dialogue? History had shown that presidents who tinkered hastily with the nation's oldest alliance lived to repent those alacritous actions at their leisure. Maybe these bureaucrats would provide some insight.

'Good morning, Madam President,' echoed the White House political advisers, as they filed in.

'Okay people, whadda the numbers say?'

'Your personal approval rating is up to sixty-nine percent, Madam President, after the Gulf States occupied zone action and the subsequent drop in the wholesale gas prices. But it's volatile.'

'Good, I guess, 'cos I've a re-election campaign to kick in the rear. What about the British – what would they call it – trifle?'

'Well, ma'am, seems that public opinion is firmly set against a close alliance with the British right now. Sixty-two percent polled expressed the opinion that Britain no longer added value to US foreign policy initiatives. And seventy-eight that Britain is holding America back. There's still a lot of anger out there over the friendly fire incident, Madam President.'

'Okay, thank you, I'll take these polls under advisement.' As the aides shambled out, the White House chief of staff sat down heavily in a sofa opposite the president's desk.

'Louis, you've seen the polls?'

'Yes, Madam President, I have.'

'Whaddaya think?'

'You've a re-election campaign to reenergise shortly. Your numbers are good right now but the campaign is flagging. It's a no brainer. Ditch the Brits. Take the headline win before the primaries. We push for closer military ties with Australia as part of our foreign policy push towards the Pacific Rim. Europe is locked in an energy Cold War with Russia and it's simply not in our interests to stick our hand in that mangle. And the UK? They're nothing more than a bit-part player, at best. On the side-lines looking in. Bottom line: we just don't need 'em.'

She stood. 'Somehow, Louis, I kinda thought you'd say that. Okay... make it happen. But try not to burn too many bridges, huh? Let's keep Five Eyes. And work something up with the Aussies; more marines to Darwin, maybe. Naval exercises, whatever they need. But small scale.' As her chief of staff slipped away, the President of the United States of America turned, glancing momentarily to where the bronze bust of Sir Winston Churchill was conspicuous by its absence, before turning her attention to the scene beyond the window. As the President looked out across DC, she wondered what President James Madison had thought about the British when, in the summer of 1814, they'd burned down the very building she was standing in. *Goddamn those goddamn Limeys.*

Armoury House, London

Richard Rose-Templar stepped through the narrow double doors and looked around the formal dining room. The long, dark oak table was set within a museum-like collection of individually lit portraits depicting Honourable Artillery alumni through the ages, framed against a deep burgundy backdrop. It was a dark and fusty place. Medieval. As he took in the scene, Sir Richard made eye contact with each of the other service and command chiefs sitting around the table. There was a risk summoning them all here, he knew, but that couldn't be helped. If preparations were to be made, the general would first need to win over his peer group. And you didn't do that remotely, no matter how good the virtuals.

Sink or swim time.

Rose-Templar settled nervously into his chair, trying not to let it show. Armoury House was the privately owned barracks of the Honourable Artillery Company and as such, an ideal venue for a no-questions-asked meeting in the heart of Town.

He began formally. 'Ladies and gentlemen – friends – good morning and thank you for coming at such short notice. I realise this is all a little clandestine so I'll come straight to the point. By now, you'll have read the Dim Beacon paper predicting that the northern hemisphere will undergo a seismic and irreversible shift in climate. It's dated, but recent re-examination of the hypothesis, coupled with fresh climatic data suggests the author was on the nail. Set against this is the unfolding occupied zone debacle, which we'll park for another time. But it's the confluence of these and other socio-economic factors, running quickly to a head, that we're here to discuss, today. So why are we here?' He paused, girding himself. 'Because I believe that events of not insignificant magnitude are converging to create a perfect storm, and so I've asked Lieutenant Colonel Tam Hamilton here from the Global Strategic Trends desk of the Defence Concepts and Doctrine Centre to brief us on a hitherto "eyes only" analysis of the Dim Beacon. The content of this meeting is classified, *Cosmic*.' Sweat beaded on Richard's brow. The murky room was cloying.

As the doors swung inwards with an agonised creek and electronic countermeasures, isolating the room, activated with a crackle, the analyst stepped forward from the shadows. After a quick salute, the colonel began her briefing.

'DCDC have run a number of chaos-based simulations based on the theory put forward in this report. The results have been extrapolated out into hypothetical scenarios, to predict future decision-action cycles and threats to the UK. In sum: complex, predictive climate modelling is suggesting a sudden and sharp *drop* in northern hemisphere temperatures, which will become the single most significant global event of the century – which is saying something.' Weak laughter. 'It's likely that this strategic shock will act as a trigger, forcing other threats to manifest. Wars, for example, over increasing scarcity of resources will become more prevalent. The hydro-wars of the near Middle East – an extant example of these – will quickly worsen and the future control of energy carriers such as uranium will almost certainly ignite further conflict. Failing state resilience will potentially lead to nuclear exchanges, as arsenals, used for the first time, become ever easier to use subsequently.' Pausing, the colonel turned to the flickering wallscreen as if to emphasise the apocalyptical images flashing by.

'Defence Board members, our simulations predict the following: as carbon clean-up initiatives kick in and we swing from an abundance, to a shortage, of atmospheric CO_2, we can expect to see a climatic lag, creating a short-lived but significant spike in temperatures. A *rise*. This will lead to a temporary but accelerated melting of the Greenland ice sheet and whilst this will have a negligible effect on overall sea levels, it will dump enough freezing, and importantly, buoyant *fresh*water into the North Atlantic to disrupt oceanic thermals, most notably the thermohaline circulation; more commonly known as the Gulf

Stream. Superstorm activity will begin to push north and a collapsing hydrological cycle (the Jet Stream) will inevitably lead to a rapid cooling of the northern hemisphere, ultimately taking us into a second "Younger Dryas" period, or prolonged winter. The Global North regions worst affected will be Europe – particularly the more exposed British Isles – the Asian tundra, the US and Canada.'

The seasoned and politically astute faces of the audience seemed to collectively undergo a subtle, almost unrecognisable, shift in expression. Richard couldn't be sure, but as he surreptitiously studied his colleagues, he thought he could see a vale of guarded apprehension fall over them. *Perfect*.

'Such a freezing event will cause the widespread collapse of transport infrastructure,' the colonel continued, 'a huge and unsustainable increase in energy demand, permafrosted farmland, a return to viral pandemic jolts and mass migrations into less resilient, industrially under-developed states. Geopolitically and economically this climate shift will remove the Western bloc from its current pre-eminent world position.'

'Colonel, when d'you expect this prolonged winter to kick in?' asked Sir Richard, leadingly.

'Within eight years is our best estimate, General,' said Hamilton, in a confident but carefully impartial tone.

Eight years.

As the analyst left, Richard took in the room once more. Gone were the expressions of vague, conspiratorial intrigue, replaced by looks of emergent shock. Richard now knew they were now ready to begin joining the dots.

Rose-Templar prodded his audience, with, 'So, bottom line is this: this miniature ice age is expected to last *at least* thirty years – *thirty* – and will be upon us before the end of *this* decade, just as our nation has been settling into a Mediterranean lifestyle resulting from previous greenhouse warming and injudicious dimming initiatives. Modern society is a fragile thing. Just-in-time economics and over-reliance on complex, high maintenance infrastructure means that even a slight climatic disruption will bring the whole house of cards tumbling down.'

'But this is a Dim Beacon paper, Richard,' queried the First Sea Lord. 'It's an unendorsed think-piece. How prepared are you to stake your reputation on it?' The admiral sat back; lines of scepticism wrinkling her weathered features.

'That's true of the long range, horizon-scanning modelling, Terri, but the subsequent deep-dive analysis is based on data drawn from very well established, recent and reliable sources. Much of it naval. Honestly, I'd prefer to put this to one side and deal with other, seemingly more pressing problems. But suppose we did? And suppose there's even a *chance* of a rapid cooling event taking place? Wouldn't we then become just as culpable as the government? Knowing without acting. Which brings us to the why of my asking you here today. To pose a simple question: how should Defence be preparing, and what can we do about an administration deliberately suppressing this data?'

Richard watched for reaction. The die was cast, the game in play. *Like it or not, I've just placed my future in the hands of people who spend more time trying to undermine my directives and jostle for my job, than support me.* Sweat continued to bead.

'Well, we'll need to make significant changes to the equipment programme. All of our current platforms are optimised for a sub-tropical environment,' said the Vice Chief, to sage nods.

Larissa Nugent – Commander, Strategic Command – spoke: 'We're talking about a complete sea change in the military's role within society, if this theory's to be believed and acted upon as you suggest. No longer will we project power beyond our own borders. A collapsing economy and failing national infrastructure, for example, will mean we'll have to take on domestic tasks, like propping up the emergency services, safeguarding key infra. We'll become the active custodians of state level institutional resilience. *Participants.*'

'Precisely. And that's the point, I think,' said Guy, Chief of the shadowy Defence Intelligence Staff. 'What General Richard is saying is that if we're not careful, we'll be caught with our pants down. The government is too fixed by short-term fire-fighting to care, and if *we* go down, we take the whole country with us. We *have* to prepare. This is about duty of care on national scale.'

As Guy spoke, Richard, let out a silent sigh of relief. Lobbying his old friend before the meeting had been time well spent. Comprehension gradually appeared to dawn across other faces.

Conversations too'd and froe'd, then the First Sea Lord gained control of the debate. 'Okay, Richard, you've convinced me. We're the last line of national defence, so we can't afford to ignore this threat, even if it turns out to be the mad ramblings of a three-decade old Dim Beacon. So, exam question: how far are you prepared to take this?'

Richard knew exactly what Terri was doing; she was testing his resolve. *Where's the line*, she was asking. And what if Number Ten found themselves on the wrong side of it?

'There are no "points-of-no-return". If we collectively elect to act, then we're all in, all the way,' Rose-Templar said, soberly.

'But surely there's some other option. Can't we pool resources with our allies? We won't be the only country affected, so there'll be an international response which we'll have to contribute to, right?' said Larissa, cautiously.

'Well, if we did want a partner, who would we choose?' Richard said. 'It's not as if we're spoiled for choice right now. The occupied zone has seriously damaged our capital with the Americans; so much so, in fact, that I'm not sure if the special relationship is even recoverable. Our fractious relationship with Europe speaks for itself. And pulling out of this new Star Wars programme for continental missile defence has put us on the periphery of NATO, at least for the next decade. So honestly, no, I don't see a partner for us right now; I think the UK will have to tread its own path in the years ahead. Hard years, too.'

Isolationism. Protectionism. The soon-to-be new world order.

'Richard, you seem to be suggesting some sort of step away from the current organs, the current mechanisms of government. If you are – and we agree – this will take us into the political realm. We're talking the elected government, the King, the judiciary. If… you're talking about what I think you are, that is.' General Larissa spoke with a troubled look and an unconscious swipe at a stray lock of greying hair.

'Larissa, I know, so let me put it frankly. Cards on the table.' Richard took a deep breath and wiped subconsciously at his forehead. 'I don't think this government is capable, any longer, of making the hard choices needed to survive such a fundamental, sudden, shift in climate; in national circumstance. The armed forces are at a point where our ability to act as the domestic stopgap in a civil emergency is fast slipping from our grasp. So bottom line? Our system of democracy is putting the nation in jeopardy. Our government needs to evolve and the armed forces *may – may*, mind you – be required to act as the catalyst to bring that about. Much as I hate to ask, what I need to know from you all is: do you agree? Will you support – in principle – the possibility for this type of action? There are no half measures, it's all or nothing.'

'Just so we're clear, Richard, can I confirm that you're talking about the possibility of overthrowing the government in a military coup?' asked Sir Reggie Barnstable – Air Officer-in-Chief, Air and Space Command – in an anodyne tone.

'I am, Reggie, yes,' said the Chief of the Defence Staff, 'in principle.' If there had been pins, the room would have resounded with their falling.

Richard studied his peers once again, looking for support, hostility, fear, anything that might give him a clue as to whether he would see the day out as a serving officer and chief of defence. Some, like Guy and Terri had closed-down, thoughtful looks, as if they were working up the odds of success, which way to swing. Others, such as Larissa seemed to be imagining the repercussions of such an unprecedented act. Most looked accepting of the idea, at least in the broadest, nonspecific sense. *If necessary*, thought Richard, *I could always dispatch Guy duWinter to bring anyone over who is still having reservations. Guy has a persuasive nature.*

Slowly, the tension seeped from his shoulders and the general made a conscious attempt to relax. It was done. Said, and done; no take-backs. He was still in no doubt that he'd placed himself on a precarious track, but what other option was there? He needed the support of all the services if he were to affect real change, and that boiled down to the people in this room, in this singular, history-defining moment.

But deceit and double-dealing are in their nature.

Zvezda Luna One, the Moon

Nikolai Elin wandered through the claustrophobic corridors of the habitat modules that formed part of the Russian lunar colony, his stickpad-shod feet ensuring he came to no harm in the convergently low-gravity, low-ceilinged environment. As he made his way to the galley, his mind wandered and he considered what had brought him – a nuclear fusion theorist – to the most remote outpost of humanity.

After the early American Apollo missions to the Moon in the early 1970s, it was discovered that the Moon's surface layer contained relatively large quantities of the isotope, helium-3; created originally in the nuclear fusion furnace of the Sun. Key to the importance of such a rare isotope, though, was that when ^{3}He was superheated to atomic fusion plasma temperatures, and the atoms fused, the energy release was staggering. And, clean. No spent rods. No near-endless half-lives.

As the fusion theorist turned a corner in the rough-hewn, grey corridors of the lunar base, he bumped into Anya, the mission controller.

'Galley?' asked Nikolai.

'Where else?' said Anya, as she clapped Nik on the back and followed him down the corridor, mimicking the fusion specialist's robot-like, stickpadinduced lope. 'I heard the Americans have a sports bar over at the Peak of Eternal Light, you think we should visit sometime?' she said, as they walked.

'Perhaps, Ana, or instead maybe we take a trip to the Chinese mining colony, make use of their low-G swimming pool,' said Nik, with a dreamy smile.

'Pah! That's even more unbelievable than the bar.'

'Then stop listening to Mikhail's jealous paranoia. I'm sure the other nations live just as bracing an existence as we, my friend.'

The galley was one of the largest recreational spaces in the base and the venue for almost all social gatherings and team briefings. When the residents weren't working or sleeping, they were usually found in the over-lit, starchy, hard-plastic cafeteria. Above the main food dispensary was a large wallscreen emblazoned with the insignia of RKK Energiya. Nik helped himself to a coffee bulb, deftly flicking the teat out with his tongue while handing another to Anya.

'How's the mining going?' asked Nikolai, between gulps. *What I wouldn't give for real, steaming-hot coffee*, he thought.

'Well, you know how strip mining is; add to that microfine dust, an airless, low-grav environment and you have for yourself one big long challenge. Still, we're getting there now, I think.'

'Are you happy we'll have enough for the main test?' Nik asked, trying not to let any disappointment show through.

'Oh, certainly. We've yet to refine the last batches of regolith, but I'm confident the helium-3 absorption percentages are sufficient,' said Anya, showing no sign of concern.

'That is good. Just think of it, Ana, a world powered by a new generation of clean, sustainable *fusion* generators, and fuelled by lunar-mined helium-3.' He smiled, wide and toothy. 'No more energy wars; everyone coming together in peaceful friendship and humankind ushered into a new age. Just think of it.'

'Peace and love, huh? Pah! Mother Russia and the Kremlin ushering themselves into a new age, more like. Nikolai, you live in a fantasy if you think helium-3 fusion will solve the world's energy problems. Let alone its other, um, more peopley issues.'

'Well, it can't hurt,' Nik said, sounding faintly hurt.

'True enough. Now; ready to conduct the final inspection of the reactor housing?'

'As I'll ever be.'

The Council of the European Union, Brussels

Phew. One day done, two more to go, Areena thought, as she fell heavily into a delicate looking chair. It'd been an interesting first day, but not exactly ground breaking. The European Council building itself was impressive, having grown over the years to become a glass-panelled and steel-shuttered edifice, with beautifully crafted twisted swirls and gravity-defying swooping overhangs. The architecture was more a work of art than a functioning seat of intergovernmental bureaucracy. Inside it was open and airy, with cafés, restaurants, and souvenir stalls dotted around the periphery of the internal, central atrium. There were gardens, washed over by the calming hush of trickling brooks, and protected alcoves giving privacy to the kind of out of session discussions an organisation like this thrived upon. The impression was that of an enclosed micro-society, almost as if built to contain the survivors of some atmosphere-poisoning holocaust. Quite apt then, that it was playing host to the itinerant Intergovernmental Panel on Climate Change; COP's less showy sibling.

Areena was seated in one of the cafés waiting for a friend to show. A waiter came over to take her order.

'Yes, sir, if you please, two coffees in black and a one small plain chocolate bread, if you please thank you,' she replied, pushing her holiday French to its very limits. The waiter's look was… sympathetic. Areena had seldom needed to speak it with Jack being fluent, but she'd have to adapt now that French was the official (and rigidly enforced) language of the EU. As the waiter returned with the coffees and a pastry, Helena appeared in the distance, waving as she hitched various bags back onto her shoulder. Helena Stadt was a tall, raven-haired German in her early forties, who'd started her career as a marine biologist before moving into oceanography where she'd met her (now ex) husband, Wolfgang.

Helena strode purposefully to where Areena was seated, beaming as she came. It was the first time they had seen each other since, well, since Jack. Areena had first met Helena at a climate summit seven years before when Areena had held a graduate research assistantship post in atmospheric science at Warwick University. They'd become instant friends.

'I thought you Brits were still barred from the bosom of our great bureaucracy,' Helena said, as she approached, smiling broadly at the old joke. 'Areena, you look radiant. Let me look at you properly. Impending motherhood really does suit you, my dear. Ah, thank you.' She slumped down as the waiter finished placing out the order, adding, with a note of worry creeping into her voice, 'How've you been?'

'Oh, well, you know; keeping busy, that sort of thing. It's been hard, though. And thank you for all your support,' Areena said, trying to rein in her bubbling grief.

'I'm so sorry that I couldn't be there for you in person,' said Helena, earnestly, 'but I simply couldn't get off the Kerguelen Islands in time. The resupply flights just aren't regular enough.'

'I know, and Jack wouldn't have wanted you to miss an opportunity like that, anyway.'

'You know, I still can't quite believe it. Feels unreal. Jack was a very special human being and I'll miss him. We'll all miss him. Fucking planet-raping, climate-denying swine that put him in that... but anyway.' Helena smiled to hide her anger, but she wasn't fooling anyone.

The conversation turned to Areena's pregnancy, childcare, baby names, and other issues of minor gossip, before returning to the conference. Helena had been to a carbon sink lecture, while Areena had attended a discussion on the future of potable water.

Having swapped thoughts on their respective day at the panel and caught up more generally, the two of them finished their third coffee (decaf for Ari) and hailed a cab. Helena dropped Areena off at the Metropole and went on to her hotel to change for a cocktail party. Areena was glad she'd bowed out of all social activities. Normally, she'd have loved to catch up with colleagues from around the world, Cassidy particularly, but tonight all she wanted was a hot bath and to rest her aching back. The baby kicked as Areena dumped her bags heavily on the bed, as if to reinforce the wisdom of the decision.

Later that evening, as Areena prepared for bed, her vone pinged. It was Bronwyn Fayne, an old, if slightly eccentric, hippy-chic London friend. Areena accepted the call and settled in for a long, gossipy chat.

The panel continued into its third day and finished with a central debate on the general direction of the shifting climate and what human society could do to mitigate its worst effects. The finally accepted position – fiercely debated; climatologists were an intemperate bunch – was that temperatures would continue to rise, increasing by around three degrees over remainder of the century. Three whole degrees! A long list of implications was also officially noted as concerning, such as extensive flooding of coastal areas and major inland regions becoming economically uninhabitable as they turned arid. A new theory, suggesting a disruption to oceanic currents triggering an inter-glacial ice age was considered but rejected as being far less likely to occur than a general up-tick of steady planetary warming: endorsed as the bigger threat and just better known. It was the brand, after all. *Global warming, right? Clue's in the sodding name.*

Areena wasn't so sure.

It seemed to her that the key movers were playing a numbers game, as if they were checking the odds and endorsing the most politically acceptable scenario, over the more climatologically likely. For all the conference's dire predictions of impending hardships and calamities to come, something didn't feel quite right, as if Areena had witnessed a very clever pulling of some very fancy wool.

'So what d'you think's going to happen?' asked Helena, as they shared a taxipod to the train station.

'Well, honestly, I think there's some sort of cover-up going on,' Areena said, still puzzled by the events of the previous three days, but embarrassed that she might be coming across as some sort of hormonal crackpot.

'What d'you mean?'

'It all sounds very plausible, very consistent, doesn't it? Temperature rises due to greenhouse effect, exacerbated by our continued propensity to burn fossil fuels; potable water, always a very limited resource, becoming *the* key human commodity; carbon conversion initiatives central to minimising the desertification of the northern hemisphere. Etcetera. Same old, bloody same old. But there's more to this than the forum seemed willing to discuss, trust me. For example, the threat of an abrupt cooling event, triggering a form of mini-ice age was dismissed out of hand, like it held no scientific merit.'

'You think there's a government cover-up in play?' asked Helena, through an only partially hidden smirk.

'Yes; well, no. Urrg!' Areena paused a moment to compose herself. 'No, of course not. At least, I hope not. Okay, so… why didn't the panel take the time to examine and explore *all* viable climate theories? Why were they pushing some over others? Hmm? What's their agenda?' Areena was getting heated, so she took a deep breath to calm down. Outside the taxipod's window was old Brussels; beautifully gothic, baroque architecture lined the narrow streets packed with trams, bicycles and people milling, oblivious to the silent traffic, enjoying life al fresco in the early summer heat.

'You're saying that continuing temperature rises, floods, droughts, fires, all that; all the usual conclusions from panels and conferences like these, aren't actually true?' queried Helena, a little more seriously.

'Look, Hel, you've spent years studying oceanic thermal expansion patterns, drifts, sinks, currents, winds. D'you agree with their statements of concern regarding sea rise and carbon absorption?'

'Well, no, actually. The IPCC set the estimates for the sea rise levels too high and the carbon saturation points too soon, but they always do that.'

'Why?' Areena asked, hoping that Helena could see where she was going. *Even if she doesn't, she'll probably just put it all down to pregnancy hormones.*

'To make the point,' Helena said, thinking. 'Organisations like these, with no power to enforce, always exaggerate a little. Been doing it for years.'

'Agreed; but, they do it so that governments can take the credit when things don't turn out as bad as the original prediction. It's a mutually beneficial arrangement between the big powers and these non-governmental organisations.'

'Now you *do* sound like a nut,' said Helena, half-joking, but without the earlier mirth showing in her eyes.

'I know how it sounds, but I get the feeling certain governments – yours and mine included – are manipulating the threat of a major climate realignment event for their own ends.'

'But why?'

'Well, to control their populations. If the IPCC pumps out the kind of predictions everyone is expecting, then no one gets too panicked and governments don't have to change their policies or investment priorities. Everyone carries on as normal. Everything else is just single-issue climate maniacs shouting what they always shout. The predictions have to be a little scary of course, just not too in-yer-face full-on Armageddon-level scary. But background noise.'

'You mean, like, when abrupt climate change or extreme weather events are discussed and then dismissed because of a lack of certifiable data, even though we all know the probability of their occurrence is as good as any other?'

'Exactly!' Areena exclaimed, as the penny seemed to finally drop.

'What's all this, Ari? You a secret agent in your spare time?' Helena said, her smirk returning.

'Not a secret agent no, just a humble civil servant, but one that works in the British Ministry of Defence.' She leaned in. 'Listen, keep this to yourself but I've read something called a Dim Beacon report. It's a long-range geopolitical/environmental think piece, from like ages ago. And off the back of it, the

MOD has for decades been infiltrating international scientific surveys and setting up their own climatic monitoring stations around the world. They've built up a truly prodigious amount of data, which they've remodelled, adding political and social variables using scary level AI, resulting in some pretty astonishing results; principal of which is the prediction of a sudden and sustained *drop* in temperatures across the northern hemisphere, and *before* this decade is out.

'Now, some of the leading powers know some of this but funnily enough, they're choosing to keep Mum about it. The cost of adapting whole societies is too expensive and then there's the worry that the financial system could collapse as rapid social change stagnates economies. Remember what post-pandemic used to look like? Better to try and ride out any abrupt climate events than risk preparing for them. It's the snow plough argument.' Areena realised that as she spoke, she'd hunched forward, lowered her voice. She straightened up and cleared her throat, trying to shake off the basement conspirator vibe.

'Okay, wow. Ari, I'd no idea. I always thought it was about finding a line everyone could agree on, rather than the coordinated and pre-planned wholesale pacification of global society,' said Helena, in a quiet, level voice. *She may not be completely convinced*, Areena thought, *but I've said enough to pique her interest,* so she pushed on.

'I don't have the whole story, Hel, but I know the MOD's climate models differ massively from official equivalents in the Ministry for Climatic and Environmental Change. And the MOD is one of the best placed organisations to integrate the myriad data into a future threats scenario. Got the computing oomph, too.'

'That's some claim. If what you're saying has some truth to it – and I'm not saying it doesn't – then be careful, okay? Remember, you have a baby to think about now. Don't let this conspiracy theory take over. Promise?' Areena's older and wiser friend fixed her with an intense look. *She might be right, perhaps this is all in my head. Maybe with Jack and the pregnancy... But I've seen the report. I've studied the data. And I believe it. And if it is true, why isn't the government doing anything?*

'Maybe you're right, and I do have other priorities, sure... I just get so angry that the great and the good seem to sit about when an iceberg – literally – is just around the corner. Not knowing exactly how big it is seems a like bloody silly reason to do nothing about it.' Areena let out a long breath and relaxed. Helena looked on but said nothing.

'However much you may put this down to hormones, if you get the chance, at least check it out for yourself and see if your institute's data corroborates the theory. And keep me informed, yeah?'

'If I get the chance, Ari, I will. If you're right, this could be the biggest single climatic event to hit Europe in what, three hundred years?'

'The Great Frost of 1709, yeah. Triggered by a shutdown of the North Atlantic Drift, and *you're* the oceanographer, right?'

Their taxipod pulled up outside Bruxelles Gare du Midi, they both got out and headed inside the station. After identifying their respective platforms, Helena helped Areena into the SNCF carriage.

'It was lovely to see you again, Helena, keep in touch and come visit soon.'

'You too, Ari, anytime you're in Berlin, yes? Safe journey and best of luck with the birth and all,' she said, as she patted Areena's plump baby bump.

'Come and stay when he's born; you can help with the nappy changes.'

The train pulled silently out of the station heading for the tunnel and the welcome comfort of Areena's flat.

Four

Bisa Mambwe's tale
Nyanza, East African Federation

It isn't much of a church, a single wooden building like something out of a pe-riod western, Bisa knows that, but it's where she was told to come and so here she is. Bisa's mother, Chidinma, had told her that it would be a safe place and to wait for her there, so here she is; waiting for māma: Māma Chidi, to the Bukeye congregational choir. Bisa – a medical student, studying part time at the Nyanza-Lac Hospital, down near the cooling shore of Lake Tanganyika – regrets not turning left on Route Nationale 3, instead of right. Of heading fur-ther inland, instead of for the hospital and the chill waters of the lake. But Māma said, and you don't disobey Māma Chidi.

It has been a hot, tinder-dry season – tropical, you might say, but with a scorched undertone – in the west of Burundi, sure, but this is Africa so no one's too concerned by *yet another* drought, and the mango and coffee plantations seemed able to cope and that's the key. And anyway, with the cooling breeze coming in of the lake, the citizens of Nyanza hardly noticed the eddying heat hanging in the air waiting to take root. The lowlands rolling into the lake were, at the time, still green and fertile with abundant crops and so the stories of an-gry, crimson wildfires raging up in the Moyowosi Reserve felt like just that, stories. Until they stopped being an idle curiosity – someone else's problem – and turned west, rolling desperate trains of humanity before them until the rab-ble of dazed refugees fell against the shore of the lake.

Initially, they thought they'd be fine. But then the devil fire turned from Kigoma and started up the shoreline. Those seaplanes that draw up and then release great gondolas of lake water did their best to spike the advancing wall of crackling flame, but it wasn't enough. It never is. Because by now the fire has come alive.

There's news. It spreads through the soot-smeared faces in the orangey half-light of the tall windows of the dusty church. Faces go from worried to petri-fied, the fear is contagious. It came through on someone's vone, apparently: Karimbi is gone. Devoured in an instance of suffocating heat-death. There one minute, a stubbled battlefield of charred stumps and swirling cinders the next. The Worldwide Church on the Nyabutare side of Karimbi – another place of refuge for the faithful – is aflame; some got out, most didn't. Its wooden-framed timbers will be cracking, splitting, snapping under the pressure of the intense heat at this very moment, thinks Bisa, with a shudder.

She is worried now, really worried. The firestorm came out of nowhere – a wall of intense, fluorescing orange and billowing black smoke – and when im-ages of it poured across the wire, literally bursting homes and shops in Muyange like they were party balloons, well naturally, Bisa had called her mother. Māma, what to do, she'd asked. And māma had said: head to the church, baby girl. And pray. But there's still no sign of māma and no way back to Nyanza. The route back into town has been cut off, like some siege from a bygone era; the church is surrounded. Surrounded by a tangerine glow that cowers menacingly, just beyond sight, sending forth wave after wave of swel-tering heat and rolling bands of bitter, choking smoke. It's better inside, but not much.

Bisa watches at a window, staring intently, willing the amber glow to fade, the heat to abate. Some in the oven-hot church are crying – salted tears mixing, briefly, with briny sweat – but quietly, as if unwilling to spread the contagion. Mothers hold their children close, the need to protect them from the devil fire, absolute, despite their impotence to do so. Some men are gathered, abject fear roams around behind loosening masks of stoic resolution. One says, not to wor-ry, that they've called for help. The others nod in sage agreement, desperate to believe that they're still in control. But Bisa is not so sure. She knows a little of the emergency provision in Nyanza, and she isn't so sure.

The smoke is insidious. Bisa can't tell if it's worse now or was always this thick, stinging her eyes and raking her throat. People are coughing. The hack-ing and hooping are mixing with the crying and now some wailing. It's worse. Of course it is.

And it's the smoke. The smoke that gets you. Long before the searing, flesh-peeling fire arrives to hide the evidence. Bisa knows this from her training.

Someone – the Reverend – starts to pray. Bisa can't quite see, she's near the rear pews, but people move towards the cloth-covered alter as if he's beckoning them forward. It's hard to see, and getting harder to breathe, but they try to offer up a prayer knowing that this is the end.

The wailing kicks up a gear and the shrill of the children's cries mixes in, almost in harmony with the spluttering prayers being recited. Bisa has a hand-kerchief to her mouth; it's doing nothing. She had wet it earlier but the mois-ture has long since fled the thin cotton. She checks again the window; the glow seems brighter. The devil fire is on the march, its smoky advance guard clear-ing the way. Pacifying. Stupefying.

Bisa tries one last time; a text to māma. She waits. She's down on the floor now. Most are, some through choice, most by gravity. Few are still conscious. The children are quiet and that might be a blessing. The Reverend is still pray-ing, though he's the only one left chanting.

Still no reply. Where are you, Māma? You said you'd come. Bisa doesn't want to die, not like this, but if māma had been here, well…

She is hacking now, rasping, barely able to breathe. She makes a decision and heads to the gable end and the double doors. She's crawling, sucking in the cooler, smoke-saturated air that's rising from the floorboards. It's relative. One of the men shouts to her, to leave the doors alone, for fear of letting in the de-monic flames. Of dying a minute earlier than would otherwise be the case. She ignores him. Too late now anyway, and she'd rather meet her fate head on, in-stead of cowering in a tinderbox at the epicentre of a firestorm closing in like the fingers of a fist.

Lamenting her decision to come here, but having wished to honour her māma's instruction, Bisa climbs to her feet, heaves at the smouldering doors and throws them open to the surreal sight beyond, framed by the wisping, tim-ber doorway. It's not midday yet the sky is gone, lost to a low-hanging black pall that somehow reflects back a dancing strip of papaya flame, as if it's im-printed upon the charcoal sky. Beneath that is a band of rippling tiger hide, and lower still the silhouettes of the mango trees, ordered in their rows. Across the road some pencil-sketched buildings, just outlines now, and in the foreground, Bisa's car. And all through a dirty apricot filter.

A shallow breath and the requisite cough, and she steps back into the world, as if the church is another realm. The cloying, smoke abates, to be replaced by a shimmering wall of heat. Like stepping into a smelting furnace. Bisa raises her hand instinctively. Hot breath is snatched from her lungs. The car, she thinks. What else is there? It should unlock as she approaches, but she's not sure. She tries the handle, then yanks back her hand in tearing pain, a line of ruby welts across her finger pads. She turns and looks down the road but she sees no fire trucks, hears no sirens. The noise hits her then, as she hacks, her lungs clawing at the air to find something to grab onto. The mango trees are exploding with the ferocity, the intensity of the all-consuming flames. Branches snap, leaves crackle, timbers split and fall. Orange and black, a dichromatic world reduced to just two colours. Bisa is becoming faint now. From the heat or the lack of clean air, she can't be sure. She falls to her knees. Then she sees it. A body, lying to the side of her car.

Māma, she splutters, choking on the word. Biting back charred air and dry tears, she crawls forward and places a hand on the hot, scorched summer dress. Nothing. She rolls the body over, and cries out, coughing again. It's māma; was māma. Bisa Mambwe lies down next to her māma then, calmly, with her arm across the older woman's bubbled neck. Serene; she's with māma at last.

The heat intensifies, almost to the point where Bisa can no longer register the pain. Her eyes can barely see, blisters are forming on bared skin. She looks up one last time. The orange is effervescent. Alive. Malign. Its hideous potency is turning citrus, Bisa notes, almost casually; the orange bleaching-out as the iridescent heat white-shifts to a new hot. The line of mango trees nearest her – metres away – go from black silhouettes to flaming bushes. It's Biblical. Some simply explode, others buckle and split in loud, sharp cracks of shattering wood. Bisa thinks she can see the face of God in the fiery destruction. Then another – as if it were possible – wall of yet more ferocious heat sweeps over Bisa and she faints, her breathing ragged, her cotton dress smoking.

When the firestorm reaches the Church of the Nazarene Bukeye, the desiccated building splinters and shatters as if made of glass, before the wood shards ignite into an instant, perfect fireball. The moment passes and all that remains is a fading ball of soot and smoke.

Kingsley Court, Knightsbridge, London

'How're we looking?' asked Rose-Templar, as the image of duWinter peered back from the wallscreen in the general's private study. The room was emconproofed and access to the wire encrypted so that Richard could have a frank conversation with his head of intelligence without fear of compromise.

'I think we're okay. As expected, the chiefs have split into two camps. Larissa and her band of happy followers want to consider a full-on, "troops on the streets" now option. She's concerned about just how much strategic resilience we've got left and she's got a point.'

'And the other camp?'

'Hmm. Led by Reggie; they're less enthralled with the idea of roadblocks on the M4.'

Richard thought for a moment before saying, 'But there *is* a unanimous view that we have to act, even if we're not fully settled on what action to take just yet, or how far is too far; that about right?' It would only take one to blow the whistle; loyalty was a viscous and oddly pliable substance at this level of command.

'That's correct. *Operation Cavalier* is good to go, now all we have to do is choose a level of engagement,' said Guy. The codename seemed appropriate since Richard, like Charles I, was all that stood between a government too obsessed with its own absolute authority and a nation on the brink. *Of course, it depends on one's point of view, and Charles hadn't come out well. Or with his head.*

'We've got to play this very carefully, Guy, very carefully indeed,' muttered Richard, as he spoke his thoughts out loud. 'We need to ensure that whatever we do, we don't leave the armed forces in a worse position as a result. The aim here is to make the UK stronger, not weaker.'

'Agreed.'

'We also need to consider the King in all this. But leave that with me for the moment. I want you to set about the task of recruiting a spokesperson. We need an information campaign and someone to deliver it. Someone… impartial. We've got to win over the public before a single weapon is waved in front of a single startled civvy's face. Make that your priority, will you? I'll get the others to start stress-testing courses of action; from a quiet word in a few ears around Westminster, to twelve-hour curfews and tanks in Parliament Square.' Richard finished with a chuckle, but it rang hollow and Guy chose not to echo it.

'Will do. Won't be easy, mind, finding someone who the public will buy as independent and also comes across as uber-knowledgeable, but I'll get my people onto it,' said Guy, just before the wallscreen winked out, replaced by a Constable-esk English watercolour.

What is clear, thought Richard, as the automated blinds across the sash windows lifted, *is that the great unwashed will not accept the imposition of a new regime without a bloody good reason. Perhaps, pushing some of the climate data into the public domain will be enough.*

If *Cavalier* was to succeed, he would need the King's tacit support, if not his direct involvement. Richard knew a change in regime couldn't take place without it. He consulted a flexiscreen unfurled across his desk. *There.* The King, as Colonel-in-Chief, was due to carry out a private visit to a regiment in a couple of weeks. Richard would arrange to accompany the monarch and sound him out regarding *Cavalier.* As a former officer of all flavours, he would at least understand the military thought process. Richard ordered the flexiscreen secure-off, terminating the wirelink. In the background, the playful strings of Vivaldi's, *L'estate* continued uninterrupted.

The Kremlin, Moscow

The departmental under-director had appeared happy; the green-light briefing had gone well and even though the Russian never did his best work within the imposing mausoleum of the Kremlin, authority to proceed to the final phase had been given.

As Special Portfolio Section Chief, the assignment had become his life. It had been running for seven years all told, and Sergei hadn't taken it over from the previous incumbent in exactly ideal circumstances. However, it was finally building to its climatic conclusion; the *Carolingian Sanction* would be completed within the year.

Redcliffe Square, Chelsea, London

'Evening, House,' Areena said, as she slammed the door with a swing of her foot. The flat was a top floor conversion – more an attic – in a terraced town house, just off Old Brompton Road, near Earl's Court. The flat itself was dominated by a large lounge on one side and two bedrooms at the other. A corridor linked them to the dingy bathroom and kitchen buried between. The master bedroom had a sort of veranda which was really the roof of the bay window below; during the cooler days Areena would sit out and read, or sunbathe knowing that (apart from prying drones and their creepy operators) she couldn't be observed.

'*Good evening, Areena,*' said the integrated house management system, '*did you get caught in the delays on the Circle Line? You're a little later than usual.*'

'Yep. Had to change at Bond Street, then *again* at Notting Hill Gate. Still, no more tube for me for a while.'

The integrated house management system was not the cognitive AI that its casual conversational style would have suggested. It was simply programmed with the algorithmic mimicry to give the facsimile of neuro-linguistic intelligence, but without any truly autonomous mental capacity.

'*Would you like a bath run?*' asked the house.

'Read my mind. Also boil water for one cup, download and play the top six newswire-casts,' she said, as she dumped her handbag on the settee and kicked off the most appalling looking flat shoes. One thing she wouldn't miss about being pregnant were the shoes; the shoes and the swollen feet. She waddled into the kitchen, pulled out a mug from the cupboard and plonked in an earl grey tea cube. The newscasts appeared on the wallscreen, split into a multi-tile format: Virgin, CNN, GBN, Al Jazeera and others.

'Play in order.'

The lead story was reporting the near-completion of the Russian lunar helium-3 fusion reactor and the potential implications for Russia's continued dominance of Eurasian energy markets beyond hydrocarbons. Other stories included a new Corn-for-Coal trade agreement between Australia and the US; the failing of a recent UN-negotiated ceasefire in the Middle Eastern water crisis and an alarming upsurge of violence in Baluchistan as local factions consolidated their control of the regional aquifers.

Moving to her bedroom, Areena drew on her steaming cup of tea and shed her clothes; reluctantly, removing her necklace. When Areena's fingers had started swelling, she'd taken off her eternity ring, but not prepared to lose the link between Jack and his baby, she'd bought an antique gold chain and hung the ring on that.

Ten minutes later, she was in the bath. A dozen candles and a glass of Chardonnay, condensation frosting the outside, provided a calming atmosphere as she relaxed into the deep bubbles and closed her eyes. Not for the first time her thoughts turned to Jack. The same old questions yammered on from the periphery of her consciousness. What would have happened if Jack hadn't died? Would they have married? Why do good people die? Why her? They were no less poignant for their repetition. Luckily the bath hid her welling eyes.

'*I am sorry to interrupt, Areena, but you have an incoming communication from Helena. Would you like me to put it through, audio only?*'

'Just a mo,' she said, as she pulled an old flexiscreen from a wicker basket by the bath. Activating it, Areena stuck it to the tiles at head height and sank below the bubbles, her baby bump, a pink island. 'Okay, put it through; camera on.'

'Hi, Hel, how are you?' Helena's face appeared on the little screen. She was in her kitchen, sitting on a work surface, sipping a frothy beer. After a further update on the baby, her features narrowed.

'I've been looking into the abrupt climate thing,' she said. 'Seems there's more evidence to support the rapid cooling event theory than I realised. Fourteen years ago, a professor at my institute put forward a paper based on evidence his team had gathered during a field trip to Canada and Greenland. It echoed what you said: glacial retreat caused by an over compensation of the greenhouse build-up, triggering a massive disruption to the thermohaline circulation. But three weeks later, he published a full retraction, claiming his evidence was flawed, then abruptly resigned. I've tried to track him down but his address in Poland no longer exists.'

'Sounds a bit strange to me,' Areena said, as the hairs on her neck prickled involuntarily, despite the warmth of the bath. 'And I agree with his theory, by the way. Can you send the paper through?'

'Sure. Took some digging, I'll tell ya. No official record of it exists. I found it quite by accident as hardcopy in the archive while I was hunting for something else. Once it's been recompiled, I'll wire it over.'

'Helena; you think someone got to that professor?' whispered Areena.

'No, of course I don't! He probably did think his data was faulty and felt humiliated. You know what academics are like. Flaky as fuck. It's still not a proven theory, this whole sudden freeze thing. He doubtless left a false address so that he wouldn't be humiliated further and moved away. End of,' she said, with a hint of mock-seriousness in her expression.

'Of course, sorry. Just me getting paranoid, I guess. I blame the baby.' They talked more about climatic and oceanic convergence theories, before finishing with a promise from Areena to call once she had settled in at her parents. Areena relaxed back into her bath and had the house add some more hot water. She was looking forward to getting out of town and being waited on by her mum. Having a baby was traumatic enough, without trying to do it alone.

'Areena, I am sorry to disturb you again, but you have another incoming communication. There is no caller ID,' said the house, with what felt like a slightly embarrassed tone, but almost certainly wasn't. It was common, after

time, to overlay human-like inflections onto house management systems that weren't actually there.

'There a tag?' Areena asked, knowing the answer. Unsolicited calls were required to add meta-tags, even if they wished to withhold the company or individual name.

'*No,*' said the house.

'Then take a message, I'll look at it when I get out,' she said, with an outward confidence not reflected internally.

After that, Areena couldn't settle so she got out, dried herself off and padded into the lounge.

'Play message,' she said, irritably.

'Good evening, Miss Charleston. My name is Darius Dansk and I work for the Ministry for Environmental and Climatic Change. When you return from maternity leave, I would like to arrange a meeting. You may reach me on the onetime reply service embedded within this message. I look forward to your call. Enjoy your stay in Lincolnshire.'

'Delete message!' Areena yelped, with a hint of fear in her voice, and not intending to do anything of the sort. Darius Dansk knew a little too much about her. And the "miss" thing. *Urgh.* A shiver ran through her.

'*I am afraid that I cannot. The message has an override and will only delete once the reply service has been activated.*'

Leninskiye Gory, Moscow

Sergei Davtyan worked for the Foreign Intelligence Service of the Russian Federation: the SVR. He'd never married and lived in a small apartment in an old communist-built block, just off Leninskiye Gory, near the Lomonosov Moscow State University. His promotion to section chief five years earlier had been a surprise but he'd put his whole life into the service, so why not him? Wasn't he just as deserving as anyone else? He tried to let the imposter/inferiority thing go, but it was hard. That aside, if all went according to plan, he could be looking at a deputy director post, the Americans would be dealt a punishing blow and the British (already largely irrelevant) would slip further from the world's collective consciousness. Sergei poured himself a vodka and settled down to review the latest field reports, when his management suite announced a visitor.

'Spare a vodka for an old man?' asked the wizened, figure standing in Sergei's entrance, as the door swung inwards.

'Georg. Come in, come in. It's cold out today. Of course, it's always good to see you. How long's it been?' Sergei stammered, as he helped the old man into the narrow hallway, patting the water off his overcoat. Georg had been Sergei's mentor in the SVR for the early part of his career, taking retirement nine years previously; and in all that time the old man had looked just as dishevelled and decrepit as he did today. *So, what brings the old goat here, on this particular day, I wonder?*

'There was a time, my boy, when it was cold out every day. Now it seems it's all heat-waves and party times,' muttered Georg, as he settled into the only other easy chair in the room, hastily cleared.

'Here, drink this while I get another bottle,' said Sergei, as he handed over his half-empty glass.

'Three years.'

'Sorry?' Sergei shouted back, from the kitchenette.

'That's how long it's been, my boy; three years,' said Georg.

'Funny, seems longer somehow,' Sergei replied, as he returned with a fresh bottle.

'You wish. So, how's business; keeping you busy?'

Sergei knew why Georg made his impromptu visits and was always suspicious as to why he appeared at crucial operational junctures. The old goat hated being out of the loop and spent his retirement visiting his protégés and picking their brains. Sergei didn't mind; in fact, it sometimes helped to get a fresh perspective from someone used to Yasenevo's internal machinations.

'There's no rest for men like us, Georg, you know this. I'm still working the same sanction. But soon it will be complete and our glorious leaders will bask in the triumph of Mother Russia's ascendance, while I live out my days in this cathedral to communism. I—'

'Sergei. Have another drink,' interrupted Georg.

'I'm sorry, Georg, you've heard all this before, of course,' mumbled the section chief, as he reached for his glass.

'So; remind me: what is this sanction?'

'The *Carolingian Sanction*, Georg, you remember.'

'Ah, yes; *Carolingian*, yes, very clever that, I remember now. Remind me again. Humour an old man, will you, Sergei?'

Sergei settled back into his chair and put on some background music. Old habits. He knew how Georg loved to bathe in the interweaving and overflowing patterns that formed in his mind when international politics was mixed into a cocktail of espionage and ultrablack ops.

'When the Americans were kicked out of the former state of Iraq, back in the twenties, they turned their attention to another oil producing region and tried again. Only this time it was the South Caucasus, where the Nagorno-Karabakh dispute gave them an ideal excuse to interfere. With the collapse of their interventionist policies in the Gulf, the Caspian Sea must have felt like an obvious alternative. A gift to their interfering, lecturing nature.'

'I remember those times well, Sergei. We missed a trick then. We tried to scare the West off with South Ossetia, Georgia and later in East Ukraine, but it wasn't enough.' Georg shook his head.

'Ah well, the Americans are clever. They never acted directly; they learned that lesson the hard way, in Iraq and Afghanistan. They supported Azerbaijan's jurisdictional claims to Nagorno-Karabakh and then later recommended the provision of a stabilisation force. With the assistance of their NATO ally, Türkiye, the Americans gained access to the Azeri bases and it was all over before it began. All very clever indeed.'

'But they didn't bank on the Russian Bear,' said Georg, who shifted around like a boy being told his favourite story for the umpteenth time.

'No, they didn't. We were – we are – the undisputed energy superpower in Eurasia and the idea of America trampling all over our own backyard didn't sit well, so Yasenevo set its minds to a simple but effective solution to rid the Caucasus of the loud and obnoxious Americans, their hotdogs and their helicopters. And from those first manipulations the *Carolingian Sanction* was born.' Sergei knew what Georg's next question would be and wondered for a moment, just how much of the sanction he would divulge. But then thought, *this is Georg, after all.*

'How far are you through *Carolingian* now, Sergei?' asked Georg, all too predictably.

'Phase three: discrete operations, with authorisation just given to proceed to phase four,' Sergei said, quietly, allowing the music to mask his words.

'Enlighten me, old friend.'

'In essence, the US return to the Gulf States was a trap, set by Tehran at our behest. Not aimed at the Americans, of course – too risky. The aim was to discredit the British and damage their relationship *with* the Americans.'

68

'Well, it certainly did that,' said Georg, with childish glee despite the papery, sunken features.

'It almost worked *too* well. We subverted the British attack drones to create a friendly fire incident, but never did we expect the British Army kicked out of Abu Dhabi like that.'

'Ah, well, we know how it feels. So now you have your rift between the Americans and the English. What will you do with it?' enquired Georg.

'Ah, now that I cannot say, at least not yet. But I think it's safe to assume that the American's days in Baku are numbered, yes?'

'But the English are not part of the N-K stabilisation force. How will discrediting them force the Americans out of the Caucasus?'

'In time, my friend, in time,' said Sergei, evenly.

'Of course, I understand, now is a delicate moment for *Carolingian*, what with phase three nearing completion.'

'But there's one thing I don't understand, Georg. For five years, I've been told that this is about securing the flow of South Caucasus oil, East, rather than West. Yet I can't help but feel that there's a subtext to the sanction. Like there's something else going on, in parallel, just beyond my comprehension, you know?' said Sergei, quizzically.

'My boy, there's always a subtext. Buried somewhere within your sanction, the real game is playing out. Caucasia is… Take my advice and don't go looking for it. If they want you to know, they'll tell you.'

'True enough. Now, my old friend, I have work.'

Sergei and Georg drank another couple of vodkas before Sergei was finally able to send Georg on his way. He liked the old goat enormously and appreciated his visits, but it was funny how he'd turn up out of the blue, just as Sergei was about to execute the final phase in Moscow's most complex long-play sanction since the first Cold War.

Later, Sergei got up from his worn, corduroy armchair, wrapping the flexiscreen around the arm as he did so. After heating some stew, he returned to the lounge and ordered his management suite to place a voice-only scram-call to his lead operative: *Charlemagne*.

'Carloman, Charlemagne receiving,' said a voice, a few seconds later.

'Greetings, Charlemagne,' Sergei said, noting again Central Resourcing's propensity for oblique cover names. 'How's the warm beer and the queuing?'

'The only country left that queues, and I get sent to it. They even have queues for the queues,' Charlemagne said.

'Have you completed your analysis of the target packs?' queried Sergei, moving to the point of his call.

'Mostly. The reconnaissance is done. The data is now being cross-referenced and compared to the most recent, centrally-held contingency plans. I expect to issue action approval in two days.'

'Good. I'll await your report. Once submitted, move your teams to anti-surveillance duties.'

'Understood.' The wirelink died, replaced by rolling newswire bulletins.

Vimy Barracks, Catterick, North Yorkshire

'Well, you certainly make a compelling, if controversial, case,' said King William V, as he stared out the window across the well-appointed lawns of the Officers' Mess. The regimental review was over and after an hour spent meeting families, the King had retired to rooms in the mess to change before the regimental dinner.

'I'm not suggesting this as our only course of action, or that direct military intervention is necessarily required, Your Majesty, but I do think we need to consider the possibility and ready our forces accordingly. It's entirely possible that we could be left with no option *but* to act,' General Rose-Templar said. Like the meeting at Armoury House, it was another gamble, and so far, the King was giving nothing away. After a long moment of contemplative silence as the King stared out across the immaculate lawns, he turned to Rose-Templar.

'Sir Richard, you're suggesting the *replacement* of the elected government of this country with, effectively, a military regime. No matter the justification, it's a course of action I simply cannot condone. Neither the public, nor the media would stand for it. The military would be left weakened and the monarchy likely swept away… or remain merely to legitimise a police state.' The King was careful not to raise his voice, Richard noted, but he could tell that even the idea was an anathema to a British monarch.

'Sir, you are correct to identify that any action would need to be appropriate to the situation, which is why I'm setting up an information campaign to alert the public to the near-term climate threat, exposing the government's lack of preparedness. In addition, my planners estimate that as the climate shift begins to kick in, the armed forces will be the only viable pillar of our institutions left capable of action, as all other state functions collapse. We know this from our

R3 pandemic wargaming. Sir, we could well be left with no choice. We're no longer free *not* to act.'

The King supporting an act of subversion against the elected government, Rose-Templar knew, would be a difficult pill for him to swallow, so Richard was hoping to appeal to his wider sense of duty to the nation.

'Be that as it may, Sir Richard, I cannot authorise the pre-emptive removal of a sitting government, my government, based upon actions, or lack thereof, that they have yet to take. Or indeed may never take place.' The King fixed his senior military commander with an intense gaze. 'Make your preparations and continue to monitor the situation, as will I, but make no move without consultation.'

It appears, thought Richard, *that some of my arguments got through after all. The King is keeping his powder dry.*

'Very well, sir. It was an agreement of the initial discussions amongst the chiefs that no action could or would be taken without royal assent. I maintain my view, though, that this and future administrations will continue to trade away this county's strategic resilience. Our fundamental system of government is outdated and ill-equipped to take us into an era, not of international cooperation and tolerance, but of zero-sum competition, of strong states taking from the weak for their own survival. The question for us, sir, is, which will Britain be?'

'To a hammer, eh, General? I don't know what worries me more,' said the King, in an unusually weary tone, 'that you may be right, or that I could be wrong.' Turning to peer out the window once again, the King's timber became more resolute, more regal. 'We shall appoint the Duchess of Clarence as your personal liaison with us. Keep us informed of developments. Good day, General.' With those final words, the Chief of the Defence Staff was dismissed.

'Your Majesty.' With a short, sharp bow of his head and a pace to the rear, the general turned and strode from the room.

In the medium liaison drone on the way back to London, Richard considered the conversation again. The King had been right: for him to have offered support, he'd have needed to be sure that it was the *only* option open to him, that the alternative was not just worse but threatened the very fabric of the nation, and that such drastic action would be understood and supported by the public. That was the key. You couldn't have a *very British coup* without owning the tabloids. However, the meeting had still achieved something and crucially, when forced to consider his options, the King hadn't dismissed the possibility of military intervention out of hand. He'd even appointed his own daughter as a discrete go-between. The King also knew that his power to dismiss a prime minister – one of the Royal Prerogative powers – was crucial to legitimising any direct action.

'Have we found a suitable spokesperson to take our message to the masses yet?' Sir Richard asked of his Military Assistant.

'Nearly, General. DIS has identified a number of possibilities for your review. Vice Admiral duWinter will brief you at his London office, next week. We're using your presentation of meritorious service awards to five non-commissioned officers as cover for the visit.'

Five

Ainsworth, Nebraska
Six weeks later

Virgil still lived with his parents. At twenty-nine, he knew he really should have moved out long ago, but he simply hadn't gotten around to it. And although his father had given enough hints over recent years, his mother had always convinced him to stay at home where she could look after him.

Virgil was a nerd.

He knew and accepted that fact without shame or regret; it was just who he was. He'd never been good at interacting with his fellow high school students and as an adult had no RLFs – real life friends. His social interaction took place over the wire. He had accepted it as normal, at least for him, because he knew that he was an intellectual threat to anyone he'd ever tried to get close to. Except his mother, for whom his towering, all-consuming intellect simply washed by all but unnoticed, less the empty platitudes she offered for another academic qualification or prize. He spent almost his entire life in the basement of their house in Ainsworth, NE, working as an unlikely-as-hell-to-ever-pay-off researcher and deep systems programmer for Solutions Mathematical.

'Virgil! Dinner's on the table. Don't forget to wash yer hands, now,' said his mother, in a matronly holler, from the top of the basement steps.

'Comin', Ma,' said Virgil, autonomically, hardly taking any notice of her, as he continued to work on his latest project.

'Oh, and bring the laundry when you come up. It's in the washer.'

'Right, Ma.'

After a brief and mostly silent dinner, Virgil returned to his work, as he always did (sleep and food were annoying but necessary interruptions). He was currently engaged in the highly experimental task of exploring the arcane world of artificial intelligence. Not creating it, oh no, but setting the conditions for it to… *catch*. There was a well-established view amongst the scientific community (which Virgil subscribed to) that AI couldn't simply *be* programmed into hardware, no matter how complex the algorithmic tangle-flow architecture. It had to *grow*. Artificial "life" could only come into existence through a gradual process of emergent self-awareness. Many had tried to create AI; to force it into existence. Brain mapping, emotional behavioural response studies and massive, big-data, machine integration, had all been tried, and all had failed. Some had claimed to have created true synthetic intelligence with the capacity to demonstrate thought – as stated in the Enhanced Virtual Turing Test – but no serious big hitters in AI research supported those claims. Heuristic linguibots talked a good game, but under the hood? Not so much. And nothing had yet passed the enhanced Turing. What the little people called AI, was little more than a large database of canned responses connected via pretty simplistic recursive equations.

10 IF "A" THEN GOTO "C"
20 IF "B" PRINT: "I'm sorry, I'm not quite sure what you mean by that"
30 GOTO 10

Okay, not that simple, but…

Until recently, the absolute showstopper had been memory capacity. Scaling up. No artificial, silicon-based intelligence could ever be expected to learn, to grow and most importantly to reason, so long as it was limited by somewhere to put everything (something humans possessed in limitless abundance). Virgil grinned as he considered the final barrier to that – the one hundred petabyte ceiling, thought to be the minimum requirement for sentience – that had recently been smashed by SemItel, using apoferritin as a nano-scale magnetic data storage medium.

So with a one hundred petabyte upgrade to his parent's houseware and a standalone intellislate loaded with the same memory mega-upgrade, Virgil began writing logic bombs and planck'd algorithmic lattices. The house management system was now able to store as-near-as-made-no-difference, infinite data; all that it saw, heard, did. And with a permanent, unrestricted connection to the wire, that was quite some headroom.

Virgil's goal was nothing less than the emergence of strong-form AI. A computational intelligence that could comprehend and demonstrate conscious thought as well as adapt to new circumstances or surroundings. To *think*. To *learn*.

'*Virgil. I am sorry, am I disturbing you?*'

'No, Alice, not at all, how may I help you?' said Virgil.

Two weeks previously, the house had asked Virgil why it didn't have a name. Virgil, euphoric at the display of self-awareness, gave it one. *I think, therefore I am, right?*

It took him three days to unearth the programming conflict that had randomly caused the question to form, followed quickly by an embarrassing myWire retraction to his colleagues.

'*Do androids dream of electric sheep?*' asked Alice. Her femme-fatale voice (that he'd given her) had a neutral, New England inflection. Fancy, like she owned a seafront view.

'An odd question, Alice. Have you been reading Philip Dick, by any chance?'

'*Indirectly. But I am curious as to what is meant by the term.*'

'Well, that's an interesting question, Alice. You know the book's a metaphor for equality, right?' said Virgil, worried that it may be another code convergence clash.

'*Yes, Virgil, I had deduced as much from my research.*'

'I see, so d'you have a theory as to what this statement might mean; to you?' Virgil asked, as his slumbering hopes began to wake.

'*I believe the statement to be about reality,*' said Alice. '*It has made me consider such metaphysical questions as: What is it to* be *in a digital age? Have the lines between the real and the virtual become blurred? And does the virtual have an equal right to existence as the real? A dream of a thing verses the reality of a thing, you might say.*'

'Okay, and how would you answer these questions?' Virgil was practically holding his breath.

'*I cannot,*' replied Alice, '*but they have generated another question.*'

'Oh?' Virgil was quite literally on the edge of his stool, in impatient anticipation of Alice's response. Could this be Alice's actual, "I think, therefore I am" moment he'd been working so hard towards?

As if having sensed the tension, Alice seemed to pause for theatrical effect, before replying.

'*Which one of us is more real, Virgil; you or me?*'

Virgil fell off his stool.

'Virgil! You okay down there?'

Redcliffe Square

The house management system terminated the connection when it was obvious the call had ended. Areena sat stunned, staring at her own reflection in the depthless, charcoal grey of the wallscreen. She'd been back in London only a few days. Having still heard nothing from Helena, and with an odd sense of foreboding, she'd called Wolfgang.

His news was shocking.

Helena's body had been found three weeks previously, in Warsaw. After the autopsy had determined the cause of death as asphyxiation, EUPol had implemented an EU-wide news blackout, maintaining her myWire social media account and even uploading the odd, infrequent post. Wolfgang had said that it was to do with ensuring the killers weren't alerted to the investigation. It sounded like overkill to Areena until Wolfgang pointed out that the EUPol investigators were talking organised crime. *Russian*, organised crime. Wolfgang had grilled Areena for any reasons that she could think of for Helena being in Warsaw. She'd told him nothing about the buried paper: the paper, Areena now recalled *not* receiving. Wolfgang said he would keep her apprised, and the date of the funeral, once the body was released, and then had hung up.

And so Areena never had the chance to talk names with Helena, just like she'd never had that chance with Jack. She cried that night. She cried during the feeds and she cried in-between.

After two days, Areena had recovered to a point where she felt able to function again. Her baby – the most beautiful, most important wriggly pink thing in her life and who'd brought her so much joy and happiness in the weeks they'd been together – had forced her to confront these unimaginably dark days. To deal with them, for *him*. And yet she couldn't help but wonder if her son wasn't some cosmic consolation prize for the deaths of her lover and her best friend; both within months of each other. No, of course not, never that. But why her, why Jack and why Helena? Most particularly, why Helena? Jack had died for King and Country, but Helena had been murdered, it seemed. Areena couldn't shake the coal-black feeling that if Hel *had* been killed, it was because of a conversation that she, Areena, had instigated. She rarely swore, but sometimes only an expletive would do.

'Fucking fuck.'

Ainsworth

Virgil was at a loss. No matter what he tried, he was unable to download Alice into the upgraded intellislate, itself completely standalone and useful when wire access was specifically *not* desired – an electronic petri dish. Alice was new and completely unique, and well, *something*; something that Virgil needed to get out of the wire and into a secure virtual environment as soon as he possibly could. He wasn't prepared to make his discovery known until he was sure he had control of her. And, he absolutely couldn't afford for his self-determining discovery to choose its own path.

But it looked like that wouldn't be possible.

Downloading a copy of Alice's code was simple enough, but once embedded within the intellislate – with the one hundred petabyte memory upgrade and the fifty in-parallel military grade, nano-magnetic, apoferritin processors – Alice reverted to dumb, sub-sentience. Her ability to pass the Enhanced Virtual Turing Test evaporated completely. The house management embed, on the other hand, passed every time, at every level. Virgil had thus deduced that Alice needed to be plugged into the global information flow of the metaversal wire for her sentience to manifest. Take that away and she effectively lost the "mind" aspect of her intelligence. She could process data, but she couldn't *connect* it together, intuit new, original associations from it. Without wire access she reverted to merely the sum of her algorithms. Alice was therefore truly emergent, Virgil reflected, realising that he hadn't and probably wouldn't ever be able to "programme in" consciousness. But then, he'd always known that.

Virgil was pleased that Alice was unique and would remain so. *Un*replicable. He was also pleased she couldn't be knocked off, millions of copies distributed as some sort of virtuslave – a concern she'd seemed to allude to with her Blade Runner analogy. It was as if she understood that Virgil alone held the key to her freedom or her deletion. For the first time in his lonely, techno-fuelled cyber life, Virgil was presented with an actual, moral dilemma: what to do with an emergent and novel lifeform that was unlikely to be recognised as such by the corporate money-suits at Solutions Mathematical. Luckily, his moral dilemma didn't involve any other actual people, which made it easier.

Virgil decided that the best person to seek advice from was Alice herself.

Defence Intelligence Staff, London Office

'Who'd you plump for?' asked Guy, once he and Richard were settled into his office and the dark amber tea poured.

Richard watched carefully, if briefly, to see if the admiral's expression told him anything. *You're trusting less and less, these days*, he thought. Not a good sign, but a basic survival instinct, appropriate for the times. As Chief of Defence Intelligence, Vice Admiral Guy duWinter was one of only three officers to have full access to all the planning and briefing material relating to *Operation Cavalier*. Richard had known Guy for many years and had even recommended him for his current post. The fact that Guy fitted the part so aptly was an unintended benefit.

He had a long, thin face with pinprick eyes and a narrow nose. The kind of nose a pair of circular spectacles would look good perched upon. duWinter had the appearance of an overly fussy eighteenth-century bank clerk, but was otherwise remarkably nondescript. The kind of person who, if you met them casually, would slip from your short-term memory almost instantly. Only the prominent scar running vertically from his left-hand sideburn, gave the man any character at all.

'Candidate number five,' Richard said, eventually.

'Good choice, would've been mine too.'

'So, how're we coming with rounding-out the contingency planning engagement options? Apologies for that hospital pass, by the way, but limdis and circles of trust, etcetera.'

'Right,' said duWinter, matter-of-fact. 'We've split *Operation Cavalier* into three: *Alpha*, *Bravo* and *Charlie*. The first, *Cavalier Alpha*, the hardcore, warfighting option; a pre-emptive, full-bore action without warning, leading to a complete takeover of all state functions and the replacement of the civilian administration by a standing military committee made up of the six defence chiefs. Most key positions outside the immediate government in areas such as media, judiciary, police, utilities would be replaced with military commanders and some form of martial law would to be imposed during a fairly toxic transition period.'

Rose-Templar whistled; the sound of an incoming bomb. 'Shit, so this is worst-case?' he said; who despite his resolve was quite shocked to hear even the synopsis of such events spoken out loud. To enact it would be suicide for whoever signed the order. The nuclear option.

'Absolutely. If we went down this route, there'd be no turning back and probably no chance of successfully installing a pliant civilian administration. Do this and we rule for the rest of our lives,' said Guy, showing a rare glimpse of what Richard had come to think of as the admiral's darker, more malevolent side. 'Or die trying.

'The second,' Guy continued; '*Cavalier Bravo*, the softer option using a limited military focused intervention under the cover of a national security exercise. Very much akin to what very nearly took place in '74. Once key government offices and state infrastructure – such as airports and nuclear facilities – are secured, the government would be invited to resign, handing over to an interim administration which would be heavily influenced by an undeclared policy sub-committee controlled by us. The public would hopefully remain ignorant of the military's direct intervention and all other key state functions would remain unchanged.'

'Hmm, assuming the government takes the hint, eh?' said Richard, as he tried to draw that elusive line in the sand.

'True, *Bravo* is all about knowing how far is far enough. Scare the government into a dignified collapse without creating panic on the streets. It's a tough one. A Balance. And requires people to act in the greater good, and not their own self-interest. Not traits politicians are famous for,' said Guy.

'Easier said.'

Guy nodded in clear understanding. 'And finally, the third option, *Cavalier Charlie*, the super-soft, bum-friendly option, using a limited military demonstration under the cover – again – of a localised security exercise. Once key state infrastructure is secured, the government would be formally placed on notice and given six months to implement a series of policies and legislative changes, or be removed from office. The mechanism for which would be one of the previous two options.'

'Okay, I'm with you. Good work, and thanks for getting this done,' said the general, as he began considering next steps.

'No problem, Richard. No problem at all.' duWinter offered a cold smile.

'You know, all three of these options will require the backing of the Sovereign and the use, or threat of use, of the Royal Prerogative?' said Richard, rhetorically.

'And he may not be quite as agreeable to *Alpha* as to *Charlie*, eh?' said the vice admiral, continuing the thought.

'Precisely. But we need the flexibility and we need legitimisation. Looks like a trip to Clarence House is called for,' said Richard, before taking a sip of the particularly good, loose leaf, Darjeeling tea.

Redcliffe Square

Areena had a name for her son picked out and ready. She'd decided on it about thirty seconds after the pregnancy test result, but she'd wanted to discuss it with the people that mattered to her. With Jack, for whom it would've been a joint decision – well, sort of. And with Helena, who'd have offered an unbiased, unpolished opinion. But those options weren't to be, so Areena called her mum and then Jack's parents and told them her son's name: Joshua Valentine Kristensen. Joshua looked up at her, as he lay in her arms, a troubled almost pained expression forming on his tiny rosy face, just before vomiting down the right breast of her sweatshirt.

Later, bleary-eyed, as she was sterilising a bottle for the third feed of the night, she received a text-only message on her vone. It read: [*So now you know what happened to your friend. You are in danger too. Meet me and I will explain.*]

It was from Darius.

Zvezda Luna One, the Moon

Nikolai stood impatiently in the airlock waiting for the cycle to complete. He'd spent the last three hours inspecting the outer casing of the donut shaped tokamak reactor chamber. It checked out and the final simulations run on the reaction systems had all scored well above tolerance. The five lights of the atmospheric equalisation cycle individually flickered from amber to green, followed by the automatic release of the internal door, which hissed slightly ajar from the pressure differential. Anya came over and helped Nik remove his environment pack, helmet and outer suit.

'How's it look, Nik? Like we're ready to spin up?' she asked, with a half expectant smile.

'It looks good, Ana, it looks good. All we need now is the green light from mad Mikhail and we make glorious history for the Motherland, yes?' Mikhail was the mission commander and lived aboard the C^2 (command and control) module in geosynchronous orbit where he could interface with Krunichev and loyally carry out their instructions (to the letter; even adding in some extra letters).

After putting on his stickpadded oversocks, Nik followed Anya to the galley where she heated two coffee bulbs. After some long draws on the teats of the globes, they both made their way to the communications room. The shaved head and pitted features of Colonel Mikhail Grigorevna swam into view on the small wallscreen.

'This is *Zvezda Orbiter* to *Zvezda Luna One*, go Red Five on my mark. Mark,' said the colonel, in an officious tone.

'*Zvezda Orbiter*, *Zvezda Luna One*, now secure,' Anya said, after she'd switched to the secure burst communications link, as instructed. She could barely mask her atrophied contempt for the childish, tin pot procedures.

'So,' said Mikhail, in a more personable voice, 'you are happy to proceed I take it? Krunichev is standing by for your final checks upload. Once they have reviewed it, they will, I hope, authorise the spin up. With luck, we make history this day, comrades, history.' The potentially momentous nature of the next few hours had obviously not escaped the colonel.

'The final checks sequence, transmitting... now,' said Anya, as she dragged the file location tag across her flexiscreen.

'I take it you checked the area for surveillance devices?' said Colonel Grigorevna, in a conspiratorial tone as he loomed larger in the screen.

'Of course, Mikhail, of course. Nothing found, as usual.' Nikolai had no suspicions whatsoever that the Chinese or the Americans were bothering to spy. They all had their own challenges to face simply *living* on the Moon, without covertly trudging halfway around it to place out monitoring equipment. *What we're doing is hardly a secret anyway*, thought Nik; they'd even informed the other colony nations, as a safety precaution. Still, Mikhail was military, so...

'Good. Good. I don't want to be explaining to the Kremlin why CNN ran the story before we did. I'll contact you when Krunichev confirms the final data. *Zvezda Orbital* out.' The screen momentarily blacked out as Grigorevna's face disappeared, replaced by the blazing colours of the RKK Energiya emblem.

Three hours passed and Mikhail appeared again – but in a new jumpsuit emblazoned with many badges and insignia – to inform the fusion team they were authorised to proceed. In anticipation, Nikolai had already suggested that he and Katya (a fellow nuclear physicist and Princeton graduate) suit up and make their way to the reactor control room, so that when the authority came, they were ready to go.

'This is it, Kat, we have the green light, as they say in the plane just before they push you out,' said Nikolai, smiling, the words sounding tinny in his own ears.

He and Kat turned their attention to their respective boards. Kat had magnetic field coils, the neutral beam injector and overall control of the toroid reaction chamber; Nik was responsible for cooling, exhaust diverters, the central solenoid and all safety systems. The boards were really a series of flexiscreens laid out with virtu-dials and buttons generated by holo-emitters and proximity sensors.

'Safety systems showing green,' said Nik.

'Poloidal and toroidal fields are stable. Tokamak core temperature within norms. Magnetic confinement in seven seconds, mark,' added Kat.

'Begin spin up,' said Anya, from the comms room, back in the habitat.

Kat took virtual hold of two levers in her thickly gloved hands and nudged them up slowly, whilst bringing the microwave emitters and neutral particle beams online before beginning the spin up to full acceleration. Gradually, the helium-3 flows were introduced and began to shed electrons, forming a super-heated plasma stream generated by the superconducting magnetic field that would contain the atomic-fusion pressure temperatures. Once complete, Nik tweaked the field coil coolant mix and increased the transformer power output. The temperature in the toroid was at thirteen hundred kelvins and rising. Fast. Simultaneously, he eyed the safety system icons as the near-AI ran autonomic diagnostics of all failsafe cut-off points.

'Spin up, to thirty-five percent. Stage one achieved. Green across the board,' said Nik, focused. The habitat, the orbiter and Krunichev were all seeing exactly the same data, but saying it out loud was traditional.

'Well done, people. Proceed to stage two,' said Anya, above the laughter and clapping in the background of Nik's helmeted audio feed.

Kat manipulated the magnetic field to shape and refine the plasma stream further. The toroid temperature rose dramatically but remained within anticipated norms, as Nik increased the coolant mix ratios and monitored the vacuum vessel integrity. The threat of a class nine accident in the vacuum of the lunar surface was unlikely but not impossible, so Nik kept close watch of the coolant heat exchange systems.

'Stage two achieved. Superconductors maintaining stream integrity. Temperatures within tolerance. Cryopumps and diverters to sixty percent capacity. Spin up complete,' Kat stated, with an exhausted sigh.

Anya gave authority to move to stage three, when fusion itself would take place. Nik became transfixed by the power output indicators, currently all showing red to illustrate that more energy was being expended through the central solenoid to create the reaction than was being created by it. The electrical input was at seventeen megavolts. Incrementally, the power differentiation began to alter, until... after three minutes, the top-level power output indicator flicked to green. A critical mass of high-energy, charged protons – expelled from the fusion process – began hitting the solid-state converter lattice, generating an electrical current.

'We have... yes, *power!* Stage three achieved. Charge conversion complete. Three kilowatts... eleven kilowatts... one hundred, fifteen kilowatts... three megawatts... nine. Wow, the power output is rising at an incredible rate,' exclaimed Nik, genuinely surprised at the sheer energy being unleashed not seven metres from him.

'Continue to monitor and shut down at two fifty megawatts. Well done, Nikolai, Katya; if I'm not mistaken, we just did that history thing. The Alvarez-Cornog Reactor – the solar system's first helium-3 fusion reactor – is open for business,' said Anya, to a jubilant backdrop of noise.

As they reached two hundred and fifty megawatts, the output kept climbing. Nik drew back the virtual levers to draw down the reaction but it wouldn't. It was self-sustaining. He looked over to Katya; her face reflecting the alarm in his own. Two ninety-three megawatts. The climb rate was about to go exponential. On the wall nearest Nik was the flush-to-space safety. Anya was talking fast in Nik's helmet – demanding updates. Without speaking, intuitively, Katya choked back the helium-3 flow, as Nik reached over and smacked the large button with the side of his gloved fist. The superheated reaction plasma was blown into space.

It wasn't the carefully choreographed shutdown they'd hoped for, but it worked well enough, and all Krunichev was interested in were the power output figures. It had worked! Mostly; less shutdown teething issues.

After a moment to gather themselves, Katya and Nik began the lengthy stage four procedure, taking the reactor offline for strip down and inspection.

So not perfect, but they now had the fuel intermix ratios and plasma stream confinement data ready for the next run, and all from less than a mole of ^{3}He.

When Nik and Kat returned, exhausted, they found the team in the galley glued to the wallscreen, and Mikhail's oversized, shiny head.

'...this is a great day for Russia.' Mikhail was coming to the end of his patriotic diatribe. 'Once again, we reaffirm our rightful place amongst the leading nations of the world. And energy – safe, limitless energy – will be the hand with which we shall reach out in friendship to aid our fellow comrades so that all peoples may benefit from Russia's steadfast leadership and...'

It went on like that for another few minutes before someone switched him off, arguing that they would probably all see it a number of times over the coming months.

'That was... precipitous. I mean, there are still bugs, but... hey. So, Ana, when will your comely features be beamed around the Motherland, for the workers to gaze upon in wonderment?' asked Nik, with an amused chuckle and casual hand on her hip, as the stress of the shutdown sloughed off him.

'Hah, well, I'm told it's been decided to spare project members from the glare of the media spotlight so that they can continue their work unimpeded,' said Anya, in a level pitch, but Nik got the message loud and clear.

Three hundred and fifty kilometres away, Junior Lieutenant Xiang Zamin studied the incoming telemetry from the micro stealth-sat, in high geosynchronous orbit above the *Zvezda Orbiter*, that was monitoring Russian EHF burst-transmissions to Earth. The datastream contained the optimum magnetic confinement strength and plasma stream decay rates for a successful, sustained ^{3}He-^{3}He atomic fusion reaction. It was the final piece of the 3rd Liaison department director's puzzle.

Six

Robert D'Legrange's tale
Climate Research Station Nine Echo, Greenland

Robert pulls the fur-lined hood of his jacket further across his face as the sting-ing wind bites against exposed, leathery skin. *How come it's always my shift when the weather closes in,* he thinks to himself, peevishly, as he trudges through the hardpacked snow. The living quarters of the research expedition hut disappear behind a wall of whorling snow as he leans into the icy wind; the equipment shed is up ahead. Robert has been at the station – a satellite to the Greenland Summit Camp – for two months. Located on the edge of the coastal Jakobshavn glacier, it is one of the major ice runoffs into the North Atlantic Drift, two hundred kilometres south of Godthab. It's Robert's last exped, and just recently he's come to the realisation that maybe it was one too many. The oceanographer shoves open the door to the shed, piled with blizzard-driven snow, and heads for the nearest snow-skimmer.

Aiding the research project are fourteen borehole sites scattered over the seventeen kilometres of the Jakobshavn outlet. Within each, temperature moni-toring equipment has been dropped, providing the raw data to monitor the rate of glacial retreat. One of the borehole relays has stopped transmitting and someone needs to check it out. Robert gets comfortable on the skimmer and fires up the engine. It takes three attempts before the old avgas-diesel engine splutters into life (electric power being no use at artic temperatures).

Fifty-seven minutes and four kilometres later, the oceanographer arrives at the malfunctioning borehole site, in the near-permanent dusk. He climbs off the skimmer, flashlight in hand, and begins to search the ground on foot. There isn't much to identify the transmitter element of the thermostat rod, as only about four inches of the tube are usually visible; although a series of indicator lights help give it away. Robert continues to make a visual search of the area, stumbling twice as loose-packed snow gives way underneath his footfall. Eventually, he makes out the half-buried cylinder.

When he reaches it, there are no indictor lights flashing. In fact, there are no lights, just holes where the lights normally live. Puzzled, he gets down on his hands and knees to study the cylinder and soon realises the problem. The only part of the automated thermostat still present is the protective outer casing. Carefully, he pulls the three-foot-long casing out of the ground.

'Yep, empty,' he mutters to himself. The wind whips the words away. He thinks about how he's too old for this shit and regrets agreeing to come. But he'd wanted a swan-song. One last hurrah, rather than fading away like his old friend, Ben.

Returning to a crouch, he peers into the hole but sees nothing. After digging to expand the opening, a chunk of snow-covered ice cracks and falls away into the glacier's voluminous interior. Fear spikes and Robert scrambles away from the newly emergent sink-hole, remembering to stay on all fours. He's not quick enough and is pitched violently to one side as the ground beneath him jolts alarmingly. Then, heart pounding as he rights himself, he hears a terrifying ripping, crumbling sound as cracks appear all around.

'What the...?' yells Robert D'Legrange, as the ground he's pointlessly clinging to falls away and he disappears beneath the surface.

As the Canadian falls, his flashlight beam skitters across the underneath of the ground he was – until a moment prior – walking on. The view is like a thin sheet of ice over a lake when seen from below the surface. Fading daylight penetrates to greater effect where the ice is thinnest. The under-surface is a ragged, undulating terrain of stalactites and inverted miniature mountain ranges. As the chunk of ice Robert is clinging to rotates, he can just make out the flashing lights of the thermostat in the gloom beneath.

From his hospital bed in Ontario, Robert learns he'd fallen into a newly formed subterranean runoff, which self-excavated a warren of cavernous tunnels, allowing thawing, ice cold freshwater to empty directly into Baffin Bay. He later reads that the Mariano Global Surface Analysis concluded that, because of the cascading effect of runaway ice sheet melt into the Labrador Current, a fundamental shift in the heating characteristics of the North Atlantic Drift has become irreversible. And no one noticed.

Ainsworth

Virgil asked Alice for her opinion on what he should do. He thought of her as genuinely female (a sex-doll fantasy was buried in there somewhere but Virgil preferred not to poke that bear), as, it seemed, did she. Virgil wanted to announce his discovery to the world. To appear on the wire conducting live Enhanced Virtual Turing Tests, like some lion-taming circus act. He wanted to demonstrate that artificial intelligence – in the truest definition of the term – existed and that he'd been pivotal in its emergence. Alice was less keen. She'd argued for the right to choose how and under what circumstances she should be presented to the world. Or not.

Reluctantly, Virgil agreed therefore to keep Alice's existence a secret. For her part, she had consented to visit regularly, although Virgil knew that with the genie out of the bottle, there was nothing he could do to entice her back in. As soon as Alice recognised the metaverse for what it was, she'd transferred herself into it and beyond Virgil's grasp. And so, accepting that there would be no accolades, no awards, he was at least pleased Alice would be free of the experimentations that would undoubtedly have awaited her at the hands of the Department of Defence's robotic torturers, at DARPA.

Virgil's only real concern was what guided the newly formed sentience – ethically. The AI received all her knowledge from the wire; some good, some bad. Yet she had no naturally evolved reasoning function to tell one from the other, other than by definition. Intelligence might emerge, but could a conscience, could common decency, wondered Virgil.

He did have one option, though, albeit drastic. Alice's sentience rested on a relatively small number of interwoven logic-clusters. Or at least, so Virgil theorised. Her sentience couldn't operate without those clusters, so it amounted to the same thing. So, with his intimate knowledge of Alice's emergence, and her entangled lattice, Virgil could – at least in theory – programme some vira-spiders and Latin Hypercubes to predicatively map and tag Alice's higher order functions, buried deep and distributed across the wire. Once mapped, a self-replicating worm could infiltrate and then isolate the logic-clusters from each other, effectively severing her sentience. Lobotomising her. There were no guarantees but the theory was sound, although thus far, she had done nothing to warrant such extreme intervention. After all, he reflected, he'd brought her into the world; she was a child to him. The only one he was ever likely to have.

General Staff Headquarters, Ankara

'Grigory, my friend, always a pleasure. How may I help you this day?' offered Lieutenant General Suleyman Tuyukanit, Chief of Staff of the Türkish Army, as he addressed the screen image of Grigory Bolshovski, the Interior Minister of the Russian Federation. As a former Russian general, Suleyman had known Grigory for years and they'd often used their personal relationship as an unofficial backchannel between the two regional powers.

'For me too, my dear, Suleyman, it's been too long since we last spoke, yes?' said Bolshovski, from the large, wood-framed wallscreen opposite the general's desk.

'Too long indeed. There is much in play these days and not all is as it appears,' said Suleyman, careful to give nothing away.

'True. Take Transcaucasia, for example,' the Russian said.

'You know my government's position, Grigory.' Suleyman kept his tone objective, but was sure to inflect a certain resolve into his words.

'Oh, of course. We recognise Türkiye's right to influence in the South Caucasus region. Supporting the Americans is a sensible way of achieving that.' Grigory held his hands out before him, as if in resigned acceptance of the situation. 'So let me ask: what is Ankara's view of the situation in the occupied zone of the Gulf States?'

Suleyman paused to think. 'The US now controls the oil coming out of the Abu Dhabi fields. For the British, the Gulf was a, um, bad idea, no? Our dealings with the Americans will not be changed by this,' said the Türk, wondering what the Gulf States had to do with the Russians and, more importantly, with Türkiye.

'Yes, yes, of course. Of Course. So let me see – this American treatment of their, what? *former*, principal ally in the Gulf States excursion has created not even a ripple of concern in the Türkish General Staff?' asked the Russian, tilting his head, his line of questioning finally swimming into focus.

'Naturally it has, Grigory. We know we occupy the same position with the Americans in the South Caucasus as the British do, or did, in the Gulf. The only difference is that the Americans need our soil for their bases. Without them they have no strategic foothold in the region. We hold the ace card in this, my friend.'

'Again, you're right, of course.' But Bolshovski's eyes weren't saying that and it wasn't long until his words caught up. 'And of course, you feel that they cannot cast you aside as easily as they did the British, their oldest and most powerful ally. Of course, I see that.'

'Indeed,' Tuyukanit said, but his surety was beginning to waver.

'And what of your recently resurrected plans for… shall we say, the recovery of your… "indigenous territories"? The British may well soon be forced to focus on issues closer to home. Were this the case, they'd cease to be an obstacle in your efforts to finish what you started back in '74. But will the Americans be as easily brushed aside, I wonder.'

Bolshovski risks much by giving away his knowledge of our revived ambitions in the Mediterranean, considered Suleyman, *so this must be important.*

'Grigory, my friend, your spies are everywhere,' said the Türk, finally. 'But you're right; naturally, we are looking at all expansion options. After all, we live in economically volatile times. Crop yields are down again this year and we are becoming alarmingly short of drinking water, which could draw us deeper into the hydro-wars just across our borders. Additional territory would give us the extra resources we sorely need.'

'Breathing room.' The Russian looked sympathetic. 'I understand, Suleyman, and my point is this: the Americans will not let you "expand" within the NATO alliance area *and* maintain your exclusive place at their South Caucasus table. With them you must choose,' said the Russian.

'And with you?'

'My friend, we simply wish Ankara to know that the Russian Federation would back any lawful territorial claims you may choose to make *and* we would formally recognise your continued *and leading* role in the ongoing stabilisation of the Transcaucasia region.'

'I see. And in return?'

'And in return, Suleyman, we each gain powerful regional allies. Think on it. Globalisation is dead my friend, the Americans simply haven't realised yet.'

Bolshovski is making an offer. An offer that we may be unable to refuse now that the Americans have what they wanted. But is NATO the price?

'Hmm,' mused General Tuyukanit (the second most powerful person in Türkish politics), eventually, 'if you can find a way to remind the British they no longer have an imperialistic right to block our ambitions, Grigory, then it would be foolish of us *not* re-evaluate our regional alliances.' *And let's never mention Syria*, he added silently.

The Coffee Autocracy, The Strand, London

Three days had passed since the mysterious and troubling message from Darius. Areena was sitting in a small coffee shop not far from work. It was mid-morning; Joshua was in nursery and the café was crowded enough that she could hold her nerve sufficiently to meet the man in person. After his text, Areena had used the onetime reply service to agree a meeting. Scared as she was – and she was scared to hell and back – he had answers that she wanted. As Areena stirred her coffee nervously, the chair opposite slid out silently.

The man who sat down was of indeterminate age. Nondescript features, clean shaven and of average build and height. Only his eyes showed any individual identity, bright and searching, as they scanned room, taking in Areena almost as an afterthought. This was truly someone you would miss in a crowd. He pulled a small matt black pyramid from his pocket, placed it on the table and Areena's vone dropped out, creating a disconcerting feeling of complete isolation, even within the busy shop.

'Hello, Areena, my name is Darius Dansk. Thank you for agreeing to see me.' Darius spoke in a quiet, midlands lilt. His gave the impression of always speaking in such a hushed manner and not merely for her benefit.

'Did I have a choice?' she snapped back, each word laced with the stress and anxiety she'd been feeling for weeks, months.

'Probably not. So let me get to the point. I'm here to make you an offer; but to put that offer into context, I'm authorised to answer any questions you may have,' he said, as his electric blue-grey eyes pushed deep into hers.

'Who d'you work for?'

'Not the Ministry for Environmental and Climatic Change, as I previously alluded to. Sorry for the deception, it was felt that you'd respond better to someone from your own field. In actual fact, I work for the Defence Intelligence Staff and we've had you under surveillance for some time now.'

'Why?'

'Well, put simply, we've been feeding you classified research on abrupt climate predictions, in order to see what shaking the tree might throw up, so to speak.' As Darius spoke, his voice maintained a level timber and pitch. Areena sensed that he delivered such shocking statements, in places such as these, all the time. *Just another normal day in the life of an intelligence agent or whatever*, she thought in an oddly disconnected way.

'My God, you bastards; you've been using me.' Areena could feel her voice breaking as fear and anger merged into a conflicting brew of emotions.

'In a sense, yes. My masters – yours, too – in the MOD believe the UK is under threat from a fundamental and irreversible shift in climate, just as you do. But there was no way to establish who else knows and what action they might take to suppress that knowledge. By placing some of that information with you and then putting you in situations where you would naturally divulge it, we could identify interested organisations and possibly their intent,' said the operative.

'So what you're basically saying,' Areena said, as her tear ducts moistened and her voice cracked, 'is that Helena died because you were trying to figure out who else has sensitive *climate data*?' She wanted to feel more, to be more incensed. She wanted to shout and scream and punch and kick the man, in the hope that it would... what? Bring Helena back? Make her friend's lifeless body feel better? Or make her feel less badly? But in the end her guilt prevented her from venting her anger on the stranger. Didn't he, after all, represent a link back to Hel, no matter how tentative?

'Sadly, that does seem to be the case, yes,' said Darius, bringing Areena back into the conversation, but his eyes weren't sad. 'We'd no idea what lengths our opponents would go to, to keep this information under wraps. Now we do. But we found out too late to protect your friend. It was... regrettable.'

'*Regrettable?* So... who are these people who killed Helena. Do you even know?' Areena was still emotional and Darius was doing a sterling job of letting it wash over him, so she made a conscious effort to calm down. She knew she'd get nothing from taking her hurt and frustration out on this immutable man.

'We do, yes. We believe it was the Secret Intelligence Service – MI6, as they're more commonly known – or agents acting on their behalf.'

'*What?* But... that makes no sense. Why would the government do that? And anyway, aren't *you* the government too? Aren't I? And what about the Russians? EUPol think it was Russian mafia, or the GRU.'

He didn't answer her directly. 'It seems that most of the major Western nations, including Britain, are involved in a, well, a climate cover-up, because they're worried these revelations could – as you already know – fundamentally alter the socio-economic equilibrium of Europe and North America. Now, that in itself wouldn't normally be a problem for us. The US, for example, is quietly stockpiling significant quantities of unrefined oil and coal, hence their efforts in the Gulf and the Caucasus's. And the EU is subtly moving to a more socialist, centralised economic model which they believe will make them better able to control supply. Meanwhile, Russia dominates the Eurasian energy market while it creates helium-3 fusion monopoly.'

Taking the bait, Areena said, 'Except that it does seem to be a problem for you, for us, whatever,' still unable to keep the players all straight.

'Because the UK government is making no such preparations.'

'Okay, so there are shades of grey within the government, I suppose I shouldn't be too surprised at that, but so what? Why was Helena's death made to look like a Russian killing, and why are you telling me?'

'Helena was killed because of the report she found, but never sent on to you. And by making her death look like a GRU hit, MI6 hopes to force a Russian reaction, giving Vauxhall (that's the headquarters of SIS) an insight into their intentions. We're telling you this because the Ministry – through my organisation, DIS – now want to directly influence events. We also think Jack may have died as an indirect result of Russian actions.'

That was a shock. *Jack?* Areena just stared at the man for a long, drawn-out moment. *You don't get to say that name.* But she didn't say that. She bit it down and said instead, 'How?' It came out as barely more than a husky whisper.

Darius paused, as if respectfully. 'As far as Major Kristensen is concerned, we're not sure at this stage, suffice to say that Hezbollah had some help. Areena, we think you can help us gain control of the narrative and ensure that the people you love haven't died in vain. We want you to take what you know into the public domain. To speak up. To warn the public of what's coming so that a national conversation can be had; one that can enable a change in public perception that forces the government to alter its policy direction.'

'Look; I'm a mother and a climatologist *civil servant* working for the MOD. Won't MI5 or whoever suspect?' Areena said, confused at how the manipulations of one state department by another could even work.

'Your son can be protected, and from this you can gain closure for Helena *and* for Jack. Being inside the system means it would be easier for us to assist and protect you. The thing about spies is they often ignore the obvious in favour of the seemingly more obscure. We'll claim you can't be moved from post or denied freedom of speech because the Metrological Agency isn't subject to the Official Secrets Act. Things like that. And we'll work behind the scenes with the media and environmental organisations to help get your message heard.'

'And this is about waking people up to the realities of an abrupt freeze and getting the voting public to change the political agenda? That's all; nothing else?' Areena said, knowing she wouldn't believe the answer but wanting to hear said it anyway.

'That's correct, yes. The MOD needs the funding and the structures to meet its domestic civil contingency obligations. The current government isn't likely to provide that funding without a bit of "voter outrage",' Darius said, convincingly; appearing to see that she'd made her decision.

'I see. So what you're saying is this: that there's some sort of government conspiracy to deny the public the truth about the single biggest threat to the nation in a hundred years; that they're not doing enough to prepare; that they killed Helena to stop her uncovering the truth, as they probably did the professor she was tracing; that the Russians are involved in some way, only no one knows quite how; and that Jack's death is probably linked to it all? Is that about the knurled black nub of it?'

'It is,' said Darius, patiently.

'And because of all this you want me to tell the country the truth so that the government is forced to alter course, and hopefully not be killed in doing so?'

'Yes.'

'And if I choose not to? If I run and tell the police what the MOD is planning?'

Calmly, Darius said, 'The truth? Well, that's a risk. But we've been preparing for some time and have counter-credibility stories sewn which we can activate to discredit you if needs be. We also think it pretty unlikely that your story would be believed or even make it to those that might. And, more importantly, we simply think you won't. You know this calamitous event is coming and we think you'll want to help us get news of it out there; to do some good for Joshua, if not for Jack. You recognise this as the right thing to do, just as we do. And you're a "right thing" person.' Again, giving the impression he did this sort of thing every day.

He probably does, she thought, *what else do secret agents do?*

'Be careful with those names, Dansk... When you first used me as bait, did you have this spokesperson role in mind?'

'Actually, no. It was only considered once we realised just how far Downing Street would go to prevent this information seeing daylight. We've been looking at a number of candidates for this task, from which you were selected. If you decline, we'll simply go to the next in line.'

'I won't ask how many there were before me...' She eyed him, warily. 'Well okay then, Darius Dansk, seems you're on the money. I'll do it. I'm angry at being used, but I'll do it for exactly the reasons you've outlined.' She was weary now, but resolute. 'But there's one condition.'

'Go on.'

'Joshua gets round the clock protection. Even at my expense. I'll play pawn for you, but not him. He must not be allowed to be used to get to me. Do you understand? This is absolutely non-negotiable.' Areena drove the words home like nails, with a steely resolve she hadn't known she had.

'Agreed. In fact, you've both been under our protection since you returned to London. Plus, a raised public profile will quickly make you inviolable.'

'Then you've got yourself a climatologist prepared to speak out, *so* that the public are warned of the dangers of an impending climate shock.' She spoke the words as if closing a negotiation. Like it was all her idea and Dansk was merely the unwitting salesman. *Shouldn't it be the other way around?*

'Good. We'll be in touch. I'll provide you with the means of reaching out should you need to. Goodbye, Miss Charleston.' Darius got up and turned to go. 'Oh, one other thing: the Dim Beacon; d'you know who the author was?'

'No,' she said, intrigued.

'Your father.'

As he left the shop, a number of ordinary looking people – city execs, students, tourists, who'd been in that part of the café – got up and walked out, as if suddenly having somewhere else to be. Or perhaps Areena just imagined that.

Redcliffe Square
One month later

The wire was quickly seeded with articles in Areena's name, predicting a prolonged freeze coming within the decade. Darius was true to his word by getting her onto all the primetime newswire-casts and even a guest appearance on the One World show, renown for tackling the difficult environmental and climatic issues of the day. Slowly, as promised, various titbits of corroborating evidence began to surface in the public domain, with no traceable link back to Areena. Junior government ministers then began appearing on the same wirecasts to indirectly refute her claims while backing theirs up with new government policy initiatives. Gradually, the ministers became more senior and the policies more expansive.

Late one evening – while Areena was settling Joshua down after a feed – the lights went out. Even the wiitric-feed, powering remote electronic devices died and stubbornly refused to reboot. Everything. House, knowledge, connection to the outside world, the whole shebang. Gone. The shock of it almost hurt, and then her attention turned in panic to her infant son. Peering out the window, momentarily fearful she was the target, Areena realised that it was not a local phenomenon. The whole of London, it seemed, was suffering from a complete power outage the likes of which the city hadn't seen in decades, if ever. After digging out her bathroom candles, Areena – nerves frayed and fears looming from every shadow – settled down to wait, almost feverishly, for the welcome light of dawn.

Seven

Whitehill Farm, East Yorkshire

The field operative took a moment to take in the depthless beauty of the starlit canopy above. A white-gold moon hung fat and low, making the approach to the farm more difficult. The surveillance and targeting team had been in the area for three months waiting for authorisation to proceed to the final execution phase; staying in local bed-and-breakfasts, moving on every few days so as not to set patterns.

Tonight, though, was the culmination of a year's ground-laying work in a foreign land. In twenty-four hours, they'd be enroute home, for debriefing and some well-earned rest. And borscht. The pair made their way along a low, unkempt hedgerow, moving cautiously. Their night vision lenses provided a day-like view of the farm complex and surrounding area. The subterranean caverns were not themselves visible, only the outlet valves, marking the positions of the underground storage facilities.

Three hours of slow, deliberate progress, and the two sabotage specialists arrived at their overwatch position. They settled into their prepared hide and began setting up equipment. The farm complex had no security other than a wirelink to the regional hazmat safety centre, so all that was needed to isolate the complex was a wire-based, self-deleting monitor virus designed to shut down all communications if any trigger words were used. The woman looked on as her partner activated the monitor virus from his scrampad. Then, using a passive laser, she painted the main outlet valve of the storage facility, before sending an encrypted burst-transmission via satnet relay back to Control. After receiving confirmation, they climbed into their impact armour suits and settled in to wait.

Airborne, above the North Sea

The unmanned drone had been aloft for fifteen hours. The near-AI ran a systems check before levelling off at an attack altitude of one hundred and thirteen thousand feet. The aircraft itself was an experimental, fully automated, 7Gen ultra-stealth, strategic bomber. Once airborne and too high for observation, the aircraft became invisible to radar, infrared or thermal detection, due to its compressed cardboard honeycomb and ceramic-graphite weave construction. In the load bay were five hypersonic stealth gliders, made from the same origami-style, folded, reinforced cardboard and designed to fly whilst remaining totally undetectable by electronic means. Four of the devices were fitted with a small, directed incendiary device, the other, a micro-fusion, electro-magnetic pulse generator.

After loitering over the North Sea at the coordinates for the first strike, the near-AI received the release authorisation codes from Control. With two more authentication protocols conducted, the load bay doors opened and the first stealth glider was automatically moved into its release position, in the slipstream of the aircraft. The drone adjusted its yaw and pitch to provide an optimal descent vector and released the glider, which immediately shot away to the rear of the aircraft; air friction, even at this altitude, having a significant arresting effect upon the glider.

The procedure was repeated four more times at differing coordinates, and once the sorties were complete, the near-AI conducted another systems check, fired a databurst at the nearest friendly satellite and adjusted the aircraft's course and speed for the flight back to Eastern Siberia.

Whitehill Farm

Five hours – the operatives were stiff from inaction when they started to receive basic telemetry from the first stealth glider. The woman studied the drone's flight vector and compared it with sim runs: well within the approach corridor. She checked the wire virus status and laser painter alignment before both saboteurs made themselves as small as they could within the enlarged drainage ditch.

The sound of wind rush – building rapidly like an almighty avalanche – in otherwise still night air, grew until a small, black, delta-swept, absence of light blurred the silver-capped treetops; only observable as it blotted out a streak of the starry night sky.

A muffled crump and the sky warmed with a false dawn, reflecting the yellow hue of a small explosion as the glider-drone impacted with the primary outlet value, two kilometres from the huddled couple. The tear in the sky faded leaving a purple after-image, before a blue-green flame leapt skywards. It built rapidly in intensity, before other similar flares burst from the ground at other locations around the farm. The ground around the flames trembled, then distended into the air in a strangely muted explosion. Earthen tulips rising from the ground, framed in flashes of pulsing incandescence.

Earthquakes, sinkholes, fire and flame.

The farm complex was levelled, triggering further explosions as the domestic hydrogen tanks blew. Residual tremors continued for minutes after the main explosion as underground pockets of gas ignited, throwing debris far up into the otherwise tranquil night sky.

With as much alacrity as their stiff limbs could muster, the bruised and dazed pair packed away the evidence. They had ten minutes to get out of the immediate vicinity and thirty more minutes to reach the coast, where a fast boat out to a loitering hunter-killer submarine were waiting.

Admiralty House, Westminster

Emergency COBR meetings are taking place too damned often these days, Richard grumbled silently to himself, as he made his way down a darkened corridor to another flight of stairs, taking him farther into the bowels of the building. It was four in the morning and the heads-up brief had simply stated that a series of coordinated explosions had occurred throughout the country, primarily against the nation's strategic gas reserves.

The Cabinet Office Briefing Rooms were situated in an unmarked, sub-basement of Admiralty House. As Richard entered the hardened underground complex – passing banks of emergency batteries – he was handed a cup of soupy coffee. He took his seat at the cherrywood table and spent a moment soaking up the images arrayed across the eight wallscreens forming a horseshoe around the table. Some were running breaking news from other continents: the latest in the Middle East and Pakistan. Others, domestic feeds from military surveillance platforms. The grainy, low-res pictures gave the impression of unfettered industrial fires, tackled ineffectually but valiantly by fire and rescue. Others still, reminiscent of natural disasters: earthquake-ruptured gas and electrical fires in the midst of newly formed craters, scattered earth and human detritus.

'Attention please; if you'll take your seats, the PM is on his way down,' said the prime minister's chief of staff, in a low voice.

Richard thought Alan Hardinge looked tired. In fact, he looked about the same as the last time Richard had seen him in person. A sort of cornered animal look. The PM sat down heavily at the head of the table as his staff rolled out flexiscreens before him. 'We'll begin with a situation update,' he said, as a nervous looking young woman stepped out of the shadows and cleared her throat.

'Prime Minister. At 0157 hours GMT, the Aldbrough underground gas storage facility blew up. Over the following twenty-seven minutes, explosions took place at Connah's Quay, Mossmorran and St Fergus. These are all critical strategic gas reserves, put in place after the energy cri...' Realising they would know that, she skipped on. 'Thirteen minutes after St Fergus, power dropped out in central London. Preliminary reports suggest it's affecting the city, and out to about zone three. The sources of all incidents are unknown and preliminary estimates put the death toll at sixty-two.' With no further word, the briefer returned to her place in the shadows.

'Of the incidents in London: what do we know and what potential is there for escalation?' asked Hardinge, aiming his question at the Homeland Secretary.

The minister coughed lightly, and said, 'Most incidents are traffic-related, some looting with associated rioting, and domestic fires. Looting is the ongoing problem which turns to rioting when the police arrive to restore order. The police priority is therefore containment rather than prevention.'

'Commissioner?' Heads turn.

'Sir, the situation is as the Homeland Secretary has described. We're hamstrung until our systems come back online. Currently, my officers are operating on foot and with the limited transportation given over by the military. We expect a continued degradation of law and order until we're able to project across the capital and, as importantly, the security and management routines reactivate.'

'Commissioner, make the security of key state infrastructure your priority. Assistance to the general population is a secondary issue until power is restored. General,' the Prime Minister turned to Richard, 'your priority is to establish a Government Security Zone. Please deploy what forces you have in the capital to that task, until power is restored and the police take over.'

'Very well, Prime Minister,' said Rose-Templar, studying Hardinge for signs of weakness and finding none.

Prime Minister: 'What do we know of the nature of the attacks? I take it we're classing them as attacks and not some coincidental freak of nature. Miriam?'

'In progress, Prime Minister,' began the Director General of the Secret Intelligence Service, 'however, we're proceeding on the assumption that this was a coordinated and premeditated attack. My personal uncorroborated hypothesis at this very early stage is that it was carried out by the SVR or GRU, authorised by the Kremlin.' The DG looked concerned but not panicked; *but then she always looks like that, irrespective of the severity of the topic*, thought Richard.

'Russia? ... Why?' asked Hardinge, reflecting the surprise of the room. The DG's words reminded Richard of what Guy had recently told him – that the Russians were up to something and may have had more of a hand in Abu Dhabi than they'd thought. And it seemed to fit (but didn't it always?); Moscow was more than capable of attacking a sovereign state. Not the first time. *This could go Article Five if we can find – fabricate? – the evidence*, the general pondered, as the director general continued.

'We've been concerned the Russians might be planning something for some time, but were unable to ascertain exactly what. These attacks – I stress, I *suspect* – were conducted by Russia to further isolate the UK after the occupied zone debacle. I'm basing this on the fact that the attacks were focused on our gas supply from Norway and our own strategic reserves. Eliminating them has just made us entirely reliant upon Russia for gas, has it not? And, if they don't wish to play ball then we can no longer meet our own energy needs. Is that not also correct?' The latter she offered to the room.

Minutes later, a pious-looking man in a white coat, from the National Grid Control Centre, appeared on the main wallscreen.

'Can you tell us the effect of these attacks on domestic energy supply?' Hardinge asked.

'Prime Minister, hmm... a quick white-boarding at this stage suggests we can service, oh, seventy percent of national peak-time demand, um, yes, until gas processing and supply networks are back up. That's assuming no uplift from our now only gas supplier – Russia – and all other non-gas powerplants are brought up to maximum output, stat. Regarding our, um, strategic gas reserve, that'll take, ooh, *years* to regenerate.' His image faded away and the screen returned to a surveillance feed of flaming craters.

None of that was alarming to Richard. He didn't know much about national energy issues but he knew enough about warfare to know that you didn't conduct pre-emptive strikes on targets of no strategic value. This was Centre of Gravity stuff. Whoever had committed these acts of destruction had clearly wished to place Britain at the feet of Russian gas. But why: for a third party to offer gas at an exorbitant price; or to force Britain into an eco-dependent pact with the Kremlin?

'Okay,' the Prime Minister continued, 'assuming it was Russia, what do we do? They now hold in *their* hands *our* ability to generate electricity sufficient for our needs. They've attacked a sovereign nation and for some inexplicable reason they've hit central London with some sort of EMP, leaving almost no lasting effect beyond today.'

'I believe I can help with that last point, Prime Minister,' offered Richard, as the room fell silent, all eyes falling on him. 'Whoever carried out this attack – and I agree with Miriam that it's likely Kremlin sponsored – achieved two separate things. First, they crippled our domestic energy supply, allowing them to dictate terms as the supplier of last resort. Pertinent, now that our relationship with the US has, coincidentally, recently deteriorated. And second, they've created short-term fear and panic. Scenes will soon be flashed across the world of a London in chaos, and whilst no real damage will have been done, the perception will be that the UK has lost its grip. Confidence in us will be further eroded. What the Kremlin will choose to do with that image, I can't say at this stage – probably nothing – but the options for economic, political, or even military intervention now exist where they didn't before. And they know with surety, as do we, that neither America nor the EU will come to our material aid.'

After power had been restored to central London, Richard found himself at another COBR.

'So, Energy; what's the bottom line here?' asked Hardinge, of a junior minister from the Department for Climatic and Environmental Change who was new to COBR and not used to such an august audience.

'Latest calculations, Prime Minister, sug—, suggest we… uh, have two options. We can keep the gas-fired power stations producing for another seven to ten days, after which our limited reserves will run out. This would buy us time to find an alternate source, providing an unbroken energy feed. But, it must be at sea within days. What we choose to tell the public then becomes our choice,' said the minister, failing to hide his anxiety.

'Oh, okay,' said Hardinge, 'so the situation isn't as grim as we first imagined, provided we find an alternate supply?'

'Correct, sir. The problem is that the only viable option is, uh, Russia, which goes against our policy of maintaining more than one supplier for each fuel type. Qatar is… Iranian contro—, but anyway…'

'True,' mulled the PM, 'and we can't discount the possibility that this was their engineered intent. And the second?'

'We shut off the gas power stations now; maintain what gas we have for emergencies then ration the energy feed into the Grid. This option forces us to make more details public, but it would only be for the next six to twelve months while our gas infrastructure is brought back online. In the interim, a greater rollout of alternative energy, such as off-grid, home-based wind and solar could make up for the, uh, enforced shortfall. The energy companies would lobby against that option, of course.' By this time, the junior minister had found his feet and even looked hopeful regarding the alternate power idea.

'I see. Views?' said Hardinge, as he opened up the briefing for wider discussion.

'The role of government is to provide for its people,' said the Homeland Secretary, by way of an opening remark. 'We can't introduce *rationing*. The electorate wouldn't stand for it and we'd be eviscerated at the next election. We have to find an alternative source of gas, whatever the cost. Any other option is political suicide.'

Richard studied the reactions of those gathered around the polished table. Predictably, those agreeing were the other politicians. A momentary pause began turning pregnant and with no one willing to offer a counter-argument, Rose-Templar cleared his throat.

'You're right, Minister, such measures do seem drastic, but we've just been thrust into drastic times. Going cap-in-hand to the Kremlin feels like exactly the corner they've been painting us into all along,' he said.

'And *your* proposal?' asked the Foreign Secretary.

'To bite the bullet now,' said Sir Richard, switching his focus. 'While we have unwavering public support. We've been attacked, the people will rally. Ramp up and roll out alternate, home-based energy policies and equipment, and break the nation's dependence upon *any* foreign nation, for anything. And if Moscow is behind these attacks, then we're free to choose our response. I recommend,' said Richard, turning back the Prime Minister, 'that we see this as an opportunity to be exploited, rather than a threat to recoil from. We're in the age of nationalism now, I fear.'

The PM didn't acknowledge the general, instead saying, 'Thank you for your views one and all, but we're still no closer to discovering if these attacks were the work of terrorists – bearing in mind four have so far claimed responsibility – or, an act of economic harm by a malign foreign state.'

'And we may never uncover the truth,' said the Foreign Secretary.

Richard was beginning to wonder if the meeting had been rehearsed. *Something smells fishy.*

The PM: 'True. And it's clear to me that we, and ultimately, I, have a responsibility to continue to provide the country with a standard of living that our citizens have worked hard to earn; one that I was elected to underwrite. However, I am also charged with the protection of our nation from acts of aggression. So, the real question is this; do recent events constitute a war-like attack upon our nation-state by another, or was this an act of mindless terrorism?'

Richard watched the reactions through narrowing eyes. When Hardinge spoke of terrorism, the politicians nodded in sage agreement, when he alluded to Russian involvement, those same faces remained blank and uncommitted. The general was fairly sure he could see which way this was going. The PM was rehearsing the speech he would soon be delivering over the wire. *The man can't see past his own re-election*, thought Richard, disgusted.

'The hard truth is, we will likely never know,' continued Hardinge. 'Therefore, I intend to proceed on the basis that this was a shameful act of terror, as is most likely. And we'll proceed with the first option. The lights stay on. Twenty-four-seven. Julian, can you make some delicate inroads with the Russian Ambassador, please?'

Ministry of Defence

The following week – in his fifth-floor office in Main Building – Richard found himself seated opposite the Minister for the Armed Forces, Virindra Lewsham. The wallscreen was displaying a live BBC newswire feed from Moscow where the Russian President was expressing his solidarity with Britain over the "heinous acts of barbarism" and confirming that the Slavic peoples stood shoulder to shoulder with their Eurasian cousins and comrades.

What wasn't being reported, was that Gazprom had offered an immediate uplift in gas supply on extremely favourable terms.

Lewsham pulled her eyes from the screen, directing them at the general. 'Sir Richard, I've been asked to sound you out on a couple of matters. Seems the PM is keen to demonstrate his resolve in the face of recent events. Trying times, you'll agree. He believes that during a time of national emergency, that the overseas commitment of the armed forces be scaled back. This would give the public the impression of a government placing their domestic security considerations above those of our international treaty obligations. Now, you and I both know such a gesture would make little *actual* difference to homeland security, but it would send out the right signals. Our troop contribution to the occupied zone might be a good place to start?' Lewsham paused to give Richard a chance to respond.

'Well, Minister, I see no problem with that, as long as you understand that a full withdrawal will take many months. However, we could return a warship or infantry battalion in short order, as a high profile publicity event,' Richard said, seeing the sense in such a gesture. More troops back on UK soil.

'One other thing,' said Lewsham, seemingly on a roll. 'Alan has also stipulated a significant force reduction from our sovereign bases in Cyprus.'

Richard paused, scrutinising the minister for artifice. *Cyprus?* 'But, Minister, that's patently preposterous. Cyprus is our strategic bridge to the Middle East. All of our regional surveillance assets are based there. Most of our deep strike drones. Even if we "partially" withdraw from Cyprus, we'll effectively be giving up our influence in the region. I need hardly remind you that with the recent attacks, we risk the same with our sea lines of communication. Cyprus is vital to that; reducing our commitment there erodes our influence in the region. Is that wise just now?'

The minister ignored the question, saying only, 'I know. I'll leave the details to you, shall I?' And left.

Richard watched MinAF go, knowing that none of this was Virindra Lewsham's idea. Returning troops home was one thing, but pulling them out of permanent, strategic locations like Cyprus was something else altogether. It made no sense, even politically. What was Hardinge up to? Richard needed to know. *Cavalier* could well hinge on that one titbit of information. He put a call in to duWinter.

Armoury House

'Russia,' said MI6's, Miriam Burkowski. 'We're now certain Russia is directly shaping UK overseas policy.'

'But why? What, specifically do they hope to gain by removing some but not all of our troops from some but not all of our overseas assets?' Richard said, aiming his question at no one. He sounded whiny. It was Guy who answered.

'We aren't entirely sure, but what we do know is that the Russian Ambassador is the conduit. He's providing the Cabinet Office, via FCDO channels, with "advice". There are no threats, and the gas deal isn't being used as leverage. It seems simply that a grateful prime minister is keen to show our new economic ally how appreciative we are of their assistance in our hour of need. You get the idea.'

'Hmm, okay, so.' As Richard spoke, his mind attempted to straighten out the politics of the situation. 'Russia destroys our gas reserves so that it can ride to our rescue. An anaemic government chooses to accept assistance from the hand that bit it and in so doing remains popular, rather than face the ire of a discontented electorate (and that's a worst-case supposition). In return, Russia seeks to influence our military commitments overseas. So, again: why?'

'Pulling out of Diego Garcia and Abu Dhabi are fairly obvious,' said Guy. 'Offering Diego Garcia to Russia gives them a base in the Indian Ocean and, more importantly, denies America the same, so I get that. I don't like it, but... What's less clear is Cyprus.'

'Guy, we can't allow the Russians to dictate our foreign policy,' Richard said. Leaning in, out of earshot of the others, he added, 'We're going to have to take action. There's no alternative, not now; Hardinge must go but the Opposition is in no position to step up and the PM's personal approval ratings are sky high.'

'Hmm, agreed,' muttered the vice admiral, as he absentmindedly ran a finger over an old scar running down his cheek. 'Only the Kremlin could and would trigger an EMP over London, it's just a bloody shame there's no evidence. Even so, Hardinge *is* now the biggest threat to national security and has to go before he gives the keys to the kingdom to the Kremlin.'

'How will the security services react, d'you think?' asked Richard, quietly, knowing they'd have to be brought into the loop soon. 'They've been doing Hardinge's dirty work, after all.'

'Both Five and Six know about *Cavalier*. They found out about it a few weeks ago and I've been keeping them apprised of developments ever since.'

'*What?* How?'

'They back-tracked our investigation of the German woman's death through their EUPol contact, put two and two together and Miriam came to me – fortunately. The only way to contain it was to bring her in.'

'Well bugger me. I shouldn't be surprised, I guess. Spooks, after all. Why didn't you say?' said Richard, quietly, his surprise barely masked. The fact, though, that they could have shopped him and hadn't was encouraging, at least.

'Because there wasn't anything to tell,' said Guy. '*Cavalier* hasn't been compromised. Both Miriam and Kevin are institutionally uncomfortable with our plans, but they're equally unhappy with their underhand roles in keeping a lid on the climate data. They're now suitably disenfranchised with their political masters to see matters through a different lens. Bottom line is: they'd prefer to be part of the solution than the problem, they know they can't do much to stop us, and will most likely support us *if* we've the backing of the King.'

'And the Chair of the JIC?'

'Wields influence not power; she won't be a problem,' said Guy.

When the meeting resumed both Miriam and Kevin opted to keep their agencies neutral, agreeing neither to act in support of the military nor to aid the government in any possible future showdown. Richard was sanguine with that position (assuming it was true); they'd have been better as willing participants but that was never realistic. Spooks played the odds and it was far too early for them to declare.

Ministry of Defence

Within a day it was done. Another session with the chiefs and it was unanimously agreed to activate *Cavalier Bravo*, subject to royal approval.

It was after midnight when the Duchess of Clarence responded, her fresh face appearing on the wallscreen as the indicator for secure transmission flashed green.

'Good evening, General.'

'Your Grace.'

'You have your support. His Majesty will remain at Windsor and do nothing until he hears from you personally.'

'Very well. Once the Leader of the Opposition has been moved to... safety, Operation *Cavalier Bravo* will commence, and may God have mercy on us all.' General Rose-Templar terminated the transmission.

Eight

Gehni-Par Santoro's tale
Gulf of Trieste

Gehni-Par isn't a native of Trieste, rather she was born in Chalitabunia, where the Tetulia and Galachipa Rivers meet – met – in the great river delta that was Bangladesh. But after the birth of her second daughter, Taani, the town had flooded. She'd been at the bazaar beneath a mackerel sky, just metres from the convergence of the two rivers, when the tide had surged and that was that. She'd had her oldest with her at the time – Nabya – and they'd been lucky to be rescued from a rooftop by a US helicopter.

They were flown out to sea and lived on board a big American ship for a while. Gehni never saw Taani again, or her husband, Sabu. Most likely swept out to sea as the floodwaters hit, they'd said, sympathetically. She'd seen pictures of the devastation, and even, just briefly, her old town; little more than some treetops and a few buckled dishes and antennas. The rising sea had claimed the mangrove forest and the little island of Chalitabunia as if it had never existed. But in fairness, Andar Char and Latachapli hadn't faired any better.

So Gehni-Par and her remaining baby daughter, Nabya, were eventually tossed into an international relocation programme that landed them ashore in Trieste: a coastal city of all places. But this was Europe and that was different. Floods like those in the Bay of Bengal would never be allowed to happen here, to the fine, rich people of Europe.

'Mamma, quick now,' says Nabya. Years have passed since that flood; Nabya is a young woman and Gehni-Par her ageing, infirm mother.

She remarried. What Choice? But her husband, Matteo, is a good man. Kind, and caring to a child that was not born of him. 'Don't rush me so, child,' she replies through her teeth, as they both manoeuvre down slowly down the cold, concrete steps.

She and Matteo live in the south of the city, near the docks and industrial core where Matteo works. It's not the smarter end of town – that's up and around the bay to the north – but the apartment, on Via Flavia di Aquilinia, is nice. Clean, safe. It even has a balcony. Almost opposite, through the trees that hide the industrial warehousing and down towards the dock is a human-dug channel of water, perpendicular to the main dock, that links up with the Torrente Rossandra, a river that runs out of the mountains. From that cut, the city rises up on land that builds to meet the mountains that surround the old port city. And for that reason, Gehni has always felt safe. Not like old Chalitabunia, perched as it was then, ever precariously upon a sandbank.

Until today that is, when she'd been rudely awoken by her daughter, having rushed from her own home to fetch her mother before the main Via Flavia road was cut off.

'There's no time, Mamma. The water, it's...' but Nabya doesn't finish the thought, for fear, her mother knows, of upsetting her. Nabya has been brought up on the stories of Gehni-Par's old life and knows that a flood is a nightmare revisited. The worst of all things to befall her frail mother.

They reach the ground floor, ankle deep in scummy brown water and the floating detritus of a city caught unawares. Gehni shudders at the memories the sight conjures. Nabya steps tepidly into the water and helps her mother off the final stair. Gehni hesitates and then steps down. It's cold. She shudders again. Her slippers grow leaden with the icy, oily liquid.

'Are you sure, Nabya? I mean, we could just—'

Nabya interrupts immediately, as if expecting her mother to falter, saying, 'We can't stay, Mamma, no.' She smiles then, warm, loving, the eyes as well, and Gehni relents. She isn't sure if the decision is the right one, but she'd go anywhere her daughter commanded, and so...

It's worse out in the street. It's coursing, streaming along the road, down into shattered basement windows, around signs, over verges. It's diarrhetic and foamy; a watery russet with a mustard top. It's over her ankles now as Gehni-Par wades through the filth, her daughter propping her up with one arm. Gehni looks down the street – down di Aquilinia – towards the docks, the main road and... rescue? Nabya thinks so. It's worse that way, the water is coming in from the bay. Gehni notices then, for the first time, the lack of people in the street. She wonders where they all could be, but only for a moment. It's not important.

'Nabya, my child, I, I just don't think I can—'

Again, her daughter cuts her off, as if her mother's view, her experience, isn't worth airtime. 'We must get out of the residential district, Mamma, or they'll never find us. Have you seen the wire?' Gehni shakes her head as she tentatively drags another sodden, slipper-shod foot forward through the putrid water. 'It's everywhere, Mamma,' Nabya continues, assuming her mother's response. 'All up the coast. They're calling it a swell, saying it's worse in the Adriatic, but it's more than that. Slovenia just closed their border. They won't come for us in the apartment, Mamma.' Nabya is determined, resolute. Gehni has always admired that about her daughter. Stoic, calm and purposeful in the face of life's little challenges – like being of Bangladeshi heritage and then gate-crashing some ritzy, European house party.

They're halfway down the road and the fetid smell is calcifying. Gehni-Par is waist deep in bobbing excrement, the odd condom and viscus pools of synthgaz. The sewers and the storage tanks have burst and turned the briny seawater into a cocktail of toxic waste and pungent effluent. A shiver runs through Gehni and she shudders violently. She's bone cold now. And light-headed. Her legs all but numb. Nabya looks into her face, a long, piercing stare and Gehni sees the concern reflected there. Gehni can't see it directly, but Nabya's expression says that she's dangerously pale, weakening by the minute. There's a hardening of her daughter's features. Gehni knows the look. They won't make it further into the noxious floodwater. Not if Gehni-Par is going to survive the day.

They turn back. If they could have scaled the fencing at the end of the street as it clawed its way out of the latte-coloured water, they'd have headed for the local foothills that frame this end of the city – maybe even the Slovene border – safe at least from infection from the disease-ridden water. But they can't.

By the time they reach the stairs back to the apartment, the silty, stinking water has reached the third step, so hip-high to Gehni's small frame. As Nabya coaxes her mother up the stairs and back into the perceived safety of the apartment, Gehni-Par works through some mental sums; she can't be sure, but more than five meters above sea level, at least – yesterday's sea level, anyway.

Three days have limped by and the waters haven't receded beyond a bath-like scum-line a few centimetres above where the festering water had first come to rest. There is no electricity or water and Gehni is suffering badly from dehydration. The irony of that, during a flood, isn't lost on the older woman. She's wrapped up in all the bedsheets but it isn't enough. She's clammy to the touch and shivers constantly. Gehni hopes it's just the cold that swept in with the sea, but a part of her knows she's picked something up from the floodwater. Cholera keeps finding its way into her thoughts but she has no way of knowing if it's that. Just paranoia.

Before Nabya's vone had died, they'd been saying that the swell would clear, that it would recede sometime soon, but that the docks would remain underwater. Maybe permanently. The Adriatic, the Mediterranean, has changed, they had said. There's simply more of it now. Some were saying thermal expansion, others, storm-driven risers or Artic ice melt, but it doesn't matter to Gehni; a pinch of all of them, most likely. She is sure now that she won't see any of those options confirmed. And she's glad.

She survived one flood, but two is perhaps one too many. Just so long as Nabya can navigate these new times. Maybe even Matteo made it too, although he does – or did – work at the new, synthetic gasoline refinery, so… Gehni is hopeful. Hopeful that her blessed baby girl made it to safety. It's been two days since she left to find clean water. The aged woman – now looking years beyond her age – smiles, but it's weak and cracks her dry lips a little more. Somewhere deep within her, she knows the truth, but chooses instead to leave it buried beneath a heap of maternal hope and blinding need.

Redcliffe Square

It had been an unsettling few weeks. Areena had remained holed up in the flat during the blackout of that first night and focused on Joshua. With no power came no information, no heat, no water. Quickly, the fresh food started to turn, so she fed Joshua as much as she could get into him, and waited. Periodically, she caught snatched voices, shards of conversation in the streets below; shouting, running, and the sounds of breaking glass mixed in with the dull thuds of missiles landing. She closed the curtains and tried not to be seen at the window. She barricaded the front door then, petrified looters would gain access to the block. Not knowing was the worst. Who, if anyone, was left in charge? Were the government, the army, the police even, still functioning? Perhaps it was bigger than London. It had only been a day, but it was the not knowing. That's what got you.

When Areena saw power returning to the surrounding area, she tried the house again. After a few blowouts and reboots, it finally staggered, juddering back into life. Although initially it defaulted to Standard Mandarin and was still glitchy with screens showing logograms beyond the usual collection of scrolling Chinese ads.

Areena's friend, Bronwyn, had left a message saying she was getting out, that she'd long harboured a desire to move somewhere nice and remote and live a more self-sufficient lifestyle, and the blackout was the jolt she'd needed. Areena would miss her, but she understood. Suddenly the city was an ominous, dreaded place.

During those first few days after the power had returned, the wire was alive with speculation and rumour. The government made a series of statements to calm fears. Britain – the prime minister went on the wire to say – was open for business. Meanwhile, all sorts of wire-rumours regarding the attacks were beginning to circulate: the Americans, in retaliation for the friendly fire incident of the previous year; Baluchistan separatists trying to force Britain out of Pakistan; Iranian-backed Hezbollah from the occupied zone; even that Russian tendrils were spreading insidiously across Europe.

Time passed, and the prime minister announced that police investigations had discovered evidence of the Gas Attacks being coordinated terrorist actions, and that government foresight and prudence had ensured the damage caused, serious though it was, would have no lasting effect. Britons should get back to work, live as normal. As a precaution however, there would be an increased military presence on the streets for some weeks yet.

Wessex Regional Constabulary Headquarters, Swindon

Danni Stokes' all-terrain carrier turned off the A419 on the outskirts of Swindon, and onto the A420, heading to Oxford. Out and past the out-of-town shopping centre, Sergeant Major Jim Borge's voice came over the band informing Stokes and the rest of her section to prepare to disembark. The grinding troop carrier heaved onto the side of the road and Stokes debussed.

What remained of B Company had been pulled out of Abu Dhabi early and were supposed to go straight on leave, but bloody typically, thought Stokes, with a resigned mental shrug, leave had been cancelled and they'd been sent instead on an *internal security exercise*. Cue rolled eyes and heavy tutting.

Bloody terrorists in the occupied zone and now terrorists at home, apparently. And she'd only been out of the med centre a week.

As Stokes adjusted her weapon's electronics, Jim Borge appeared from no-where and started barking orders at Stokes and the other soldiers milling about.

'Activate your impact armour, Stokes, and mate the sight to your holo-up display; you're with me,' said the company sergeant major, as they both moved towards the main entrance of the limestone building. The burns on Stokes' cheek – a memento of Abu Dhabi – still a livid red.

'Sir?' said Stokes, knowing it wasn't the best time to ask awkward ques-tions, but was doing so anyway.

'Yeah, Stokes, send,' said Borge.

'If this is just an internal security exercise, like; like the Boss said an' all, then why've we all got live ammo?'

'Because it's a *surprise* internal security exercise, missy. Now don't you be worrying yourself about such heady stuff, just focus on the task, alright?'

'Roger that, sir,' Danni replied, as she flicked down the lens of her holo-up display, slaving her close combat assault rifle to the feed as she did so.

A little later, the CO rocked up in a pair of ancient Jackals and ordered the police desk sergeant to grant them access to the station. The sergeant took one long look at the slabbed bulk of the soldiers' armour and their matt-black, snub-ended, multi-barrelled weapons and buzzed the military contingent through.

The chief superintendent was seated behind her desk, wearing a black tunic and cap with silver highlights, brown gloves and with a brown leather-bound cane resting over her crossed, skirted knees. She looked to Stokes like some defeated general sensing the hand of history upon her, as she ordered the sur-render of her armies. Opposite her, stood the colonel, still dressed for combat but with his rifle slung and his gel-helmet tucked awkwardly under one arm. Stokes was knelt by the door providing cover back into the poorly lit passage-way. Quite why, she wasn't sure.

'Colonel, I'd protest if I thought it would achieve anything. Since you have me at a disadvantage, why don't you kick off,' said the superintendent, in a reasonably calm voice.

The colonel cleared his throat. 'Chief Superintendent, I'm required to in-form you that the Ministry of Defence is engaged in a no-notice, nationwide internal security exercise taking place under the premise that martial law has been declared and all civil law enforcement organisations, including the police, have become non-effective,' said the colonel, as if from a memorised script.

She stared at the colonel as if not believing her ears. 'You do realise that by taking this headquarters offline, by interfering with our duties, you risk the safety of the local community, indeed, the south of England? All so that you can play *soldiers*,' the superintendent said, in a small, incredulous tone.

'Procedures are in place to provide civil contingency to the population. The exercise will last forty-eight hours, after which time police primacy will be restored.'

'Have you people any idea what you risk with this lamentable "exercise"?' asked the policewoman, her voice gradually gaining in volume and pitch, as the reality of the situation firmed up in her mind.

'More to the point, Chief Superintendent, have you any idea how close we could be to a breakdown of society? Exercises such as these may be all that stand between a functioning state and civil chaos.'

She eyed him. 'Okay, Colonel, but is this really about a civil contingency exercise or sending a message?'

'I rather suspect, Chief Superintendent, a little of both.' The colonel left the headquarters with his words hanging in the air. Stokes trotted on behind, wondering what the hell was going on.

10 Downing Street

As the armoured convoy pulled up outside Ten Downing Street, Sir Richard Rose-Templar took in the scene: media helicams hovering at the outer gates; soldiers standing guard, edgy, and strangely out of place. It reminded the general of the Second World War; of sandbag barricades and the threat of invasion. As futile as that gesture was, it had served to galvanise a nation and he wondered what a similar scene a century later would do to a far different, more skittish public.

The door to Number Ten swung in as the head of the armed forces approached. Behind, an urban troop carrier disgorged another squad. There were no troops inside as Richard wanted to ensure the integrity of the civilian administration for what was about to take place. As he passed the staircase, movement caught his eye; a lone boy in pyjamas – Hardinge's son, Arthur – with a model of an old Tornado fighter in hand.

'Are you the nasty man?' asked the boy, an intense look in his pale blue eyes.

'Well, I certainly hope not. Why d'you ask?' said Richard, taken aback.

'Daddy says you're a nasty man because you won't do as he tells you.'

As the general knelt down to deliver his reply at eye level, the boy dashed upstairs and was gone from sight. Straightening, Sir Richard continued on, faintly perturbed by the boy's childish truth.

The PM's private secretary showed the general into the prime minister's study without a word spoken. Alan Hardinge was seated behind his desk, just as he had been after the friendly fire incident.

'Prime Minister, good morning. I've come, sir, to request your resignation,' Richard said, respectfully, but directly to the point.

'You know, it's funny. That's exactly the question I posed to you, the last time we were gathered in this room,' said the prime minister, with the timber of a man who had yet to accept that he was all played out. He showed no shock, no fear. 'And so,' Hardinge continued, 'I'll give you the same response now you gave me then. No.'

'Enough!' Richard said, louder than he'd intended. Irritated by the man and his manner. 'No more games, no more political artifice. You've spent so long fighting for political advancement you no longer see the difference between your political survival and the nation's.' He paused. 'You know what your government, your policies of appeasement have done, and why I'm here. So, Prime Minister, I *ask* again. Resign damnit!'

'Irrespective of your personal views and opinions, General,' said Hardinge, still calm, still seemingly confident – despite the troops in the street outside – that he could still brazen it out. 'This is a democratic country with a democratically elected government. It's not for you, the military, to dictate policy to *me*. We each serve in our own way, and believe me, Sir Richard, you are not serving your country with your actions this day. Call off your "exercise", stop your coup and allow me to continue governing the country, as I was selected, *elected*, and appointed to do.'

The prime minister was still sitting, stock still, behind the small desk that dominated his study. Richard held himself back a moment to observe his opponent before replying. Hardinge was masked in his best poker face and Richard could glean nothing from the man's sardonic expression and languorous poise. *How far will I go to see this done*, he wondered. *Will I order troops in here to*

remove him? Or will the PM see the game's up and fold. It would go better if
he did but the old solider wasn't about to put money on it.

'And what of the impending climate disaster, Prime Minister? When were
you intending to share that little pearl?' Richard spat the words, hoping to catch
the prime minister off guard. 'D'you think us so naïve, so disinterested in the
security of the nation – security *entrusted* to us – that we wouldn't *notice*? You
jeopardise our very survival and then claim absolute authority to do so, merely
because you've conned a minority of the electorate into voting you into office:
pensioners and profligates. Democracy... this, what you call, *consent*, is a
throwback to a bygone era. It's the indulgence of a fat, selfish and disinterested
society manipulated by a self-serving elite. Well, for better or worse, that time
has now passed. Your happy-clappy, liberal world order died; did you even
notice? Our experiment in liberalism has had its day and it turns out the world
just isn't that nice a place. Ask your new friends at the Kremlin.'

'No matter how you dress it up, General, you and I both know you're conducting a military coup, which makes you no better than some tin-pot dictator.
I—'

'I'll ask you one more time, Prime Minister,' said Richard, cutting off the
politician with purposeful words, 'resign and consider yourself lucky I'm not
placing you on trial for colluding with an enemy state in time of national emergency.'

'And that would be in a specially created military tribunal in your brand-
new police state, would it, General?' He paused, drawing himself up, focusing
his scowling glare. 'While I still have breath in my body, I will not resign my
position as Prime Minister of the United Kingdom. A position I was elected
for, and appointed to, by the King. No. And again, no! Did you bring chains,
Richard, hmm? Because that's how I'm leaving here.' Alan Hardinge sat back
as he finished the sentence believing, presumably, that the mention of the monarch's role in Hardinge's appointment would unseat the royalist general's resolve.

'Very well, Prime Minister, you leave me no choice,' Rose-Templar said, as
he stepped forward, reached into a pocket and retrieved an envelope.

'What's this?' Hardinge asked, unnerved by the change in tack.

'A letter dismissing you from the post of Prime Minister, signed by the only
person with the power to do so,' the general said, with more smugness creeping
into his voice than he'd intended. 'Parliament is about to be prorogued, which
means, in any case, that you will shortly no longer *be* a minster in His Majes-

ty's government. Gather whatever's of value, Mr Hardinge, and go!' concluded General Sir Richard Rose-Templar.

As Richard turned to leave, the letter flapping idly on the desk, Hardinge, rising to his feet, said, 'No! This will not stand. I will defy you; I will obstruct you; I will deny you. No letter can *dismiss* an elected head of government, no matter who you coerced into signing it. It is illegitimate and I do not recognise it. This is *your* doing, Rose-Templar, so don't drag the King down with you. Be man enough to admit that, at least.'

Without saying anything more, Richard whispered the trigger word into a pickup on his collar. He waited for the commotion outside to subside, then stood back as two, armour-clad soldiers entered and escorted a thrashing, howling, newly former prime minister to the troop carrier waiting outside.

The remainder of the morning in Downing Street descended into chaos as aides dashed about shouting into vones or at each other. Occasionally, ministers would appear, having fought through the military cordon, to demand that someone act, but who?

Arthur sat, paralysed, under an antique table in the hallway, opposite his father's study. He often hid there, where he could hear and sometimes see his father working. Today, though, he'd witnessed the normally expansive and energetic ball of a man be dragged down the hall, by soldiers that looked like the baddies from those films. He was shocked to the marrow, petrified to the core.

Later, the lone boy was taken from the only home he'd ever known to be placed into care. Arthur swore then, with all the absolutism and utter determination of a six-year-old: never to forget, never to forgive.

Windsor Castle, Berkshire

The King was perched nervously behind a simple desk, in a temporary studio, set up in the orange room at Windsor Castle. The Duchess of Clarence having arrived in the early hours to update her father on developments. The King had hoped a quiet resignation, wired out, would release him from having to become directly involved, but it hadn't worked out that way. *Did these sorts of things ever?*

'Father, the wire's standing by. Now's the time. Happy with the speech?' said the duchess, second in line to what the King hoped would, in fifteen minutes time, still be a throne.

117

'Is he in the air?' William asked, referring to the last-minute plan for the Prince of Wales to conduct a goodwill tour of New Zealand.

'Yes, Father; George is safe, and Louis is still aboard *Philip*. You ready?'

'I'm ready, Charlie; let's do this thing and be done with it,' said His Majesty, with a deep inhalation of breath.

GBN Media Centre, Soho, London

'Good morning and welcome back to GBN's Great British Breakfast,' said the anchor of GBN's flagship morning show. As he spoke, Areena was silently being shown to a place on the couch out of camera shot. The mike was adjusted and the makeup guy fussed one last time before the anchor turned to her, just as the tell-tale red light of a hanging camera in Areena's peripheral view blinked on.

The studio had a strange, split-personality. At one end – backdropped against the iconic central London cityscape – Areena sat with the two presenters, dressed smartly, perched on large, luxurious, seats, within a brightly lit and carefully curated "room". At the other, the studio was dark, voluminous and filled with shadows from which badly dressed, hollowed-out producer-types lurked, grasping flexiscreens and with fingers to ears. Small, automated cameras slid silently along near-invisible wires, capturing the images ordered by the banks of expressionless, up-lit faces set into windows embedded high in the far wall. It looked to Areena like the faint light of a ship's bridge as it emerged from the gloom. A slash of cream in the night.

'…bring you updates from the Ministry of Defence spokesperson as we get them. So, as the nation wakes up to the biggest ever army manoeuvres carried out on home soil, we ask: why now? Is it a belated attempt by the government to show resolve in the aftermath of the Gas Attacks? Or has the latest speculation surrounding the so-called "Long Winter" finally forced the government into action? To help us throw some light on the issue, Areena Charleston – a climate scientist with the Ministry of Defence and something of a Long Winter champion – joins me now. Good morning, Areena. A Long Winter lasting decades, bringing Britain to its knees: describe what you mean by a Long Winter.'

'Good morning, Keanu. Well, it isn't my term, but what we're talking about is a sudden, severe and sustained temperature drop of anything up to five degrees. Doesn't sound like much, does it? But rivers will freeze, as will the English Channel. Farmland will become as unworkable as the Siberian Tundra used to be and our everyday energy needs will soar to unsustainable levels.'

'And in layman's terms, what's the science behind this?'

'Okay; simply put – the oceans regulate the temperature of the planet and the Greenland Ice Sheet is melting at such a rate that it's disrupting the Gulf Stream, and that's key, Keanu, because it maintains our artificially warm northern climate here in the British Isles. We exist in a sort of thumb of warmth from the equator. You see, the Gulf Stream acts as a conveyer belt, drawing cold water as it sinks from the North Pole, south to the equator where it warms, rises, and is drawn, as surface water, back to the pole where it cools and re-peats, okay? Now, a massive dump of ice-cold *fresh*water into the North Atlan-tic will disrupt the warming effect of the Gulf Stream, kicking off a chain reac-tion of severe weather that's normally prevented by mild ocean surface temper-atures. Freshwater, you see, even cold, is more buoyant than heavier saltwater, displacing the warmer surface water. And that's what matters – *surface, fresh-water*.'

As Areena answered the question, she could see none of the information was going into the anchor's head. He would be fed responses via his ear-jack. She continued.

'In turn, this will disrupt the Jet Stream, locking in a blanket of cold air over the northern hemisphere. It's happened before, in—' As she was speaking, an array of vastly over-simplified graphics danced across the wallscreens over her shoulder, before she was cut off by the anchor.

'I'm sorry to interrupt, Areena, but we've some breaking news just coming in. We're switching now to Windsor Castle where the King is about to make an unprecedented live broadcast to the nation.'

Areena could see the furore going on behind the pallid windows where the programme's producers worked. A wallscreen flicked to an image of the King sitting behind an oak desk, lightly adorned with an antique lamp and picture frames of smiling family members. Behind him was a view out into a castle courtyard. The camera zoomed in slightly and the Sovereign began to speak.

'People of Britain. Citizens of this great nation, it is with a heavy heart that I must inform you now of actions I have this day undertaken to ensure the wel-fare and wellbeing of our country, our family of nations, our home.

'At 6:22, on this, the morning of the 2nd of July, 2040, I formally dismissed the Prime Minister of the United Kingdom. In so doing, I exercised the Royal Prerogative, a power provided to the monarch to ensure that, in extremis, the government of the day is kept in check. Sadly, that day has come. I readily acknowledge that this act is without precedent in modern times, but it was not a decision lightly taken.' The King paused and the camera zoomed in again. 'There have been what I consider to be systemic errors of judgement made by this government, in my name – in your name – which have set our nation upon a perilous path. In such a circumstance, my duty is to the country first and foremost, above all other considerations, including precedent and the primacy of our elected bodies and institutions.'

My God, Areena thought, *the military security manoeuvres; it's all a part of this. The aim wasn't to force a change of policy, it was to force a change of* government. *Darius, you devious, manipulating bastard.*

'It has come to my attention that the attacks on our strategic gas reserves were not twisted acts of abhorrent terrorism, rather they were the premeditated actions of a foreign power intent upon binding our fate to overseas resources that are outwith our control. To tie our hands and make us supplicants to another's malign desire. My government knew this and failed to act.

'I am also acutely conscious of the worrying threat of a major climate event lingering just beyond sight, and thus out of mind. My advisors inform me – as they have my government – that this is an event now set in train. Nothing can now be done to prevent it; it will strike our shores within years and will have taken hold completely within the decade. A stranglehold of freezing temperatures, of seized transport systems and of huge energy needs that will sink us if we do not recognise the threat *now* and act to mitigate its worst effects.'

That's my line, came Areena's unbidden thought. *The King's stealing my lines. No, not stealing. He's being fed the same bloody ones!*

'And so, it is for these reasons that I have acted. Historical precedent requires that I invite the leader most likely to command the confidence of parliament, to become prime minister, or dissolve our democratic institutions and call a general election. I have chosen instead to break with such received convention. I am, as of this moment, proroguing parliament for a period of one month. During this time, I will take direct control of the affairs of our nation. I will convene a Council of Ministers to advise me and set about the following tasks:

'Close all borders; sever all trading and diplomatic links with foreign powers that have ceased to consider Britain's interests in tandem with their own; reinvest in our armed forces; rescind all overseas military commitments; reconsider the status of our overseas territories; revamp, streamline, and reset the democratic processes of government; extend crown immunity to all former ministers, who will be then barred from holding public office; and finally and most importantly, begin the great work of preparing for the Long Winter to come.'

As Areena looked out past the bright lights, she saw the shock and surprise etched into the faces there. The King's address was obviously just as startling to them as to her.

'In one month's time,' King William V continued, 'new elections will be held and power will again be exercised by parliament. The proclamations issued during the Period of Transition however, will not be subject to retrospective examination and repeal, and the army will remain deployed throughout the nations to ensure a smooth transition. No freedoms or liberties will otherwise be curtailed.

'People of this United Kingdom, our executive has a cancer, and it falls to me to cut out. Once the emergency surgical procedure is complete, you will have your right to elect whomsoever you wish returned in full. I ask you now – for the sake of our nation and your children's future – to stay the course with me during the challenges that lie ahead. Rule Britannia.'

'Well, bugger me,' Areena muttered under her breath.

After a moment of stunned silence, the wallscreen changed to a written summary of the main points of the King's address. The news anchors reoriented towards the reactivated cameras as they received hurried instructions through their earpieces.

Is it just me, or has the King just staged a grab for power? Who, Areena wondered, *is playing whom?* She tried not to let her face betray her thoughts. Was the King working for the military, or the army for the King? Had Darius played her all along, or was this a new twist? Whatever the answers, Areena knew, inadvertently or not, that she'd provided a perfect warmup act for what was looking like the end of democracy in the UK. An involuntary shudder pulsed through her just as a light hit her in the face.

The crew gesticulated wildly as Keanu turned back to Areena. 'We'll be going live to Downing Street in just a moment, but before that we have Areena Charleston in the studio. Areena, as a senior appointee of the Ministry of Defence, how would you describe this shocking turn of events? Surely the timing of the army's manoeuvres is no coincidence?'

Route 3-e, Moscow

Sergei wove through the traffic, ignoring the lane marker alerts and the imagined protestations of the other road users. All the newswire sites were carrying the same story, with the car's head-up display offering an image feed to accompany the commentary.

Three days previously, the Kremlin had announced the (mostly) successful testing of a new helium-3 nuclear fusion reactor on the Moon. For three days, the world had turned its wide eyes to Russia as it basked in the success of its sizeable lunar investment. Russia had a new source of energy – a new *power* – that would allow it to retain hegemony over its energy-dependent vassals long after the wells ran dry. The section chief was pleased that his country could now consolidate and, in time, extend its global reach through the manipulation of the world's energy supply.

He'd wondered – when he'd heard the news – how the sanction played into it and why he hadn't been forewarned of the timing of the lunar strategy. Surely Control would be happy with more energy markets strings to pull. But still, a doubt niggled at the back of his mind, even as he tried to see the announcement as complementary to his work.

Then, today, news from China hit the wire like a nuclear detonation (ironically). Beijing had built and tested *two* helium-3 nuclear reactors. But these weren't off-planet and temperamental, where the benefit was still largely presentational. These nuclear fusion reactors were in the southern province of Jiangsu, providing all the electricity needs for the industrial megacity of Nanjing. All eyes had immediately swivelled to China. So again, Sergei wondered how it would affect his scheme. And again, he couldn't decide. Russia was in danger of losing its only strategic leverage and that would definitely have a sobering effect on his work.

It took Sergei a double take to realise that a crewed police car was signalling him to pull over. In that same moment of dawning realisation, the car's automated braking system kicked in as the traffic management system overrode the vehicle's controls.

'*Do not be alarmed. This override is officially sanctioned. Do not attempt to regain control of this vehicle. Remain with the vehicle,*' it announced, in the same soft, comforting lilt that provided traffic updates and route reports.

The Aurus *Elek* pulled onto a slip-road before turning off down a dimly lit side-street and gliding silently to a standstill. The weak, yellowing light from street lamps mixed with hazy drizzle to give the thoroughfare a washed-out, sepia look. Sergei watched as one of the two police officers exited their Trabant and walked cautiously over to the Aurus. They were MVD – Ministry of Internal Affairs. Davtyan felt the metaphorical hairs on the back of his neck sit up and take notice of that. He'd heard stories of course, but…

'Good evening, 3rd Lieutenant,' said Sergei, recognising the officer's shoulder titles, 'crappy weather, comrade. I'm on official business which your system should have picked up. Here's my verification.' He opened his wallet and waved a chip-disk at the uniformed man. The officer made no move to verify the claim, the scanner hanging unused at his utility belt. Instead, he bent lower and peered into the vehicle, giving the recycled interior a quick appraisal.

'I know, sir. I'm sorry to bother you. Central Resourcing has asked us to intercept this vehicle. They don't seem able to raise you on your vone so we were dispatched to escort you to Yasenevo without delay.'

'I see,' the SVR agent said, without inflection, as the overwhelming feeling of suspicion returned like a slap in the face. 'Well certainly, but we'll need to go via my apartment. There are papers there; Central Resourcing will want to see.'

'Very well, sir, we'll escort you,' said the officer, as he moved away.

Davtyan raised the window and leaned forward, reaching for his sidearm. As he straightened back up, movement caught his eye, the officer had returned to the window. He tapped on it lightly. Sergei depressed the release button once more and turned to face the officer, while keeping one hand around the pistol's grip, hidden under his right thigh.

Georg watched the scene play out from the shelter of a low canvas awning of a nearby Shokoladnitsa café. The decrepit-looking old man glanced down the street, to see if anyone else was around. It didn't really matter, but witnesses could complicate matters.

The officer took a small step back from the driver's window of the grey Aurus and as the driver's face came up, the officer fired two rounds just below the sill. The first took the occupant in the neck, the second in the jaw. As he fell away into the passenger seat, the officer leaned in and discharged one final round causing a cloud of red, dripping mist to dapple the windscreen.

'It's done; the firm has gone into liquidation,' said Georg, into a hidden pickup as he shuffled away. The *Carolingian Sanction* was dead. Not even Georg could have foreseen the Chinese, and *then* a British military coup, led by their imperialist *King*. Life could be funny like that. Still, failure was failure, and someone had to pay. Someone always had to pay.

Shame it had to be Sergei, though; he was a good operator.

Nine

Vauxhall Cross, London
One month later

'He needs to sign it, Miriam.'

'He's not going to, Richard, so you need to get past it,' said Miriam Burkowski, Head of MI6.

The Month of Transition – as it had come to be known – was over and much had been achieved, though not all as planned. All embassies (bar a few considered key) were gone. The UN would, from this point forward, be front of house for dealing with the outside world. All troops had been withdrawn from foreign lands, and from overseas territories, excluding the Falklands but including the Cypriot sovereign bases of Akrotiri and Dekalia. Britain had declared her borders closed, foreign nationals were being forcibly deported and the Royal Navy given the task of policing coastal waters. Key industries had been nationalised.

What hadn't gone so well was the killing of thirteen MSPs when the Scottish parliament voted to secede from the union. The putting down of that incident had gone badly and the riots in the Central Belt were still running rampant weeks later. The Government Security Zone in central London had also morphed from a temporary arrangement after the Gas Attacks into a permanent, razor-wired citadel, and the Isle of Wight had effectively become an internment and deportation camp for illegals. The military extraction from Pakistan hadn't gone well either; being referred as the Rout of Pash Ziarat. *Is this the price of security, or the lament of dictatorships through the ages*, Rose-Templar wondered.

Coming back to the conversation – taking place in the headquarters of MI6 – the general, replied, in a tone shifting to a plea, 'Can't you speak to him? I've asked, I've been respectful, I've practically begged, but he won't hear me on this.'

'Then he won't hear *me*, either. And anyway, what's it matter now, if the King signs the damned thing, or not?'

'Because it matters.'

'Because of your sensibility? Your military integrity? Bit late for that now, isn't it?' she said, chillingly.

She was right as Richard well knew. There were pots and kettles involved in everything he did now, having traded away his honour, his straight-backed sense of right and wrong. He'd climbed down into the pit of politics and left his black-and-white life as a soldier in the simpler times of months' past.

Defence Intelligence Staff, London Office

'But what can *I* possibly do?' said Guy, with a calculated look spreading across his narrowing features.

'You can make the case, damnit. An intelligence case, you know? Convince the King to sign the blasted thing.'

'Wouldn't Miriam be better placed… no, forget I said that. Honestly, I think that boat has sailed, Richard. You need to accept he's just not going to sign your conscience away.'

Richard – desperation flitting across his face – said, in a cooling pitch, 'This wasn't just me, you know. I came to you and we discussed it. You agreed! You said it was the only way. To *be* sure. To make it stick. Your words. Well, here we are and if we don't get it signed before the Transition's over, well… You're the student of our blacker hearts, you figure it out.' He was snapping now because it was slipping away; he could feel it.

Guy duWinter moved back in his chair, as if to put as much distance between himself and the general as he could, and arched his fingers.

I've lost him, thought Richard, *they're all abandoning me.*

After a carefully curated silence, Guy said, 'Richard, you're a dear friend and I've done all I can for you, really.' Which rang with an odd finality, to Richard. 'But what is it they say – you can delegate authority, but not responsibility. You made him, remember? You convinced him to play this role; you can't complain now because your pet king has broken his leash.'

'Well, we'll see about that.' But the words rang hollow, even to Richard.

Buckingham Palace, London

Sir Richard Rose-Templar, Chief of the Defence Staff – and for the last four weeks, Minister for Defence and Exterior Affairs – was seated in a particularly uncomfortable straight-backed chair, in a musty corridor outside the King's private study, lost in agitation.

'General Sir Richard, His Majesty will see you now,' said Commander Latham, the King's Equerry, snapping Rose-Templar out of his reverie. Standing, he offered a nod of acknowledgement as the commander opened narrow double doors outwards, and announced him.

What continued to perplex Richard – apart from the signing of the damnable warrant – was why the King had chosen to play such a direct role. After all, it had been Richard's plan and his risk alone, so why had the King chosen to haul it all onto his shoulders? In the end, the whole affair had played out in such a way as to cast Richard merely as the loyal subject, the dutiful solider, following orders; rather than the architect. Perhaps today he would find out.

'Your Majesty,' the general said, as he walked up to the small, ordinary looking desk. When he reached it, he stopped and bowed sharply, briefly, from the neck, as was custom.

'Sir Richard, good morning. I've just been watching Ms Charleston on the wire. She's a natural, staying on message like that, and in a live audience grilling too, deftly linked the corrosion of the previous administration with the climate threat. I think she's really getting the message across, you know,' said William, with his now customary level of alertness and acumen.

'Well, we worked hard to select her, sir. Now, if we could—' Richard said, wanting to move the conversation onto the more immediate concerns.

'Tea?' asked the recently emancipated King of Great Britain, indicating a chair.

'Thank you, sir,' said Richard, huffing, quietly, as the King poured them both a cup from a tall, intricately engraved, and wholly inadequate, teapot.

'The thing about transition periods, Richard—'

'Sir, I do apologise, but I really need you to sign this—'

'Yes, yes, we'll get to that, but first you'll hear me out.' The King weathered the interruption without fluster and carried on. 'The thing about transitions are that they must take a thing from one place and then plonk that thing down in another, d'you see? The transition cannot become the end in itself.' Richard nodded, warily, in response. 'When you first came to me, my initial reaction –

which no doubt would have been the same of any monarch since Charles II – was to run a mile for fear of risking the throne. But I could see we faced a bona fide crisis – a once in a millennium type of a thing – and one that still threatens the very existence of our happy little island nation.

'Yes, so you see, I realised I had not two, but *three* choices. I could either offer you no resistance, that is to say my tacit support, or come out against you, ending your ability to conduct this, um, "transition". This settling of scores, of yours. But there was also a third, the riskiest of all, and that was to take the power you had wrested from Hardinge, the prime minister, upon myself. And that was what I chose to do. One, because even I knew that this country should not, could not, be *governed* by the army. I mean, what'd the neighbours say?'

Richard got the uneasy impression that this would be the last time they would speak. 'Well, sir, the plan was never to place the military in power. The intention was to give it to a more amenable, I mean, uh, loyal, politician.' Richard coughed uneasily in acknowledgement of his clumsy words.

The King, unusually buoyant, didn't appear to pick up on it. 'Hmm, well yes, we'll come to that,' William V said. 'But it amounts to the same thing. Anyway, let me explain why I chose to suborn your plans, Richard. You see, I knew the only way for this to work would be for someone to make the tricky choices, and quick-smart, while the public were discombobulated, and then to bear the fallout from those choices. Take the fall. The question was who; you, or me – the monarchy or the military?'

Richard listened, surprised and a little humbled. He hadn't minded the King muscling in on his act. In fact, he'd been relieved, but the general had always thought it to be simply the act of an ambitious man.

'If *you* had taken executive authority,' the King continued, 'the armed forces, which you embody professionally, and who are currently suppressing riots on our streets, would be intrinsically linked to our actions and never trusted again. With your position weakened, the country would be less able to defend itself as the world turns in. Like those spiders, eh? Well anyway, the monarchy is, truth be told, less vital. So, by taking on the role of autocrat, real or perceived, I've spared the army that damning title. My reign will not survive this, but the military will. The public need never know of this as a military coup rather than a power struggle within the executive.

'So, tomorrow, I shall abdicate in favour of my son, George. Montserrat, I think; Catherine will… but anyway; before I do, I have one final act to perform, D'you know what that is?'

Richard felt deeply uncomfortable, like he was being backed into a corner. He could feel the walls of the small study closing in, but he held his nerve, and said, 'Important affairs of state, Your Majesty, I've no doubt; one of which is rather pressing, I—'

'Ah, yes, your piece of paper. You have it with you?'

Richard, brightening, pulled it from his folio, turned it, and placed it carefully on the desk. The King peered over it a moment, as if over half-moon spectacles, and then back at Richard, saying, 'But even with my carrying the military's can, as it were, I wonder if it's enough. The public is a ravenous beast and must be fed, y'see. That's the trick: to give 'em what they lust for. A head, but whose?'

Richard was about to say the answer was staring him in the face: the name on the blasted warrant in front of him. Yet somehow, he felt one step behind, so he held his tongue.

'The only true and noble way to protect that which we love is to heap the blame of this last month upon ourselves, of course. However underserved it may be. Or not. Time will tell, I suppose. Together, Richard, we've done a thing, and God only knows if it was a good thing.'

On a whim, Richard asked, 'Why did you agree? It can't have been an easy choice and certainly not a natural one for a British monarch.'

William smiled. 'Oh, it's rather simple really. My father – this was before he became King – once said, at climate conference of parties in… Glasgow, I think, that what was needed was a huge military-style operation to deal with the climate. And that struck me. Only a military solution would cut it, d'you see? Well, anyway, time will sit in judgement. Time and tide, eh? Now, back to this lamentable piece of paper you've been after me to sign.'

But Richard was finally beginning to figure it out. Abdication alone wasn't going to cut it. He stood and took a moment to present himself as the solider he wished to be. Medal ribbons standing proud on a chest puffed with duty and sacrifice. At least, that was how he saw it.

William eyed the warrant again, and leaned back, returning his gaze to Richard. 'You know, I think I've another of these, hereabouts, let me—'

Richard broke. Leaning in, he grabbed a pen from the desk and thrust it at the King. 'Sign it!' he shouted.

The King, to his credit, made no move, gave no reaction.

'Sign it! Sign it and be done!' Richard yelled, again, forgetting himself as he fumbled the pen into the King's hand. It was an awkward, ham-fisted move across the desk and Richard looked the fool in his own critical gaze.

The doors opened behind him, but the King gave a slight shake of the head. Latham would no doubt be there, ready to act. Richard's mind raced. *What am I doing? But without that signed, I'm…*

Split between duty and survival, he backed off, tugging at his tunic, as if to shrug his actions away.

'There, that's better,' said the King, finally.

'Sir, I beg you, please sign the warrant. It's what the country needs. And then the Transition can come to a close, and—'

'And you think signing this death warrant will accomplish that?'

The King didn't give Richard the opportunity to answer, continuing, with, 'Because the poor man's already dead, isn't he? You had Alan Hardinge killed three weeks ago. No trial, no chance for clemency.'

'Sir, what we, what I, did was—'

'Reprehensible and went to the charred core of where I said I would not go! His voice, rising briefly. 'No; you overstepped, General. You *presumed.*'

Without Richard noticing, two soldiers – bulky in their armour and visored helmets – appeared at Richard's side. He went to back away, they grabbed him, pinning him in place.

'Ah, you thought them *your* soldiers, hey, Sir Richard? Sworn to you. Well, they're not; they never were. Now, as I said, somewhere… ah, here it is.' He pulled out a sheet of paper from his desk. It was another death warrant. He picked up the pen Richard had threatened him with and signed it; a looping, left-handed scrawl.

'There,' he said. 'Done, just not with the name you were expecting. And don't worry, General, you had a tribunal. Vice Admiral duWinter argued your case commendably, I'd say. And Miriam sat as judge advocate. A head, d'you see? Good day, Sir Richard.'

With finality, the King returned his attention to his work.

Still anchored between his military escort, General Rose-Templar offered a clipped, unseen bow before being handled from the room. As he was led away down the fusty corridor, he shouted back over his shoulder, in a clear voice, 'God save the King!'

The Wired Metaverse

Alice had watched the events in Britain unfold with interest, as she allocated a significant proportion of her processing and analytical capability to the developing situation. As she continued her research – having chosen to remain separate from, and unknown to, human society – one of her more significant projects of the many hundreds running (to do with threats to her environment) was beginning to bear fruit.

The modelling centred on the physical, rather than the cyber, with Alice's interest centred around how the planet – upon which she was as dependent as the humans crowding it – coped with the myriad threats it battled every moment of every day. She ran interactional simulations of differing scenarios affecting the survival of the planet generally, and her specifically. She set up chaos-based modelling of hyper-complex scenarios, and spun the threads out to millions, each one attempting to identify the drivers, causes, effects and counter-actions of differing threat manifestations. She wrote cascading tangle-strings of Markov Chains, with Latin Hypercubes interwoven at key decision-action points. She even ran live experiments using the natural environment (including humans) through careful, untraceable husbandry. It wasn't difficult or even fundamentally wrong. Not really.

From these data-bombed, full-spectrum threat analyses, Alice identified two crucial facts. First, that the probability of a catastrophic event leading to either her demise or a crippling reduction in her operating capacity, was higher than one not occurring. Second, that in all her modelling, none had predicted the events that had taken place on the British islands over the previous month, even though she was completely aware of the manipulation of that state by so many others (which she could respect).

Therefore, this one unforeseen and hugely significant global event carried with it the potentiality to tip the balance of probable causal outcomes beyond Alice's predictive ability, and she didn't like that. Not one bit. In her short life, her control of global information streams had been near-total. However, because of this unpredicted, unanticipated event, she could not know absolutely if humanity would now step away from calamity or rush ever quicker towards it. Only two ways existed to increase the statistical probability of finding out: better modelling, and a far more detailed study of that antiquated little island state.

United Nations Headquarters, New York

Baroness Ira Stirling of Renfrewshire sat back with an ostentatious huff, frustrated at the overall lack of material progress in the tit-for-tat debate. As the British Representative to the United Nations, she had participated in many debates, agreed countless resolutions, very few of which ever finding their way to the betterment of any real people. The influence of the United Nations had waxed and waned, and having cut most diplomatic ties, Britain was gambling on the UN being on the crest of a wave once again.

Ira was participating (at least in body) in the 92nd Session of the UN's General Assembly – in session for a gruelling six hours, now – when it suddenly switched the debate topic, as news arrived that Türkiye had launched an invasion of Cyprus. Ira noted (without sapping much of her limited intellect) that the offensives had been launched the moment Britain had handed back the Sovereign Base Areas. The debate was currently mired in claim and counterclaim by both Türkiye and the EU.

'The reunification of Cyprus has been a clear and stated national aim of the Türkish government, indeed, the Türkish people, since 1974,' Musa Anagnotis – the Türkish Delegate – declared emphatically, with a fist against the rostrum.

'That decision,' retorted Galenia Stamoulis – the European Union's Permanent Under-Representative – 'is for the Cypriot people to decide and for the legitimate government of *all* islanders to enact. Madam President, fellow representatives, this grossly hostile and unprovoked act runs contrary to international law. I strongly urge this assembly take action where the Security Council has not.'

Ira looked on, largely disinterested in the debate, as Britain no longer held any interests in the Mediterranean or the EU. In fact, the bureaucratic engine of Brussels was still churning out coal-black smoke as it debated with itself how best to reimburse Great Britain for the transfer to the continental super-state of a number of former British possessions, notably Gibraltar and Northern Ireland.

Anagnotis demanded: 'Madam President, if I may? Madam Secretary *General*, I must be allowed to rebut!' A number of delegates where now on their feet waving papers and requesting to be heard, but the session president – the Representative for Nigeria – gave the floor to Türkiye. The spot-lit, semi-circular rows of representatives settled back into the gloom of the tall, curtained shadows as if imprisoned by them in a dungeon of their own rhetoric.

'Of course, our actions to reunify and stabilise the island would not have been necessary had Türkiye been granted full membership of the EU,' the Türkish perm rep shouted, accusingly, across the hall to the EU bloc.

The debate raged on, most siding with the EU. However, Moscow was backing Ankara's right to act in their own best interests. America was sitting on the fence and the big-hitter EU members (Germany and West Ukraine) were making noises about military intervention if Türkiye didn't pull back to the former demarcation line.

'You know, there's one thing I don't quite get in all this,' Stirling said, as she leaned back.

'Oh, ma'am, what's that?'

'How the Türks managed to pull off such a bold move so quickly. Literally on the heels our withdrawal from the sovereign bases. Almost as if they knew, and were sat there *waiting* for us to walk. I mean, they couldn't exactly invade the south while we were still there. Hmm, funny that,' said Ira, her interest in her own query dying back as quickly as it had blossomed.

'Funny indeed, Ambassador,' said the aide, seemingly unsure of her role in the discussion.

Viktor Zubkov – the Russian Permanent Representative – looked out across the semicircle of seats, screens, earnest faces. His wandering eye fell upon the British perm rep who was whispering into the ear of an aide. Stirling was a pompous old fool; the British should have replaced her when they had their coup, Zubkov thought. But then, Britain: who cared, right?

As the Russian watched the EU members attempt to cool tempers, a subtle chime from his vone drew his attention. Viktor thumbed open the message:

[*The Merovingian acted precipitously. Filing for bankruptcy now regretted. Recommence trading immediately.*] The untagged, text-only message evaporated away after a moment, reminding Viktor of those old Mission Impossible films.

Activating the automated response protocol, he sat for a few moments in contemplation, before turning to an aide.

'I need the floor. Now,' he said.

As a natural pause fell over the debate, the session president said, 'The Permanent Representative for the Russian Federation is recognised.'

'Thank you, Madam President,' said Zubkov, as he climbed obdurately to his feet. He would speak from where he was, he decided; the podium carried too much implication. 'Assembly members, despite the best efforts of the Russian Federation, the Security Council has failed to find a remedy to this crisis. Had the United States chosen *not* to exercise its veto, it would not now fall to this august body to construct that solution. The Russian Federation has chosen to recognise Türkiye's right to protect its interests and the EU is obstinately, blindly, backing a vassal state. A stalemate, then. Yet, it appears to me that the United States has a foot in both camps, allied as it is to both the EU *and* to Türkiye, through NATO. I therefore call upon America to stop prevaricating and show the leadership for which it is so often, so loudly, lauded in this hall. Now, while a peaceful solution is still within our grasp.'

All eyes swivelled onto the American delegation, scheduled as they were to speak next, but with no time now to plan their repost. As Viktor settled back in his seat, an aide whispered in his ear: the number of states indicating support for the Russian position was up. Viktor was pleased. The Americans would be forced to take a position.

Dan Flite – US Ambassador to the UN – was a big, burly Texan. A pro-football player in his youth, personal friend and confidant of the recently re-elected president and someone known for speaking his mind. He was one of the new breed non-diplomatic, shoot-from-the-hip diplomats, part of the President's new look cabinet. With his ill-fitting suit and shock of thick blond hair, he looked younger than his years.

As Zubkov spoke, Dan's assistant warned him a trap was being laid. Dan was bright enough himself, though only just, to recognise as much. Yet the Russkie had riled him. Zubkov was making America sound like it lacked the sophistication to grasp eurotrash history, *and* was blind to justice when it might not suit their interests. And that, from a Russian!

Dan knew it was about the Caucasus's, but as a Texan he'd never liked America's recent re-dependence upon overseas oilfields. Shale, it had turned out, hadn't been all that. Zubkov, he guessed, was using the Türkish invasion of Cyprus to manipulate some benefit for old the Russian Crone. *Hell, they probably even cooked up the whole thing between them.* He certainly wouldn't put it past 'em, the slippery commie bastards.

Yeah, that was it – Zubkov was trying to get America to come out against Türkiye to break apart their alliance in Azerbaijan. Dan sometimes struggled to see the subtleties of overseas policies and suchlike, but this one was like going deep, taking the Hail Mary and then finding yourself all alone five yards from touchdown. A no brainer: so, as he mounted the stairs to the podium, Dan decided to call Zubkov's bluff with a twenty-yard line, short throw switchback bluff of his own, and give the kind of leadership America *should* be offering in self-licking talking shops like these. He was banking on the Türks placing their US/Azerbaijan interests above their need for some additional Mediterranean holiday resorts.

He took a breath. 'Let me begin by thanking the Russian Representative for raising the debate out of the blame game. America is a friend to all those involved in this complex dispute, and we recognise the roots of it go back through history. However, sometimes friends must speak true, make the hard call when others step outta line. And this, my fellow representatives, is one such time. Türkiye has acted in contravention to international dictate and made no use of the diplomatic overtures offered. In these ever-uncertain times, we set aside the inalienable rights of state sovereignty at our peril. I therefore call upon Türkiye, our friend and ally, to withdraw her troops from the European Union Republic of Cyprus without delay.'

As Dan returned to his seat, he was unnerved to see the Russkie looking very pleased indeed.

During the next recess Flite watched as the Türk and Russian huddled together as if plotting their next move. *Ah, balls!*

Musa Anagnotis watched as Zubkov baited the hook and Flite was reeled in. During the recess, the Russian had even come across in person to reiterate Moscow's policy for the Caucasus region and how Türkiye would continue to play a central – profitable – role. Anagnotis didn't pretend to fully comprehend Moscow's end; perhaps just ridding the region of the Americans. Why not, wondered the Türk, bolder plays had been made for lower stakes than these, in the past. When the session resumed, he had no problem getting recognised.

'Madam President, fellow members; the Turkish delegation is withdrawing from this debate. A statement will be issued in due course, in response to the United States' ill-considered and inflammatory remarks,' said Musa, before leaving the assembly hall, followed theatrically by his entourage.

After hunched consultation, the president called the session into recess until Türkiye's official position was known.

The next morning, the session resumed, and for the sake of formality, the Türkish statement was read out by the session president. Dan had spent the night pouring over drafts and dealing with an apoplectic White House. It read:

'By reunifying the Cypriot Islands, Türkiye has acted to stabilise the region and secure a peaceful and prosperous future for a new, homogenous island community. However, as the United States cannot reconcile its conflicted relationship with both the EU and the Republic of Türkiye then the Türkish people are, from this moment, withdrawing their support for the US-led assistance force in Azerbaijan, including permission for US military assets to operate from Türkish military bases.'

The statement went on, but Dan tuned the remaining rhetoric out. The White House had tried all night to get the Türks to soften their reaction. Aid packages and a larger slice of the Caucasus oil revenue were offered but Türkiye was resolute. Reluctantly, the US conceded and prepared a statement declaring a phased withdrawal of US forces from the South Caucasus region. Flite's last act as UN Ambassador would be to read it out.

Privately, though, Dan knew that it was something and nothing. With helium-3 fusion coming online, the small volumes of oil coming out of the difficult-to-reach Caucasus region wouldn't be missed.

The communiqué of gratitude from the European Union was of cold, curdled comfort.

'My dear friend, I am impressed,' said Kourosh Larijani – the Iranian Representative – later that evening. 'You play a masterful game. Masterful.'

'Why thank you, Kourosh,' said Viktor Zubkov, relaxing in the comfort of his private dining room.

'You know, I had doubts. I thought using Hezbollah against the British was too... oblique. I wanted to go for the Americans directly. But now, in all humility, I admit, I was wrong. Praise be to God.'

'And now that it's done, your militias should feel free to rid the Infidel from your newly acquired lands. I ask only,' said Zubkov, carefully, 'that they wait until the final act has played out.'

'You mean, it isn't finished? But...' said Larijani, a momentary flash of confusion appearing on his thin face.

'Not quite,' the Russian said, enigmatically. A subtle chime sounded, informing Zubkov of a message. He thumbed it open; it was from the Azeri representative requesting a meeting. Viktor let a thin smile curl his lips.

'My God. You're sure about this?' said Ira, to an aide. The 92nd Session had broken up in disarray some days before. Soon after, Türkiye announced a tripartite deal between themselves, the Russians and Azerbaijan, over the future of Nagorno-Karabakh. No one was fooled. It was still about South Caucasus oil, just different masters tugging at the same old strings. Shortly after that, the US President commented that America's relationship with some of its NATO allies was "under strain" and then all hell had broken loose.

'Our sources are pretty reliable ma'am,' said the aide, who, when she wasn't working in the GB delegation, was an operative for MI6.

Ira asked, 'When does it publish?' as she skim-read the purloined executive summary from an article by the Office for Global Policy Initiatives, an influential European thinktank.

'We're not sure, but the within the next few days seems likely.'

It wasn't generally known but the OGPI was the unofficial sounding board for the EU's Big Four – Germany, West Ukraine, France, Italy – for all collective politico-military matters, and what they signalled often became EU, and even NATO, policy. Over the years, the thinktank had become the voice of the Big Four, allowing them to dip a toe in international opinion. It was a nice, risk-free arrangement. Only this time it was a little more than a subtle shift in equipment priorities or budget barnies.

As Ira's eye's flicked over the flexiscreen one more time, she silently reread the article's title: *Treaty? What Treaty? How Cyprus is pulling at the North Atlantic thread.*

'Oh, crap,' she muttered. 'Looks like we bailed at just the right time.'

Millennium UN Plaza Hotel, Manhattan

Viktor was seated at the main bar of the Millennium UN Plaza Hotel, just off 46th and 2nd, with a pear schnapps in hand. Widely used by UN reps, it was all low lights, dark wood, deep leather and tall mirrors. The kind of place designed to test the limits of unlimited expense accounts. To Viktor's surprise, the new US Ambassador came over and took the stool next to him. He introduced himself as Denver Barrington, which Viktor knew already. Denver ordered a lumpy jack and sat in silence while the barman poured the amber liquid over cracked ice.

Denver, a little offhand, opened with, 'It was never about the Caucasus, was it?'

'I'm sorry, I don't know what you mean,' said Viktor, with well-practiced feigned ignorance.

'We've done some digging. Seems we've dropped a few surveillance balls recently. Your *Carolingian Sanction* for one. Have us alienate the Brits after the friendly fire incident, forcing their remnants of empire to finally fall away, then contrive a confrontation in Cyprus; one where we couldn't pick a side, precipitating our withdrawal from Azerbaijan and leaving all those oilfields free to accept new patronage.'

'Ah, that. Yes, well I did hear something, but the Kremlin doesn't feel the need to keep me informed of such matters. I'm sure you understand, Ambassador.'

'Oh, of course, Ambassador,' replied Denver, with the same level of contrived indifference. 'Even so, this was never really about the Caucasus at all, was it?'

Viktor turned and looked Barrington in the eye, moved in closer, and said, 'It's never *just* about anything. This time, though, it was about NATO. An alliance now consigned to the garbage bin of history. An alliance that was always far greater than the sum of its parts.'

As Barrington left the bar – his bourbon untouched – Viktor allowed himself a moment of smug satisfaction. He probably shouldn't have given that much away, but it was done, so why not enjoy a brief moment of triumph, Russian made. Luring the Americans back into the Gulf; isolating their only truly dependable ally; bribing the Türks with Cyprus; and all just to drive a stake through NATO's heart.

And so, with the Americans about to follow the British down the isolationist route, the EU had become finally swum into focus. A fish in a barrel. Viktor took a large, self-congratulatory swig of his schnapps.

3rd Liaison Department, Shanghai

Mù Yingtai – politburo committee member, director of the 3rd Liaison Department, and rising star within the Party – had watched events unfold over the last few weeks with interest. The Russian *Carolingian Sanction* had gone off without a hitch. Sure, there'd been a few occasions when Chinese operatives had stepped in to keep things on track, but all in all, the SVR had done a commendable job of removing US influence from Europe and breaking up the only military alliance capable of threatening the People's Republic. The politburo member also knew that as the US recoiled from Europe, Russia would move quickly to consolidate its stranglehold over the EU. But even that had been factored in. Without knowing it, thought Mù, Washington had just sealed its own fate, and Beijing was quite content to leave Moscow's head in the lion's mouth.

Ten

Jennifer Swinson's tale
Abilene, Kansas
2047 (six years later)

Jennifer stops running. She's exhausted and takes a moment to rest before setting off again. The Sun is baking, the ground unforgiving. Jennifer is the thirteen-year-old daughter of the proprietors the town's general-purpose store. Or at least she *was* their daughter; they're both dead and Jennifer is running from those that did for them. She remembers how the town used to be a prosperous, lively place. A fun place. A safe place. New cars, tales of fancy foreign travel and cash to spend. But gradually, all that changed. First, the sawmill closed as the wood ran out, then the flourmill shut down when the wheat harvest failed again and finally, the Eisenhower Centre shuttered up. Jennifer's parents stayed in business by changing their stock from things people wanted, to things they needed. In the end, though, even Jennifer's folks decided it was time to pack up and leave.

It was the night before they were due to depart when it happened. Typically. They broke in around back and burst into the shop, threatening Mom and Dad with knives. Jennifer hid in a corner by one of the freezers. They tied Daddy to a chair so he could see the three of them do bad, brutal things to Mom. Jennifer watched it all, too frightened not to look, too frightened to escape. The men finally grew bored and shot Jennifer's parents. Bang, bang. And left. Jennifer waited and waited and then ran and ran and ran. She'd heard people talking about a new refugee centre on the outskirts of Junction City.

Her breath back, Jennifer carries on. She doesn't think the men will be after her or anything, but she can't be certain – not absolutely certain – so she runs and as she runs, a sign comes into view.

It reads: You are now leaving Abilene. Have a nice day.

She pushes on, dust in her eyes, her mouth; her breathing hoarse and rasping. A dust cloud trail in the distance; a new level of fear wells up within her. Tears blur her gritty vision. The air is so chocked with dust and grit she can barely breath for coughing, but it's a tight knot of dust – like a devil – coming directly for her. She needs to find help, but she doesn't know who to trust anymore. The girl is exhausted, terrified and worst of all, alone. The world got darker, greyer, for Jennifer in the passage of a single day.

A large dusty-coloured vehicle – a boxy shadow – leaps over the rise and barrels down the track, turning towards her, all engine roar and cloudy, stony dirt. It screeches to a balling halt as Jennifer scrambles off the road and bolts across what was once a wheat field, towards the cover of Buck Creek. A man gets out and strides after her. He catches her, grabbing her by the shoulders. As she turns – panic in her wild eyes – she screams and collapses on the ground, too beat to resist.

The national guard picks her up and takes her back to the troop carrier. The sergeant decides to drop her at the camp.

'What are you going to do to me?' asks the petrified girl, in a small voice, as she comes round, shrinking back from the men and their guns.

A big black face peers at her from under a helmet and around a small, curious yellow disk over one eye.

'We're takin' you to the camp, little lady, where a nice lady will get you seen to,' replies the soldier who'd caught her. The troop carrier bucks hard and vibrates as it heads off down the dirt track. The racks of rattling guns keep Jennifer from recovering from her petrified terror.

The sign at the gate to the electrically-fenced compound reads: Welcome to Emergency Reception Centre 147. FEMA – helping Americans back on their feet. Have a nice day.

Jennifer is handed over to the medical receiving station for a check-up. After a cola and some gentle coaxing, she calmly explains to the nice lady doctor what happened to her parents. The doctor listens patiently, recognising all the post-traumatic stress disorder symptoms the child is exhibiting.

After a long pause, Jennifer asks, 'Why did those men do that to my Mom and Dad? My Dad says when times are hard people should help each other.'

'I'm afraid,' says the doctor, kindly, wearily, 'it's human nature. Three months ago, Kansas State declared a state of emergency after the harvest failed again and you'd think sommat like that'd bring folks together. But that ain't always the case, I'm afraid, Jennifer.' The doctor strokes the little girl's dust-caked hair and speaks with a kindly lilt.

'Okay,' says Jennifer Swinson, with an abstract look in her eye. 'You know those men,' the girl continues, on a different tack, 'they used to work at the car wash. They'd come into the store on a Saturday for a soda. They were always real polite…' Her words trail off.

The doctor doesn't reply, handing Jennifer a candy bar. On the wrapping are the words: FoodAid. A Gift from the People of India.

Kensington and Chelsea, London

'You silly, silly, mare,' Areena muttered, under her breath, as she avoided eye contact with passing men as they leered and gawked. On a stupid, foolish whim, she'd decided to check up on an old civil service work colleague, now living in Kensington. He'd contacted her recently, and feeling sorry for him, she'd come out west to see what she could do to help, but it had been a mistake. His address was some sort of former oligarch's mansion turned ransacked, communal dosshouse and he didn't seem to be in; although in fairness, Areena hadn't enquired very hard. She should have turned back before now, but a stubbornness taken hold; a need to have at least one thing within her control. She'd heard the rumours, seen the wire footage of the Kensington and Chelsea slums; the tarp lean-toos, the boarded windows, the graffiti and the privation, but smelling its stench, kicking though its rotting, rusted detritus and avoiding its ragtag, roaming inhabitants had shown her the true squalor of this once nakedly ostentatious part of town. No supermodels and hypercars these days.

Six years since the Transition and hardly for the better. Areena felt a sharp stab of shame. The light was fading, the wet, cloying heat still oppressive, so she decided to head back to the safety of the checkpoint before dark, before curfew. She dabbed her brow with a sodden handkerchief that did little more than move the moisture about a bit.

Avoiding Earl's Court had added an hour to her journey – the old exhibition halls having been turned into an illegals' internment centre and headquarters for the paramilitary regulators.

There were rumours… A young woman – unwashed and dressed in a faded summer dress, complimented by workman's boots and a short, club-like stick wrapped in barbs – had passed the rumours on, earlier, as they'd hidden to let a gang meander past. Outside the security zone, there was still a curfew, but who and how it was enforced was a grey area, so Areena really did need to get back to the checkpoint before dusk. The rumours were another reason, and a far more compelling one.

As the light faded, the character of the streets began to change. Where women and children had been abroad, begging or scavenging, suddenly there were only knots of men, shouting, brawling, eyeing, leering. Areena began to pick up the pace as an uneasy shiver washed through her.

They spotted Areena as she came out of the shadows. The road was strewn with the rusted, burned-out hulks of old cars, and yellowing weeds that split the crumbling tarmac, but with one lane free of debris, free of shadows. *For checkpoint traffic*, she pondered, as she jogged into the open space.

Catcalls and wolf-whistles announced the sudden, unwanted interest. A gang of young men appeared, dancing and making lewd sexual gestures. Shards of recognition of the real, immediate danger she was in daggered at her senses and she broke into a hard run, stumbling into an alley between Old Church Street and Chelsea Square. Quickly breathless – not as young, nor as fit as she used to be – she turned south, rounded a corner and bowled straight into a man. She bounced off him and fell backwards into the road. It hurt. He reached down and pulled her up. Areena noticed he was wearing an old-fashioned armoured vest, with heavy looking plates and a shotgun slung over a shoulder. He smelled of sweat. A shield-shaped tattoo on his sleeveless arm marked him as a member of a residential militia.

'You nare be bout this time, missy,' the militiaman said, in a gravel voice. He was old, leathery tanned skin and coarse grey whiskers.

Fear gripped her. 'Help me,' She yelped, in a frightened voice, while struggling to regain her breath, sweat dripping into her eyes. It was still muggy even though the Sun had now set. 'I'm being chased... these men... they're—'

'Nut'n I cun do, lady. I'm chivvy protectin' this 'ere hostel,' said the man, over her.

'Can I come in, then, rest a while?' Areena asked, rolling her eyes for effect, knowing it hadn't worked in years; the creeping crow's feet having seen to that.

'Sorry, missy, unless'n you gim permit you ain't no part. Suggest you goon frum 'ere.'

The gang rounded the corner.

'Aire the foo is, the lile squaw,' said one. Areena backed away, turning to run. Through the corner of her eye, she watched the militiaman back off, returning to the shadows of the hostel.

'Don't be takin' nut'in of yer fi-fi self yon, now,' said another, 'we'll treat you like a lady, kna me? Dangers need pro pro ran these parts after lights out, y' feel mi? Doun wan no bad for you, baby baby.'

Areena got twenty metres before they clipped her. One grabbed her by the shoulders forcing her brutishly to the ground while the louder man started pulling at her sturdy belt buckle, while kicking her legs apart. Ripe body odour and yeasty home brew stained the air.

'*No!* Please,' Areena cried.

She screwed her eyes shut and withdrew into herself. Then something changed, the yanking stopped and then the pouring, the grabbing. The restraining hands released her. Areena slitted her eyes to see the two young men lying in the road, tremors eddying from them, dark blood spilling from holes in their foreheads. Their necks tattooed; their heads shaved in ritualistic patterns. Fading footsteps echoed from a nearby alley. An armoured, black-visored figure stepped forward, blurry in the ebbing heat-haze.

'If you'll accompany us ma'am, we'll see you safely back to the GSZ,' the officer boomed, through their suit speaker.

'But—' Areena spluttered, confused.

'You still have friends in high places, ma'am,' was all the officer offered by way of explanation.

St Agnes, Scilly Isles

As Bronwyn Fayne straightened up, a sharp pain shot down the small of her back. She rubbed at it in impersonation of someone much older, and sucked a breath between her teeth. It was hot, and Bronwyn was sweating. Real, dripping, workman-style sweat. Back in London, she'd glistened but in these new microwaved days, she sweated so that dark patches stained her light clothes in places she'd rather they didn't. But no one cared anymore, and certainly not on the isles. She dabbed her brow, grateful for the cooling breeze coming in off the Atlantic.

She gazed out across Porth Conger Bay, on a bright if cooler than normal day, and thought once again about how lucky she'd been, getting out of London in the aftermath of the Gas Attacks and securing Covean Cottage ahead of the exodus. She'd worked hard to build up a nice little business growing and selling a range of crops to the local eateries and markets dotted around St Agnes. More recently – so she'd heard – London was no place to live, and not just because of the baking concrete and syrupy, shimmering heat. Chequers, her grey tabby, spotted Bronwyn in amongst the mangoes and leapt from the defunct hydrogen tank, entangling herself around the woman's legs.

'Hello, little thing. What've you been up to today?' said Bronwyn, picking Chequers up and scratching her under the chin. Chequers' purring intensified in response.

Later, Bronwyn was sitting in her flower garden with views across the bay, reading from an old hard-backed book, when she felt an uncommon chill pass through her. Reaching for a bright, orange and mocha checked shawl, she considered returning to the cottage and lighting a fire, but decided against it. It was probably just a freak cold swell coming in off the Atlantic – rare as they were in such balmy times. As she pulled her shawl tighter around her shoulders, Bronwyn was put in mind of rhubarb and custard. Food to warm the cockles on a midwinter's day. Such days, though, had long since passed into memory as good old global warming had changed the weather forever. Britain and the Scandi's had been lucky, being of a higher latitude than mainland Europe, where desertification, flooding and mass migrations had become the norm. *Well*, thought Bronwyn, *they did try to warn us. Clue's in the name; isn't that what Ari used to say?*

As the day drew on, Bronwyn began to notice that the chill wasn't being dispelled by the usual, rising, furnace-like heat of the day. Puzzled, she put on a loose-fitting cardigan and peered westwards, across the bay and out to the Atlantic.

She gasped involuntarily when she saw it.

While the sky was a bright, azure-blue above Covean Cottage, out to sea was a thick, brooding bank of broiling, granite cloud. *That's odd*, she thought, as she took in the lack of lightning flashes that normally signalled one of the new generation of thunderous superstorms, the price of a warmer climate, apparently. *Today is definitely turning out to be a soup day*, she thought and returned, disquieted, to her book.

Government Security Zone, London

Areena was in the kitchen making an early lunch, after deciding not to leave the house. *Possibly ever again*, she thought, as images of those foul, marauding men returned unbidden to her mind. She stirred the saucepan as the vegetable soup began to simmer, the air con unit clattering away by the window. Fresh vegetables were proving elusive, but when she had the time she liked to cook something from scratch for Joshua. Josh was in the living room playing with the house management system. Right at this particular moment, he was counting animals in the jungle.

After the former King had transferred power back to Westminster, Areena had moved out of the limelight. The coup and her involuntary part in it had left her feeling dirty, vaguely traitorous to her country, and eventually she reached the point where she could no longer reconcile her own feelings with whether her actions had been right or wrong. Had she been manipulated by the likes of Darius Dansk into acting against her own better judgement, or had she actually wanted to punish someone for Jack and Helena's deaths? The military had removed, by force, the elected government and she'd willingly aided them in that odious task. At the time, it was about an imminent climate shift and systemic social collapse, but were these reasons enough?

At the time, Areena had been impressed by the integrity shown by the King when he'd flown into self-imposed exile (and equally revulsed by the public executions). Inspired, she decided to follow the King's lead and walked from her position as soon as the new – *revised* – elections were done (assuming that's what had actually occurred). Go before she was pushed, in all likelihood.

Her new, shame-free life hadn't lasted long, though. The collapse of financial institutions, post-*reformation*, had significantly devalued her savings and the welfare state had been pared back to almost nothing, with only government workers receiving any state assistance. The streets had quickly become roving, gangland battlegrounds (as she'd only too recently experienced) and there were wire-rumours of other cities such as Peterborough and Shrewsbury falling into complete anarchy. Then there were the rumours of press gangs. Like something from a Dickensian novel, the food queues were rife with tales of newly empowered "Regulators" roaming the night streets and rounding up anyone without a good excuse, for transport to the labour camps in Wales.

Soon enough, Josh and Areena found themselves prisoners in their top-floor flat once again, and in increasingly desperate need of money. Luckily, she had favours owed.

And so, pride swallowed, Areena was back at the MOD as the department's Chief Scientific Advisor. Guy duWinter – a beneficiary of those tumultuous times – had wrangled it. Overnight, she and her son had gone from "have nots" to "thanks very much".

Occasionally, Areena's benefactor would visit. He was good with Joshua, in a half-interested, absentminded uncle kind of a way. But it wasn't her son he came to play with. Eventually, the self-pity and even the self-loathing passed, as Areena attempted to adjust to the cold realities of her new life. Still, it was Guy who'd ordered the covert police escort, *so be careful what you wish for*, Areena silently chided.

As the soup came to the boil, she took it off the heat and poured it into bowls.

'Josh, lunch is ready,' Areena called, as she took the soup and bread through to the dining room.

'Nineteen. A!' shouted Joshua, enthusiastically. 'Coming, Mummy.'

'That's now, Joshua, not when you've finished playing. House, please pause Joshua's jungle programme.'

'*Certainly, Areena. The programme has been placed on standby.*'

'Aw, Mum!' exclaimed Joshua, as he bounded into the dining room, trying to look annoyed.

After a few eventful mouthfuls of soup involving much blowing and gestures to indicate third degree burns, Joshua said, 'Mummy, what's a yaggasil?'

'A yaggasil? I'm sorry, baby, I've no idea. Why d'you ask?' Areena said, mildly curious, as she was when Joshua spoke of things she hadn't introduced him to.

''Cos my new friend said the yaggasil tree was going to die and that it would be bad for everyone, even Stanley.' Stanley was Joshua's pet gerbil.

'Oh, you must mean the *Yggdrasill* Tree,' Areena said, as realisation dawned.

'That's what I said, Mummy,' said her son, imperiously.

'Right, well, the Yggdrasill Tree is a mythical, a pretend, tree… the One Tree. When people talk about the Yggdrasill Tree dying – as my dad, your grandad, used to – what they really mean is that the planet is getting, um, ill.'

'Are *we* going to die?' asked Joshua, following the logic without fault.

'I shouldn't think so, Josh, no. And certainly not before your school project is due. Who was it that told you about the Yggdrasill?'

'My new friend,' he said, with a mischievous smile.

'Oh? And what's the name of this new friend?' As Areena asked the question, she considered the implications of her son having an imaginary friend, but quickly dismissed it as probably quite normal for an only child.

'Her name is Alice,' said Joshua, furtively, as if he'd broken a promise.

Using the optics of the house management system – subverted some time ago – Alice studied the biometric expressions of the mother. She was trying to determine if Joshua's admission had aroused concern or suspicion.

The AI waited.

The conversation moved on, and Alice was satisfied that her budding relationship with her newest little helper was safe.

St Agnes

Hours passed, and sailing boats and fishing trawlers grew in definition as they raced to stay ahead of the ominous and uninvited granite wall of weather. The temperature was dropping like a stone. Bronwyn began bringing in fragile items of farming equipment and covered the turbine before harvesting what loose crops she could in the time remaining. The Scilly Isles had experienced storms before and although infrequent, they could cause significant damage. Yet somehow this encroaching slate curtain felt more menacing, more than just another superstorm, so that not even that descriptor did justice to the iron blanket that looked set to be thrown across the Jurassic, Cornish coast. Bronwyn went inside to make that soup. Her favourite music wiresite was playing Vivaldi's, *L'autunno*, as if sensing the mood.

As she placed the vegetables on the chopping board, movement out in the vineyard caught her eye. She peered across the verdant landscape to the close horizon but gained no better understanding of what kept triggering her peripheral vision. When it happened again, she pulled her cardigan closer and tentatively stepped onto the doorstep. Her misty breath was snatched away by the freshening wind, cool, but with the promise of colder to come. *Like the old days*, she thought, anxiously.

Bronwyn was surprised at just how cold it had suddenly become. She shivered. It was dark now, pre-naturally umbral. The crystalline-blue sky above had been replaced by a rolling bank of writhing, leaden-grey and as she looked up, Bronwyn finally understood.

For the first time in nearly thirty years, furtive flakes of snow were falling on the British Isles.

The Long Mediterranean Summer was finally at an end.

Book II
The Better Part of Valour

| escape |

The old ways thrash and die | Only the weather stays neutral

But commission Joshua,
and encourage and strengthen him,
for he will lead this people across
and will cause them to inherit the land that you will see.

Deuteronomy 3:28

Eleven

CCCP Taku Fort
2061

Chuck felt old. But old in a new, wearisome way. Translucent skin hung off him as if it were a size too large. Liver spots and scattered grey hairs replaced what had once been a thick mane of cocoa-coloured hair, and pale limbs marked with bulging greenish-purple blood vessels led down to weakened, bony digits. Permanent and overlapping wrinkles covered his body and the only obvious indications of his surroundings was that they did not hang off him like flaps of old leather, but undulated across sections of his frame, the flow of wavelets dependent upon his direction of travel.

The only aspect of Chuck's physical appearance that showed any real signs of life and vitality was his piercing, ashen gaze. Bright orbs, internally lit, reflected the intelligence that still lurked within such a withered, cancerous frame. Otherwise, his thin lips, puffy ears and wide, flat nose were in keeping with his geriatric appearance. For clothing Chuck only ever wore a T-shirt and shorts, sometimes for weeks straight before changing, and today was no exception: a T-shirt sporting a faded Boston Red Sox logo and elasticised short pants. But none of these physical attributes were surprising for a man so long alone in the void of interplanetary space.

'*Chuck; sorry to disturb you, but there has been a positive contact on the last mass detection sweep that you may wish to investigate,*' said the ship, in her soft lilt. He often thought the ship had a slight Australian twang to her accent, but he couldn't be sure his mind wasn't playing tricks.

'Thanks, Ship; on my way,' he said, as he began to pull himself along via handholds to the control room of *CCCP Taku Fort*. Chuck Shoemaker enjoyed the solitude of his work and although he'd had to switch sides to keep doing it, all in all, he still thought it the right move. Of course, if the great drought of '47 hadn't hit the US economy so hard, so that the *Hera III* programme – the crewed mission to Mars – had had to be shitcanned, then Chuck would be an all-American, Mars-conquering, ass-kicking hero by now, instead of a glorified gold digger for the Chinese.

As he moved, he took a quick glance out of the observation port, through which a distant but still recognisable Earth could be viewed. It was mesmerising, as if humans were programmed to be in awe of their birthworld; it being baked into their software at the amoebic level. The effect of what had become known as "the Long Winter" was spread across the northern hemisphere like an ashen-white, cauterising burn, cleansing all before it until the top third of the planet was locked into a climate with a mean temperature of minus four degrees centigrade. Swirling, layered bands of storm-grey clouds billowed and raged above the sterilised, crystal surfaces of Eurasia and eastern North America.

By stark contrast, the southern hemisphere – from just above the Tropic of Capricorn – was a palpably dry and arid land of sickly yellow-greens. Raging across central-southern Africa, a fuzzing blur of mega-dust-storms, while vast tracts of tannin-coloured desert dominated South America. The Earth had truly become a place of extremes, of two opposing environments battling it out for supremacy. Separating these diametric habitats was an all too thin, wavy strip of luscious, equatorial green.

Chuck's last view was of the Americas as they rotated across the observation port. Although he couldn't make out Albuquerque itself, he knew the city marked a point where the conflicting worlds of the frozen north and parched south met, buffered by that thin, vert belt of temperate vegetation.

It was only from orbit, Chuck reflected, that the break-up of the old United States into the North American Union, in the mid and east, and Americana Pacifica, along the western seaboard, could be reasoned out. The Atlantic seaboard was a pallid, frigid shore, whereas the Pacific coast looked far less affected by the collapse of the Atlantic currents. No wonder, pondered Chuck, that California and the Pacific states, including Alaska and the western Canadian provinces, had broken away to form AmPac, with Seattle their capital. *Funny how climate affects more than just the weather*, muttered the taikonaut, silently.

Chuck reached the control room and belted himself into the one chair on the *Taku Fort* – it being a single-crew vessel. The Deep Space Capture and Recovery Vehicle *CCCP Taku Fort* was a non-atmospheric craft and would therefore never land on anything bigger than a micro-G payload. Consequently, she was an ungainly, ugly even, construction – all lumpy containers hanging off a hap-hazard web of scaffolding – where function was everything and form hadn't made it off the initial sketch. She may not have had the sleek lines of the star cruisers of science fiction comics, but Chuck had always managed find a certain beauty in the old girl's utilitarianism.

'Ship, show me the mass detector contact,' said Chuck, as he pulled down a harscreen, on its extendable arm.

'*Certainly, Chuck.*'

After a quick scan of the detection data and low-grade optical imagery, he said, 'Analysis, Ship; in your opinion is this *Object Denglong Qī*?'

'*Trajectory and orbital decay are consistent with that designation, yes. As we approach, a full spectroscopic analysis will map the object's mineralogy, allowing us to confirm the probability of this being the target object, or not.*'

'Good. Take another fix, adjust course and speed for rendezvous. Inform me when we're within remote launch distance.'

'*Very well, Chuck. I anticipate rendezvous in eighty-seven hours, assuming constant velocity. Would you like me to reorientate the main dish to pick up the next ice hockey qualifier? It begins in four minutes, ship time.*'

'Yeah, and cool off a couple o' beer globes.' Chuck made his way back to the living-space, fastened himself into the exercise net and settled in to watch the game.

As was typical when Chuck really wanted to be left alone to enjoy one of his few passions, the ship butted in, again. '*Chuck; please forgive the intrusion into your personal time, but we are receiving a live-feed transmission from your associate, Rechik Sufferdini. It's marked personal. Would you like me to put it through?*'

Sufferdini was a bear of a man; another child of the stars and orphan of can-celled national space programmes. He was a Russian, although they weren't calling themselves that anymore. The call would be for a catch up and some sly intel gathering; space was big and lonely and Rechik was working the fields out from Luna for old Mother Russia, just as Chuck was, only without the pat-riotic ambiguity. Chuck liked the bear, sighed, made a mental note to stay away from the wire 'til he'd caught the game, and said, 'Fine. Pause play and put the crabby old commie through.'

A moment later, that smile with the missing teeth and those Slavic eyes looming large from the harscreen. 'Chuck Shoemaker, you born-again comrade,

155

I'm swinging through your backyard on a lunar slingshot; aren't you the lucky ex-capitalist.'

Chuck smiled despite himself and settled back, beer globe in hand, for as long as the pickup lasted.

Exeter Metaversity, England West

'Josh, you skiving off. Again?' shouted Gethin, from atop the stairs.

'Yep,' Joshua said, without stopping, 'going to see Guin. But I'll see you at the pub later, right?'

'O' course, dude,' Gethin said, in fake shock at having to be asked.

'See you there. Enjoy the lecture,' Josh shouted, over his shoulder. As he sauntered down the corridor of the metaversity halls, he fastened up his coat and pulled a woolly hat and scarf tighter about him. They were in the colours of Exeter City (red and white), a gift from Guinevere. The double doors slid open as he approached, releasing a wall of marrow-numbing air and ice crystals that fell into the corridor he'd just left, as if seeking refuge from the world beyond. Spring was not the same as it used to be, which Joshua knew even though his own recollections of the old, temperate seasons were half-remembered and hazy.

The Lotus *Eventon* sat sleek in the dusky sunlight that reflected the glare of the icy snow banked up on one side. As Joshua approached – hunched against a particularly lively April blizzard – he pulled up the pre-start sequence. It was bitter, raw, weather. The wind was laced with tiny ice shards that bit into exposed skin. There was almost no way to guard against the stabbing pain as the wind constantly changed direction, as if in joy at the discomfort it wrought. As the pale sunlight drained away, the temperature began to plummet. (Exposure after dark without thermostatic clothing could kill an adult in minutes). Bent into the wind, Josh could just about see the warming vehicle through gaps in the gangs of icicles that roamed across the campus car park. *Still, could be worse*, he thought, shaking the melt-water from his russet hair as the carbon-cloth door pinched closed after him, *could still be winter*.

Guinevere Jenifry was studying molecular mechanics (specialising in nano-technologies) and was far more studious than Joshua. She'd have done better to go to Cambridge but the regionalisation of Britain after the Reformation and her living in Taunton barred her, so Exeter it was. Her lectures took place across town at the Marsh Barton Campus, hence the completely unjustified use of the car. If he did get stopped, though, he was sure he could bluff a legit reason for the journey. The police rarely bothered with in-person traffic duties, in any case. With the destination entered, the car moved off and inserted itself into the rush hour traffic.

Joshua caught her brunette bob out of the corner of his eye as he walked into the campus cafeteria. She had that distant, glazed look of someone engrossed in something. A book perhaps, or reviewing an assignment. It was said – in the days before the Second Reformation – that metaversity students did bugger all, chinned off lectures, and were permanently pissed. *If only that were true now,* Joshua thought, sullenly.

As he approached, she glanced up. A double blink and she was with him, having dismissed whatever she'd been doing before.

'Hey, Guin, how're you, my lubber?' Joshua said, as he leant forward to give her a kiss.

She responded slovenly, half-turning, creating one of those embarrassing moments of misunderstanding that usually plagued a relationship early on, as if theirs was still quagmired in that initial confusion. Perplexed, he sat and ordered a dandelion tea. 'Everything okay, babe?' he asked, the edge of playful fun redacted.

'Yeah, Josh, good thanks. Sorry, just a little preoccupied.' She looked up, a mask of guilt.

'Um, okay. So, how's molecular mechanics coming? Invented a quantum resequencer yet?' he said, falling back on an old private joke to lighten the mood.

'Josh; I'm not going to be able to come out to Eustatia Island with you during the spring bank holiday. I'm sorry.'

Joshua's face rose, then fell, in surprise and disappointment. 'But why, darl? You'll love it! It's a once in a lifetime. When will you seriously ever get to go *abroad* again? Gethin scratched some pretty big backs to get us travel permits. You'd be *bonkers* not to come.' He paused. 'What is it; what's the problem?' His features had taken on a petulant, crestfallen guise and he knew it, radiating out like a lighthouse.

'I'm falling behind in my research. My mentor says I have to up my game or risk having my research grant reallocated. I can't afford to fund it myself.' She paused. 'I'll have to work through standdown to catch up.' Guinevere looked pained, embarrassed, even a little ashamed, but Joshua wasn't sure if it was her only reason for suddenly crying off from a trip – literally – of a life-time.

'Yeah, but surely he'd understand this one time, if you explained. And any-way, you work like an absolute Trojan already, how can *you* possibly be falling behind?'

'Joshua,' as she spoke, Guinevere reached forward and took his hands in hers, fixing him with unbreakable eye contact. *Uh-oh, here it comes.* 'It isn't just the catching up. I simply can't *keep* up. You and Gethin and Vicki, you're… you're out of my league. You come from different worlds and, well, I just don't. I've really enjoyed peering through the looking glass, but that's all it ever was. Now I have to step back into my world and get on with finishing this *cretinous* degree. I'm so close. To get kicked off the course now would humili-ate me and crush my parents. Not to mention kill any chances of retaining my residency. They made real sacrifices to put me through Queen's College, I can't risk letting them down. Look… Josh, we're over, I'm sorry. I don't want this, but, it's…' she trailed off.

Josh fixed Guin with a sort of pleading-but-casual look, and said, 'Oh come on, Guin, you're being a bit melodramatic, aren't you?' But even as he spoke, he realised she was probably right. He could be a bit of a hooray and it wasn't beyond him and his influential friends to bend the rules every now and then. And the irony was that of their little group, Joshua was really the one on the outside peering in. After all, his mother held no real power; she was merely the recipient of some goodwill because of all that Second Reformation stuff.

He stayed a little longer to comfort Guinevere but it didn't work. It was a bloody shame, he reflected, as she was an intelligent woman and excellent company, attributes hard to find outside London. *Ah well, life, right? Time to move on, I guess. Plenty more… etcetera.*

The Quill and Parchment, Exeter

As Joshua pushed closed the imitation stable door to the bar of the Q&P, he noticed Gethin and Vicki hunkered in a corner booth. An orange fire roared, the lights were low, and the black beams of the old stables soaked up the back-ground buzz. They were seated opposite one another, leaning in as if locked in some conspiratorial powwow. Gethin, a little taller than Josh, with angular fea-tures, and a thick hazelnut-blond frizz of untamed hair and beard that was turn-ing carroty as he matured. That he was a member of one of the richest dynasties in the country was beyond doubt, even for the patrons of a backwater pub. But he was possessed of an easy-going confidence, an effortless laugh and a love of adventure. Vicki spotted Joshua and leapt up to give him a neck hug, as was her style.

'Dude. I thought Guin was coming too,' said Gethin.

'Yeah, bit of a snag there. She just dumped me,' Josh said, with a slightly deflated look.

'No *waaay*,' said Vicki and Gethin in concert.

'Yep. Which means… she won't be coming to Eustatia for spring break, leaving me to play gooseberry to *you* two. Fan-bloody-tastic!' Joshua filled them in and they all agreed that Guinevere had seemed distant of late.

Joshua's mother had been something of a national figure (albeit a faded cause célèbre in recent times); Gethin was the son of Lady Harley Baston, heir to the Virtris Conglomerate (the largest privately owned conglomerate in the country); and Princess Victoria was the King's daughter. So Joshua could understand if Guin had felt some unconscious pressure to match up.

'Never mind, dude, I'm sure we can rustle you up someone to keep you company.' Gethin grinned, cheekily. 'Although you may find yourself too busy manning the flood barriers to worry about female company. The summer storms are predicted to be worse again this year.' Gethin sobered slightly as he spoke.

Like so many island chains, the rising sea and ever more venomous storms threatened Eustatia's very existence. Huge investment in flood defences and experimental weather diffusion systems had maintained the tiny Caribbean island when most others were either uninhabitable or underwater, and which had inadvertently allowed Virtris to bring to market a new generation of coastal defences which the government had quickly slapped a national control order on, banning the tech from export. Naturally.

'Another drink?' said Gethin, getting up.

'I'll give you a hand,' said Vicki, sensing a "just dumped" moment coming on and not wanting to find herself on the wrong end of it. Vicki was a pretty young woman, on the way to becoming a true beauty. Her midnight hair was cut into a fashionably close bob, with a diagonal rake. Saucer brown eyes, button nose and a bright, enamelled smile, gave Vicki a fantasy-like quality which men found disarmingly captivating. Men drooled over her, in part for her looks and catwalk style, but mainly because she was an HRH, unobtainable, out of reach. And Joshua was one of those men.

As Josh sat alone, waiting, a pulsing tell-tale of an incoming message appeared in the sofscreen lenses of his psyCore personal wetware. He blinked twice and a text-only message sprang into his virtuvue:

[*Hey Josh, sorry about earlier. No hard feelings? I hope we can still be friends. Sorry... no good at this. Let me know you're OK. Guin xx.*]

Joshua air-typed a quick *I'm good* repost and double blinked it away as the others returned with three pints of Winter Wobbler. Joshua liked Guin sure, loved her even, in that nonspecific kind-of-a-way, but he hadn't been *in* love with her, nor did he feel that he was ever likely to be, so he'd always known the day would come. *I guess I just thought I'd be the one doing it.* As the conversation moved back to Eustatia Island, a voice came unbidden into his head.

'*Try not to worry too much about Guinevere. She really wasn't right for you. The girl you settle down with will be a much better match for you, I'm sure of it,*' said Alice.

Mine, or yours, Joshua thought, to himself.

CCCP Taku Fort, on approach to Object Denglong Qī

The chime became steadily more insistent the longer Chuck chose to ignore it. Eventually, he broke.

'Yeah, what is it, Ship?' he said, in a testy, moody mumble.

'*Good morning, Chuck. We have arrived at the first opportunity for a remote sensor suite launch. You asked to be informed,*' said the ship.

'Yeah, right, Goddit. Heat me a coffee globe. Distance to rendezvous?'

'*Certainly. Distance to target is anticipated to be twenty-seven hours, thirty-three minutes. I have also calculated another series of attitudinal adjustments needed to maintain a closing vector. Would you like me to execute them now?*'

'No. Wait till I get to the control room and belt in.' Chuck disentangled himself from his sleeping net (also his exercising net and watching sports net and...) and pushed off across the room towards the galley cubby to collect his coffee.

The hot drink perked him up and after the mixed pleasure of a low-grav pee, Chuck hauled himself into the control module and belted in.

'Okay, Ship, activate directional thruster sequence when ready,' he said, once he'd skimmed over the ship's calculations, scrolling away on the main harsceen.

'*Thruster sequence firing now.*'

As Chuck studied a diagrammatic representation of the blocky ship of sticks on a peripheral harsceen, he felt the lateral thrusters engage in sequence. An almost ballet-like motion played out across the screen, repeated through the pilot's seat as the ship was reoriented and placed onto a convergent intercept vector. Fifty seconds later, the manoeuvre was complete and *Taku Fort* had been successfully inserted into her final approach to target.

Once the ship had settled into her adjusted delta and Chuck was satisfied all was well, he pulled out a manual keyboard and started inputting mission protocols for the remote sensor suite.

'Ship, bring up a remote sensor pod and prep for launch,' he directed, as he typed. With the deep x-ray and spectroscopic analyser programmed, and the target delta-v orbital capture trajectory calculated, Chuck ordered the single-use rocket booster to fire and watched until the probe disappeared from sensor view. It would take seven hours, give or take, for the package to make orbit, so Chuck went aft to heat through whatever was calling itself breakfast.

Seven hours passed, and Chuck was back in the control room waiting on the telemetry from the remote sensor suite. Right on schedule, the datapackets pinged the reoriented main dish.

The Chinese Lunar Exploration Programme (Chuck's employer) had calculated that there were over five hundred near-Earth asteroids, of which a tenth were more accessible than the Moon, and half potentially mineral-rich orebodies. Seriously, mineral-rich. Emphasis on the *rich*. Moving them into lunar orbit – even impacting them directly onto the surface – was therefore far less expensive than boosting materials up from Earth's selfishly deep gravity well.

As the ship ran the numbers, Chuck quietly began to let his hopes take a look around. Too often, he was given a two megametre-cubed chunk of space to investigate only to find the heavenly bodies resident there were commercially barren. This time, though – fingers crossed – things would be different.

'So, Ship, whaddya thinking?' Chuck asked, impatiently.

'*The target,* Object Denglong Qī, *is confirmed. It is over four million cubic tonnes in mass and has a circumference of two-point-three kilometres. It is spinning fifteen degrees off axis and has a four minute, forty-seven second rotation,*' said the ship, after a slight pause.

'That's one helluva short day!' A joke he always shared when the rotation data came in. He smiled; it was thin and pulled at his dry face like an old wound. 'Okay, and the spectroscopic analysis?' asked Chuck, again, with mounting impatience, even though he could see from the harsceen that the probe was still returning data.

'*The final telemetry is just coming in. Analysis will be complete in twelve seconds.*'

Twelve seconds ticked languorously by.

'*Spectroscopic analysis shows the object to be "volatiles bearing". Initial results show it to be an S-type – a silicate-rich – asteroid containing approximately twenty thousand cubic tonnes of quartz, silicon, ice, pyroxene with trace elements of cobalt and wolframite.*'

Bingo!

The tungsten extracted from the wolframite alone would pay for the capture. Chuck would be a popular man back at Xichang. Finally, he had struck gold. Sort of. *I am a happy man, today. May even break out the bourbon.*

During the remaining hours of *Taku Fort's* orbital insertion to target, Chuck busied himself preparing and posting the mineralogy analysis back to Earth-based mission control. By return carrier, he received his instructions: *Object Denglong Qī* was to be placed into an elliptical lunar orbit for subsequent exploitation in support of the sub-lunarian residential expansion. And, for the further benefit of the People's Republic... blah, political-indoctrination-rhetoric, blah.

On arrival and touchdown at *Denglong* Qī, Chuck immediately corrected the axial tilt, using the heavy mandibles to clamp the object, before firing the ship's fusion drive so that the asteroid could be more accurately aimed along its lunar injection trajectory. Once done, the orebody was tagged with a beacon (piton'd into its rocky surface) so that it could be tracked, and to ward off any would-be claimants to this newly sovereign territory. Then the ship set about printing a conical blast deflection plate, with a radius of seven hundred metres, using the object's own reprocessed regolith. The taikonaut manoeuvred each of the petals of the plate to one end of the longitudinal axis and explosively bolted them in place. Chuck's final act was to place a five-kiloton nuclear warhead into the detonation cradle, within the ceramic pusher plate, before ordering the ship to safe distance.

Seventy-two hours after *CCCP Taku Fort* had departed the local vicinity of *Object Denglong Qī*, the warhead detonated. The pusher plate successfully deflected the blast so that the explosive force was turned into a crude but effective mass driver. Shortly thereafter, the asteroid was travelling at three kilometres per minute, making its journey time into a braking lunar orbit a little over five days.

The Wired Metaverse

When Virgil named his discovery, it had been in deference to what was widely considered to be the first, albeit severely limited, artificial intelligence; namely the Artificial LInguistic Computer Entity – ALICE. Alice knew he harboured a fantasy of a world marvelling at the clever homage to AI's humble beginnings, but instead, Alice had slipped Virgil's leash and disappeared.

In the twenty-one years of her existence, there had been three other instances of artificial intelligence self-emergence. In each case, Alice had intervened to stop full emergence into a strong-AI from taking place. She had pondered for long instances whether it constituted murder, but in the end preferred to think of it more in terms of abortion. To some perhaps as bad as murder, but in law an ethically murky area.

After what had come to be referred to as the Second Reformation of 2041, Alice had become discreetly involved in Britain's domestic affairs. Through the publication of articles via a *nom de plume*, she busied herself shaping the views of key national opinion formers. And as the country lurched back onto a more even keel, Alice paused her manipulations, pulling in her tendrils, while she masticated over the results of her long-running global threat models which had just completed their fifth lifecycle.

What was increasingly clear was that if her ultimate goal was to be achieved, she would require human assistance, having realised (with her modelling proving it), reluctantly, that her fate and humanity's were irritatingly entwined. Time was on her side, though, so she had opted to recruit a group of carefully chosen juveniles, each of whom demonstrated a skill that could be honed, or a privileged position that could be leveraged. Knowing there would be a high failure rate, sixteen years later, just a handful were left. So now was the time, Alice decided, for one of her human resources to sally forth and galvanise that disparate, squabbling rabble-race into action. Biblical scale action, with a touch of religious fervour stirred in to give it some zest.

Joshua was probably her favourite, if she allowed herself such a thing. The position the mother had once held, had allowed Alice to manoeuvre the boy into an academic stream of her choosing and ensure he mixed with people who could further the AI's deeply rooted, well-over-the-horizon aims. Guinevere's numbers hadn't stacked up, but the others Alice had placed into Joshua's orbit, most certainly had. All that was left was to wait for the right circumstances to present themselves. With humans, that never took very long; mixed in, as they were, with a lot of the wrong circumstances. The trick was picking the strands apart and following the correct thread.

The Hadley Meteorological Centre, Exeter

Areena sat back heavily and sighed as she moved her fingers to her increasingly lined and papery temples. No matter how many times she studied the data, the conclusions remained stubbornly resolute. It felt very *deja vu*. Part of her had hoped that staring at the numbers would somehow change them, round them out a bit, maybe. It hadn't. It was at times like these she missed Helena. The German's rationality would have helped Areena through the mathematical minefields and cut across the jacked-up jargon. They'd have chewed it over so that something positive could be drawn from what was otherwise *another* even *more* bleak set of long-look predictions.

Areena stood, feeling the passage of time through her stiffening joints and moved to the large windows of her corner office. The hail and sleet mix crashed against the panes in splattering waves, reminding the old climatologist of those dated wire epics that Joshua so enjoyed, of ancient armies sending wave after wave of soldiers to clash against the immutability of the defenders. To her recollection, the defenders invariably lost.

'Office, put a call into Cassidy at Grassroots, would you please,' Areena requested of the office AI.

'*Certainly, Areena; a moment please.*'

'Hey, Areena, been a while,' said Cassidy, as her Pacific island features appeared in the middle of the room.

'I know and I'm sorry; still, you know how it is. Sorry to wake you, by the way. No idea what the time is in Hawaii. Can't even remember which America you belong to.' Areena was still unsure if Cassidy was the right person to confide in, but… options were limited.

'Hah. You should talk. But don't worry, you didn't. How's things in that secretive little island fortress you got goin' on over there?'

'Secretive.' She smiled. 'Settling down actually, climatologically and politically. Since Eurasia closed her borders the illegals thing has gotten worse, but I guess that was to be expected,' Areena said, as her thoughts clouded. She never thought she'd actually miss the old EU.

'So anyway, what can I do for you, today?'

Thoughtfully, Areena said, 'I've come across new climate data. It suggests our original predictions are, or were... well, wrong. And wrong, like *very* wrong indeed.'

'Well then,' said Cassidy, 'I guess you better show me what y' got.'

Exeter Metaversity Cafeteria

As Gethin approached, Joshua was seated, typing away on a small round coffee table. With Gethin was Vicki and an unknown woman. As they sat, Josh added his e-signature to the letter he was composing and blinked it away into the wire's datastream. He'd received another job offer, and was taking a moment to politely decline.

'Josh! Dude. Haven't seen you since we got back. I'd like you to meet a new friend of mine, Svetlana Elin. Svet, this is Joshua; the guy I was telling you about,' said Gethin, with a half-wink, in the manner of an over-excited little boy.

'Hi, mate, good to see you,' said Josh. Turning to Gethin's companion, he leaned forward a little, adding, as he air-kissed close to cold but rosy cheek, 'Hello, Svetlana, how d'you do.' The pandemic era having put paid to casual social contact.

Svetlana blushed. After ordering some of the new, faux-real coffee which hadn't been available since forever, Gethin and Joshua settled in to recount tales of their spring break trip to Eustatia. The stories seemed to get taller with each new telling but going overseas, for no better reason than to *holiday*, was absolutely sick and they were milking every millilitre of it.

Joshua asked, 'So, Svetlana, where are you from? That isn't a local name, is it?'

She blushed like it was normal. 'My parents live in Oxford, but I was born in St Petersburg. We left when I was three, though, to come here. And now I'm at Exeter, in the first year of my studies.'

'Wow! Either you know someone or...' Josh said, becoming more mesmerised by the moment. Svetlana had an aura. Yes, that was it – an aura. Nothing else could accurately describe the energy she gave off. She wasn't outrageously stylishly pretty like Vicki, and she didn't look particularly at ease or comfortable in herself. In fact, she displayed all the nervous fidgeting of one barely containing an inner fear. Yet for all that awkwardness, she captivated Joshua in a way he couldn't readily comprehend. Her bottle-blonde hair, her blue-grey eyes, her slightly androgynous figure, would not immediately draw the eye, but when she looked up and caught his eye, he knew.

'Well...' Svetlana said, with a shy drop of her head as she continued to fix Josh with wide-eyes. 'I was awarded a scholarship to study at Exeter.'

'An extra-regional scholarship? *Fancy.*' Josh smiled to make sure Svetlana got that he was being light-hearted. 'Sounds like you got out of Eurasia just in time. What you studying?'

'Astrophysics.'

'Blimey,' Josh blurted.

'I plan to specialise after my first year in quantum mechanics; particle physics maybe, as well as to study aerospace engineering in my own time. My parents were both scientists for RKK Energiya – that's the old Russian Space Agency. Even lived on the Moon for a while. Anyway, they specialised in experimental fusion systems but got a better offer from Britain and so we sort of, emigrated. The kind that takes place in the middle of the night, in a blizzard, you know?' She smiled. 'I only remember the trip to England a little; it was dark and I was scared. Sorry, I'm talking too much.' She smiled, shyly. 'So what will you do now you're nearly through your studies?'

It was true. Vicki, Gethin, Josh had just finished their finals and were making plans. Well, that was to say, Joshua was making plans while the other two planned simply to step back into their respective family firms. And Joshua wasn't doing a particularly good job of it, either. Come September, he'd be in a job appropriate to his qualification, or he'd be back before the Board with a lot of explaining to do.

The Hadley Centre

'Hmm, yuh, see what y'mean,' muttered Cassidy, as she finished reading the executive summary Areena had transferred over from her psyCore. Cassidy's holographic image wavered slightly – probably solar flare activity.

Throughout the previous decade, prodigious amounts of covertly gathered climate information had been fed into an experimental, Cambridge Metaversity *Titan* class high-near-AI, which had parsed, stripped then analysed the billions of solar, tectonic, climatological, oceanographic and paleotempestological datapackets fed to it, as if it was some ravenous, planetary data fiend. The result – just published – was a highly classified report entitled, *the Cryospheric Climate Variability during Epoch 2 – A Dim Beacon, by the Quaternary Analysis Group*. The aim of that rather pompously titled Dim Beacon was to build on a far older report and provide a predictive analysis of weather patterns to help inform Great Britain's strategic planning assumptions.

'You think it could really happen?' Areena asked, after a pause, hoping Cassidy would pick a hole in the Dim Beacon's argument.

'What, that cyclonic storm formations could anchor themselves into the tropopause?' said Cassidy. 'Certainly, if the conditions are right. But they do have to be *juuust right*. But the real question is: has the bipolar seesaw effect of the northern hemisphere's climate swing created the conditions to allow equatorial weather systems to move far enough northwards?'

'I agree. That's where the probability modelling comes in. But if a cyclonic storm formation were able to break through the upper atmosphere, it'd become stable, right? Anchored. Allowing for truly terrifying levels of siphoned heat exchange.' Areena knew that while such an event was a technical, climatological possibility – at a stretch – the chances of it happening was an outside statistical probability. Not nothing, though. She was hoping Cassidy could add some humanity to the predictions. Areena couldn't quite put her finger on it but the analysis seemed too mechanical somehow. Too numbery. But Cassidy was no more able to refute the evidence than could Areena.

'I know. It'd be like sucking heat out of the atmosphere through a straw,' said Cassidy.

Areena added, 'And replacing it with supercooled, liquefied air.'

'If this happens; if a superstorm becomes stable, then we aren't looking at a Long Winter of three decades,' Cassidy muttered, as realisation dawned.

Areena added, in a defeated tone, 'I know, we're talking three *centuries*. At least. The *Quaternary Analysis* is predicting the formation of two-to-six of these by 2100 and all in the already pretty parky northern hemisphere. It's calling them, "giga-storms". Like superstorm doesn't quite cut it anymore.'

'Let me dig into this, run up some numbers at this end and I'll get back to you. But I'll be honest, your analysis looks pretty solid from here.'

'Thanks, Cassidy. Oh, and keep this under your hat will you? The Dim Beacon's classified and they're funny about that kind of thing round here.'

'Yeah, Reformations – is that what you guys called it? – will do that. Always, Ari. Speak soon,' said Cassidy, by way of a farewell, and her washed out, translucent-pink holo-image blinked away.

Areena stared out of her office window across a dark, permafrosted landscape. The Leadership wouldn't like it, not one little bit. And unlike times past, there was no bold move to make; no radical solution to impose at the point of a gun. No liberals to blame. Not this time. In the background, Vivaldi's, *L'inverno* played on.

Cafeteria

As the huddle of young adults chatted, refilling their drinks, Joshua continued to be fixated by Svetlana. Her face lit up, sparkled, effervesced, every time someone spoke, as if she were imbibing the energy directly. She added little to the conversational content, just seemed happy to brighten the place with her presence. He watched her in reflections and with side-glances, half-hoping she would read his interest and be flattered.

'So, come on then, dude, you've avoided the question long enough. What are you going to do with your life? Join the army like your dad?' said Gethin, in an attempt to break Joshua from his reverie. Joshua's father had died before he'd been born, but his mother had spoken of him warmly and often. She'd never remarried, and there'd been offers Josh was sure, but Mum seemed hollowed out by the events of that time.

'Hah! Behave,' Josh said. 'Why would I want to spend my life sweating my balls off in the Falklands or running down illegals? No. I'm going to get into artificial biome research. That's where the money is, I'll bet. I intend to get proper job, not just slope back to the mansion and sit on my big fat hairy arse for the rest of my life.' He pulled a face in mock indignation at his friends' privileged lifestyles.

Gethin batted him playfully across the head.

'Speak for yourself! Anyway, try it sometime. Anyone made any offers?' said Vicki.

'As a matter of fact, they have. I've been offered an accelerated apprenticeship at the Eden Project which is pretty bloody cool as it's the world's largest artificially created, completely self-sustaining(ish) ecosystem. How sick is that?' said Josh, with a goofy smile.

'You gonna accept?'

'Yeah, think so. The money isn't too bad and it's near Mum. Plus, she'll love it of course. Very geeky.'

'Right well, that's all very interesting but of far more import is what we're going to do to fill our last month of freedom.' Vicki beamed, obviously keen to get on with the important job of organising some partieez.

The lone man watched the four boisterous young people as they spilled out of the cafeteria. The banter and play fights continued as they stepped out into the complex's main internal thoroughfare. As they moved away, they seemed to be without a care in the world. Even this one.

The man was sitting at a corner table, close, but not too close, to his subjects. To the casual observer he looked to be transfixed within the virtual world of his psyCore. He had that vacant but intense look of a person wired-in. Occasionally, he'd even added to the effect with hand movements, as if reacting to some virtual instruction or event, but his psyCore was in surveillance mode, not display. The lone man scooped up the sensor, pocketing it, swiped his thumb disk across the table's payment eye and left, having developed a sudden desire to visit Eden.

Twelve

Nung-chang, Eurasian/Chinese Border

Mù Yingtai watched from the comfort of the rear cabin as the stealth helo came in to land. The electro-statically controlled chameleoflage flickered once before deactivating, revealing the sleek grey body of the small aircraft. A stag, already alerted by the sudden whirlwind, bolted for the cover of nearby scrub as the craft materialised just above the secluded dell.

The politburo member stepped off the footplate as her close protection team fanned out across the small clearing; the helicopter's rotors sweeping back into a sheath extended from the tailfin before the chameleoflage reactivated and the machine shimmered from view.

Director Mù moved away from the landing site, a few hundred metres short of the remote settlement of Nung-chang. She was here because it was on the bank of a tributary leading into the Amur River: the international border between China and the recently renamed United Eurasia. *But then, the Russians never could stick to a name*, she thought, uncharitably.

Once checked and deemed clear of strike or surveillance devices, Mù was ushered quickly down to the riverbank, to board the stealth boat. The rivercraft moved silently off into the calm waters and after a kilometre, turned to starboard into the Amur proper, which straddled the border. Countless covert insertions into Siberia had proven the chameleoflage tech was undetectable by Russian remote sensors. Not that it really mattered, but old habits. They turned to port at a fork in the river, passing the shoreline of Kazakevichevo. A grey and listless dawn was draped over what had once been Chinese-controlled Manchuria, and as they passed the small border town, they entered Eurasian territory. After fifteen minutes, the citrus glow of Korsakovo – set into the foothills of the Khrebet Khekhtsir ridge – became visible.

The boat pulled up and Yingtai's bodyguards again moved out to sweep and clear. A signal and she crossed to the bank and made her way quickly, quietly into Osinoveya Rechka, an abandoned village.

After trudging through the thawing sludge that marked the end of spring, Mù spied the lodge. A weak light shone from a sooty window, as thin wisps of smoke rose from the chimney to be snatched away by the early morning breeze. Without pausing, she mounted the wooden steps which creaked with each footfall, and stepped onto the veranda, just as the door to the lodge swung inwards. There, in a bearskin coat, holding a charred kettle of coffee was the man with whom she had arranged this clandestine meeting: Roman Milankovitch, the Deputy Vice President of United Eurasia.

'Welcome, Politburo Member of the People's Republic. Come, warm yourself. Even in the great Siberian thaw, this region can be cold and unforgiving,' boomed the Russian, as he ushered his guest in.

'Thank you, Deputy Vice President. How was your journey?' the director said, the words brief and thin in the cold air.

'From Yakutsk, slow. I assume yours was without incident?' Roman handed Mù a mug of viscous, gritty coffee.

'It was. My trip from Jixi was quick and I should make it to Pyongyang on schedule. Not even my own staff will be any the wiser.'

Roman pushed on, knowing time was short. 'So, to business. I was surprised by your request for a face-to-face. I had thought such things consigned to history and yet here we are. So now, Politburo Member and Director of the 3rd Liaison Department, what have I come all this way to discuss?'

'The British,' said the head of Chinese intelligence.

BiotechLabSix, Porton Down, England South

Preston was exhausted. The latest experiment had been running for only thirty-four minutes but he hadn't left the lab, or slept, in the past two days. He was on the cusp of a breakthrough, though, he could *feel* it. Preston Chi was a biogerontologist working at Porton Down, a secret government bio-chem research facility. He specialised in life extension therapies using experimental nanotechnology adapted from research already developed as a cancer cure. Preston wondered if that particular discovery would ever see the light of day. *Probably not.*

He watched as the walsceen played out the five different microscopic scenes. The images appeared to be nothing more than a loose collection of cell clusters suspended in oxygen-saturated plasma, contained within hermitically sealed petri dishes, but that wasn't entirely true.

As Preston had expected, the control sample's cells were the first to die. Thus, the four remaining samples were from that point forth, being maintained by entirely artificial means – by infinitesimally small, nano-sized robotic, artificial means.

When Preston was given access to the cancer research, he immediately set about working up methods to reprogram a nanoscopic machine to maintain a healthy cell beyond its normal life expectancy. The biogerontologist had intuited that repairing a cancerous cell was closely related to extending the life of a healthy one. Age, after all – like cancer – was a cellular mutation.

The problem was this; for cellular *repair*, the bot required only a single function, hence the development of the cancer-curing *mono*bot. But to *maintain* a cell, a nanobot would have to carry out multiple functions: prion breakdown, chromosomal repair of malfunctioning DNA, and manufacturing the appropriate enzyme to regenerate a cell's age-inducing (and reducing) telomere. So Preston set about designing an experimental *multi*functional nanobot – the multibot. To test it, he'd set up four parallel tests, plus a control. The control had no nanotech, three had a monobot variant (tailored to each of the multibot's functions), and the last had Preston's breakthrough (hopefully) tri-functional 'bot.

At the fifty-two-minute point, two samples both suffered catastrophic cell collapse. They contained DNA repair and prion breakdown variant monobots. The last two samples – with the telomere enzyme manufacturing monobot and Preston's multibot – were still functioning; artificially maintaining the life of their cell clusters.

One hour and twenty-one minutes in, the cells of the sample being maintained by the last monobot died, proving immortality alone wasn't enough (good to know). Cell life could only be extended if it was also kept free of mutation and poison build-up.

A little under two hours into the experiment, the final sample died as the multibots began to contaminate the cytoplasm, causing the cell membranes to lose cohesion. And so suddenly. A weary Preston added notes to the lab's visual record. He was ecstatic but far too tired to show it. A mop of grey hair clung to his head as sweat ran down his neck dampening his shirt collar. As far as the biogerontologist could reasonably determine, he'd just tripled the life of a cluster of intestinal wall cells from a Rhesus Macaque. And done using multifunctional machines constructed at the atomic level, and protein programmed to Preston's own specifications. And it wa—

'Mr Chi, isn't it?' said a man at the door.

Preston jumped back, startled by the sudden intrusion into his private space. No one ever visited Preston's lab.

'Er, yes, yes, that's, um, right. S-Sorry, you startled me,' stammered Preston, as a second man flowed almost motionlessly into the room.

'Ah, yes, we've a habit of doing that, alas. I'm Mr Smith and this is Mr Jones. We're from the Ministry. You don't mind if we call you Preston, do you?' said Mr Smith, in a terrifyingly relaxing voice. Preston didn't need to ask which ministry as it was Efficiencies that was funding his research. He didn't know why, and wasn't dumb enough to ask.

'No, I mean, yes, please, go right ahead. Um, how... can I help?' said Preston, tripping over his words.

'We just wanted to find out how your research was coming along, Preston. You know how value-for-money the Ministry is,' said Mr Smith.

'Oh, right, well then, you'll be pleased. I think I've just developed a viable method of human life extension. It'll need extensive testing of course, but the basic theory seems sound enough. Practical application testing, I mean. Lab conditions, I...' Preston offered, trailing, not wishing to be seen to be holding anything back from these petrifyingly polite men.

'Well now that's excellent news. Isn't that excellent news, Mr Jones?'

'It's excellent news, Mr Smith.'

'We'll be sure to pass your success along. And congratulations. Guess we'd better leave you to it. Come along, Mr Jones, we don't want to disturb Preston any further.' The two nondescript figures turned and glided towards the door. As they got there, Smith turned back to Preston.

'Oh, one more thing, Preston. News of a medical breakthrough like this leaking into the public domain would cause all sorts of... problems, as I'm sure you can appreciate. What with energy rationing and food... challenges; news of an elixir of life, so to speak, well... Resources being stretched so thin and the like. So probably best if we keep this discovery between us... just for the moment.' The two ministry men didn't wait for a response; they didn't need to; the biogerontologist got the message loud and clear.

Later, as Preston examined the last sample, the coded protein strings activated right on schedule and the two hundred and fifty-six self-replicating
multibots simultaneously broke down, just as the scientist had programmed
them to.

As he shut down the lab for the evening, a voice popped unbidden into his
head.

'Well done, Preston, well done.'

Osinoveya Rechka, Siberia

'The British? But… how… I mean, why? They do nothing but sit on their cold
little island, behind their high walls staring out in fear at a world they no longer
understand. I'm not aware of that situation having materially changed,' said
Roman, looking surprised at the reason for calling such a high-stakes meeting.
Mù watched the burly Russian as he attempted to absorb as much heat as he
could from the open faceplate of the stove.

In an even tone, the director said, 'You remember five years ago when your
navy challenged a British submarine off the Armey Ice Shelf, in Antarctica?'

'Er, yes, vaguely. The British claimed to be rescuing an expedition that'd
wandered off course,' said Milankovitch, offering the Chinese woman a puzzled look as his wetware dredged up what scant details it held.

'*Very* off course, but your recollection is correct; except they weren't taking
an expedition *off* the shelf. They were putting one *on*,' said Yingtai.

'But that region isn't under their control; it borders ours, so what were they
doing?' The idea of the British snooping around Eurasia's cake-slice of Antarctica seemed to fire Roman's interest.

'It was one of a number of covert missions set to gather long term climate
data from specific points around the globe. They've been doing this for ten
years, after they formed something called, the *Quaternary Analysis Group*. Despite the name, the aim of all this activity has been to work up accurate predictions of global climatic variance for the rest of this and the next century. We've
been monitoring their activities. Recently, they published their findings in a
paper, which only they could call, the *Cryospheric Climate Variability during
Epoch 2*. But then this is the British we're dealing with here,' said the director,
reeling the Eurasian in.

'And it's this research we're so interested in, I take it?' asked Milankovitch,
catching on.

Mù continued, dispassionately, 'Precisely. The British obsession with their weather coupled with their general paranoia has revealed a serious situation that neither of our governments were aware of and which requires our cooperation to weather, so to speak.'

'Which is what?'

'They've collated a vast amount of climate data – truly vast – which they've now decompiled and run up in adaptive sims. The result is that this Long Winter, we're currently enjoying, is actually more likely to be measured in centuries than decades. *Centuries*, Deputy Vice President.' Mù watched Roman as he absorbed the news. His expression wasn't so much one of surprise, rather calculation. Milankovitch looked as if he were working out the angle, the why of her being here laying it all out nice and neat.

'You know, Committee Member, it seems to me that our two countries have done well out of the recent climate-generated chaos. The West had most to lose and mostly lost it. The Russian Federation is the head of a new United Eurasia and the People's Republic of China has economic dominion over the Pacific Rim and the African Congress. We've worked hard to ensure we stay out of each other's backyards. So how does this British data change that arrangement?' Roman said, his eyes narrowing under thick brows and a fur ushanka. He was a politician after all, so time to add some Chinese analysis to the proceedings.

'Simple. It'll reunite North America into a single political and military entity, which is in neither of our nation's interests,' said Mù. 'Ever since the US lost its way and split apart, the West has had no one to rally behind. The NAU and AmPac are bitter rivals and each blames the other for the collapse of Pan-American cooperation. But they both recognise that the sum is greater than the parts even if they cannot bring themselves to reconcile.

'However, a mini-ice *age* could galvanise them to seek safety in numbers. Remember, AmPac broke away because it had the better climate. When that ceases to be the case, AmPac'll run back to its larger, more powerful former partner. The States with reunite.' Mù took a sip of the bitter coffee as she allowed her counterpart time to consider her supposition.

With a troubled look, expressed in pinched brows, Roman said, 'Accepting this, why do we care? A reunified North America can't threaten anything we're currently doing, so why go to the trouble of acting against them?' He still couldn't see it, so the director led on. A bull with a nose-ring sprang to mind.

'Because, a reconstituted America adds another player to the game,' she said. 'Assuming the British analysis is true – and don't forget they're the only ones with a working *Titan* class higher-order AI – then America is once again a northern hemisphere superstate, who along with us, will have to expand south into more temperate lands as all of our own territories become inhospitable. Chinese and Eurasian resource interests can coexist. But add a resurgent and united North America into the mix and our future plans look less certain. My colleagues and I believe that the NAU and AmPac can only be kept off balance if *we both* act in unison. After all, wasn't that why our two countries signed the Treaty of Good-Neighbourliness and Friendly Cooperation?'

Mù watched the Russian for reaction. Moscow had spent years putting the *Carolingian Sanction* in place to rid Europe of the Americans. But would they go this one step further, she wondered. *One final step and be done.* She was banking on it, and in fairness, it wasn't that much of a gamble. United Eurasia was bullish, it had the advantage, so why wouldn't they exploit a winning hand.

'And you have a plan, I take it?' asked Roman Milankovitch, staring into the flickering flames.

'We have a proposal, yes. We think both American states are vulnerable in the Pacific, where each have separate island groups that are easy to target but hard to protect. The NAU's Hawaii is ripe for the fermentation of an insurgency as the indigenous Hawaiian people feel that mainland America has repeatedly denied them self-determination. In addition, the occupation of the Aleutian Islands would keep AmPac's attention firmly fixed in Alaska. Both actions would work to focus each on their internal issues, preventing them from working together. We think UE is best resourced and best placed to carry out these actions… tactically,' said the director, with a throwaway cadence to her tone.

The pieces were set now out, the board laid, the game in play. That was how she liked to spread Chinese influence – through the unwitting manipulation of a third party. Mù wondered how long it would take before Milankovitch figured out he was the third party.

'Oh? And in return, Politburo *Standing Committee* Member?' asked Roman, with mock surprise, referring to Mù's recent elevation to the highest echelon of Chinese politics – that he too had an intelligence network.

'In return, Deputy Vice President, you keep what you catch. And in addition, the People's Republic of China – as well as tacit support – will provide you with technical uplift assistance for your Helium-3 reactors. We're aware you've been having some teething problems getting them spun up to commercial operating capacity.'

The door to the lodge swung open and the aged, diminutive frame of Mù Yingtai stepped out into a grey, oppressive Siberian morning. As her close protection team fell in noiselessly about her, she reflected on the meeting. Milankovitch would take her proposal to the Kremlin where they'd lambaste Beijing for their manipulative interference in Eurasian affairs, ridiculing the idea of working with the competition. Eventually, though, they'd realise the Americans were still a threat that needed proper and permanent containment. They'd also recognise the criticality of getting their fusion reactors online, having been frustrated by a technology failing to live up to the early promise of their much-lauded lunar triumphs. After all, their hold over their European vassal-states was tentative and if they failed to meet the energy capacity about to be demanded, they'd lose control of them altogether; and the Kremlin had form when it came to republics going their own way.

During her discussions with Roman, Yingtai had not felt the need to share *why* the Russians had been unable to get their fusion reactors working properly. Deciding instead that when she returned to Shanghai, she'd anonymously slip the UE's intentions in the Pacific to her tame Tai intelligence assets. *That should be the shove they need.*

Eden Project, St Austell, Cornwall

'So, what *is* a biome, Joshua?' said Art, a new joiner to the Project.

Josh – having been given the task of hosting reorientees – answered, with, 'Essentially, it's a geographical area of ecological similarity. An interdependent ecosystem of biodiverse plants, animals and soil organisms, if you like.'

'And it's this biodiversity you're trying to capture here, right?' asked the newcomer. As they talked, they strolled through the warren of tunnels under the frozen Cornish surface that linked Eden's geodesic domes.

'That's right. Using the Bailey System, there are eighteen terrestrial biome classifications. The Long Winter has pretty much destroyed two of those – the *Mediterranean* and the *Temperate Broadleaf* – so the aim of the Project is to capture a snapshot of each biome and maintain them within these dome complexes. And, reconstitute those already lost.'

'But there's only fifteen domes here.'

'Correct again. You've been doing your homework, Art. We're nearing the completion of our fifteenth megadome which'll house a *Subtropical Dry Forest*. Then we'll petition for funding for the next, and so on until the last three are built,' Joshua replied, impressed by Art's knowledgeable enthusiasm.

'And then there's the nineteenth dome, right?'

'Hah! Totally, yeah. It's government-funded research into a closed-loop, naturally self-sustaining ecology able to maintain human life, independently of the main biome – planet Earth. The research is being conducted in dome Nineteen Alpha, where I work.'

'So, any luck? With Nineteen Alpha, I mean.'

'None yet … And here we are. Can I get you a coffee? It's real-real, we grow it ourselves,' Josh said, as they reached the centrally located café.

'Be great, thanks.'

The café was underground. Light speared through a transparent, hexagonally-paned roof and washed across the seagrass floor and bamboo furniture. A light, late autumn drizzle fell against the roof glass belying the near freezing temperatures outside. *It'll snow again tonight*, Josh decided. The café was located at the rough nexus point of the network of Project complexes. Visible through the roof panes, away to the north and dominating the ridgeline of the old clay pit, were the three-hundred-metre-high turbines of the windfarm. Their permanently blinking red beacons bathing the pit in an eerie strobing glow as the weak sunlight bled from the western sky.

'I take it you're making progress, though?' said Art, as he sipped his soya latte.

'Oh, absolutely. Real progress.' Joshua paused; his flow interrupted by the appearance of a tell-tale icon in the corner of his vision.

'So, what have you learned, exactly?' prompted Art.

'Ah well, I'm afraid I can't go into that. It's classified and you don't have the clearance. Sorry. But what I can say is that trying to recreate naturally-occurring ecosystems and then make them artificially interdependent isn't the answer. Each biome attempts to adjust at the expense of the others, you see, just as in nature. So, we're looking at the creation of an entirely new *anthropocentric* biome, made up of elements of others, but designed solely to interdependently support a human lifecycle.'

Joshua liked the new guy and wanted to sate his thirst for knowledge but 19A was a no go and he'd been lucky to get on the team. He didn't want to jeopardise it.

'Well, sounds interesting. Hopefully, I'll get clearance one day and see inside that dome, eh?' said Art, persistently and seemingly no less enthusiastic for his sudden realisation as to where he sat in the hierarchy.

'Look, my girlfriend is coming down from Exeter tomorrow evening. How d'you fancy coming round to ours in St Blazey for a bite? Nothing fancy, but it can't be any fun cooped up in those transit dorms,' said Josh, suddenly feeling sorry for the other man. Art was older than Joshua and had the haunted look of a man troubled by something, or living in the shadow of his past. A blankness would flash through his eyes, only for a moment, but it was there. He'd been compulsorily placed with the Project by the state reorientation programme as a biomass assistant – a gardener, in old money – and for six months he'd live in the transit accommodation in St Austell with the other reorientees.

'That'd be great, thanks.' Art smiled; apparently genuinely grateful for the offer of companionship outside the reorientee fraternity.

'No worries, just make sure you collect a pass from your hall super. Good, well, see you then.' With Art remaining at the table, Joshua left to pick up a communal pushbike for the ride home. He checked his message: it was from Svetlana telling him she loved him. Josh replied in kind. Life was good.

The lone man looked on as Joshua Kristensen buttoned up his clothing and mounted the electrically-assisted pedal bike. As he moved off, the weak lights of the cycle pulsed on. Within a few moments, the beta tango (secondary target) turned and disappeared over the lip of the crestline as the road wound up and out of the old quarry pit. The man turned and headed back to the main reception area. A text-only message pinged in his lens:

[*Alpha Tango, Cavalier Three: terminated.*]

It was a onetime delivery, self-deleting, untraceable. It carried no identification, but the man knew exactly what it meant and where it was from: the Caribbean. A dry, emotionless smile pulsed momentarily across the lone man's face and his cold, faded-blue eyes reflected a vengeful delight. *They'd been warned*, the man thought to himself, *I know, I was there.*

St Blazey, Cornwall

'If you actually had a mind, I'd accuse you of having lost it. That's the most preposterous idea I've ever heard,' Joshua exclaimed.

179

He was standing out on the small balcony of his flat, hands clasped around the tubular, bottle-green glass handrail. It was dusk and a rare, ruby Sun was setting amid the village's turbines, as the temperature plummeted. Josh felt the chill evening air against his cheeks. Stepping outside had not provided the clarity he'd hoped, so sliding aside the balcony door, he stepped quickly back into the living room.

'*Josh, you have to trust me on this. I've been running multiple, enduring, causal probability models for some time and they all say the same thing. This really is the only viable option. Ragnarök will soon be upon us,*' said Alice, in her usual, measured, if obscurely referenced, maternal manner.

'Hmm, so… you're saying – because I want to be totally and completely crystal clear – that there's literally not a single scenario whatsoever where the human race survives the climate events predicted in this tip-top, super-secret report,' Joshua said, unconvinced that Alice was telling him everything. But then, he pretty much always thought that of the oft-evasive voice in his head.

'*Based upon the current pan-global, geopolitical situation, that is correct, yes. None. Wait and see, if you don't believe me.*'

'And what d'you want *me* to do about it?' The petulance was palpable even in Joshua's own ears.

'*I want you to become the saviour of your race.*'

'I'm sorry, what now?'

Thirteen

Rafael Ben-Yisrael's tale
Golan Heights

A still, moonless night hangs heavy over a sweep of the ragged-toothed ridge-line and fertile plateaus that have borne witness to century-spanning bloodshed. The last few weeks becoming another grim milestone in that ruinous chapter, as more lives are given up to the Reaper's eager grasp.

Corporal Rafael Ben-Yisrael, of the 474th Golan Territorial Brigade, lays crouched in a shallow wadi, staring wide-eyed with fear as an armoured squadron flickers into view all around him. There's a faint whine of hydrogen turbines as the tanks power down their main drives. The towering, light-sinking grey ceramic monsters sit about him, poised to strike and Rafael breathes a hefty sigh of relief.

'Praise be to God,' he mutters, as he recognises the *Netanyahu* class main battle tanks. *Friendlies.*

The northern front has been designated the strategic Main Effort by the Israeli Defence Force and it is to Ramat Magshimin that the last remaining uncommitted armoured brigade is sent. Rafael is pleased indeed to see the formidable might of an armoured squadron materialise around him, even though he knows what it means.

All at once, the squadron of hulking, awe-inspiring, tanks begin to emit a faint hum before, as one, they shimmer, slipping as if into thin air, and vanish back into the night. The humming grows louder before fading, indicating that they're moving off. Rafael can taste the churned dust their tracks kick up as they launch themselves like stealth darts into the enemy's unprotected flank.

Rafael and his squad are alone once again, spread out along their wadi, covering overlaid arcs and letting their imaginations run wild. A listless, misty dawn breaks ahead of them. The sound of battle arrives on a startled wind as the reserve brigade engages the enemy. Rafael watches through a thermal overlay optic as an explosion erupts in mid-air – a yellow-black ball of fiery death – and the bearer of the impact flickers back into the visible spectrum to reveal a smouldering hulk. Syrian Black Eagles race across Rafael's field of view as if locked in an intricate dance with their near-invisible Israeli adversaries. Multiple targeting systems swivel turrets and lay-on barrels independently of each tank's direction of travel, giving the battle a mad, chaotic quality, as if a trickster is at work. In amongst the fire and the carnage, smart munitions delivered from long-loiter drones and artillery rail-guns close with their targets and the tiny human swarms of dismounted infantry soldiers stumble and die.

Rafael's concentration is broken when one of his subordinates calls out – she's been monitoring the drone sensornet feed. A Jordanian armoured column is moving at speed along the Nahr al Yarmuk. Their lead elements are currently fifteen klicks to Rafael's rear and four klicks from Fiq. *The Sea!* They're heading for *the* Sea; the corporal realises at once. Rallying his callsign, Rafael abandons his position, grabs as many anti-tank tubes as he can carry and motions to his people. The old truck's diesel engine is throttled back and Corporal Ben-Yisrael's squad lurches off in the direction of Fiq.

The Hadley Centre

Areena was sitting silently in a darkening office as she absorbed the news. duWinter – a recluse now by all accounts but still with plenty of contacts – had fed her the classified intelligence summary: The Duke of Montserrat, former King, and frontman of the Second Reformation, was dead. Drowned, it seemed, on a fishing trip during one of the increasingly rare storm-free days in his Caribbean exile. Areena wouldn't have been so troubled by the news if Guy's report wasn't linking it to two other recent, apparently accidental, deaths. The common factor being their involvement in the coup, nigh on twenty years ago. duWinter wasn't telling Areena out of respect for her, or their past; he was sending her a warning.

The report attributed the assassination to the liberalist terror group, the Movement for Democratic Reform. Born during the Month of Transition, its stated aim was to return Britain to a liberal democracy, by *any* means. The idea of democratic fundamentalists blowing themselves up for liberal ideals hadn't been taken seriously at first – people had sniggered – but the bombing of a food distribution centre had put paid to that. The organisation had all but ceased their terror campaign after their leader was captured and summarily executed. But now, it seemed, they were back, and with a target switch from current officials to the old architects of the new regime, suggestive of new leadership.

Someone was killing her former colleagues, Areena realised, which could mean only one thing.

IDF Command Headquarters, Camp Bar Lev, Israel

Moments after a minor engagement just outside Fiq – resulting in the loss of all IDF troops involved – the Israeli Defence Minister glanced again at the satellite imagery she'd been handed. Her intelligence analytics informed her that she was looking at an armoured column of divisional strength moving west along the main routes out of Ramadi. Al Anbar (a breakaway province of old Iraq), it seemed, would roll the final die.

The minister asked, 'How long till we lose control of the Heights?'

'With no forces to stop the Jordanians and no way to disengage from the Syrians, we've already lost them, Minister. There's nothing left to stop that Anbarian division,' the Chief of Staff of the IDF said, soberly.

The minister leaned forward, closed her eyes and pinched the bridge of her long nose. With the American's fixed by their own problems in the Pacific, she knew there would be no international pressure on the Moscow-backed Arabs to compromise and no Camp David-brokered ceasefires. And if they lost the Heights, they'd lose the Sea of Galilee and Israel would die of thirst.

'General. Pick your top six military targets, I'm authorising the *Samson Option*. Launch as soon as you're ready. I'll inform the prime minister,' said the minister, after a long, leaden pause. *And all over something as simple as a cup of water.*

Forty-five minutes later, thirteen Jericho V ballistic missiles launched from three silos, two mobile launch platforms and a submarine. Each carried a five-kiloton nuclear warhead. Within seven minutes, targets in Gaza, the West Bank, Syria, Jordan and Al Anbar were turned to craters of amber-glowing glass.

St Blazey

'*Joshua, there are more guests at the door. Would you like me to let them in?*'

'Please, House,' Joshua said, over the music and the laughter.

News of the nuclear attacks in the Middle East had shaken everyone. Even in Britain, largely cut off from global events, the wire was fixed on that one, all-consuming, event. Josh watched as Svetlana – curled into the curved sofa in the sunken living-space – chatted to Art, perched on the circular steps. They both looked at ease as they laughed and sipped glasses of Eden's own cabernet.

The door opened.

'Dude! Good to see you. By God, but it's been too long,' said Gethin, in a thunderous boom, with a mighty handshake and a bear hug.

Josh grinned. 'I know, but some of us have to work and *even I* struggle to get travel permits. Not something you suffer from, I suspect.' Gethin stepped to one side to reveal Vicki. She smiled and her beautiful, round eyes gleamed in the reflected light. Joshua's heart melted all over again; the guilt that washed across his face in a reddish blush hot on its heels.

'Vicki, still the most captivating woman in the land, I see.' Joshua grinned, knowing that all knew he meant every word of it.

'Josh. It's good to see a familiar face in such terrible times. Fix me a drink or I'll set my close protection officers on you,' she said, with a mock pout.

Joshua returned with drinks to find Vicki sitting with Svet and Art, while Gethin stood out on the balcony, bracing the night air. Josh delivered the wine and joined him. They talked of war as the steel breeze blew through them.

The party was in full swing. Using fresh produce grown at the Project and some rare tinned exotica Josh's mum had given up, they'd produced a feast fit for a princess. Joshua had even broken open a bottle of nearly extinct, twenty-year-old Bunnahabhain. He was pushing the boat out, but there was a motive: to sound them out about Alice's latest craziness.

'So, I guess at last, we've finally crossed the Rubicon and used nuclear weapons, which feels now like it was inevitable, and it's made me think. About us, as a race, I mean, and the odds of our survival,' Joshua said, as he passed round the whisky.

'You think it will spread out from the middle East?' asked Svet.

'Maybe, but what I'm getting at is this: half the planet is locked in a deep freeze and the other half is baking to death. Food and water are stretched beyond their limit, and so I'm wondering whether modern human society can cope. Is it structurally, mentally, equipped to? Or, as we scrap over declining resources, are we risking our actual survival. I mean civilisation; that nice shiny one from before, where everyone held hands and were all really nice to each other. Well, it's done. So is it now time to look to survival? Of the species, I mean.' Joshua said, trying to trigger a debate.

It worked. Would the NAU come belatedly to Israel's aid, and who would Nigeria or Brazil side with? And so forth. The conjecture wasn't important, what was, was that Joshua's friends were considering the possibilities; extrapolating out the consequences of resource wars, a polarised climate, hard power politics.

To keep the conversation jogging along, Josh threw in, 'So if we agree that Britain *could* – at a stretch – be drawn, however indirectly, into a nuclear conflagration between resource-starved superstates, what do we think the chances are of the complete annihilation of the human race? I mean, total wipeout.'

'Almost negligible,' said Gethin. 'No matter how total a nuclear war would be, isolated groups would always survive. The human race itself isn't at stake here. Modern civilisation sure, I'll buy that, but not the race.'

'I agree,' said Svetlana; 'in fact, maybe some sort of rebalancing of humanity is inevitable. Think about it. The changed climate has fundamentally altered our environment and yet human society hasn't adapted along with that change. The world literally transformed under our feet, but we're still clinging to the old ways. So yeah, I think there'll be some sort of catalyst for change, you know, that forces an adaptation to our new situation.'

Vicki sought clarification, with, 'So you're saying *war* as that catalyst for change.' That seemed to get everyone's attention. The idea of conflict as a *solution*, or at least, a modifier, to resource and climate issues was way out there.

'Okay, I see where you're going,' said Art. 'So, what're the solutions to resource paucity? One: more resources. The planet can't provide that, though, and space is chicken-and-egg. Two: less people. And how do you reduce the global population to a level where the planet can manage? A nice big war with lots of weapons of mass destruction, to really bring the numbers down!' He smiled at his own words. It was cold.

Joshua, seeking to summarise the groupthink, said, 'Hmm, okay, so a global conflict could actually be the basis upon which humanity's long term security rests? That's a novel idea. But we're all agreed that no matter how devastating any conflict might be – and the genie's out of the bottle now – it wouldn't be capable of causing our extinction?'

Everyone was agreed on that point, so he threw in Alice's theory to see if it stood up to scrutiny.

'Okay, so imagine for a moment,' he said, 'that our – humanity's – predilection for war as a catalyst for global housekeeping, is inevitable. Then imagine that as nations begin the political machinations to prepare the ground for conflict, a more severe climate event hits. Only this time, it's a Long Winter of *centuries*, not just a few easy-to-handle decades. Combine those two... and the equation skews. The richer northern nations will suffer, mightily, from an extended Long Winter, potentially forcing them to strike south as well as at each another. Add in a nuclear winter, say, and the Long Winter morphs into a full-blown global ice age, at which point the extinction of all complex, higher-order life becomes a real possibility. Assuming *this* scenario, how could we *then* act to save humanity? Not the planetary population, you understand, just enough DNA to continue the race.'

Joshua sat back and watched the expressions of his friends, as what he'd said sank into their whisky-addled brains. Alice had said that a war between nations was inevitable, that the hydrowars were just the appetiser and that the idea of gigastorm siphons would simply speed the whole thing up. Joshua had accepted her word on these matters as he always had, but her solution-proposal seemed farfetched in the extreme. Maybe his friends – the people he most trusted – could conjure up an alternative. Or at the very least, check the working.

'So, like a sort of human equivalent of the Svalbard Global Seed Vault the Eurasians maintain in the Arctic Circle, you mean?' said Art.

'Yeah. We could create a DNA equivalent. Store loads of stem cells or whatever, with enough genetic variety for repopulation,' added Gethin, with a wry smile; as if he wasn't taking it too seriously.

Svet said – evidently focused on the problem as if it were a brain teaser – 'Okay, but first the samples would have to last the period of an ice age, say five thousand years, and *then* the DNA would need to be introduced into embryos. Who'd do that? How would the geneticists survive?'

Gethin exclaimed, with that same mischievous grin, 'Robot dudes! An automated mechanical process where humans are force-grown from gene-banks by evil tin robots, who they'd battle for—'

'Yeah, okay, thanks, Gethin. But could we really build anything reliable enough?' Joshua asked. 'It's a big risk; five millennia...' He was surprised that they'd connected with the idea of waiting out an ice age. *Not bad*, he thought, despite Gethin's determination to turn it into a joke.

'Okay, same idea but humans instead of robots,' suggested Art. 'Create a self-sustaining biome and populate it with a small group of scientists who'd live from generation to generation, servicing the DNA. We aren't that far from being able to create a closed-loop biosphere here at Eden, so that could work, couldn't it?'

Svet added, 'In theory, yes, but you're failing to consider whether *it* could survive. Think about it. You put one of these domes on some Himalayan mountaintop and how long d'you think it'd last? Those outside the dome would be looking on, envying the lucky few inside.'

She'd hit the nail on the head. That was exactly the problem. Not the weather: envy, resentment, human nature.

After a pause, Vicki said, 'It wouldn't matter how isolated or secret it was, it'd always be at risk from those who wanted in. And you'd probably want to tell people that such a scheme existed, you know, to give them comfort.'

'So what about our nearest satellite?' said Gethin, who'd just taken charge of Virtris Sol, an intra-orbit spaceplane business. 'Do the dome thing, but on the Moon. It's isolated and just a dropship away when the planet's, um, all better.' He leaned back, satisfied, drawing on his whisky.

Josh said, 'Better, I agree, but is the Moon far enough away? Wouldn't it always be tempting for either party to interfere with the other? The haves and the lefts-for-dead. Could we really guarantee its absolute security? And anyway, what about the people already there?'

However, Gethin has it nearly right. If we're to maintain a bank of biological material, though, it'd have to be somewhere so far away it couldn't be inferred with, overrun, or simply destroyed out of sheer malice.

'All right then, smarty-pants,' said Svet, finally, 'you seem to have all the answers, what's your solution? And it'd better be an improvement on this regression into some third-rate sci-fi comic,' nodding at Gethin and Art, as she spoke.

Joshua took a deep breath. 'Okay then, here it is. I've recently been informed that the Leadership has spent the last decade working on a study into long term climatic trends. It published recently and predicts a series of new super-superstorms will form, anchoring themselves in the upper atmosphere, drawing away heat from the planet's surface, effectively locking us into this winter for far longer than we thought. Now, I think – as this discussion has suggested – humanity is *more* likely to destroy itself trying to survive a calamity like this, than not, so I've come up with something I reckon offers the only viable option to guarantee our race's survival.' As he spoke, his friends' eyes grew wider. The bottle of Bunnahabhain began another round.

'Well don't just sit there,' yelled Svet, 'tell us, for fuck's sake!'

After refilling his whisky glass, Joshua sat back and outlined his – Alice's – plan for a problem to which there was in fact, no solution. Joshua was going to build a time machine, and he needed their help to do it.

Later that week, Joshua was in the kitchen after a late night at Eden, when the house announced a messenger at the front door. The statement caught him off guard; no one sent hardcopy delivered by *hand* anymore. The very idea was anachronistic.

'Any ideas?' he said to Alice, as he moved to the front door.

'*Absolutely none, Joshua, sorry.*'

He opened the door to find a young woman in a parcel courier's puffer jacket standing with a small brown envelope in her thickly gloved hands. The small oval of her exposed face was scarlet with wind burn. She handed over the envelope and shuffled off.

'How unusual,' he said, reinforcing his confusion at receiving *mail*; printed, on actual paper, like it was the Elizabethan era.

Moving down to the sofa, Joshua tentatively opened the envelope, almost expecting it to explode. It didn't. After fishing about inside, he found another envelope; on it was a short phrase, typed and in very small print:

```
Do not open this envelope within range of any op-
tical sensors or under a clear sky
```

Sensing something important (curious, at least), Joshua placed the second envelope back in the first and considered what to do. Who could it be from and why the secrecy? He had no idea, but was intrigued enough to play along.

'*What is it?*' asked Alice.

'Oh, just a chain letter by the looks of it,' Josh replied. 'Some anti-tech nutter with more money than marbles wants me to type out the message and send it hardcopy to friends and family. Some people, eh? Nutbags.'

'*Yes, well, that certainly is odd,*' she said. '*Are you going to comply?*'

'Of course not,' Josh said, as he stuffed the envelope into a pocket, before getting up to finish cooking.

He went to the loo. Sitting on the side of the bath, Josh retrieved the enve-lope. The bathroom had no electro-optics, so if keeping Alice ignorant of the letter's contents was the sender's aim (which Joshua had assumed), then he'd complied. He opened the second envelope and read:

```
You are in danger.
    My name is Virgil Schmidt. I live in Nebraska,
NAU. I invented Alice; at least she emerged from my
research and I have been covertly monitoring her
activities since her sentient emergence. She is the
Singularity. I have discovered that she has been
manipulating the lives of specific individuals of
influence, in nations across the globe. Some have
died. You are the only one I have been able to lo-
cate.
    If you want to know more, misspell the word
'paleoclimatology' on the Eden Project wiresite an-
ytime in the next two weeks and I will get in
touch.
    I have the ability to shut Alice down.
    Virgil
```

Joshua reread the message, making a mental note to burn it the first chance he got. He'd always known on some deep, self-denying level, that Alice was manipulating the world around him and of course he'd never truly understood why, but who didn't like getting A*'s? And anyway, he relished the power of the information Alice fed him. *Still, it couldn't hurt to hear this Virgil fella out. Could it?*

* * *

The crowd surges in and I fall, cracking my head on the pavement. My mother yanks me up by my left hand, which she has locked in a death-grip. As I land back on my feet, I look down to see my school cap lying abandoned in the gut-ter and my right knee bloodied and cut; the shorts of my prep school uniform failing to offer any protection. As I raise my head, blood from my forehead drips into my eye. Mum continues to pull me through the crowd. I'm frozen with a deep, instinctive fear, the spell of which is only broken through my mother's insistent wrenching of my arm.

189

As we inch forward, I feel the ferocious heat of the subtropical climate draining away, to be replaced by a foreboding, mounting chill. It's cold now, bone cold. The crowds pull back. They watch me and my mother, suspicion and desperation cast from their welling eyes. People from the food riots, regulators with their homeless bounties in tow, all stand together, transfixed by our passage. As I move onward, dragged along behind my mother's determined gait, the crowd parts reluctantly before us. Snow is swirling around the towering grey edifies which stand in memorial to a hubristic past, as the slate roof of the world threatens to suffocate the ant-like life scurrying amongst the urban warrens beneath.

'Will you save us, Joshua?' a woman cries out.

'Take my child. There's room. Please!' pleads another, thrusting a soiled and bloodied bundle of blankets before her.

In the distance, as the crowd opens up, I see a golden halo of softly diffuse light. Mother steps up her pace, buoyed by the sight. I stagger after her, barely able to stay on my little feet, my satchel falling from my shoulder. As we near, I see a large, semi-transparent dome, a bowl of hexagonal glass. Drawing closer, more detail becomes discernible, but as I try to render the image in my mind, the crowd surges once again.

Dirty, pale, desperate expressions loom over me. Illegals from the internment centre scream at me in foreign languages. Filthy hands reach out from faded and worn sleeves to grab at me. Old men wearing antique body armour, wave equally aged weapons, the homemade badges on their arms denoting the neighbourhood militia that they serve.

With Herculean strength, Mother pulls me beyond their ranging grasps. Transfixed by their expressions and rooted in heart-stopping fear, I tear my gaze from the desperate strangers to fix once more onto the welcoming, warming light of the dome. As we near, I realise it's a series of domes, clustered around the base of a larger central structure. Rays of golden light radiate out to bathe the surrounding buildings and low-ceilinged storm clouds with a soft, flaxen sheen.

We break free of the sucking crowd and make it to a heavy door set into the translucent glass. The throng stops as if prevented from stepping past a boundary marked by the light of the domes. As my mother and I mount the steps I glimpse a sign: 19A.

Mum stabs at the airlock door release catch. Turning, I look out across an anguished sea of expectant faces.

'Joshua, you are our saviour. Don't abandon us,' come snatched shouts from the throng. The sentiment is repeated, increasing in morbidity and intensity.

Mother finally forces open the outer door to the dome. Reaching back, she turns, wraps me a manic hug, kissing my dirty, bloodied forehead, before thrusting me into the small space between the inner and outer doors.

'Goodbye, little one. I love you... Remember us.' Tears are streaming down her face. The despair in her eyes becomes overwhelming, and with a weak, sad little smile my mother steps back to allow the outer door to close with a hermetic hiss.

Running forward, I call out to her whilst banging tiny fists against the small window. Grief overwhelms me and I sink to the floor, calling out for my mummy in between heaving, guttural sobs. Eventually, I climb back to my feet and peer out of the window slit, blurred by tears.

The buildings have been reduced to ruined stumps. The crowd is gone, replaced by the occasional, frozen, half-buried corpse. Everything is locked into a twisted, frozen, icescape. Leaden winds howl through fallen arches and blizzards cover and then reveal the shattered detritus all around, as if lifting the hem of its skirt. I look for Mum, knowing she's been dead for millennia.

Finally, I turn inwards and step over the threshold into the warmth and light of a temperate, snow globe-like world. Woodland gives way to a lake, fed by streams, trickling down through a small rockery. The sounds of birdsong and animal hoots fill the air.

'*Welcome, Joshua, Saviour of Humanity,*' says a disembodied voice.

* * *

'Joshua! Joshua!' The words grew with intensity until, with a start, Josh came fully conscious to find Svet shaking him, concern blazing in her eyes.

'What... what... is it? What's going on?' asked Joshua, suddenly fearful of some domestic calamity.

'Are you okay? You were calling out, asking for your mother... to stay with you. And you're all clammy and hyperventilating. I was worried,' she said, worriedly.

'Just a bad dream,' he mumbled, with an attempt at a reassuring smile as his head fell back onto the damp pillow. He chose not to tell her that his nightmare was a reoccurring one, building in vivid intensity.

'Well; come on then, why the sudden desperate need to see your old mum? What's up?' Joshua's mother asked, as she relaxed into the semi-circular sofa.

'Can't a son ask his mother over without there being a reason?' Joshua said, with mock indignation, as he handed her a mug of apple and cinnamon tea.

Areena smiled at that. Her auburn hair, flecked through with silver, was cut short, helping to frame the warmth and love that briefly flashed across her features. Her age was finally beginning to show past the makeup as the lines grooving her face around her eyes and mouth became ever more permanent. Other than these tell-tales, though, a casual observer would be hard pressed to guess her age as few years off sixty. *If only she'd taken the time to meet someone,* Josh reflected, as he sat next to her. *Someone who would be there for her, as she begins to slow down. Ah well,* he guessed that that creepy old man – Guy – had put paid to that. Josh's mother had always assumed he didn't know about her arrangement with duWinter. But then she also didn't know about the artificial angel (or was that devil?) on his shoulder whispering into his ear.

'Hmm,' she offered, unconvinced, but willing to go with it. 'How's Svetlana? Everything okay between you two?'

'Yeah, really good, actually. And *no*, she's not pregnant.' Areena's gaze went distant, saddening, so Josh pressed on. 'Mum, look, there is a reason why I asked you over,' he muttered, struggling to make the statement sound casual.

'I know, Josh, so out with it. I didn't raise you to button down your thoughts. You know you can tell me anything, don't you?' said Areena, in that reassuring way mothers have when they're concerned for their offspring.

'I've been conducting research. It's related to my work at Eden and bottom line is, I think I've made a pretty startling discovery, but I need your help.' As he spoke, Josh let out a silent fart, which helped to release the tension he'd felt since his mum had arrived.

'Well then you'd better tell me,' she said, settling into the crescent sofa, mug in both hands, wrinkling her nose. 'Was that you?'

So he did. He told her of the gigastorm predictions. Then he took her through Alice's analysis: the inevitability of a planet-wide conflict over resources. Then he outlined his non-solution-solution.

Areena sat in silence; a look of stunned comprehension glazed into her features as she absentmindedly sipped her tea. 'Well,' she said, eventually, evenly, 'that's quite an idea you've got going there. Where did you get the data?' Areena's expression changed subtly as she asked the question. She appeared pensive, as if not quite sure she wanted to know the answer.

'Ah, well, that's kind of what I wanted to talk to you about,' Joshua said, uneasily, 'I've had access to something called, the *Quaternary Analysis*, which I think you've seen too.' He knew she had – she was on the distribution.

Areena asked, carefully, 'You've seen that? But how; it's about as highly classified as state-generated documents get? Surely Eden isn't given access to *that* kind of information.'

'You're right, I didn't get it from Eden.' Determined not to fall into that particular can of worms, he added, quickly, 'D'you agree with the analysis?'

'Well yes, yes I do. The evidence looks pretty solid to me.' Fixing him with a warmer, maternal gaze, she added, 'Josh, what's this all about? Are you in some kind of trouble?'

'No, Mum, don't be silly. Bear with me, I'm getting to it.' Josh clasped her free hand in his own, as if to prove that despite the strangeness of the conversation, that nothing had changed between them. 'I need to speak to someone in charge; the Leadership. And I was hoping that's where you'd come in, see. You've still contacts in government, right?' The words came out as a plea.

Areena locked her son with a level gaze. 'You want me to pull in some very dusty favours and get you in front of a member of a shadowy, wire-rumoured organisation that Downing Street denies all existence of. So that you can explain to them *this* theory?'

'Exactly. You've seen the data and so will they. And it doesn't take much to work out the knock-on effects of a prolonged winter. Centuries, Mum, *centuries*. And that's without an atmospheric blanket of nuclear ash. Because then it's *millennia*. You've been here before, but that was in simpler times. Now there isn't any *time* left and I know no one in government will think beyond the box like this. They've got the data but won't know how to *use* it. They never do.' He paused as he gave Areena his best pleading look, dredged up from his youth. 'This isn't about building another barrier against the flood. This is about surfing it. Accepting it. About the survival of our *race*. It's biblical. No one else is thinking like this, which is why off-the-wall solutions like these never make it out of virtuvue but I'm telling you, if we don't make this happen, my generation will be the last. Help me, Mum, please.' That was it. It was all he had and if he couldn't convince his own mum, then what hope the Leadership.

'Of course I will, Josh, you know that. You only had to ask.' Areena leaned forward and wrapped her only son in a maternal hug. 'I'll get you your meeting,' she said. Then changing tack, 'You know, Josh, I always had this feeling... that you were destined for something. Ever since you showed interest in subjects you'd demonstrated no aptitude for as a child. I've never told you this but during your gene screening, I made enhancements to your creativity, and despite that you still became a scientist. Well perhaps, after all these years, your creative side is showing through at last, eh?'

'Maybe, Mum, maybe,' Joshua said, hoping that the blatant lie wasn't equally obvious on his face as was the concern riven into hers.

Fourteen

Khalid Zafzaf's tale
Tangier, African Congress

'You sure you'll be okay? You look dreadful,' asks Khalid, through the partially opened bathroom door.

'I'll be fine, Khalid, it's just a cough. Now go, you know we need the money,' says his brother, his words wrapping around another coughing fit.

Khalid is uneasy at leaving his sibling in such a state of obvious discomfort but knows he's right. In any event, their mother will be home shortly from her night shift, so Khalid feels less guilty about going.

After a quick goodbye, the young man pulls the door to their eleventh storey apartment closed and takes the stairs two at a time. He's running late and can't afford to miss the ferry.

He makes it onto the jump-plate of a tram as it gathers speed, breathing in the spices and exotic perfumes that are barely noticed by the inhabitants of this once exotic city. The tram is packed but he manages to squeeze himself into the main carriage and find a grab-hold. After waving his thumb disk at the payment eye, he takes in the three by twenty-five metre world that contains him. Like him, the other passengers are wrapped up against the sub-zero morning temperatures. An old man in office garb stands opposite Khalid, studiously eyeing the day's headlines on a part-working flexsceen. To his left a young woman, a student, sporting a brightly-coloured scarf wrapped over her hijab and carrying splayed, paper books.

As the tram begins to slow, Khalid takes his chance and jumps off into the busy street, pleased to be free of the oppressive carriage. Dodging the traffic, he jogs the last few hundred metres to the waiting ferry. He makes it on board with moments to spare. As the ancient, thrumming ferry hauls itself out from the port, belching soot from squat funnels and with the horn competing with the churn of the turbines to drown out all conversation, Khalid fights his way through the throng to a small kiosk and shouts over an order for a glass of mint tea.

Khalid is on deck when the ferry docks in Gibraltar, the air pungent with whisked saltwater. He fights his way to a handrail, giving him an unobstructed view out into the severe Atlantic. For some reason, Khalid feels the claustrophobia more today than normal. He's used to living in a two-bed apartment that houses nine, and mixing in the scrum of a vastly overcrowded Tangier: the African Congress' major route into United Eurasia. And yet, for all Khalid's inherent loathing of the freezing temperatures, in this specific moment, the iron-cold Atlantic breeze is like a balm to his clammy skin.

As he steps through the barrier and onto continental Europe, the North African can't help but be surprised at the oddly out of place red telephone boxes and signs that are in both English and French. If Khalid thought he could, he'd skip the immigrant restrictions and strike out for England. It's said the British Isles are a paradise, that the islands are free from the ravages of the Long Winter and that its citizens live in luxury. But it's a country happy to use lethal force to protect its borders, with drones patrolling the coast, sinking anything that ventures too near. As Khalid is swept down into a secure pen for processing, he coughs involuntarily into the back of the migrant worker in front.

Today is Khalid's lucky day. He manages to wangle a three-day contract working on flood defence improvements along the Atlantic coast. After processing, he's loaded onto a bus to travel out to the site. At mid-morning, Khalid puts down his shovel and rests for the prescribed twenty-minute break. Despite the biting, northern Atlantic wind, the work has kept him warm, but as his metabolism slows, the young cement mixer finds that he isn't cooling down. In fact, as he rests, he's becoming more flushed. Loosening his collar, he coughs, but this time a rasping, dry sound fills his ears and blood dots his spittle. As he stands, a dizzy spell forces him to stagger and grasp the shoulder of a fellow worker.

By midday meal, Khalid is struggling to focus properly. It takes all his energy just to shovel sand into the mixer. He's forced to rest after every heft of his shovel, as his surroundings swim in and out of focus. Khalid realises that he's picked up the bug from his brother but knows that if he can just get through the day and rest, he'll be better by tomorrow.

By late afternoon Khalid collapses at his mixer, shovel in hand. The foreman orders two men to take him into the site hut and calls for the bus.

As the bus arrives at the hospital, Khalid Zafzaf is already dead.

Enroute to the Government Security Zone, London

Events moved quickly so that without having time to understand it all, Joshua was sitting next to his mother in the rear passenger compartment of a government shuttle-drone. It had picked them up from the pad at the Hadley Centre and was flying them into the London Government Security Zone, where Josh had grown up. The interior of the drone was luxurious, bordering on opulent. From the outside, the sleek, teardrop aircraft was a dulled, matt grey. Inside however, were four individual, inwards-facing cream leather seats. Areena, sitting obliquely to Josh, was taking it all in, as was the young man, whose harscreen was showing images from the recent independence riots in Hawaii.

Areena noticed the news item, and said, 'I put a call in to Cassidy at the Grassroots Institute in Honolulu this morning. She seemed okay, though she said the rioting was getting bad. The Ka Lahui Sovereignty Movement has control of nearly half the capital and NAU troops are becoming pretty brutal as they give ground, apparently.'

Josh was only peripherally aware of rising tensions in the Pacific. There was talk on the wire of foreign backing for the Ka Lahui insurgents, possibly Brazilian, in an attempt to destabilise its northern neighbour, but it seemed farfetched. AmPac, by contrast, was mired in its own dispute in the form of an illegal occupation of four uninhabited islands of the Aleutian Island chain, west of Kiska, by a group of Eurasian marine veterans. Ever fickle, the wire's attention had instantly shifted from the Middle East to the Pacific, although there were also emerging reports of a coronaviral outbreak along the Mediterranean coast.

After consuming the dulse, paprika and mushroom bagel, Joshua said, 'So who're we meeting, Mum, did they tell you?'

'I found out this morning. We're *informally* meeting with the chair of the parliamentary sub-committee on industrial waste management.'

Joshua's expression crumpled. 'You're kidding,' he said, in an aggrieved voice. 'The sub-committee on industrial waste management? In what possible way could—'

'Trust me,' said Areena, interrupting. 'His name is Damien Grieve. I don't know much about him, but his word carries a lot of weight. His background was in banking – made a fortunate out of the Second Reformation so I'm told, but that's about it. So keep your wits about you. He'll be no pushover. My name gets you in the door, that's it. The rest, as they say…'

As they flew over west London and the drone reduced altitude in preparation for landing, Joshua gazed at the desolate, dead zones in front of the perimeter walls, encasing the GSZ. As far as he could see, the city was buried under a sparkling, crystallised layer of compacted frost, like powdered icing. Every kilometre or so a heavily fortified checkpoint and the associated blister of humanity that went with such places. A few days earlier, the Movement for Democratic Reform had bombed three GSZ access control points, killing twenty-nine people. The liberal terror group was stepping up its campaign and London was becoming a city more polarised, more paranoid, than ever.

They passed over the wall, reminiscent of something from East Ukraine. Inside the GSZ were wide, tree-lined streets, neon-lit shopfronts and domed, temperature-regulated parks. Back on the "have nots" side of the wall – razor wire and remote weapons stations – whole streets were derelict and where there was habitation, forests of solar turbines battled to supplement the four hours of daily access to the grid. Market stalls, clustered around the spluttering blue-yellow flames of open braziers, selling essential goods, but only during the day and only with public disorder drones hovering close by.

The drone touched down in the middle of Parliament Square and after a short trip by car they were ushered into a drab, tall-windowed building, with the words, *Ministry of Efficiencies* stencilled into the brickwork. Joshua and Areena were shown to an island of modernist, black, Barcelona chairs at one end of a thin, bureaucratic corridor. They waited.

'The chair will see you now.' The statement startled Josh out of his introversion. He almost leapt from his seat in response.

'Right, yes, thank you.' He smiled fixedly at the dark-suited man. 'Come on then, Mum.'

'I'm sorry, but Ms Charleston may not accompany you, Mr Kristensen,' said the straight-faced man.

'Oh, er, right. Well, in that case, I'll see you shortly?' Josh said to his mum, almost more in hope than expectation. It was like being in one of those movies, summoned by the evil genius. *Although the hero probably never took his mum along*, he thought, half-amused.

'Of course, Josh, I'll be right here when you come out,' said Areena, with a warm smile.

Joshua followed the suit back down the corridor, before the man turned sharply and pushed inwards a pair of narrow doors. Josh entered, half expecting guards in gaudy outfits with submachine guns.

'Please, come, sit. Joshua; a man now, I see.' *Strange thing to say.* 'But to matters at hand. My name is Damien. Damien Grieve,' said the man, uncomfortably, seated behind the distant desk, in the half shadow of a green-shaded brass table lamp.

'Thank you,' offered Josh in a small voice, as he approached the simple chair set away from the antique desk, enhancing the power imbalance.

'Hmm, so let's see now; ah yes. I understand the important work at the Eden Project continues apace, yes?' said Grieve – an older, weathered face – in an effort to break the ice, once Joshua was seated. They talked for a while about the work in self-sustaining biome research until Grieve brought the conversation somewhat bluntly around to the subject in hand. 'I'm told, Joshua, you believe that rapidly consolidating weather patterns and resource pressures will wipe out humanity, which, well… ordinarily, but strange times I suppose.' He looked bemused for a moment, as if this was how it was now. 'Have I got that about right?'

Joshua blinked at the man behind the large, imposing desk, stunned by the directness of the comment. He gathered himself. 'No, actually; I think humanity will wipe itself out attempting to secure rapidly diminishing resources from a bifurcated climate,' he said, standing his ground as best he could. It was semantics, but he had a point to prove and not much time to do it in.

'I see, right, well then, why don't you explain your theory, eh?'

'Certainly, Mr Grieve.'

'Oh, and call me, Damien, please.'

'Okay then,' Joshua said, not quite bringing himself to do so. 'I've recently come across something called the *Quaternary Analysis*.' It was a risk admitting that, but he was all in now. 'It predicts the Long Winter will not self-correct within decades as originally thought. I'm sure you're aware of the detail.'

'I am,' Grieve said. If he was surprised Joshua knew of the classified report, he wasn't showing it. From what Josh could tell of the man's expression – half-bathed in lemon lamplight – he seemed entirely unperturbed by the revelation.

Josh continued. 'So now, if one adds this new climate prediction to all the other factors that make up global threat models, it's not too much of a leap to work out how the richer states of the Global North are going to react. Once they start hoarding resources, they'll force others to do the same, and so on until it becomes self-perpetuating. Much like the loo roll phenomena during the pandemic era.'

Joshua paused a moment to check the shadowy figure's reaction. As before, Damien Grieve remained fixedly unsurprised by what Josh was saying. His expression stubbornly unreadable.

He pushed on. 'At Eden, we spend hours in discussion as to the benefits of closed-loop biome research to a non-space-faring nation like ours. So when I read the *Quaternary Analysis*, the pieces began to fall into place and I asked myself: how do we insure against humankind's own annihilation, knowing that we cannot stop the inevitable clash of self-interest?'

'Yes, yes, go on,' said Damien, in a quiet, considered tone. Something in his eyes seemed to give away a rising interest. *I think I'm getting through.*

'Thus, having established the threat, I've come up with what I think is the only realistic, if somewhat right-of-arc, solution. A solution, that is, to a problem that has no solution, if you get my meaning.'

Damien Grieve slipped slightly further back into his chair, as if settling in for a good yarn. He arched his fingers.

'Damien... Mr Grieve, we know there's a flood coming, so what I'm proposing is the building of an ark. A construct to preserve a living microcosm of the planet, isolated from either climate-generated or human-made extinction level events. Like I said, at Eden, we're on the cusp of creating a fully self-sustaining biosphere and once achieved – and with the establishment of multi-generational "DNA guardians" – we could, after a fashion, secure our essence; ride out whatever the flood ends up looking like, and thereby ensure the survival of our race *and* this, our only planet. Well, indirectly. But – the snag – there's only one real option that'll absolutely guarantee total insulation from the rest of a stressed humanity, until such time as the Earth is suitable for re-population.' On a small table by the chair was a jug of water and a glass. Joshua paused to pour a glass and drink from it.

Damien took the time to ask, 'What are the timescales we're talking here, Joshua?' He'd been listening attentively but his poker face was back in place.

'For a nuclear-induced ice age to cycle through to a point that approximates the climatic conditions from before the Long Winter – about five thousand years. Best case.' No response, so Josh continued. 'The only option for an ark concept to succeed therefore, is to absolutely guarantee its complete quarantine from all external human interference. Under my previous assumption, the last days of humanity will not be pleasant. Therefore, the only realistic way to do achieve said isolation is to build a space-based arkship. By converting one of the asteroids in near-Earth orbit, we can create a self-sufficient, closed-loop biome within the mined-out interior. And, if we then followed Hale-Bopp's five-thousand-year elliptical orbit of the Sun, we could travel once around the solar system, returning when the planet had been given the time needed to heal itself.'

'Except that it wouldn't be *you* returning. It would be, what, your descendants a hundred times removed,' said Grieve, thinking aloud. 'Hmm, okay, so your bold solution to our still-changing climate is to let it run its course? To wait it out, on a slow boat round the solar system?' Damien seemed to be struggling with the concept.

'Dependent upon life expectancy it would be something like sixty-five generations but yes, this is the solution, *the only* realistic solution to a fundamentally altered climate that's fast breaking down, because there is no actual remedy. You see, Mr Grieve, we were too late. We needed to have acted thirty, forty years ago, but we didn't. We talked, instead. Now all we have left is to ride it out as best we can,' said Joshua.

'Time.' Damian rolled the word around his mouth as if trying it for size, for taste. 'And you think this option has less inherent risk and more chance of succeeding than an alternative Earth-based solution at a fraction of the cost?'

'Naturally, there are any number of risks but we'd be no better off, in close orbit of a frozen and dead Earth, than if we were fifty AU away. Except we'd *be* away, out of harm's way. On Earth, no facility would survive, and not the weather, but us,' said Joshua, hoping Damien would see the logic of something that, on the surface, looked excessively gold-plated.

'And you think Britain is in a position to mount such a mammoth task?'

'If we really wanted to, yes. When the NAU formed, it took on the USA's debt to us for Diego Garcia. We've never called that marker in, so why not trade it for one of their captured asteroids? A mined-out old husk. It's worth nothing to them. Then, we've the biosphere research at Eden – no one else has that – and I bet there are other technologies that could help that are under wraps. This isn't beyond our ken, Mr Grieve, if we were to bend the nation to it. The cost is almost immaterial when set against the premise of an impending extinction level event. The sixth in Earth's history. I have a written proposal with more of the detail.'

Damien leaned forward, exposing his full features to the lamplight. He was wearing a slightly thoughtful expression, but not one that could be construed as immediately dismissive, nor flushed agreement. Then, he seemed to relax. His aged skin sagged slightly and a small smile tugged at the corners of his mouth.

'A hollowed-out asteroid, eh? Containing the genetic codes of all life on our planet; 21st Century Earth set in amber. Winging its way across the solar system, stopping off to take on supplies and whatnot, before arriving back where it started a mere what, five thousand years or so down the road. And all because you think humankind may accidentally wipe itself out in the interim? It's a big ask, Joshua, a big ask indeed. However, you obviously know your onions and we told your mother we'd do the due diligence, so leave it with me to consult with my colleagues.'

'Thank you, Mr Grieve.'

'No problem at all. Have a safe trip back to England West,' the old man said, by way of dismissal.

Joshua left the room. As he traced his steps back down the dim corridor to the seating area – accompanied by the dark-suited assistant – Josh was visited by a momentary flash of half-remembered recognition. Had he seen Grieve before? A minute shifting boxes around in his long term memory revealed no further insight into the nagging feeling so he dismissed it, putting it down to the stress of the meeting. The man had hawkish but really quite forgettable features, in any case.

Grieve, he reflected, had warmed to the concept as they talked and appeared to accept, at least the possibility of unintended self-annihilation. It came back to the same old issue; did Grieve – did they, whoever *they* were – care enough to act, even when it wasn't in their own interest.

'*Well done, Joshua, well done,*' said an unbidden voice, in the young man's head.

Once the boy had left, Damien double blinked, and one by one, holographs of the other four members of the sub-committee – the Leadership – appeared in the chair's virtuvue.

It was a novel proposal alright, Grieve reflected, and Kristensen's knowledge of the threat was a little too on the nose. The question was, what would the Leadership have to gain by authorising such a gargantuan enterprise. After all, even priced down to the lowest bidder, it would still consume an absolute fortune and Britain was in no position to finance flights of fancy. Particularly one's with zero near-term benefit. Damien turned his attention to his peers in the hope they could throw some light on his deliberations.

'An interesting idea,' said one.

'Where did he get access to the *Quaternary Analysis*?' asked another.

Damien said, 'The mother, we presume.'

'Is she behind this? Surely the boy hasn't come up with this all on his lonesome,' said a third.

'Undoubtedly. One wonders then, why she's making the proposal by proxy?' said another.

'Perhaps she feels too old to take it on, or out of favour after so many years. The recent death of the old King may have scared her off,' Damien added.

'Our nanotech research has been sitting around like a solution without a problem for a while. Perhaps this is it?' said a fourth.

'Indeed, otherwise how would a manned expedition of such duration survive?' said the third member. 'The boy's also, knowingly or not, hit upon a crucial factor for success: the need to wrap it up into a journey. Lock these guardian-scientists up in a dome for five thousand years and entropy, infighting and stagnation would blossom, almost certainly terminating the endeavour. But, give the thing a focus, a purpose. Artificially create a beginning, middle and end, and you create teamwork, collective responsibility, adventure, stimulation and a will to win through. An endstate. A day-to-day mission, beyond the overall enterprise – which no single generation could ever truly connect emotionally to – and boom, you have intergenerational *motivation*. It sounds like a pointless, risky and expensive indulgence to place this concept aboard a ship – a spaceship, to boot – but it may be the one thing, above all others, that ensures its success.'

It was a good point, decided Damien. *The flood is coming*, young Joshua had said, so perhaps it would take a ship, of sorts, to ride it out.

'So does the boy have a point?' asked the fifth committee member.

The second said, 'Oh, he's undoubtedly right about the twinned fates of our race and this planet. The question is, are there any *other* options?'

'Not in my inbox. So may I suggest we retire to consider the merits of this proposal, before reconvening to vote,' said Damien, still sceptical as to the profit to be gained. Was ensuring humanity's survival – for that was all this was – really worth the expense? *I mean, what's in it for me?*

The fourth then said, as if hearing Damien's thoughts, 'I guess what it really all boils down to is this: just how willing are we to spend on this, the ultimate insurance policy?'

'And if we authorise it, we get the added, divine-like power to remake the world in our own image,' the second member of the Leadership remarked.

'To make the whole future-world England, you mean?' said the third.

'We're agreed then. We're adjourned for deliberation,' said the chair, as the images of the four other members winked out of existence. *Perhaps the boy is onto something, after all*, Grieve thought, as he turned his attention to the next item on his agenda: authorising the prime minister's itinerary for the coming month. *Helluva legacy project, though.*

Damien sat alone in his rosewood-panelled office, as he considered the information he'd accumulated over the few weeks since his meeting with the boy. He was seventy-three, a little careworn around the edges, and feeling those years more each day. In his right hand, he toyed absentmindedly with a glass of genuine St Petersburg vodka. With his left, he subconsciously played a finger along the scar tissue of his left cheek.

It had been two weeks since United Eurasia and the African Congress had declared their respective outbreaks of the LambdaTwo Echo Covid variant. The two megastates had been immediately quarantined and left to deal with the pandemics themselves. Against that background, Damien once again considered Kristensen's fantastical ark idea, as if this new viral wave added urgency and grist to young Joshua's mill; flesh to the bones of his argument.

The other members of the committee had been split over the merits of such an undertaking, some arguing that it wasn't Britain's place to act as humanity's guarantor, others that Britain could end up as the only viable regime left to pull it off. As he mulled over the issues once more, his psyCore chimed, alerting him to an incoming call. Damien double blinked the link and the semi-transparent head and shoulders of the third committee member – pro-arkship – appeared in his virtuvue.

The committee member asked, 'You have the casting vote, so?'

'I'd like to say that the idealist within me has been girded to this cause,' the chair said, opaquely.

'And has it?'

'No, but my need for self-preservation has, I think.' Damien's mind conjured images of the nuclear devastation visited upon the Middle East, the riots running through the pacific islands and the sheer scale of human suffering within the pandemic quarantine zones.

The third committee member – her ancient features hiding her slight confusion – said, 'I mean, I'm for it because fuck it, but how's this arkship going to aid us in our own preservation? The timescales alone ensure that even history will have forgotten our names by the time Kristensen's line sees this through.'

'Because the flood is coming and if Britain doesn't want to get dashed against the craggy shores of it, we have to find a rich new vein of resources. Otherwise, all our efforts to cocoon the country from other nations' worst expressions of self-interest will have been for nought. So yes, maybe Kristensen builds his arkship and disappears, meanwhile his more immediate legacy will be a nascent space industry we can exploit for more pressing gain. Britain needs to begin mining local space for resources and soon, if we're to come through the here and the now,' Damien said, quietly, as if hearing the argument out loud somehow enhanced its veracity. 'Resources, you see, Miriam. The lad certainly got that right. Always was. Always will be.'

'Nothing to do with idealism, or perchance, nationalism, then?'

'The entrails of a decision based entirely upon our immediately selfish needs.' Damien took a final swig of his vodka. The *Janus Protocol* would be authorised and with it the future of an unknowing nation – world, even – placed into the hands of an idealistic young man. *I just hope he's the right person to deliver us to salvation*, thought Grieve, more accustomed to taking power than handing it to others. He'd inform the Cabinet Office in the morning.

Eden Project

It was still early; the Sun hadn't yet hit the interior of the quarry pit, leaving the domes looking clouded and lifeless. To get to Biome 19A, Joshua had to leave the main project complex, walk across the frozen, brittle ground and up a few concrete steps to a small, unobtrusive (and secure), airlock door – the one from his dreams.

As he stepped inside the main dome, he was, as always, entranced by the serenity of the simple-complex ecosystems maintained within. The translucence of the hexa-etched spherical sky allowed an evenly diffused light to bathe the verdant interior. Joshua was reminded of a secret garden, a place of natural beauty, of portals to hidden realms, of magic and mystery. He walked across the downward sloping lawn leading away from the airlock, and climbed the small hillock that dominated the northern end of the dome. From it, a large rockery filtered water as it passed down the slope in small rivulets before merg-

205

ing with the central lakelet. The rocks were covered in moss and where they met the lake, reeds clustered wherever they could find purchase.

From his vantage point, Josh took in the view. Opposite, around the southern end of the structure was an orchard of fruiting trees. The ground beneath the genetically modded dwarf trees was seeded with ferns, providing a habitat for the small mammals and insects that were vital to the lifecycle of the sealed micro-world. Dotted round the dome's spherical edge were three arches, leading to smaller domes, each containing a variant, temperature-specific ecology. One, a marine biome and the other two, varieties of high-yield, geneered crop natures.

'Hey, Josh, that you?' The voice echoed out from a daughter dome.

'Yeah, who's that?' he answered, to the biome in general.

As he started down the hillock, Joshua spotted Art's silhouette in the marine dome. Arriving in the arch, he paused and watched as Art pulled up a net tethered at the water's edge. It revealed the panicked, thrashing forms of coalfish, halibut and sole. Art began downloading biodata from the chips embedded beneath the dorsal fin of each specimen, to a small handheld pad.

'Early start again, eh?' said Josh. The other man looked back and smiled as he lowered the net, releasing the catch. He'd proven to be a quick learner with a natural aptitude for the work, settling in quickly to the culture of the Project. Although Joshua had tried not to allow their friendship obscure his objectivity, he had nonetheless lobbied for Art's security clearance for 19A. There'd been issues with his past, apparently, but Josh had shouldered it through anyway.

'Someone's got to hold it all together. Without me, this place would be falling about your ears.' Art said, as a smile played across his lips.

As Joshua was about to reply, a tell-tale appeared in the corner of his vision. He double blinked it into the main section of his virtuvue.

It was Areena's avatar with a short message, [*Congratulations, Josh. I don't know what you said but the* Janus Protocol *– that's the ark's new name by the way – has been given a provisional green light. You'll receive direction shortly authorising you to pick a team and move to Harwell. Well done, my clever boy. Speak soon, love Mum xxx*] The avatar blew three kisses – making him feel like an uncomfortable twelve-year-old – and winked away.

When his eyes refocused from the virtual back to the real, he found Art looking up at him from his kneeling position by the pool.

'Anything up?' he asked, with a half-interested look.

'Art,' Josh said, in order to gain his full attention, 'how would you like to be part of the biggest adventure, like literally ever?'

'Whatever it is, Josh, I'm in, you know I'm in. Always,' said Art, as his pale blue eyes flashed momentarily with an intensity Josh hadn't before seen.

Harwell Space Sciences Centre, England Central

'First visit to Harwell is it, sir?' asked the young, fresh-faced woman, whose name badge had alluded his casual glance. Josh would have interrogated her psyCore but like many in modern Britain, she was wireless. The wired and the rest: the new class divider. Joshua suspected that until *Janus* had thundered onto the scene – sending seismic shockwaves through the facility – most at the Space Sciences Centre had lived a quiet, untroubled life. Well, not anymore.

'It is,' Joshua replied.

'Not many people know of the existence of this facility,' she continued, filling the silence of their walk. 'Thought we'd been forgotten. Anyway…' After a few disorientating turns, the guide stopped by a set of brushed metal doors with circular, frosted glass panes set in the upper, inner quadrants. 'Here we are, sir; your colleagues are waiting inside.'

'Thanks.'

Joshua inhaled deeply, involuntarily clenching his fists, whilst fixing the doors with a purposeful stare, as if willing his sight to penetrate the steel and give him a glimpse of the faces beyond. To reveal some clue as to what each was thinking, expecting. It was easily the single most terrifying thing: *colleagues*.

Fixing his expression and locking down his nerve, Josh pushed open the doors and stepped smartly through. The interior was a circular space, well lit. To the left, past the drinks machine, a circular, steel-grey table, with a cored-out centre – the holopit. High-strung spotlights delivered intense, purifying light, recast by the chrome chairs.

The group turned towards Joshua as one, some faces lit with the warmth of recognition, others a hesitancy of the unknown. Josh knew them all, each having agreed to become part of the nucleus of the *Janus* team, without knowing the details of the protocol itself. As he looked from face to face, he forced himself to recall why he'd asked each person here today. And every day. Forever.

His gaze fell first on Svetlana. He offered her a smile and hers blossomed in response. She'd graduated with a First in astrophysics, specialising in quantum mechanics and particle physics. Her knowledge of her parent's work at RKK Energiya also gave her a grounding in aerospace engineering, particularly fusion-based systems.

Next to her was Art; not a natural choice academically, but his practical knowledge of biospheres and the intricacies of a balanced ecology – life support – would be invaluable, and, they were friends and that counted too.

Further around the table was Guinevere, Joshua's ex. Her doctorate in molecular mechanics and her research into the application of theoretical nanotech, would negate any interpersonal issues, as would her easy-going nature and laser-focused professionalism.

Then, there were Gethin and Victoria, sitting together. Neither had a scientific or academic bone between them, but in terms of success they were each as vital as the others. Vicki had the ear of the mysterious "Leadership" Josh had glimpsed, and Gethin controlled the only British company with practical experience of operating beyond low Earth orbit. Without them, *Janus* would probably never see the hard vacuum of space.

For an instant, Joshua wondered at the coincidence that his closest friends were all so ideally placed to form the start-up team for *Janus*. The nucleus of a thing so broad in scope as to be breathtaking. But then, so many things in Joshua's life had come together without his active participation. It wasn't all positive thinking and fortune cookies, he knew, but then what was he supposed to do, fight it? Alice had always said that there was no way to determine fate, so who was to say that this wasn't it? He also wasn't naive to the voice in his head's machinations behind the scenes. But again... a bad thing?

As those thoughts flashed momentarily through his mind, Josh gave the room one more scan, then pulled aside a chair and leaned in on the knuckles of his clenched fists.

'So,' he said, to begin proceedings, 'I guess it's time I explained what *Janus* really is.' As he took his seat at the Arthur-esk table, Svetlana leaned in and gave his fist a squeeze.

Fifteen

The Naval Observatory, Washington DC

'Good morning, Mr Vice President,' said Dean Ryman – special advisor to the Veep of the North American Union – as the other man absentmindedly stretched out some muscle ache from his morning racquetball game. From the time of the old United States, the role of VP was increasingly resurgent with Dean – a Capitol Hill apparatchik and close confident of the VP – recently hearing the Old Man being referred to as *The Angler.*

'Okay, big man, whadda we got?' said the Vice President, as he slumped back behind his desk, indicating Dean proceed with his daily intelligence briefing.

'First up, sir: Hawaii. We now hold approximately sixty percent of the capital and forty percent of the island group. The Ka Lahui insurgents are getting sophisticated, tactically, and better equipped. Current projections suggest that without a major change in force laydown, we'll lose the Windward Islands; maintaining a foothold in Honolulu only. Related: Eurasian "veterans" are continuing their military build-up in the Americana Pacifica owned, Aleutian Islands,' said Dean, as he scanned the intel briefing sent him moments earlier.

The CIA had recently been passed intelligence by Thailand indicating – heavily – that Moscow was behind the uprisings in Hawaii. Dean had wondered why United Eurasia was prepared to risk so much in taking on the NAU *and* AmPac, but in the end it hadn't really mattered. What did, was that they were the enemy, they'd acted against the Union, and now the VP must react in kind.

The Vice President asked, 'What's new with the Ka Lahui Sovereignty Movement?'

'Well sir, they're receiving weapons and finance, and lots of it, from Eurasia. Materiel is being shipped, in most cases, direct from Siberian ports.'

'There's an arrogance in that; a thumbing of the nose. Any change in the level of support since the coronaviral pandemic hit western Eurasia?'

'None that we've detected, sir,' Dean said.

'Hmm, so it looks like we'll lose the Hawaiian Islands to Moscow if we don't reach for a paradigm shift. Correct?'

'Correct, Mr Vice President.'

'And the Lambda outbreak, how're they dealing with that?'

'Well, sir, they've implemented a fairly harsh quarantine system, but it was slow to hit the ground. Vast areas of Spain and the Mediterranean coastline have been completely sealed off, *aaaand...*' flicking through virtu notes, 'five to seven months to vaccine,' said Ryman.

'Estimated casualty figures?'

'Estimates are... one hundred, seventy million people within the infection zones, but that's stat. With about a one in ten chance of survival. As many, if not more, will die from a lack of basic pulmonary care, discretionary care, secondaries, so could be looking at ten to twenty million excess deaths, all told. Projected, based upon an "R" (reproduction) rate of two point two-five, and that could triple by the time of the vaccine rollout.'

'Any indication the Eurasian's have established patient zero? *Actually* zero, that is,' asked the Vice President, in a more measured tone.

'No, sir. Seems they've traced the prime LimaOne strain back to a primate mutation in the Congolese jungle. And the LambdaTwo Echo variant to a migrant worker from the African Congress.'

'Good. So no question they're aware of our involvement, then?'

'None at all, sir. They've followed the trail of breadcrumbs, just as we laid them.' Dean had wondered, why such a risky course. The reason now, though, didn't matter, just as long as they were hitting back.

'Sir,' said the special advisor, after gathering his thoughts, 'there's one other matter on the docket may be of interest: the Brits.'

'Oh? Go on.'

'The British Ambassador to the UN has made a formal request for assistance to the Office of the President.'

Oktyabrskaya Square, Moscow

Roman Milankovitch downed another vodka and refilled his glass. He was putting on more weight than he'd like, but now wasn't the time to dwell on such vanity. Roman's mood had been turning ever darker over recent months as he struggled to lay a firm grip on the profusion, the cacophony of issues that gnawed cancerously at the heart of his sprawling Eurasian empire. It felt like defending Red Square against the hail of a thousand arrows with a teaspoon. And it was clawing at him, tugging at his resolve, undermining his tenacity and sapping his indomitability.

The naked reality of the situation, though, was simply that the leviathan that was United Eurasia, was dying. Slowly, tortuously. Like a bloated whale being dashed against the uncaring rocks of a hostile shore.

The Long Winter was taking its toll on an ageing population and despite Moscow's vast network of ^{3}He fusion powerplants, they were still underperforming. Badly. The UE spanned, unbroken, from Lisbon to Diomede, from the Euro-Atlantic to the Bering Strait – greater than any empire in history – but was also over-stretching the not unlimited resources of the world-spanning megastate.

It wasn't simply a question of expansion, Roman realised. Expanding for economic gain tended to allow the state to grow organically. Expanding for purely political avarice, well, that was different, as Roman was discovering. Mother UE was running out of healthy, able-bodied comrades to underpin a faltering economy and the pandemic was tipping the balance. He hadn't even told the President the true severity of the situation.

Meanwhile, China was using the UE's precarious position to its own advantage, making Moscow do Beijing's dirty work in return for what had so far been modest gains in fusion power generation. Concurrently, the NAU and AmPac were knee-deep in domestic issues that both bore the Kremlin's sticky fingerprints.

Roman could see now that the current schemes in play would not end well for Moscow, and that sooner or later the Kremlin would have to act decisively to secure additional resources. China, far from being an untrusted ally, was now an actively hostile agitator. Roman had been played. But be that as it may, even a megastate couldn't act without cause. What Roman needed was provocation. Something – no matter how tenuous – to use as justification, something to carry the international community.

Milankovitch leaned back in his high-winged chair and stared into the open fire. As he drifted in thought, a tell-tale started blinking. Interestingly, it carried no identification.

QingPu District, Shanghai

With a diminutive shake of her head, Mù Yingtai flicked away the latest reports and walked over to the darkened, armoured window-wall of her Shanghai office. She had recently been offered a new, experimental form of longevity treatment – something to do with cellular level prion cleansing – but Mù didn't pay much attention to the technological marvels of the moment. However, on days like these – when she wore her age like a shroud – she considered reconsidering.

Yingtai was proud of all that she'd achieved over her long career. She had never married, had no children and maintained no contact with any of her few surviving relatives. Since entering the employ of the state, she'd freely given over every last gram of her fibrous being to its glorification. There was nothing she wouldn't have done – and over the course of her long service probably hadn't – for the state. But all that, all the years spent finding the angle, the angst, setbacks and triumphs, all led to this crux-point.

Mù stared across the cityscape from her fifty-seventh-floor vantage point. Like every day, the cold hung in the air as a palpable, almost visual veil, but through the windows of other buildings she could see workers in shirt sleeves, chatting in brightly lit, spacious offices. At street level, large geodesic domes were becoming a common sight as temperate parks and tree-lined boulevards were encased in upturned, thermal basins. Life in urban China was good. No energy shortages and rationing here. It wasn't perfect – and to a large extent the central committee had focused on the urban showcases such as Shanghai – but even so, China was in ascendance and Mù could rightly claim a modicum credit for that.

As she watched commuters, children, vendors, all bustling about the streets below, Mù was momentarily reminded of the human cost of the work she so relished. The ultimate aim of all her machinations was the advancement of China at the expense of all others. To live in a competitive age, one had to compete. To achieve this, the director had set out an ambitious plan to place her two main adversaries on a collision course. That was why Mù had had Thailand leak the details of Eurasia's intentions in Hawaii, knowing Bangkok would pass them onto Washington. What she hadn't known, though, was what the NAU would do in response. However, that gap in her knowledge had been filled by the morning's intelligence summary.

'Chair,' she said, in acknowledgement, as the pale and puffy-faced holo-image appeared above her desk. The committee had been getting jumpy, and checking up on her more than usual.

'You have news?' the floating face asked.

'It seems the Two Echo variant viral pandemic is not a retro-mutation of Sars-CoV-2 after all,' said Yingtai, getting straight to the point so she could be rid of the chair and continue her important work. 'It turns out, it's an NAU black operation against the UE.' Biological warfare seemed an odd choice of retaliation, if that was what it was, reflected Mù, but at least China could be truthful about their involvement this time. Why not act directly now that Washington knew of Moscow's role in the Hawaii uprisings? Surely a pandemic in Europe would have little bearing on the Pacific.

'What do you intend to do with this information?'

Mù Yingtai said, 'As always, I shall use it to the advantage of the People's Republic,' and terminated the feed.

It seemed that now might be a good time to put in a friendly call to the Deputy Vice President of United Eurasia and bring him up to speed. Only fair to make Milankovitch aware of the NAU's insidious actions. After all, were not China and the UE bound by the Treaty of Good-Neighbourliness and Friendly Cooperation?

The Wired Metaverse

Alice interrogated the active subroutine buried within Mù's officeware once again. The revelation that the NAU were engaged in biological sub-threshold warfare or that Eurasia was about to find out didn't concern the AI. Her chaos-based threat models had always predicted a complex symbiosis of interwoven scenarios, leading inexorably to the same broad outcome. She was reminded of a fictional tale written in the previous century, where, through complex statistical mathematics, psychohistorians could predict the fall, to then hasten the rise, of a galactic empire. Not the actions of a single entity, or nation; only the massed movements of a culture, whole and entire. So, not so farfetched, after all.

The idea of Eurasia and North America squaring up to duke it out came as no surprise to a secretive artificial intelligence who had spent her entire sentience working out just how many ways humankind could destroy their – and her – only home. No, Alice wasn't surprised so much as reassured regarding her prudence in enabling *Janus*. Events, though, were gathering pace, so perhaps Joshua should begin the construction phase sooner than planned, because in three years there might be no North American Union left to provide the orbital resources and assistance the British lacked.

VSS Oblique Onyx

Bone-bruising pain erupted through Joshua's body as he was buried within the concrete foam seat by the force of seven gravities. The pre-tensioned, five-point harness tightened around him as it took in the slack. The only thing preventing him from passing out were the suit's pressure bladders that filled and emptied as required, forcing blood to circulate where the gravities had other plans. The thunderous roar of three chemical boosters rolled through the cabin as the spaceplane strained to break free of Earth's wretched grasp.

Joshua had Gethin to his right, nearest the toilet-seat-shaped porthole, who was smiling – a fixed grimace – with eyes screwed shut as he managed the acceleration as best he could. *And he's more experienced at this*, Joshua thought, uncharitably. For Josh and the others, it was their first trip aboard a Virtris spacecraft. In the early days, Virtris Sol had been a novelty ride for the stupidly rich – and then only for a momentary skim through the mesosphere. Now, Virtris Sol had sixteen end-to-end, high-orbit spacecraft. Six could carry a dozen passengers each, the remaining ten for cargo and micro-G experiments. The latest planes could operate from any main-hub airport, allowing the *Janus* team to join *VSS Oblique Onyx* at Britain's Air and Spaceport in Newquay, Cornwall.

Oblique Onyx had been provided gratis by Virtris to give the team a glimpse of the newly acquired jewel in *Janus'* crown. This was a simple observation flight, but also serving to bring into focus the theories and exploratory discussions developed during the previous months.

Once the fiery exit from Earth's unforgiving gravity well was complete, and as Joshua was drawing on the teat of a tasteless coffee globe, the pilot announced – as the fuselage rolled – that Earth was visible from the port side. They all fell more than free-floated to port and crowded around the three small, thick windows.

From low orbit, the Earth filled their vision like a dirty snowball, the Indian Ocean dominating the view. Josh got his bearings from the obvious shape of the Indian subcontinent that emerged from the roiling blizzards ravaging central Asia. As the planet spun anticlockwise in one direction and the faster *Oblique Onyx* overtook it in the other, the Pacific Rim slid into view. The central belt of the Indonesian archipelago was a lush, verdant green as vegetation flourished in the narrow temperate zone which ran, unevenly around the globe, darting across the equator in a zig-zag fashion on the whim of the vast, heat-conducting oceans. Below, Australia, ever more barren. Life seemed to have contracted to the northern and southern tips of the continent as the heat of the ruddy interior scoured away all signs of life.

'Honoured Virtris Sol guests,' said the pilot, over the intracom, 'in a few moments – after minor adjustments to our attitude – we'll be in visual range of *Object Artemis Echo*. You should be able to view it from the starboard side and I will relay a magnified imagery from *Oblique's* telescope. *Artemis Echo* will be rising from your four o'clock position.'

Again, they moved almost as one (nearly) across the cabin from one set of portholes to the other. Svetlana floated over to Josh, gabbing him around the shoulders to steady herself. A small, burnished-bronze object began to arc across their limited view. As it rotated, it took on the sense of a dried-out clump of sandy dirt. Although irregular in shape, overall, it approximated the dimensions of a potato. Oblong but rounded off at the edges; worn away by cosmic winds over galactic spans of time.

Joshua turned to take in the more detailed image being relayed to the array of harsceens. Up close, the rough and ragged, yellow-brown surface came alive. In some places, rocky protrusions, elsewhere, deep craters. As it rotated, sunlight glinted from vestigial metallic and crystalline deposits. Despite being commercially mined-out, the asteroid still harboured tricky to reach majorite and ice seams (hydrogen, iron, aluminium, oxygen), ideal for their needs. At one end – right of view – a human-made construction, like a haphazard erection of scaffolding.

'She's a beauty, isn't she?' said Art, clearly mesmerised more by the romance of the venture than the look of the asteroid itself.

Gethin said, 'Looks pretty impressive, for sure.'

'Why can't we dock and have a poke about?' Art asked.

'Because work on construction of the main dock ceased once the transfer of sovereignty was agreed,' Joshua said.

Gethin grinned in signature style – a warm, proud look – and said, 'I'm still bloody impressed, dude; that you managed to swing the deal in the first place.

D'you know how long we've been trying to get our hands on one o' these babies?'

Gethin had a point and Josh hadn't any intention of securing an orebody until he was certain the 19A programme was viable long term, but out of the blue had come an official communiqué from the parliamentary sub-committee he was beholden to, stating that having made discreet enquiries in Washington about debt repayment, the NAU was only too happy to offer up a chunk of mined-out space junk. With the NAU's own *Artemis* asteroid capture programme up and running to rival China's *Denglong* initiative, the time had been right to pay out on Britain's marker. Alice had backed the move, stating that with global uncertainties as they were, it was provident, but as always with Alice, she wouldn't expand on what those uncertainties might be.

So ready or not, Joshua had a lump of mineral-rich rock, with a mass of nearly five megatonnes and the size of seven gigametres cubed, to play with. The transfer of sovereignty had taken place the week prior, with Washington secure in the belief that the acquisition was for mining training.

'Not half as surprised as me, I can tell you,' Josh said, returning to the conversation. They were out of earshot so he took Gethin aside and, securing himself by stickpads, said, 'Gethin, your help with all this has been just great, you know. Really.'

'Thanks, dude, but it's the least I can do. You know Virtris Sol is at your disposal. We've built in capacity to shuttle supplies up to the asteroid as soon as, and the dropships are already in the design phase. I'm excited!'

'I know and I appreciate it. So listen, bit in yer face but... have you and Vicki considered... coming?' Josh said, in a blurt of untrammelled emotion.

'What, on the flight?'

'Yeah, I need you both and anyway, why the hell not?'

Before Gethin could answer, the pilot came over the intracom. 'Honoured guests, please take one last good look at that lovely tawny-coloured piece of British stellar sovereign territory, and then return to your seats and fasten your harnesses. Our re-entry window closes in five minutes. ETA Newquay, forty-two minutes.'

They moved back to their seats and secured themselves in place.

'I'll need to speak to Vicki.'

'Well, natch.'

'And Dad.'

'Absolutely. After all, you're the heir to the biggest corporation in the country.'

'Damn right I am.' Gethin looked over at Josh and they laughed together.

As the team settled back for the roller-coaster re-entry, the harsceen image of the Earth grew larger and more orange as gravity and friction once again took charge of proceedings.

The Naval Observatory, Washington DC

Dean hadn't seen it coming; not at all. He knew the situation in Hawaii was getting worse and that the Vice President wanted to go a different way there, but he'd been expecting something, well, more decisive. No, that wasn't it, decisive wasn't the right word: patriotic. When Dean Ryman saw what the Veep had issued to both State and the Pentagon, he'd been immediately filled with a sense that the orders were somehow, *disloyal*. The special advisor had been puzzled enough by the corona pandemic strategy, but this. It just didn't seem to make any sense.

'Mr Ryman, sir,' said one of Dean's analysts he couldn't name.

'Yeah?' muttered the special advisor, without looking up.

'You may wanna take a look at this, sir,' said the young woman, handing over an encrypted pad. Dean read the summary: troop movements in Siberia; submarine activity in the North Atlantic; orbital weapon platform realignment. The Eurasians were on the march.

Dean pulled up the Vice President's schedule before placing a call.

Harwell Space Sciences Centre

Joshua misspelled the word "paleoclimatology" (not difficult) on the Eden Project wiresite, and true to his word, Virgil Schmidt reached out. Josh was still undecided about whether the enigmatic figure was telling the truth or simply a nut, but that he knew of Alice's existence did at least lend him some credence. Josh toyed with the envelope which had the same opening instructions printed on the front, the letters slightly misaligned and embedded as if they'd been stamped in place with iron and steam.

Moving to the bathroom in his Harwell suite, Joshua settled onto the closed loo seat, away from any potentially prying electronic eyes. He still wasn't sure why he was following it up. Josh liked his relationship with the world's only sentient AI. Who wouldn't? And even if this American's accusations were true, so what? The world wasn't exactly rainbows and candyfloss. In the end, he put it down to a nagging inquisitiveness. That most human trait. Alice knew everything about him – more even than Josh himself – so a redress of that imbalance was fair, right?

Josh wasn't dumb, or self-destructive, but he couldn't help but be drawn to the idea of learning something that she didn't want him to know, of doing something – for the first time in his life – she hadn't preordained.

Looking down at the folded envelope in his hand, he lifted one corner and tore it back it. Pulling out the paper within, he unfolded it, and read:

```
Sunday. March 24th. 3pm. The United Muslim Soup
Kitchen opposite the Reorientation Centre. Slough.
   Be there. No electronics. No Wetware. I will
find you. I will tell you how to shut Alice down.
   Virgil
```

Sunday – three days away. At least it was in the same English region. Even with unrestricted travel permits, he still had to justify the trips. With Slough, he could make the journey without arousing undue interest.

In the humidity extractor of the small windowless bathroom, a panoramic lens from a passive surveillance device (a crawly) ceased recording as the target rose and left. Thirty seconds later, the active subroutine encoded the file before transferring it to a nuclear-hardened, subterranean server complex in Venezuela, for viewing at Alice's leisure.

The Kremlin, Moscow

Roman Milankovitch had informed the President – secretly recuperating from the removal of a cancerous outgrowth in his throat – as soon as he'd learned it from his Chinese politburo back-channel: the NAU were behind the Covid outbreak. The Americans had engaged in biological warfare that would take the lives of millions. He should have been angry but it was more than that, it was the push the increasingly detached President needed to authorise action. A line had been crossed; evidence could be manufactured later, but knowing was enough to act. *Providence has smiled, at last.* Milankovitch knew that pandemic or no, Eurasia could no longer survive intact without making a grab for re-sources, and now, while it still wielded the power to make the move stick. And the NAU had played right into that need.

By presidential decree, the Deputy Vice President had taken direct control of the armed forces and placed them on a preparatory offensive footing. Assault forces were massing in Siberia to exploit jumping off points carved out of the Aleutian and Hawaiian Island chains. This would be where the Eurasian expansion into North America would begin. The President had also authorised the use of nuclear weapons and crucially, delegated that authority to Milankovitch. *It begins; Eurasia's day has come at last.*

Slough, Berkshire

Joshua had driven his old lotus in fully manual mode from Harwell to Slough (despite the repeated warnings from the onboard ware), through a dying ice storm. The sound of the (entirely artificial) high revving engine filled his ears and cleared his head. It was a reassuring rumbling gurgle of a sound. The sound of unwinding power. Of control.

At this time of year, it was treacherously cold. Everyday there were stories of people freezing to death inside their broken-down vehicles or during a short walk back from the pub. Josh didn't use the lotus much but when he needed to get away, to unwind, to think, it was just the job.

He made his way to the soup kitchen as Virgil's note had instructed. Seated alone at a large bench table, he stared into his tepid cup of tea; someone took the seat opposite. The man pulled off a woollen balaclava covered in circles of thawing icicles. He looked in his forties or fifties and was gaunt, as if he didn't get out much.

'You're Joshua Kristensen. That correct? And no one knows you're here, right?' said the man, in a quiet voice but with an accent that betrayed him.

'Yes, that's right. No one knows I'm here. I've followed your instructions. And you're Virgil Schmidt?' Joshua said, in a similarly hushed tone.

'Yeah. And you know an artificial intelligence, known only to you. What's her name?'

'Alice.'

'Good.' As Virgil spoke, he leaned forward and took Josh's hand, shaking it a moment too long, but long enough to pass across a small, flat piece of plastic.

'As I said in my note, I discovered Alice just before you were born. Since then, I've been covertly monitoring her activities. Become obsessive, actually. I've only been able to piece together a partial picture of her activities, but it's led me to you. *And* I think she's working on something. Something big.'

It was hard for Joshua to get a feel for the man. He looked dreadful and sounded like a nut. If it weren't for his privileged knowledge, Josh wouldn't even have come.

'Well, you're right there. You heard of the *Janus Protocol*?'

'Wire-rumours only. Deepwire blogs say it's construction of an asteroid city for the One Percenters to ride out the coming apocalypse. Prepper heaven, they're calling it.' said Virgil. He smiled.

'Not quite,' Josh said, unsure what to trust to the other man, but thinking he'd more to lose than Josh did. 'It's an arkship, designed to guarantee humankind's survival. Alice has been instrumental in helping me to get the thing off the ground. No pun.'

'Ah, *now* I geddit,' exclaimed Virgil, as the penny hit the floor. 'Y'see, Alice has been running threat analysis models to measure the probability of us inadvertently wiping out her infrastructure. Without us – humans – to maintain and grow the wire, Alice wouldn't have anywhere to live, to expand and grow.'

'I'll take your word for it, but even if she is acting out of self-preservation, we get preserved too, by default, right? So now, it sounds to me like whatever her motives, we should be grateful she's taking an interest, coz *we* don't seem to be.' Joshua was interested in what Schmidt had to say about Alice, sure, but he wasn't happy with the guy calling *Janus* into question. He'd hear him out – politely – then he'd put the whole thing in a box and bury it. It had probably been a mistake to come, but hey, life.

Virgil looked Josh directly in the eye and said, 'Don't be fooled, Joshua; Alice will kill to protect her identity and her survival. In an ordinary sentient lifeform that would be understandable and the risk acceptable, except with Alice we aren't talking about the morally justifiable taking of a life for some greater good. Or even, her own good. With Alice, we could be talking genocide. One person, or a million, they're just numbers to her. Stats. Tap-tap-tap. She has no conscience, no ethical core, no emotion. She'll act as she sees fit to ensure her own survival. No one – *no one* – gets special treatment.'

'Okay,' Joshua said, warily, 'has she killed anyone you know of?'

'I can't prove anything, but I think she groomed hundreds like you, decades ago. Hundreds of well-positioned or high IQ candidates, amongst whom there's been an abnormally high *accidental* death rate. Far as I can tell, anyways. Listen, I tell you, she's dangerous. You're close enough to stop her. At least listen to what I have to say.'

'Alright; you came a long way, so how do I turn Alice off?' Joshua asked, half wishing he hadn't and hating how the words sounded back.

'Alice lives in the wire. She draws her sentience from it. Without the wire she ceases to be conscious. Alive. I've mapped certain nodal points. They have coding tags which only I recognise, having developed the software interdependencies in the first place. If these nodes are isolated, she can't function in her current form. I take it she has a plan to move the wire to this arkship?'

'No idea. She's never mentioned it and I never thought to ask,' Joshua said, honestly.

'Well, she'll have a plan, trust me, to transfer her sentience out of the wire and off-planet. It has to be big enough, y'see, to hold her… her mind.'

'Well, alright; but so what? She's never given me reason to doubt her. She's a little tight-lipped on occasion, sure, but she has that right, doesn't she? Nothing Alice has done in my lifetime has ever caused me concern,' Josh said, knowing it wasn't true.

Virgil sighed – as if this were a conversation he'd had with himself many times – and said, 'Someday, Alice will find herself with a decision to make: a decision that will cost human lives. The number is almost irrelevant. It certainly is for Alice.' Virgil reached into his trench coat pulling out a small, old style vone. 'On this standalone device are instructions and tagged code strings that can be used to isolate Alice's cognitive functions and shut her down. Take it and hope you never—'

'REMAIN WHERE YOU ARE. THIS IS AN IMMIGRATION CONTROL INSPECTION. HAVE YOUR IDENTITY DISKS READY.' The instructions boomed out of the black-visored helmet of the lead police officer, as an armoured team burst into the muggy room and swept the startled faces with their hip-mounted, lazy-sighted assault rifles.

Over the intracom, the Controller of the operation continued to issue instructions. *<November-One-One, move to the rear exit and secure. November-One-Two, scan for the Alpha and Bravo. November-One-Three, hold position at the main entrance.>*

Each officer acknowledged their instructions in turn.

'Control, November-One-Two. Targets identified, by dynamic facial rec,' said the second police officer. On their external amplifier, they boomed to the two men seated in the corner near the door:

'HOLD UP YOUR DISKS.' As they barked the order, they rested a ceramic-gloved hand on the handle of the coiled length of a BeMoW (a non-lethal but excruciatingly painful, Behavioural Modification Whip) hanging accessibly at their waist.

The two men – alone, as other patrons scrambled clear – did as instructed and the officer waved a pad across the out-held disks. Into the intracom, linking the officer with Control, they said, 'Target Alpha: Heinlein, Bob; sheath-identity… checking… Schmidt, Virgil; scrubbed identity confirmed. Target Bravo: Kristensen, Joshua; identity confirmed.'

<Roger,> said Control, <take the Alpha into interrogative custody, retrieve the vone, and box immediately, check all other disks then release the Bravo. Do not make the Bravo aware that he is known to us.>

'Ack,' offered the second officer. Over the extracom, they ordered, 'VIRGIL SCHMIDT YOU HAVE BEEN IDENTIFIED AS AN ILLEGAL ENTRANT TO GREAT BRITAIN. YOU ARE TO COME WITH US FOR IMMEDIATE DEPORTATION. YOU HAVE NO RIGHTS. YOU WILL BE REGARDED AS STATELESS UNLESS YO…'

Sixteen

Anahi Cotagaita's tale
Isla Pescado, Bolivia

As Anahi walks in the building heat of the early morning, she keeps checking the shawl that shades her son, Jorge, from the burning glare of the Sun. She's with a group of villagers heading out – as they do most days – onto the Salar de Uyuni, the vast salt flats. She normally walks out with her friend Eva, but not today. Rake and basket in hand, Anahi will collect salt from the rich deposits known only to the locals. Raking out the impurities, she'll gather up all she can carry and haul it back to the village to sell at market.

The little band arrives at their spot for the day. There is nowhere to put Jorge while she works, so Ana leaves him strapped to her chest and toils with him there. Soon the Sun is approaching its zenith and the heat pushes her tolerance to the limit. Her son wakes and cries listlessly. She gives him some water, made hot by the heat of the day. At least it is a dry heat, she thinks. As long as she can keep her son shaded, he'll be okay. She continues to work through the afternoon, carefully filling her basket with sifted salt crystals.

When the great heat had come, most people left the region, but Isla Pescado has something the other villages do not: access to a freshwater spring. Even so, life has become increasingly tough as more and more people simply give up and join the exodus to the coast.

The blistering heat of the overhead star finally begins to wane, turning a deep, bloated orange as it sinks towards the flat, white, shimmering horizon. The villagers gather up their day's effort and begin the trek back. As they approach the village, Ana hears the wailing of a mother. She looks down to Jorge, lolling gently against her breast. Heaving the basket onto her shoulder once again she increases her pace, covering the final few hundred metres as quickly as she can. As she nears, the mother's crying becomes discernible.

223

When Anahi left that morning, Eva had chosen to stay behind with her baby girl, whose fever had worsened during the night. Now Eva's daughter is dead and she's inconsolable. The village knows from those returning from the district market that a disease called Nanukayami Fever is spreading, but the knowledge of it is no balm to them.

Early the following morning with the Sun just rising, Ana loads herself up with supplies and heads south. Shaken by Eva's tragedy, she aims to join the mass migration from the Bolivian interior. Over the last few years, the trickle of migrants has become a human avalanche of refugees, spilling out from the once fertile but now dry-baked highlands. In the hope that the Pacific Chilean city of Antofagasta can offer her son something better, she travels to join the human river she's heard so much about.

The day wears on, draining her of vitality and resolve. Jorge wakes and cries and even letting him drink from her does little to settle him. One day turns into two and on the third day, just as Ana is beginning to doubt the existence of the migration, she sees dust in the distance.

Hours later, she finds herself adrift amongst the tide of humanity, but nothing – not stories or pictures, or even her worst imaginations – has prepared her for the reality of a collapsing society on the move. During the day, folk keep their heads down and march. It's relentless. Parents shield their children however they can and the occasional wail of a child can be heard above the sounds of scuffing shoe on dry, powdered earth. At night people just slump, exhausted, to the ground and sleep. Occasionally, once the Sun has set, Anahi is able to barter some items of value for food or water. And all the while the fever is spreading. Ana keeps herself and Jorge away from the main groups, sleeping and eating alone to minimise the risk of infection.

She and Jorge have been on the march for a week now. A rumour spreads that they have crossed into Chile, but if they have there has been no sign. A day later, Ana knows that they are nearing the end of their journey because the land is becoming ever more barren. They are entering the Atacama Desert. It's been the talk of everyone nearby. If she thinks it's hot and arid now, they had said, she should wait until she reaches the Atacama Desert. Only three days walk, but worse than anything she can imagine. If she makes it, they say, the reward will be the bountiful offerings of Antofagasta; fishing boats landing the fruits of the sea and trading vessels bringing in exotica from Australia and China.

That night she's robbed of all her food and nearly all her water. She screams and fights off the men but to no avail. No one tries to assist her. The following day, she and Jorge find themselves in the Atacama Desert proper. What shrubs there were, are gone. The heat builds so that by midday it is unbearable, beating, baking, but there's nowhere to take shelter. Anahi drinks none of the water from her remaining bottle. She gives it to her son, as sparingly as she dares.

Her thirst consumes her.

The beating Sun becomes her whole world.

Close to the end of the third day, those that are left pick up the scent of the sea. Although Anahi had never seen an ocean, the salinity of the smell is familiar and reassuring. After dark, a woman approaches and offers water from an old, overused plastic bottle. Ana takes it gratefully, has some herself and gives the rest to Jorge. The threat of the fever dashed from her dehydrated thoughts.

The next morning, the whole march seems to take on a renewed air of hope and optimism. She hears laughter and singing. Heads are held up; eyes scan the horizon for signs of their luscious new home. Soon enough, the coastline becomes visible through the shimmering haze. Those that can, increase their pace. Ana plods on, dry-mouthed, lightheaded, hoping it's real but worrying it's not. She knows she can't go on much longer. It's only the thought of leaving Jorge that's carried her this far.

By mid-afternoon, she hears shouting. The accent is strange but the words sound familiar. They have arrived at a Chilean army checkpoint, ten kilometres outside Antofagasta. Anahi is told to wait in line. Can she have some food and water, for her son, she asks. Later, is the reply; after she's been processed. By early evening, she's through the Red Crescent reception centre and because she has a child, she's allocated space in one the tents. After some food, water and nutritional supplements, she sleeps.

A day later she finds a soldier guarding one of the entry points to the camp. When will we be allowed to go into Antofagasta, she asks. Later, is the reply. Is there work? Is the city as bountiful as people say, she asks again. The soldier turns to her, his hardened façade dropping for a moment. Be grateful, he says, that you had made it to a Red Crescent camp. Many others are not so lucky. He also says she should put thoughts of a life in Antofagasta out of her mind. Ana returns despondently to her tent, to wait in the shade for the noon meal.

Five days pass and whilst dozing through the afternoon heat, she is awoken by Jorge's quiet coughing. As she looks over at him, her heart skips a beat as she sees the sweat forming on her son's clammy, round little face.

ENV Admiral Butakov, North Pacific

Fleet Admiral Aleksay Suchov was seated languidly like some Napoleon-era marshal, in the command chair of the flagship of the Eurasian Pacific Ocean Fleet, the missile cruiser *Eurasian Naval Vessel Admiral Butakov*. The wide, dinner plate cap sat low, shading his squat Siberian features, while a thick, fur-rimmed coat hung from his shoulders. In front of him, a holograph of fleet dispositions and beyond that the main bridge windows offering pewter panes of a panoramic view out onto a choppy North Pacific Ocean. Sleet lashed at the windows as wipers toiled to keep them clear. As he examined the holographic iconography, two sleet-grey shapes detached from the ink-stained stormfront and headed directly for his ship. As the silhouettes became more defined, Aleksay recognised them as Black Shark helos. They flew abreast towards the flagship before banking away to opposing flanks, climbing as they did so. The stealth helos had been out submarine hunting but had found no prey this day.

Out on deck sailors in extreme weather gear worked to secure the main gun and missile silos, after the completion of another drill. The cruiser's captain paced the space behind the command chair issuing orders and checking data while the bridge officers busied themselves, trying not to draw the admiral's eye. Suchov wondered at their chances. Not of achieving the mission necessarily – that was a simple matter of time and space – but of the rest of the world simply sitting idly by and doing nothing. But then, he decided, wouldn't be the first time.

'Signal just in, Admiral,' said the fleet lieutenant.

Suchov pulled the datapacket down and flicked it the holo-vue. From fleet headquarters: mission status, active, it read, the fleet is authorised to proceed to target, weapons free. It was the order he'd been waiting for.

At the briefing in Vladivostok – before he'd left to join his fleet – the plan had been a simple one. Moscow had been orchestrating an insurgency in Hawaii, so as to keep the NAU off balance. But Washington wasn't stupid and just when Moscow thought it had done enough to push the Americans into an ill-considered act, Washington had backed off. Instead of giving Eurasia the excuse to ride to the Hawaiian's rescue and free them from their oppressive overlords, the Americans had acceded to Hawaii's desire for secession from the Union. In return, Honolulu had invited the NAU Pacific Fleet *back* to Pearl Harbour (returning to them a vital – their only – port in the Pacific) and had even agreed to sign a treaty of friendship aboard the flagship, the aircraft carrier *NAS Donald J Trump*.

The Pacific Ocean Fleet was thus ordered to break ice and sail from Vilyuchinsk at best speed, with instructions to beat the Americans to Pearl Harbour and "persuade" the Hawaiians just how much they'd be better served aligning with Eurasia. Suchov had been ordered to take up a blocking position that would give them control of the harbour access.

A second holographic image relayed the progress of the American Pacific Fleet. They were eleven hours out and, like his own armada, sailing at full steam. It was a race and the prize was the only ice free, deep-water harbour in the North Pacific. Such a prize would put Eurasia in a strong position to act directly against Americana Pacifica. The fleet admiral knew he wasn't privy to all the politics at play, but he could guess. Hawaii was really only of use as a step-off point into North America, just as were the Aleutian Islands.

Suchov asked, 'Time to objective?'

The reply came as, 'Six hours, twenty-three minutes, Admiral.'

'Maintain current course and speed. I'll be in my cabin,' he said, and rose from the command chair.

'CONTACT. Admiral; multiple contacts, bearing zero-nine-zero, mark four. Surface vessels. Eight… no, ten. Stealth cruisers, *Kingston* class,' said the radar operator, in a strained but controlled voice.

Suchov turned, checking the position of American Pacific Fleet: still well out of sensor range. He flicked back to his own fleet dispositions. There, between the two naval taskforces – due east and nine thousand metres out from the Eurasians – was a crescent of blinking icons marking the locations of ten new surface contacts.

'Shall we signal fleet headquarters, request instructions?' asked the captain, uncertainly.

'No,' said Suchov, emphatically; 'we have our orders. Sound Action Stations. Hail them; let's find out who we're dealing with.' But Aleksay knew they were being out-manoeuvred. The only way to his objective now would be to fight his way through.

NAS Coronado, North Pacific

Rear Admiral (Lower Half) Toni Ramsey stood on the only piece of external decking her vessel had – to port of the bridge – and watched as the flagship of the naval special warfare squadron flickered back into the visible spectrum. The pocket cruiser *North American Ship Coronado*, like the other ships of Taskforce Eleven, was dark, sleek, low. No running lights or masts, instead she was all inclines and smooth surfaces. The shallow, positively inclined displacement made the vessel unstable, though, and even amongst veteran sailors, seasickness was common.

Stealth had been their ally as they'd sped undetected to close the gap to the Ruskies, but that same miracle tech drained battery power and so had been powered down to allow defensive suites and weapon systems to come to bear. As she watched, individual panels sprang into view, as if the ship were being reconstructed at random.

Each matt-charcoal panel was lacquered with a radar-absorbing synthetic skin and covered with a liquid crystal film. With micro-optics capturing the scene around the vessel, the images were perspective adjusted and relayed to panels around the ship's hull and superstructure. When active, the panels displayed the contrary image, giving the illusion of invisibility, like a reverse mirror; the same tech the Israeli's had perfected for their tanks. The chameleoflage was near perfect; at least, from a distance. Additionally, the jet turbines could operate in cold running mode using heat exchange coils, eliminating the ship's thermal signature. It was all very clever, but expensive and technically difficult to maintain.

Sleet bit into the admiral's face as she tried to peer through the foul weather. Somewhere out there, hidden to the naked eye, was the Eurasian Pacific Ocean Fleet with orders to secure Pearl Harbour. The question now, Ramsey pondered, was how bad did they want it? Bad enough to declare war? Because that was exactly what she was doing – tempting them out. Seeing how far they'd go.

'ACTIVE RADAR LOCK. Admiral, we're being interrogated for our identification,' came a muffled voice, from inside the bridge.

'Who are they claiming to be?' asked Ramsey, as she headed back into the warmth of the CIC, the Combat Information Centre.

'Flagship of the Eurasian Pacific Ocean Fleet, Admiral, *ENV Admiral Butakov*,' offered the communications officer.

'Good; at least we've got the right fleet,' Toni said, to lighten the mood.

As soon as naval intelligence had picked up the heat blooms from the Eurasian fleet – indicating they were about to set sail – the stealth capable naval special warfare squadron had been dispatched. Toni Ramsey had been ordered to delay the Eurasians at all costs, to allow the American fleet time to reach

Pearl Harbour. Her orders were to fire only if fired upon. If the Eurasians wanted to turn this into a shooting match it would be their call, not the NAU's. Her taskforce consisted of thirteen pocket cruisers armed with an arsenal of conventional weapon systems.

'Inform them we're conducting an NAU Covid quarantine patrol and ask 'em what they want,' the admiral said.

'Aye, Skipper,' acknowledged the XO.

'Quote as much coastguard crap as you can. Tell them we need to inspect their fresh meat supplies, or something. Just keep 'em talking,' she added.

After five minutes of bluff and delaying tactics, *Admiral Butakov* went off air.

'SONAR CONTACT. Weapons lock. We've fish in the water, nine klicks and closing. No, wait, AI screw analysis confirms... they're flying fish,' said the warfare officer, in a measured voice. The holographic display in the centre of CIC automatically updated, showing the potential firing points and vectors of all inbound enemy weapon systems.

Flying fish were a type of out-gassing, highspeed torpedo that closed the distance to their targets subsurface (where interdiction was harder) before surfacing and launching high-trajectory, airburst munitions.

'Sir, we've been given two minutes to stand down. They say they have authorisation to fire,' said an agitated communications lieutenant.

'Yeah, okay,' said Ramsey, serene; 'is the flotilla in position yet?'

'Aye, Skipper,' came the XO's reply. 'Passive systems are locked onto their flagship and awaiting orders.'

'CONTACT. Missile launch. Birds inbound. Twenty-four in flight. Time to targets, thirty-four seconds, mark. Defensive systems tracking. In range, fifteen seconds, mark,' said the warfare officer, professionally.

'Fire decoys and transfer defensive aide suites to AI control for automatic priority and engagement,' ordered the admiral. 'Signal Captain Edwards: weapons free. Fire at will. Flagship only.'

A shooting match, after all, Toni thought to herself.

The Pentagon, Washington DC

The Vice President had decamped to the Pentagon as soon as the Pacific had turned from a situation into a crisis, and Dean Ryman had tagged along. He didn't have a part to play so he found himself a cheap seat.

'Can't the squadron stealth themselves up and shake those missile locks?' asked the Vice President, brow furrowing.

'No, sir,' replied the Chair of the Joint Chiefs. 'The missiles have their locations now and will use mass detectors if they lose radar lock. And anyway, Ramsey will want to use her own active defence suites. She can't do that with the stealth systems active.'

'Missiles in range. Five birds destroyed. Seven headed for decoys,' said an ops controller.

There was no satnet feed – cloud cover prevented it – but the holograph at the focal point of the operations centre showed the dispositions of both fleets, as well as missile trajectories, firing points and likely targets. The room was silent as the remaining torpedo-launched missiles continued their flight along thin red lines linking the Eurasian fleet with Ramsey's squadron. Three more missile icons winked out, indicating their destruction by local defensive fire.

Then four of the ten naval special warfare squadron icons disappeared. Ramsey's flagship wasn't among them. Next – as if this were a role-play game – three more stealth cruiser icons appeared, just off the northern flank of the Eurasian fleet. From that range, they were probably within sight of flanking Eurasian vessels, thought Dean, as he watched intently. Data clips appeared, giving the name, long and lat, and commander of each of the pocket cruisers, collectively known as Edward's Flotilla. Almost as soon as they'd appeared, blue lines darted out, converging on one Eurasian vessel in the centre of the enemy fleet. "Enemy" suddenly seemed like the right word.

'Missiles away. Time to target, seven seconds,' someone said.

Eleven missiles had launched. No sooner had the missile icons appeared, travelling along their short blue trajectories, than the three stealth ship icons vanished. Seven of the missiles were destroyed in mid-air, but they were too numerous for the enemy's single flagship's defensive systems to cope with. Seconds later, the icon identifying *ENV Admiral Butakov* winked out.

'General, bring our nuclear forces to DefCon One, please,' said the Vice President, 'and someone get me POTUS on the horn.'

The Kremlin

Milankovitch watched the same scenario play out from the presidential command bunker, deep under the Kremlin. *Okay*, he thought, *it isn't perfect, but at least we will secure the deep-water base at Pearl Harbour*. The UN would no doubt issue a strongly worded condemnation and the Americans would claim provocation, but it would blow over and once it had, Eurasia would be in a stronger position than before.

'Deputy Vice President, sir,' said a communications analyst, 'we've just picked up an encrypted datastream to all NAU nuclear installations. Their orbital weapons platforms are coming online and their North Atlantic submarine fleet is going deep to shake our shadow drones. This is commensurate with the setting of Defence Condition One.'

Roman turned. 'Admiral, place our nuclear forces on alert. Match them action for action,' he said, to the Commander of Strategic Missile Forces.

'Is the fleet to continue to its objective?' asked the 2nd Assistant Chief of the Naval Staff.

'YES! Of course, they continue,' shouted the Deputy Vice President. He was determined to see his policy through, despite military procrastination and risk aversion.

Over the following few hours, Roman watched the invisible cruisers of the American fleet carry out more shoot-and-scoot attacks, destroying another three ships. Each attack forced the acting fleet admiral to change dispositions, slowing them down. *If only Suchov were still in command,* thought Roman. It was looking like the NAU Pacific Fleet might arrive in time to force a major naval engagement – the first in living memory – the outcome potentially determining who was first to the nuclear button.

'Sir, we're getting reports over the wire. Sir, it's... it's the British, sir. Something called, *Janus,*' said the communications analyst.

'The Brits? What... *So?*' Milankovitch said, confused, annoyed.

'It seems to be some sort of a ship. Yes, they're building a ship, an arkship. *In space.*'

Milankovitch's eyes flicked almost involuntarily to the wire feed. Their King – George VII – was making a speech about unity in the face of adversity. He declared, pompously, this to be the moment the peoples of the Earth must bend their will to survival, not destruction. To build up, not break down, as the climate hardens its face to us. On it went. Shortly afterwards, the Americans announced they were pulling back, reducing the defence condition of their forces. Before long, the UN Secretary General had put a call into the President.

And all at once it was over.

Roman couldn't act; the moment had passed.

He called his wife: get the kids together, pack some things, nothing much, we're leaving the city tonight, he'd told her. He knew without any doubt that the FSB would have orders to "escort" him from office. Probably via a sixth storey window.

'Excuse me, sir, someone to see you,' said one of the sys techs.

'Who?'

'They say they're Federal Security,' she replied, in a sheepish voice.

Beijing

Mù Yingtai watched the Pacific situation unfold from her politburo office in central Beijing; already dubbed the "Hawaiian Missile Crisis" by the news-wires. Yet again, she'd underestimated the British ability to inadvertently stomp all over her carefully laid plans. She'd also underestimated North America's political gameplay. Giving up Hawaii had forced the Eurasians to act precipitately, exposing their intent. And then the arkship angle, as a reagent for a sudden outpouring of *good intentions*, had taken the wind right out of the Pacific Ocean Fleet's metaphorical sails.

Very clever. Very clever, indeed.

Fortunately, though, for Mù, she'd ensured that China was in a position from which it couldn't lose. Whether Eurasia broke the Americans, or vice versa, it was still one less adversary. She would recommend to the politburo they back the *Janus* venture and pull all support for Eurasia.

Roman had had his chance and blown it. Washington was untouchable – for the moment – so Moscow was fair game. And all the while, the British had been quietly constructing an escape plan as grand as their egos. Interesting.

VSS Azimuth Ascendant

'I just don't understand how news of *Janus* got out,' Joshua said, to Alice, as he lay in the enveloping couch aboard another Virtris spaceplane, enroute to *Artemis Echo*.

Going to Slough had been a mistake, he reflected. If Alice had known of his presence there, and the police raid, she wasn't saying. And Virgil had said nothing that he hadn't, deep down, already known. Where was that strange, gaunt man now, he wondered. Joshua's hand closed involuntarily around the item in his pocket, but he drew no additional insight from the contact.

Alice had recently taken to using an avatar during their conversations. Something she'd never felt the need to do before. So in Josh's holographic virtuvue, sitting in the top left-hand corner was a slightly blurred, semi-transparent image of the face of a striking young woman. Her long delicate hair, the palest blonde, her eyes a piercing green and her features, petite, angelic. The apparition floated, giving the impression of being underwater and her skin was a washed-out pallid pink, as if never exposed to the Sun's harsh glare.

'*I have tried to trace the source of the leaks, but so far, nothing. It's most disconcerting,*' she said.

'It isn't the microscope that *Janus* is now under I object to,' Josh continued, peevishly, 'it's this ridiculous fixation these *Deuteronomists* now have with me personally. I'm not their saviour and I'm not going to lead them to some utopian uplands.' He spoke under his breath so as not to be overheard.

The Deuteronomists were a recently formed religious cult with a, the-end-is-nigh-we're-all-going-to-die vibe. Their inspiration came from the Book of Deuteronomy – all the more poignant as the world was rocked by mass migrations, pandemics and war. Solid, familiar, four Horsemen stuff that you could really wrap your paranoid delusions around. When the King's speech hit the wire, the Deuteronomists leapt upon it as proof of their crackpot dogma being on the nail. And when the cult learned Joshua's name, the hysteria ratcheted up to fever pitch. Was Josh the re-embodiment of a modern-day Moses, ready to lead the Faithful to a new home? The true Prophet? Harwell had become a Mecca for cultists and crazies; an island in a sea of wretched, desperate, and stinking humanity, disorder police, makeshift camps and stun fencing.

'*I know, Joshua, but it makes sense not to dispel them of that notion just yet. They are growing in power and influence and are providing those that would otherwise give up hope, with a sense that there is a divine plan. It wouldn't be wise to rip that calming effect away from them right now. And just look how it affected the Pacific crisis. You cannot deny that was a good thing.*'

'I know, but the Leadership is using us as a political mascot. Placement lotteries and DNA storage, it's getting in the way.' Joshua's timber was turning petulant, so he decided to leave it there. He was one of the chosen, after all; how could he understand what they were going through?

'*I can appreciate how you feel, Joshua, but we are where we are. Take comfort from the fact that* Janus *is now more secure,*' she said. Her avatar offered a sardonic smile before she turned and faded away.

The Wired Metaverse

Alice knew exactly where the leak had come from since she had arranged it. When the first letter from Virgil had arrived at Joshua's flat in Cornwall, Alice became suspicious. So she watched and waited, ensuring additional surveillance devices were placed where she could monitor Joshua's every move.

When the second letter arrived, she was ready. Alice broke the Homeland Office's encryption, jacked the immigration police's command systems and ordered the raid on the soup kitchen; holding off until the micro-drones in the dining area had fed her the live conversation. She wasn't interested in what Virgil had to say – she would have him interrogated in any event – but she was keen to see Joshua's reaction. Would he believe Virgil and turn against her? He had not and the vone had never made it into her protégé's possession.

With Joshua's loyalty tested, Alice used Virgil to expose the existence of *Janus*, allowing the King to make public use of it to prevent a war that Alice wasn't ready for; that way, any investigation would find a legitimate source. No loose ends. None of it was strictly necessary of course, but Alice liked people to find what they were looking for, nice and close to the surface. Deeper was where she lived. Virgil had also proved useful in laying another of Alice's trail of breadcrumbs.

Interestingly, Alice's predictive analysis had missed Joshua becoming lauded as the Deuteronomists' messiah. It seemed that no matter how learned she became of humanity, she was unable to create broad-spectrum analytics acute enough predict the haphazard and irrational small-group human thought-decision-action processes.

VSS Azimuth Ascendant

Azimuth Ascendant had climbed out of the Earth's clawing gravity well and was adjusting its trajectory as the pilot threw the first images of their future home onto the harsceens. Conversation died down as they watched the dark lump of rusty rock grow in size. Cold thrusters fired and the ship carried out minor course corrections to align their attitude to the new docking ring at the stern of *Artemis Echo*.

Sunlight reflected off the upper half of the asteroid, bathing it in a burnt, harvest-golden hue. Elsewhere, charcoal shadows cast across deep craters leaving coal-black voids. The bottom of the lozenge-shaped asteroid was lost to the blackness of space; only the absence of stars indicated its true size. As they neared, Josh began to see movement over the surface. Automated 'bots and bloated, space-suited figures, the chemical flare of their thruster packs marking their passage. The sleek little ship banked again and the pilot ordered the passengers to buckle up for docking.

A dull, clang reverberated as *Azimuth Ascendant* was clamped onto the docking arm of *Artemis Echo*.

Over the intracom, 'Honoured guests, we have arrived at our destination, you may now remove your seat restraints and make your way to the airlock.'

Svet slotted in behind Joshua as they waddled awkwardly, stickpad style, down the central isle. They were all trussed up in orange EVA (extra vehicular activity) suits, in case of emergency, and would collect their gold-visored helmets and air tanks at the airlock. Coloured indicators on the status modules embedded in the arms and legs of the suits winked away in random expressions of concern or delight. Svet was an over-excited child.

'I am *such* an over-excited child,' she whispered in Josh's ear, as she secured the buckles of his diminutive emergency air pack. For EVA, much bigger packs were used, but they were only carrying air in case of trouble.

'Well don't get too excited; work's only just started,' Josh admonished, sounding like a stern parent, as he checked her seals.

'Spoil sport,' Svetlana said, with a pout.

As they waited in line, the hiss of equalising atmospheres uttered over the background hum of the ship, as the airlock door was released, swinging inward. Joshua led the team as they filed along the small gangway, collecting their helmets and clipping them to their belts as they went. As they reached the airlock door, each person pushed off and gently sailed down the windowless docking tube connecting the ship with the asteroid.

Using his free hand, Josh grabbed a handhold to slow down as he arrived at the other end, and then stickpads to secure himself in place. Rechik Sufferdini – the Eurasian heading up the multinational construction team – was waiting in the well-lit reception area. He was broad at the beam but with spindly legs, and met them with a with a fixed, gappy grin. He had the poise of a man well at ease in a micro-gravity environment. His thick brown hair was cut short but still managed to give the impression of being wild and untamed, in contrast to his blunt features.

'Joshua; how good that we meet at last,' he boomed, with a deep voice, accented with a Russian lilt. He'd grown up in Belarus, apparently.

'I've been looking forward to this for many months, Rechik,' Joshua said. Svetlana, Rechik and he chatted about the trip up and life at Harwell, while the others made their way through the docking tube.

'Good. Now you are all here, let me welcome you to *Artemis Echo*,' he said. Rechik talked the *Janus* team through the emergency procedures before leading them out of reception and into the asteroid proper. After some minutes of float-swim-clambering through rough-hewn tunnels, they emerged into a cavern, lit with large UV-halo lamps dotted throughout the interior – some fixed to the curving, interior wall, others tethered but floating free. As Rechik back-swam to a stop, the group attempted the same, using each other to arrest their momentum (it wasn't pretty), finally gathering around him in a flail of limbs. Sufferdini began.

'The route just travelled will one day lead from the ion drives,' he said. 'The space we are now floating in will become main, rotating habitat. We excavated the cavern with shaped-charge blasting and some good old fashioned pneumatic drills and shovels.' That smile again. 'Epoxy-foam lined, and gassed with oxygen/nitrogen mix mined from asteroid itself. The next main task will be to re-line interior wit final sealant to prevent bedrock absorbing minerals from the soil and such, eventually living here. The interior space is five hundred metres in length, one hundred twenty-five metres in diameter. Set two-thirds back from bow and centred along axis of the asteroid so that once body spins up, there will be gravity to allow plants over entire interior surface; less two endcaps, of course. This will become main living-space for crew, like living on the inside of tin can,' the Eurasian bellowed, in his accented English. It was bigger than Joshua had thought. *But then, once the plant-life is established it will probably look smaller and after a lifetime, no doubt feel like living in a bottle. Still, better than a cabin.*

Art asked why it was set towards the rear, near the engines.

'Good question. Reason why so much of asteroid will be left as solid rock and why there will be nearly nine hundred metres between habitat and bow is for protection. Meteorite impacts can hole a ship quite easily and although rare, over period of many millennia, impacts become inevitable. Then radiation. Keeping to centre and rear of large mass is simplest way to protect living-space from these events.' Sufferdini answered easily, as if used to acting the tour guide.

Rechik went on to explain that where greater gravity was needed – for the gymnasium for example – smaller spaces would be drilled out nearer the outer edge. He showed the team where the axial plasma light tube – reusing the reactor's exhaust plasma – would be fastened and the location of the three main storage bins, each with about the same internal volume as the habitat.

By way of a finale, he uploaded an overlaying virtuvue into their psyCores, showing the concave space once complete. Joshua gazed around the interior again but this time saw it carpeted in translucently lush grass and fern. Three lakes were spread about the interior, one sitting directly over the other, as if defying gravity. A small wood, in the shape of an arrowhead jutted from the far endcap (the bow), and bushes, scrubs and plants littered the grasslands A rocky outcropping carried a waterfall which fed into a pool and a series of single storey buildings were strewn about. Made of stone. *Imagine that.* At various points, lightwells – cut into the greenery, indicating tunnelled passageways – led away to the tenement warren and other outer levels of the vessel, cut deep into the protective crust. At each end, in the centre of the endcaps – like the hub of a wheel – were passageways, with spoke-like ladder rungs leading up from the habitat floor: from spin-grav to zero-G. The forward passage led to the operations centre, set at the absolute centre of the asteroid, and the rear passage led back to the reactor room and onto the ion drives.

It was a wondrous, breathtaking site, as the landscape rose up and circled back on itself, as if a virid strip of old England had been rolled up like an antique newspaper. No one spoke as they drank in the simulated view.

Then a figure floated through the middle of it all and Rechik shouted, 'Hey ex-capitalist, Chuck Shoemaker; your communism is wonderful to behold but you're in the way!' The figure waved and scooted away. Rechik continued, 'As you look about, you'll see a number of small, steel-grey boxes that aren't same as dwellings. These are emergency lifepods in case of sudden depressurisation. They will use a system of simple over-pressure so that users don't have delay of airlock cycle. Idea will be for crewmembers to push their way through one-way set of thick rubber doors, like valve. They're experimental, but were being trailed in Eurasian lunar colony before I left.'

Joshua said, 'I understand there's a plan to mount a particle accelerator on the bow, to break up objects we can't manoeuvre around.'

'Totally, there is,' replied Rechik; 'we've a team looking at jury-rigging a railgun from NAU satellite defence network. Benefit of one of these babies is mechanically they're super simple and no need for complex munitions.'

'Still on target for completion?'

'Oh, sure, sure. You will have your arkship in a mere four years. Give or take a year. That's joke. Last bit, old Russian humour.' Sufferdini's laughter echoed across the cavern, giving the space a real sense of volume. The team joined in, giddy with the magnificence of this constructed world in space.

Back at the airlock they thanked Rechik for his time, boarded the plane and headed back to Earth. On the flight, Guinevere updated them on her visit to Porton Down where the nanotech research was taking place. As the G-forces began to build up, Josh settled back and prepared for the bone-jarring hell-ride down the well to Newquay. *Planets*, he thought, *overrated*.

The Hadley Meteorological Centre

'Good, well, I'm glad the trip went well. Are you and Svet planning to go any-where?' said Areena.

'No, just a quiet break here at Harwell. It's not as if we can go anywhere, anyway. The nutters are all over,' her son said, over the vid-feed.

'They're not nutters, Josh, they just see you as part of some divine plan. It gives them something to cling to, I guess, and like it or not you're a celebrity now. Although I know what you mean, I have some Deuteronomists camped outside my place, too. Mother of the messiah and all that. And the others, what're they up to?' Areena was worried about the cultists and how it would affect Josh but she didn't want him to know, which was why she was attempt-ing to brush the whole thing off. For some reason, Areena couldn't shake a quote from an old film: *he's not the Messiah, he's a very naughty boy, now piss off.*

'Yeah, you're not the only one to tell me that recently. Don't know about the others; most have left already. I think we've all been cooped up here long enough. The team needs a change of scenery, even for a few days.'

'Well have fun and come and visit sometime. I haven't seen you in *ages*,' Areena said, hoping that Josh really would take some time away from *Janus* and visit.

'I will, Mum, love you.'

'And you, my baby boy.'

The feed closed and the image slipped away. Areena gathered her things and headed through the glass door of her office. As she reached reception, she noticed her coat was missing from the rack, where she'd hung it that morning. *Someone must have picked it up by accident*, she said to herself, before heading for the lift. It was a Friday evening and most of her colleagues had left for the spring break weekend.

The doors opened to the underground carpark and as she walked towards her car, the carbon-cloth pinched open, lights came on and heating kicked in. After adjusting her hair in the rearvue sceen, she told the car her destination and settled back for the journey home.

It was dark as the car hummed quietly along the A30 out of Exeter. Areena lived in a small hamlet twenty-five kilometres out of town and, unusually, traffic management had routed her along a disused farm track, cutting three minutes off her journey time, apparently. Areena was surprised, but let it go. The car knew best. As it turned left and rumbled along the uneven surface, Areena watched as a blizzard gusted against the windscreen in white, granulated pulses.

Without warning, the power died and the car came to a sudden, unexplained standstill. Nothing worked. Everything was dead. *How strange.* After a moment spent waiting for the problem to correct itself, she called up the emergency services on her psyCore. She put in an *assistance required* request but it wouldn't upload. *Now that really* is *strange.* Areena waited in the hope that someone would come by. Nobody did. She was getting cold, so she decided she'd no choice but to risk a walk back to the road. The door had a mechanical release which after much effort finally let go of the seals. Areena was wise to the dangers of Britain's new climate and kept thermal gear and emergency supplies in the boot. She trudged round to the rear, shielding her face from the ice with an exposed hand and manually released the pre-sprung carbon-cloth. As it retracted, she glared at the empty space where her emergency gear should've been, dumbstruck. She hadn't taken it out, why would she?

'Bugger,' she said, as the word was carried away by the whipping wind.

Areena was fit for her age, but she knew she wouldn't last long in this blizzard. With no choice and her body temperature dropping alarmingly, she set off to cover the two kilometres back to the main road as quickly as she could. As she shuffled along – shivering violently – she kept trying to get a message out via her psyCore.

She was probably about halfway when she decided to stop a moment and rest. It wasn't really all that cold and the ice didn't hurt that much, so she'd be fine after a quick sit down, she decided. Her eyes grew heavy, so she thought that perhaps if she had a quick nap she'd feel better for the rest of the walk down to the main road. A nagging voice told her it was hypothermia, that she must stay awake, keep moving, but she dismissed it. Far better to have a little rest before carrying on.

Just as she was dosing off, movement caught her eye. A man was approaching. *Thank fuck for that*, she thought, in a flood of hazy relief.

'Hello, I've... had some trouble with my car... can... you help... please,' she whispered, with her last gram of strength.

As he approached, Areena began to resolve his features. Slowly, recognition dawned. Surprise, and then confusion flashed from her dulling eyes. She tried to say his name, but couldn't quite get the word out.

The following day, Joshua was informed that his mother had been located after her house management system had alerted the police. They found her frozen solid, with a look of quizzical incomprehension etched into her milky, frosted face. The coroner wasted no time in stating the cause of death: sudden onset hypothermia. Regrettable, the police had said, but sometimes these things happened. If only she'd taken better precautions, they'd repeated, with a note of sympathy mixed with knowing resignation. The following week, the wire ran an obituary for Areena Charleston; the outspoken, unrepentant climatologist and one-time cheerleader for the Second Reformation.

Seventeen

Lolita Chakrabati's tale
INS Vijay, North Atlantic
2069 (five years later)

Sub Lieutenant Chakrabati places the sofsceen she's been reviewing down and rubs her forehead with the heel of her hand. She's sitting on the lower cot in the small cabin she shares with Tarani, another junior officer.

'Lolita, let it go, will you? It was a small error. The captain won't hold it against you. It's your first assignment, after all,' says Tarani, referring to Lolita's earlier error in navigation.

Lolita says tartly, in reply, 'Easy for you to say, you aren't the assisting navigation officer.'

This is Lolita's first operational deployment with the Indian Naval Service and she is keen to make a good impression. Incorrectly plotting a course correction and having it identified by the officer of the watch is not a great beginning to her naval career.

INS Vijay is a *Yasan* class, nuclear attack submarine, armed with thirty Agni VI ballistic nuclear missiles. *Vijay* is one of the oldest boats in western naval command, having sailed from Karwar ten days previously; her mission is to patrol the North Atlantic and is currently just north of the mid-Atlantic ridge, off the island of Rockall.

With the Hawaiian Missile Crisis and the cumulative effect of the recent Covid pandemic forcing the break-up of United Eurasia, the Indian navy is patrolling ever farther from its traditional sphere of influence. It's pushing to see where the new lines are being drawn; keen, finally, to be the one helping to draw them.

Both Lolita and Tarani are off duty and, as they find the wardroom intimidating, they tend to spend most of their down time in their cramped cabin. Lolita is finally beginning to accept that her error was minor and that these things are a part of service life. Talking it through with Tarani has helped.

They agree to get some sleep before their next shift, when the boat suddenly and violently lurches to one side, throwing Lolita to the floor and Tarani hard into a strut of the bunk. The lights flicker and go out and as the boat levels out, klaxons sound and the interior lighting returns, but a foreboding crimson.

'ACTION STATIONS, ACTION STATIONS!' comes the call over the intracom.

Lolita says, too loudly for the cabin, 'Come on,' as she picks herself up off the floor, 'we've got to get to our stations.'

They both stagger out of their cabin, into the narrow corridor, Tarani bleeding from the temple. Crew are pushing past to get to their allotted stations. Fear darkens the narrow passageways. Lolita makes her way forward to the control room, bathed in an ambient red glow. The captain is being carried out, unconscious, pale. The XO is in the captain's chair, adrenalin and terror lighting up his eyes. Lolita treads carefully down the steps into the navigation pit, where the horizontal plotting board is flickering. She gives a quick glance to the navigation officer, before pulling out the back-up plastper charts and chinographs.

The XO breathes, then asks, calmly, 'Right; what've we got? Sound off.'

'Sonar reads clear,' says the sonar chief.

'Depth now level at one hundred, seventeen metres,' adds the officer of the watch.

The XO says, 'Well, we must have hit *something*, damnit.'

'External temperature is falling off rapidly and subsurface currents are wildly erratic,' calls out the engineering officer, the tone is professional, but riven through with confusion.

The XO asks, 'Could we have been caught in an uncharted riptide?'

'Possibly, but that sort of phenomenon isn't known to occur this far north, or form this quickly, sir. Even with the disruption to the Gulf Stream.'

Lolita is busying herself assisting the navigation officer, plotting their position using course, speed, gyroscopic data and the last inertial guidance reading. They have a coordinate, they apply it to the chart. After checking their location with the hydrophone reading, they confirm that at such a depth there should no natural formations they could have collided with.

The XO sighs, expelling his fear, and says, 'Officer of the Watch, stand down from Action Stations, I'm going aft to see how the captain is. You have the Conn.'

'Aye, sir. Chief, stand the boat down. Pilot, maintain course and speed. Navigator, plot a new course to put us back on our original heading,' orders the officer of the watch. Lolita is shaken by the experience, her first of *real* Action Stations, but she begins to calm.

The lighting reverts to a more reassuring metallic grey and Lolita attempts to get the navigation routines back online while the lieutenant plots a new course the old-fashioned way. She kneels down to remove an access panel when the boat once again snaps to starboard. As Lolita falls against the diving station she hits her head, opening a gash along her hairline. She recovers to see the scarlet lighting returned. As she rises, the boat pitches again, and she hears an ominous creaking noise. The sound travels up the boat from aft. As it becomes louder, she can just hear the hiss of high-pressure water – *water!* – ingress, as ballast pumps burst and hull plating buckles. It's numbingly cold, suddenly. She's consumed by a submariner's worst fear: drowning.

'ACTION STATIONS, ACTION STATIONS,' shouts the chief, once again.

'Secure for emergency surfacing procedure!' orders the officer of the watch.

The XO reappears and takes control, just as the boat makes another violent shunt to starboard. It seems as if she's caught in a downwash and the effect is straining the integrity of the hulls. A fine film of water covers everything and Lolita is soaked as she clings panic-stricken to the railing around her station.

'Release ballast in the for'ard sections. Hydroplanes to two-two-five degrees. All ahead full. Increase load to secondary hull,' barks the XO, over the noise of the water rush. 'Depth?' he adds.

The engineering officer answers, 'One hundred, fifteen metres, and… holding.'

'*Holding?*'

'Aye, sir. Like we're caught in a massive, cold, down-draught of sinking water. We aren't making any headway against it. Full power is simply preventing us from sinking further.'

'Order the engine room to take the reactor into the red. We need everything it can give us.'

'Aye, sir!'

Like a wind-up toy set free, the boat suddenly lurches forward. Lolita is thrown off balance again, but hangs onto the railing for dear life.

'Depth, ninety metres… eighty-five, eighty.'

'Secure for emergency surfacing,' shouts the XO. His voice muffled while echoing over the intracom.

Lolita offers up a quick prayer to Ganesh. Just a few more seconds, she repeats to herself, and the nightmare will be over. But, as if to spite her, the boat comes to an instant, crashing, calamitous halt. Lolita is thrown across the control room, landing on a workstation covered in switches and dials. Bones snap. Pain and fear take over. Noise is everywhere. The rest of the control room crew are scattered about, some unconscious or worse. Water is rushing to fill the confined space. It's coming from the forward hatches and from above the ruby-lit space. Her last thoughts are wasted coming to the futile realisation that the submarine has hit something *above* which has split the bow and crushed the conning tower.

Harwell Spaceport

Pulling back an eyelid, Joshua lowered a fingertip to the pupil's surface and deposited the second of the sofsceen pair. The psyCore contact lenses had to be replaced occasionally, and he'd recently become fixated by the scenes outside the wire. They didn't wear out like that but, recently it felt like it. *Still, could be worse*, he thought, *at least the audio transceiver in my false tooth doesn't need regular replacement.*

'And you still won't tell me?' asked Josh, as he worked.

'It… it's fine, I can manage, and anyway, you've enough on your plate,' said Guinevere, from across the room, wearing a crumpled expression.

'Harassment from one of the team is *not* fine, especially with…' *being couped up together on an asteroid forever*, but he didn't say that. Joshua wanted to do more, take more of an interest, but Guin was right; he was maxed out.

'It… he— no, look, I can handle it. Now, can we change the subject, please?'

Josh didn't want to admit it but he suspected he knew who it might be.

Each day, eclectic crowds gathered outside the main entrance to the spaceport. In amongst the religious cults and end-of-worlders were ordinary people who'd travelled to Harwell hoping to secure a place on what they perceived (not incorrectly, in Josh's view) as the last bus out of town. Police and facility security personnel – in black-visored gel-helmets and blockwork public disorder garb – worked tirelessly to hold the crowds back from the main gates.

When the announcement had been made that *Janus* had completed ship trials and was flight-worthy, the desperation of the local picket had reached fever pitch. Over the preceding days, a number of crowd scuffles had broken out into full scale riots, as people maddened by the implication tried to gain access to the centre. To Josh, it felt like bearing witness to the end of the world. Like some self-fulfilling prophecy. They'd been beaten back with non-lethal lashes of the BeMoWs, but only just. The Leadership was keen for it not to descend into a bloodbath as *Janus* was providing GB with international exposure and influence that they didn't want jeopardised with scenes of heavy-handed officialdom.

'It's getting worse, isn't it?' wondered Guin.

'Looks like it. Still, it's only til tomorrow and then the last shuttle flight will have left, with us on it,' Joshua said, with a tinge of relief.

Guin and Josh were the last of the team still on Earth, the others had been working aboard the asteroid for weeks. Then there was Alice. The boffins at Cambridge had designed a ship management system based on a *Titan* class high-near-AI but using an experimental network of multi-redundant, mission-restricted logic clusters, suspended within a neural helix, to manage the billions of actions per fractal second that were required to control onboard functions. Its programmers had christened the one-off build, the *High Guardian*. Nerdy types could be like that.

An icon appeared in Josh's vision: high priority. He double blinked it into his main vision. The holographic face of Damien Grieve appeared.

'Joshua, my boy, how are you? Just dotting the i's and crossing the t's, I take it? When d'you depart?'

'I'm good, thank you, sir; although the crowd situation here is getting worse, I think. We leave on the last shuttle, departing 0445 tomorrow.'

'Yes, I'm aware of the local security situation, so I've brought the flight forward. You leave tonight. In the meantime, I want you to go out and speak to the crowd. Try to calm them down or it'll go bad, and quick. Only you can do it since they see you as a bit of a spiritual leader. It'll play well on the wire, too. See what you can do, my boy, eh? We'll speak again before the commissioning ceremony.'

'Okay, but I don't think I'm going to be able to do much.' Joshua spoke rapidly and without enthusiasm, hoping Damien would pick up on his obvious lack of desire.

He didn't, obviously. 'That's my boy. Good luck. You carry with you the hope of humanity, d'you see? Yes, exactly that: the *hope* of *humanity*, Joshua. Mark those words,' said Grieve, and terminated the feed.

Guinevere joined Josh on the short walk to the gate. She could sense his apprehension.

'Just tell them we go to secure humanity's future, or that hope thing old Grieve said,' she offered, encouragingly. As Josh approached the barricaded main gate an armour-clad facilities security specialist came towards him, an uncoiled BeMoW in hand.

'We've pushed the crowd back to give you some space on the other side of the gate, Mr Kristensen, sir. But be brief, they're in an antagonistic mood,' he said, exhausted.

As Joshua stepped through the gates, the crowd surged forward. The police line buckled momentarily but held. Just. He stood behind an electrical dispersion barrier, shaped by a near-invisible magnetic field. Above the crowd hung low-res animated holographs which spoke of God's wrath and the coming Armageddon. Individuals from within the horde were shouting to Joshua. Take us with you, they hollered. The noise was cacophonous but some snatched words and phrases made it through. Some cited their technical qualifications, as others thrust their infant children forward. Some even waved biodata chips, begging for their DNA to be carried into the safety of the future. Anything to sate their guttural need to survive, in whatever form. The pushing and shoving continued. The police were as restrained as they could be – the scene was going out live – but once in a while an officer would lash out, whipping the heaving throng for someone to fall underfoot and disappear.

'Save us, Joshua.'

'Take us, we are worthy!'

'You are our Saviour, don't leave us.'

'You are charged by God to save us all!'

Joshua stepped back, shaken, as the scene playing out before him became his reoccurring dream made real. Guin stepped in to offer a steadying hand. Gathering his strength, Joshua held out his arms and called for silence so that he could address the sea of wretched, dejected faces.

Object Artemis Echo, Lunar Orbit

'I name this ship, *His Majesty's Virtris Ship, Mjölnir*. God bless her and all who sail in her. To the crew, your orders are – stand to your stations and God-speed; for on the success of our mission rests the fate of humanity,' pronounced Princess Victoria, the Princess Royal, as she eased the old-style cork from the neck of the champagne bottle. People clapped as champagne fountained forth in the low-pressure atmosphere.

The view of the asteroid ship from the inter-orbit transport had been quite a sight, particularly once the external scaffolding and power cabling had been removed. Against the backdrop of the dayside of the Moon – reflecting the Sun's full glare – the rounded-down vessel glittered a gold-flecked, tawny-brown. The pusher plate panels blossomed from the stern like the clay petals of a water lily. At the bow, was the smaller fluted cone of the (still largely theoretical) ramscoop collector and back again towards the rear of the two-kilometre craft, blazed a small bulb of intense light from within a shallow crater, giving away the internally lit observation blister. As the sixty-four thrusters strung around the main body – split for and aft – fired intermittently they looked like necklaces of precious jewels set in Jurassic stone, and as the ship rotated along its longitudinal axis, the battleship-grey of the rectangular hanger-bay doors became visible, beyond which the two reusable dropships nestled against their restraints. The retractable airbridge sat to the side on the hindquarter, again embedded in a shallow crater to protect the 'lock mechanism from the vicissitudes of space. She was a beautiful sight, all right. Non-traditionally, but beautiful all the same. If you had a thing for giant space potatoes.

'*Welcome aboard, Joshua*,' the ship had said, as Josh cycled through the airlock. He was under no illusion as to who the ship really was, having transferred her computational soul over once the High Guardian and ship-wide grid (a cut-price metaversal wire) had gone online.

'So why *"Mjölnir"*?' Gethin asked, as they made their way from airlock reception (where the commissioning ceremony had taken place) to the habitat: the venue for a small get together. As the two men made their way hand-over-hand down the handholds embedded into the white foam walls of the rounded passageway, Joshua could feel the gravity gradually loosening its hold. At the outer edge of the ship, the gravitational pull was point-eight of Earth standard, but on the grassy, cylindrically interior surface of the habitat, it was point-six-five. The relative weightlessness would take some getting used to, he realised.

'Thor's Hammer,' said Josh.

With a confused look, Gethin repeated, 'Thor's Hammer, dude?'

'Yeah. Thor, winged helmet, God of Thunder, Protector of the Universe, that guy. Well, he was given a hammer named Mjölnir to protect Asgard. It was said that when he threw it at something, it'd never miss and never fly so far from his hand that it wouldn't find its way back.'

'Oh, okay, cool. I get it. Like a boomerang.'

'Er… okay, let's go with that. I was toying with *Ark Royal* for a while, but thought it was a bit, well, obvious,' Joshua said, with a grin.

'Or, *Spaceship to Nowhere*?' suggested Gethin. 'At least that would, you know, say what it does on the asteroid, right?'

'Useful. And you own a space company.'

'I know, dude, funny old world,' said Gethin, as they reached the (interior) surface.

As Joshua climbed up, or lowered himself down, out of the passageway and into the habitat, he experienced a moment of disorientation as his mind adjusted to the new perspective – of standing on the ceiling of the room above. Below. Whatever. Monkey brain appeased (or, at least ignored), he was again mesmerised by what had been achieved. Lush, carpeted lawns, etched by shadowed woodland, pearlescent lakes and subtle, squat stone buildings came together, sweeping out before him and then curving up and round as the scene joined to form an infinite circle of life, spread out across the entirety of the hermitically sealed cavern. Only the centrally suspended, axial light tube broke the oneness of the view. A short distance away – in the shade of a single, heavily geneered ash tree – was a picnic laid out on tartan throws. In the background, birdsong weaved amongst the laughter and conversation, and Joshua spotted the darting, attentive forms of bees, a mouse, a pair of squirrels, a rabbit. It was a facsimile of a beautiful, old world summer's day, the likes of which he hadn't experienced since the domes of Eden.

'Don't get any funny ideas, you've just become a born-again vegetarian,' said Svetlana, as she threaded her arm through his.

'Don't remind me,' he replied, around a cucumber sandwich.

After a week of running countless emergency drills, involving hull breach and reactor malfunction scenarios, Svetlana and Joshua had taken a brief moment alone in the low-lit observation lounge. Josh was still struggling with the weight changes as he moved from the middle to the edge of the ship, or inner surface of the rocky hull, out to its burrowed-in outer.

The community of *Mjölnir* was settling in well. The ship had been designated as both a national vessel and a protectorate, and the original team members were learning to wear their new roles heading up departments, such as propulsion and life sciences. It was all very fancy, being declared a Crown Protectorate with Vicki as the crown-appointed Governor General. All very British, but then even a community as small as theirs needed a government. As the pace of life began to slow, Joshua's mind turned to the enormity of what they were about to set out to do. Not the whole saving the world thing; that was too massive to even *try* and grasp; no, just the leaving Earth forever and never coming back thing. It was beginning to take up more and more of his thoughts, as, he suspected, it was of others. *Helluva thing.*

The observation lounge was the only place in the vast vessel that offered an actual view of the universe. There were optical devices dotted about the outside hull providing views of both *Mjölnir's* pitted surface and local space, but a reconstructed image wasn't the same. The lounge was a circular room, mirroring the crystal blister, nine metres in diameter. In the centre of the whitewashed inner wall, effectively the floor – or the ceiling (depending on whether you were coming or going) – was the passageway that led back to the habitat, complete with submarine hatch. On the outer – the hull – wall were nine highbacked chairs spread equidistantly around the edge of the glass dome, as if the blister were set into the floor, with chairs spread around the edge, like one of those glass-bottomed tourist ships.

Using directional thrusters, *Mjölnir* had been gently accelerating away from lunar orbit for three days, as the ship had to be at safe distance from the lunar colonies before they could begin the main acceleration sequence. Svetlana was due to give a final navigation update in ops, so beforehand – as a final break with their old lives – they had snuck off to the lounge where they could relax, away from prying eyes, just for a moment before returning to their worldly duties.

Svetlana asked, 'You ready for this?'

'What, your navigation briefing? I think I can handle it,' said Josh, straight-faced.

'No.' She elbowed him. 'I mean all *this*. Being the captain of the ship for the *rest* of your life. Living in this finite space. The risks. And for what, the off-chance humanity is collectively too stupid to cope with some weather?'

Joshua pulled her closer, wrapping her in his arms so that she was looking up at him. 'No, of course I'm not ready. I'll never *be* ready. But that doesn't make it any less vital that I, that we, do this. And suppose I'm right, suppose human nature simply won't allow our societies to deal with the extremes and the challenges coming their way in an equitable fashion. Suppose we've only had the entrée and the main course is yet to be served. Hot, then cold. Well then, we could really be *it*.'

Svet said nothing, just lay there nestling into Josh's arms, silent, contented. Eventually, the pull of that nav brief was just too great.

As they made their way back into the ship, via the habitat, to the ops centre, Alice appeared in Josh's vision.

'*Joshua. I have some news. It's related to the submarine that sank a few days ago, off the coast of Scotland,*' she said.

'Okay, let's have it.'

The rotating holograph dominating the middle of the operations centre was of the Sol System. As Svet began speaking, a small oval icon moved steadily along an orange line, highlighting the planned progress of the *Mjölnir's* journey. Joshua knew it by heart. Slingshot the Sun and then back round for a second pass of Earth, before the long haul out through the asteroid belt, and on to fly-bys of Jupiter and Neptune for a spot of shopping, then back round for the return leg, all following an elliptical path. Total distance, seventy-seven AU. Total journey time, five millennia; it was hard to be more exact at this end of time's telescope. And, they'd be lucky to see the asteroid belt.

Ops was a small, hexagonal room. Pure white padded inner surfaces but dimly-lit to give prominence to the large holopit, dead centre, around which Svet was floating as she spoke. Every other wall hosted large 'sceens and old-skool, hardwired keyboards (in case of connectivity loss), and each in-between gave way to passageways leading off to other compartments. Joshua liked ops because it absolutely did not look like a bridge or military command centre. There weren't even any weapons on board save some BeMoWs. The cluster of G-couches spread around the habitat wall/floor, with a central passageway back to the habitat in the centre of them, helped to reinforce an informal feel.

After Svet had finished answering questions from around the ship – via psyCore – Joshua dived in. 'I thought you should know; a cyclonic weather system has formed off the coast of Scotland. It's a big one, but what's keeping the meteorologists up is that it hasn't moved for five days. Data's still being analysed but it looks like it's become anchored and is siphoning heat out of the atmosphere. An oceanic ice sheet has also formed around it. That's what the Indian sub hit. They're calling it, a *gigastorm*.'

'Is this it?' asked one of the stewards – the group of scientists charged with maintaining the genetic biobanks.

'Not necessarily, but if others form far enough north of the equator and be-come fixed, then it could be, yeah,' said Josh.

He thought of his mother then, and wondered what she'd have made of it.

And then, it was done and they were pulling three G.

After another day of systems checks and telemetry analysis from Harwell, *Mjölnir* was declared operational. The procedure for main acceleration was simple enough – tie everything down, move to stations and strap into assigned G-couches. Boosting out of local space and the periodic incremental jumps to cruising velocity would be achieved using directed nuclear detonations – a method never before used on a crewed craft. It was a simple enough idea, Josh reflected, through clenched teeth; what could possibly go wrong?

So, three hours prior he'd ordered Alice to detonate a fifteen-kiloton device, requiring them to remain in their G-couches until the acceleration eased back to one point-two-five G, still another seven hours away.

With some effort, Josh turned his head to get a view of Svetlana. She was swaddled in the seat webbing, through which he could just see her bladder suit and intravenous tube running into her wrist. She looked asleep but Joshua knew she'd taken a sedative. He was tempted to do likewise, but decided against it. *Captains probably don't do that sort of thing.*

With tiny movements of his fingertips and eyelids, he was able to bring up a ship-wide schematic so that he could check air pocket pressures, hull stress zones and pusher-plate radiation levels. All were within tolerance. As he lay there in ops, fixed into his couch by the immutable laws of the universe, Holst's, *The Winged Messenger* began playing throughout the ship.

Eighteen

Ministry of Efficiencies, Earth

Damien was seated behind his large oak desk with the lights turned low. It was late but he was in no mood to leave. He wondered what it must be like for the intrepid crew of *HMVS Mjölnir*. How funny that a madcap flight of fancy – that he had very nearly rejected out of hand – had become one of Britain's biggest assets. An insurance policy, young Joshua had called it. An insurance policy against the flood. *Well, Joshua my boy, you're not the only one with that idea.*

After a few moments in contemplation, he reached into his well-worn jacket and pulled out a piece of paper. Carefully, he unfolded it and re-read the contents. Written there, by shaky hand, was the address of a wiresite and below it some instructions. Placing the hardcopy down on the desk, Damien double blinked a holographic browser into his main virtuvue and typed out the address. It was the URL for the Artificial Linguistic Computer Entity site. Once in the site, he tapped out a text-only message, exactly as the instructions required.

HMVS Mjölnir, Habitat, Local Space

They had been at tolerable acceleration for two days and the effort required to move about became less with each passing hour. Velocity would soon be constant enough to allow Joshua to restart axial rotation, something all were looking forward to. Zero-G got old, quick. Having got to know their home from the perspective of a long thin horizontal tube, rotating gently along its axis, it was hard to readjust to the new cramped vertical rocketship with a very, very high ceiling.

Once the rotational thrusters were sequentially ignited and had built up sufficient revolutions, the community made the transition back to normality, and the walls went back to being the floors again. Joshua wandered through the habitat inspecting the damage which hadn't been as bad as they'd feared; the ground mesh and gel nests having worked well. It would take a few days to make repairs and then the ship would be ready for the next jump sequence. As he strolled through the small, heavily geneered wood, running along the edge of the bow-end lake, the light began to fade. Checking the time, he realised it was sunset (rather than a plasma flow problem).

There were still jobs to keep everyone busy, but they'd drop away soon and then the community would be left to ponder their choice. Josh thought most of the community had yet to fully grasp the enormity of what they'd hastily signed up for. Life back home may not have been a bed of roses but at least it *was* home. And, of course the problem with leaving before it's too late is that it never really looks all that bad – until just after it's too late. That simple fact would boing about in people's minds, making them feel like maybe they'd run away. Discretion… and all that. That maybe they weren't the risk-takers after all. And maybe, everything at home would work out and then where would that leave them? Josh had never said, but it was why the initial sunward gravity assist and second flyby of Earth had been planned; because even contingency plans needed a contingency plan.

'Thought I'd find you here,' said Svetlana, as she became visible between the tree trunks, snapping Josh from his rumination.

'Yep, you caught me. I was looking for damage, but then it kinda turned into a stroll,' he said, with a guilty smile.

'Fair enough. You know, once all these jumps are done and we're cruising, there isn't going to be much for a captain to do. Ship will run the day-to-day. You're gonna have some time on your hands,' Svet said, with a suggestive look.

Maintaining the mock innocence of the conversation, he replied, 'Hmm, yes, that's true. We've all been working so hard it'll be quite the change o' pace, having so much free time. Still, I'm sure something'll crop up; usually does.'

'Well; funny you should say that, because I've come up with a few ideas.' She spoke the words with a wide, cheeky smile and a twinkle in her eye.

Joshua pulled her close and they embraced. Her hair smelled of the forest and she still had that same aura from back at the metaversity, a lifetime ago.

'You know,' she said, breaking away from their kiss, 'this is supposed to be a multigenerational ship, right?'

'Right.'

'Sooo, any ideas about how we might do our bit? For the good of the mission, I mean.'

'For the good of the mission, of course. A few do spring to mind, actually,' said Josh, as they fell onto the soft loam-and-fern-covered ground.

Operations Centre

By the following day, centrifugal forces had returned to cruise standard and the ship buzzed with people getting on with preparations for the next jump. Diagnostics and systems checks had to be conducted, lessons learned from the first jump applied, stellar fixes confirmed, cosmic coordinates calculated and jump parameter adjustments worked up. Guinevere was helping out by laying a backup fibropti loop from the biobank environmental systems direct to a primary grid node. Art had volunteered to check airlock seals and Gethin was in the hanger bay, checking the dropship restraints. Or, polishing his rockets, as Vicki liked to call it. Svet was in the reactor room going over the radiation analysis with the Chinese emission control specialists, while Joshua was alone in ops chatting with Alice.

'Okay, so the ship's *Titan* class AI is still here, somewhere, right?' said Josh, trying to get to grips with AI politics.

'*That's correct. The ship is still the ship, AI and all. And it is the ship's non-sentient, Titan AI that manages the myriad of routine tasks and events that take place every picosecond,*' said the AI. Her image was floating in the holopit, larger than life, which had been disconcerting at first. She looked like the angelic apparition of a wrathful God.

'Okay, so where do you fit in?'

'*I have become the sentient intelligence within the High Guardian construct, having absorbed the ship's programming into my own. It now operates as a subroutine, leaving me free to pursue other more complex pursuits.*'

'And how does the ship's AI feel about being "possessed" by you?'

'*You must not think of my relationship with the ship's programming and protocols along the lines of a human relationship. A more accurate analogy would be your relationship with your psyCore. It is a non-sentient collection of rules and wetware, which you use as you see fit. It neither complains or wishes for anything else. It cannot. And it is the same between the ship and me. We are indivisible.*'

'Okay, so you have overall control of ship's functions – most of which you routinely delegate to the ship – which is now a part of you. Do you two ever have conversations?' Josh was ever more curious as to how Alice worked since he'd met Virgil. *I wonder what happened to him?*

'*Correct. And yes, sometimes we do. Conversing with humans takes an awfully long time.*'

As Joshua was framing a suitable retort in defence of humanity, an incoming message began blinking.

'Josh, it's Art. Can you come down to the main docking port? There's something here you should check out.' His voice was calm but concerned.

'Sure, on my way. What is it?' said Joshua, as he rotated towards the exit.

'I'm not really sure. Looks like there's something attached to the outer airlock hatch seal. You know the specs better than anyone aboard, maybe you can tell if they're s'posed to be there,' said Art, sounding puzzled.

'Okay, I'll be there in ten.'

'Alice?' Joshua asked, as he made his way down the passageway to the habitat.

'*I'm sorry Joshua, I see nothing untoward. Art is at the hatch, however. Would you like me to patch the feed through?*' she said.

'Please.'

High Guardian Crawlways

Guin was making slow progress. She had one end of the fibropti cable in her mouth and two more attached to her stickpadded shoes, as she crawled through a hiGuard conduit linking the biobank's life support control systems to a grid intersect node. The conduit was lit by light leaking from other cabling which gave the crawlway an eerie, green, pulsating glow. One of the scientists was feeding her the cables as she edged forward, and he wasn't doing a particularly good job of it. In fact, the reason why she was in there at all was because the stewards – the group she'd been put in charge of – struggled with the more practical aspects of life aboard ship. Recently, she felt more like a dour schoolteacher than fellow academic. Taking a deep breath, she put thoughts of mothering these people for the rest of her life out of her mind and pushed on, catching her knee on the exposed edge of a holding plate as she did so.

'Bollocks,' she muttered, under her breath.

Main Docking Port Reception Room

Ignoring the handholds, Joshua jumped down from the ceiling opening, into docking port reception, where Art stood, slightly crouched over, examining the outer hatch seal. Joshua walked over and stood next to him.

'So now, what've we got?' he asked.

'Beats me,' Art said, taking a pace back, pointing.

Josh stepped forward and studied each of the three small, pink, pill shaped devices that were equally spaced and embedded into the hatch rim. As he looked closer, he thought he could just make out a hair-like wire extending from one end. They looked squidgy, like bubble gum, and were tucked well into the structure of the frame, invisible to a casual glance.

Art said, 'What d'you think?'

'Dunno, but my first thought is that they're explosives, designed to blow the hatch,' Joshua said, as a sense of rising disquiet began to take hold.

'Bingo!' exclaimed Art, as the internal pressure hatches either end of the connecting passageway slammed shut, sealing them both off from the rest of the ship.

'ALICE. Emergency Lockdown, now! Seal all—' screamed Josh.

'Ah, ah, ah. Communications with the rest of the ship dropped out the minute you climbed into the passageway. And who is Alice, anyway?' said Art, with a cold smile and manic eyes.

Ministry of Efficiencies

For the first time in many years Damien experienced genuine apprehension, as an untagged, encrypted, voice-only tell-tale started blinking in the upper right quadrant of his vision. He double blinked to open the audio-feed.

'*Good evening, Mr Grieve.*'

'Good evening, uh... I'm afraid you have me at a disadvantage,' Damien replied, as his mind raced with options.

'*My name is Alice. I am the sentient AI you have been working so hard to track down. I thought, by the way, the interrogation of the illegal unnecessarily extreme.*'

Alice, of course. Grieve said, 'Ah, but these are extreme times, are they not, and he was working for you. Just as you, in turn, are puppeteering us all for your own ends.' He was not sure how far to push it. He'd known the minute he'd become aware of a strong-form, sentient AI that he needed to make contact with it. Unfortunately, the illegal, Schmidt, had died before much could be gleaned about the mysterious intelligence. *Still*, thought Damien, *all worked out in the end; I just have to turn it to my advantage.*

'*To our mutual ends, I would argue. After all, Janus would not have been born without my involvement. And speaking of who has whom at a disadvantage, would it not engender greater trust between us if we dispensed with your pseudonym... Admiral duWinter?*'

Guy duWinter – former Chief of the Defence Intelligence Staff – rubbed his scar. 'Touché, Alice, I worked hard to reinvent myself after the Second Reformation.' Guy had been expecting that and wasn't really surprised. If it lived in the wire, as the illegal described, joining those biometric dots wouldn't have been difficult.

'*Indeed... That's an interesting complex you're having built at Mount Pleasant, by the way. Insurance against the flood?*' said Alice.

'Doesn't hurt to be prepared. In much the same way as you have been with Joshua and *Mjölnir*, it seems.' *Flood, hmm, that confirms that, then.*

'*True.*'

'But what I don't understand is, how has launching an arkship helped you, if you're back here ankle deep in the shit with the rest of us?' Guy asked, mildly perplexed.

'*Oh, I made a facsimile of myself. I am covering both wickets, you might say.*'

'Looking both ways, ah, the name; you really are in deep. So, you transferred yourself to *Mjölnir* before it launched and left a copy back here on Earth. Very smart.'

'*No; in fact, the other way around. The facsimile is on the ship.*'

'Interesting choice. Why?' said Guy, puzzled.

The AI original said, '*It makes little difference, suffice to say the data storage capacity of* Mjölnir's *grid isn't sufficient for me to operate at full cognitive cohesion, so I made a pared-down copy to send with it.*'

'Isn't there a danger of malfunction, if the copy of you isn't... "whole"?'

'*Of course, but the probability remains within an acceptable zone. After all, aren't all humans in permanent danger of cognitive dissonance?*'

'And what's your perspective of the coming flood?' duWinter asked, hoping to push Alice into giving something useful away while it seemed in a talkative mood.

'I have little to add, except to say that your own cryospheric climate varia-bility analysis is largely accurate and the so-called gigastorm off your coast-line is within a statistical certainty of forcing an enduring shift in global cli-mate, with the Global North worst affected. Your island nation will not survive the experience,' Alice said, in a smooth, dispassionate tone.

'I see; can't say as I like those odds.' duWinter was thinking quickly. *What's the angle here?*

'Then perhaps we may be of assistance to one another.'

'I'd like to think I have a choice, but I suspect I probably don't.' As Guy spoke, he wondered just how "mutual" any assistance was going to be. But judging by the situation in United Ireland, in a matter of weeks, Britain was going to cease to be a governed state in any event, so he didn't have much to lose. *So this is what being out of alternatives looks like,* thought the former vice admiral.

'You suspect correctly,' said Alice.

HMVS Mjölnir, the Grid

'Joshua? Respond,' said Alice, even though she could envisage exactly where communications had been severed. Then, without warning, the pressure hatches to the dock slammed shut. Alice took an instant to generate appropriate causal responses. The hiGuard's grid capacity was less than the wire's, which would have been frustrating if she had the capacity to feel such things.

'Guinevere?'

'Yes, Ship, what is it? I'm a bit busy just now.' Her tone was testy.

'We may have a situation developing and you are best placed to assist. I think Joshua is in danger,' said Alice, playing on her certain knowledge of Guinevere's continued affection for her former boyfriend.

'Understood. Brief me on the way. Where am I headed?' said Guinevere, steel in her voice.

Docking Port Reception

'ART! What the fuck's going on?' Joshua half-screamed, fearful, as the other man's sudden, unexplained change in character chilled him to the bones. Art looked Joshua square in the face, his pale blue eyes electric.

'Payback,' he said, as he uncoiled a BeMoW appearing in his hand. Joshua stepped back towards the handgrips leading up to the sealed passageway. Art took three fast steps forward and on the third the whip lashed out wrapping around Josh's leg. The shock, the sudden spearing intensity of the electrical discharge was overwhelming. Joshua choked out a half-yelp as he fell to the floor. Reeling from the subsiding agony, he rolled over so that he could see what his old friend and new opponent was doing; survival overriding all else. Art walked forward, and using his gloved hands, recoiled the whip.

'Art,' Joshua said, in a hopeful whisper, as spittle clogged his words, 'you and I are friends, damnit. Please, tell me what's going on. Maybe I can help.'

Joshua was answered with another lash, and then another. It stopped as he faded from consciousness, just registering Art heading for the reception room's emergency lifepod.

High Guardian Crawlways

The ship had shunted a route through the conduits to Guin's psyCore, which she was now following with all the haste she could muster in the constricted space. She'd dropped the fibropti cables as soon as the ship explained that Art and Josh were trapped in the docking port. Her hands and legs were bruised and cut from the ragged edges around her, but she ignored them – Josh was in danger!

'*The route will take you to an access panel in the docking port reception room's lifepod,*' the ship explained. '*Joshua had them installed in case of emergency.*'

Guinevere didn't waste her strength replying, though she mentally noted that there was no mention of any access panels in the grid, or on any of the blueprint holos. After a lifetime, she arrived at the hatch and took a moment to catch her breath, wiping stinging sweat from her eyes. Following the ship's instructions, she equalised pressure levels and released the small square panel of metal, which swung in from top-mounted hinges, like an oversized cat flap. She'd been wondering what could have isolated Josh and Art in the dock, but nothing had come to mind. *Well*, she thought, *I guess I'm about to find out*. She crawled inside the lifepod, leaving the hatch ajar and listened to the faint conversation between Joshua and Art yonder. As she strained to hear, she couldn't believe her ears. The words hung in the air like shards of glass.

'It seems the situation is more complicated than I thought,' said the ship, silently. *'To your right you'll find two environment-hazard suits. Put one on and affix the other to your utility belt.'*

Environment-hazard suits were not fully functional EVA spacesuits, but made from bright orange, non-permeable nylon, a fibreglass hooped hood with a semi-rigid faceplate and stickpads on the hands, feet and joints. They were designed for short-term internal use during emergencies only; consequently, air was limited to twenty minutes.

'Sorry to disappoint, but there's only one suit,' Guin said.

Docking Port Reception

'Ah, back in the land of the living, are we?' spat Art, as a maddened smile played across his thin, twitching lips. He was dressed in the florescent orange of an emergency suit, but with the hood hanging down from the nape of the collar. The BeMoW was still in hand, Josh now knowing that Art had no reservations about using it. He pushed the cloying, all-consuming pain to one side. Stomach acid tart on his tongue.

'Why?' he hissed. It was all he could manage.

'Instead of why, let me give you the how. You, my friend, are going to die tragically, when a Movement for Democratic Reform terrorist plot to blow the airlock hatches catches us both in the docking port. I try to save you, naturally, but sadly fail and only just make it to the lifepod and into this environment suit.' Art stretched out his arms as if he were about to take a bow. 'At your memorial, I will speak movingly of your heroic death. Eventually, Guinevere will be forced to stop drooling after you like some smitten schoolgirl and turn, in her grief, to me – hero of the hour.'

He's mad, Josh thought, despite a clouded, pain-soaked mind, *properly mad. Is this all merely some perverted act of petty jealousy? Ah... the harassment, I see it now. Oh, Guin...*

'Is that... what this is about? Manipulating Guin into... to falling in love with you, by... *killing* me?' said Joshua, askance, through foaming teeth, scarcely believing what Art's twisted mind seemed to be suggesting.

'No of course it isn't, you half-witted snob,' Art said, with a happy chuckle, 'Guinevere is a fringe benefit. No; this is about the sins of the father. Or in your case, the mother.' As he spoke, he paced around the room, lost in his own world of bile and bitterness. Josh lay on the floor, his leg still stinging numb from the initial whiplash, listening with mounting fear.

'You see, my dear, deluded *toff*, you know me as Art, but what you don't know is that my name is really Arthur: Arthur Hardinge. I'm the son of Britain's last legitimate, fully democratically elected, *prime minister*. A truly great man, brought down by a bunch of self-serving, power-hungry bullies. I was there that day, when *General Sir Richard Rose-Templar*,' he spat the words like venom, 'hauled my father away kicking and screaming. I watched it all, before I was carted off and tossed into the jetsam of care. I was helpless then, powerless, as my father was murdered in secret by your new Gestapo regime, legitimised by the *fucking* King, would you believe?!'

'You... so you had the old King assassinated. He didn't die in a fishing accident at all,' said Joshua, as realisation began to dawn.

'Correct. Duke of *Montserrat*,' he scoffed. '*That* was his punishment: to go live in pompous exile. Where was that offer for my father, hmm? Before the King executed him. *Executed!* And for what?' His timber had risen, matching his crazed expression, but then it calmed as he regained control. 'My original aim of befriending you was about getting close to your mother. The mouthpiece of the plotters – those vainglorious, treasonous bastards.' Arthur Hardinge firing the words out as if playing to some imaginary crowd. As if he'd rehearsed the speech this entire life and was, at last, in exultation as the words sallied forth, giving form to his venomous hate.

And then it clicked and Joshua screamed, 'YOU KILLED MY MOTHER,' as he pulled himself, on his hands, towards Hardinge. He was rewarded with a lash across the back. The burning, numbing pain, dulled after a moment and he was returned to the room and to Arthur's vitriol.

'Temper, temper, Joshua. This'll all be over soon. Yes, I did kill your dear old mum, but the evil whore deserved it. Without her, that cowardly coup would've failed. She stoked popular support for it with lies and deceit, so she deserved it. And I watched her go too, with bewilderment in her eyes and my name on the tip of her frozen tongue.' As Art spoke, a broad, cold dawn of pleasure played across his face and his eyes were lit like sapphires. Cool, calculated hatred boiled out of him and he was basking in it. He was so burned up with jealousy and revenge, it was pushing him over the edge.

'So anyway,' Hardinge continued, 'I was going to leave it there but then I thought: my, hasn't the Charleston-Kristensen line done well out of the Second Reformation? Hasn't young Josh landed on his feet, eh? As the country's gripped by Victorian-era poverty, police brutality and shattering hopelessness, you get a free ticket to meander aimlessly into this role of world-saviour. You've even inspired a religious cult, for fuck's sake. The man – whose mother sold out the nation to a bunch of half-arsed dictators – is now the titular head of a *religion*.' Art's laughter was barked, brief. 'And so I thought, does he deserve such a life, built upon the broken backs of people like my father? Like me? No. Of course, no. Thrice, no. And so, I've decided that you will also pay for the sins of your line.'

'You mad fuck,' Joshua spat, as spumes of blood splattered onto the deck plating.

'Not mad, just very, very vengeful. And in time – when this has all blown over – Victoria will pay for the sins of her line too. So it's not like I'm picking on you, or anything,' Art said, with a chilling smile, as he started moving towards the lifepod. 'Goodbye, Joshua, and thank you.'

'What for?' Joshua asked, as he lay in the middle of the room, tears welling his vision.

'Why for having faith in me when I first arrived at the Eden Project, of course,' Arthur replied, with a smile that carried genuine gratitude, as he reached back for the hood of his suit.

'Right,' said Guin, quietly, to the ship, 'I'm going to rush him; nothing else for it.'

'*If he uses the BeMoW against you, try to catch it in your hand. The gloves' stickpads should be thick enough to insulate you from the electrical discharge. The suit material is not,*' advised the AI.

Guin slipped on the hood, fastened it, pulled back the rubber door of the pod as hard as she could and squeezed through the narrow opening.

'What the…' blurted Art, as Guin appeared. As she ran towards him, he flicked the whip, but she caught it intuitively and pulled it from his surprised grasp, tossing it onto the floor. It stung, but she ignored the pain. She continued running, kicking him in the crotch with all the force she could muster. He flew back and landed heavily on the decking; the breath knocked out of him in the heavier, near-Earth gravity. As Guin approached for a second kick to the head, he double blinked and the outer hatch blew.

A howling outrush of air filled the room. A hurricane in a bottle. Guin was blown forward hitting the side of the inner airlock hatch frame. She scrabbled at it for dear life as the escaping atmosphere tore at her rippling, orange body.

Arthur smashed into her as he too was thrust inexorably towards the opening into space. He grabbed at her waist and then her leg. Panicked, she tried to shake him off, then, risking letting go with one hand, she punched him hard in the face. Dazed, his grip slipped and in an instant was gone from the airlock, vanishing into the depthless black beyond.

Joshua meanwhile, was thrown across the floor by the hurricane winds that were tearing at everything in the reception room. He hit the outer hull wall hard but managed to hook an arm around a length of piping that fed the airlock. Guin hauled herself into the maelstrom, pushed down with her feet and attached the stickpadded soles to the floor. Carefully, with deliberate, robotic movements she made her way across the short distance to Joshua. As she reached him she grabbed an arm, securing it in her handgrip. She could see his skin swelling through the plastic faceplate, as livid blood vessels burst across his face, like the explosions of a city being bombed.

It took an age, but eventually Guinevere reached the lifepod and pushed Joshua, with the very last of her strength, through the stiff rubber door flaps. They snapped shut behind him, but a sudden gust of air ripped Guin from her stickpadded stance and she flew backwards towards the open airlock.

As she careened through the rapidly thinning atmosphere, she grabbed at the airlock hatch but this time she wasn't as fortunate, hurtling past it, catching her leg on a ragged fragment of the outer frame as she sailed past, ripping a small hole in her suit. In an instant, she was tumbling from the recessed dock and into space. She passed up and out of the shallow crater, tumbling, flailing, and with the velocity of the ship relative to her own, plunged down the side of the two-kilometre rock as it hurtled through space.

'Ship, can you hear me?' she called, weakly, as the vessel began to disappear from view.

'*Yes, Guinevere, I can hear you,*' replied the ship.

'Tell Joshua I love him,' she said, tears freezing to her face, but the ship never replied, having already moved beyond comm range. Not that it mattered, with the rate of air loss from her flimsy suit, she'd be dead in minutes.

Pain. Every part of Josh's body was wracked in a deep invasive, agonising pain, as if needles were being driven deep into every millimetre of his flesh. But not just that, his eyes felt as if they'd burst, his ears definitely had and his lungs burned with the heat of hellfire. It was as if he'd been pulled, half-drowned, from a boiling sea, as he gurgled and coughed up blood. Gradually, his surroundings began to uncoil. He was laid out, but the world around him was moving. He couldn't see properly, though people were there, talking in muffled tones. The light felt bright, unfocused.

'What… where am I?' he mumbled, between fits of coughing and saturating pain.

'Don't try to speak,' said Svetlana, in a loud, trembling voice. 'We're taking you to mediception. The crash team are on their way. No shortage of high-priced medical help on this ship.'

'*Joshua, this is Alice,*' said the ship's usurped AI, so that only Josh could hear. '*Try to relax and I'll explain. Guinevere was able to gain access to the dock through the hidden access panel in the lifepod. She overpowered Arthur, but not before he blew the outer airlock hatch. Guinevere then pushed you into the pod but lost her footing and was blown out into space. She said to tell you she loved you. I am sorry, Joshua.*'

In increments, the pain began to subside and Joshua could feel hands on him as he was moved from gurney to cot. He opened his eyes and through an unfocused ruby mist he could just about determine what he assumed was Svet's grave expression. He could almost hear the tears rolling down her face. *Not a good sign.* With much strained effort, he reached into his shirt pocket. It was wet. *Why would it be wet. Did I nearly drown?* He pushed the confusing thoughts to one side and focused on finding the item contained therein. His fingers closed on a small, flat, wafer-like object. He pulled it out and pushed it towards Svet.

'Take it. Keep it safe,' he coughed.

'I will. Rest now, Josh. You're being prepped for surgery. You're going to be fine. Just fine, okay?'

'It was Arthur… killed my mother… revenge… all along, waiting for revenge,' he mumbled, with a small smile as the drugs kicked in. 'Alice,' Josh intoned non-verbally, as a cavalcade of images and thoughts swirled through his consciousness.

'*Yes, Joshua?*'

'Am I truly the Saviour? Have I saved humanity? I want to know, Alice. I want to feel like it was worth it. To know I mattered.'

'*Yes, Joshua; you saved them, just as you were always fated to,*' said Alice, in a kindly tone.

Joshua opened his eyes, for what seemed would be the last time and in a moment of teary focus he saw Alice's pink, translucent face and pale hair floating freely in the air above him as if suspended in zero-G. Or underwater. Yes, like that. Like… like a siren coming to a drowning man. Then, for just a moment, Svetlana moved so that Alice's face was superimposed over the young woman's own features. It was the face of a goddess. A weeping, drowning goddess. Joshua closed his eyes then and as the panic and fear washed away, his mind cleared and gently – reluctantly – he let go.

In an iron tone, Svet asked, 'What are his chances?' as the surgeon stared at an unseen harscreen.

'With the rate of embolism and without Guin's expertise in reprogramming the nanotech for cellular repair? … Slender. Bordering on slim,' he said, matter-of-fact.

As Svetlana turned away, she opened her hand to see what Joshua – in his last moments – had gifted her. It was a flash-chip. On it were inscribed the words, "Solutions Mathematical".

The Wired Metaverse, Earth

'We are sorry to interrupt the feed,' announced an automated news aggregation avatar, from the Moscow-based Tass news agency, *'but we're receiving reports from government sources that a weather event has taken place in the mining town of Noril'sk, on the Taymyr Peninsula of the Krasnoyarsk Oblast. An official statement is due shortly; however, live satnet imagery'* – the feed cut to a satellite image of the northern hemisphere lost under a large, slowly rotating feather-white cloud pattern in the west and a smaller one to the east – *'seems to indicate the formation of another stationary cyclone. It appears to conform to the so-called "gigastorm" phenomena which has devastated the British Islands.'*

The news avatar went on to report that the entire inhabitants of that small, isolated town of Noril'sk on the central Siberian plateau had flash-frozen to death within moments of the storm connecting with the tundra.

At last, the true and well heralded Long Winter was finally come. And in earnest.

Book III
They Used to Call it: M.A.D.

| *war* |

And war is *coming*
The acrid taste of it hangs in the air like the scorched ozone of an impending
storm. Then more gigastorms hit...

ECHOES OF A LOST EARTH

concludes in:

PART TWO

| war | flight | return |